TRAPPED BY THE POWER

Lightning flared out from the apex of the central cone in the great chamber, lancing out toward each of the lower cones, slamming into them with sparks and fire. Thunder, deafeningly loud, the sound of the earth cracking open and splitting itself apart, roared through the great chamber. Blinding light exploded out from the lightning strike to reflect off every silver surface, flooding the chamber with brilliance.

The lesser cones answered back, sending their own thunderbolts back to strike at the top of the center cone, blasting it into incandescence. Then, as suddenly as it had been there, the lightning was gone, and the cones were as they had been, unaffected by the massive power that had played around them. The sound of the thunder echoed through the chamber, reverberating back and forth like the angry war cry of some long-forgotten god.

The chamber shuddered and shook with the thunder. Chewbacca, aboard the *Falcon,* was thrown from his bunk as the ship bounced and lurched along with the chamber. He was halfway to the ship's control room before he came fully awake and realized the ship was on the ground.

Not just on the ground, but *under* it, in a sealed chamber, with no hope of escape.

The Sensational *Star Wars* Series
published by Bantam Books and
available from all good bookshops

The *Empire* Trilogy by Timothy Zahn
The Heir to the Empire
Dark Force Rising
The Last Command

The *Jedi Academy* Trilogy by Kevin J. Anderson
Jedi Search
Dark Apprentice
Champions of the Force

The Truce at Bakura
by Kathy Tyers

The Courtship of Princess Leia
by Dave Wolverton

The *Corellian* Trilogy by Roger MacBride Allen
Ambush at Corellia
Assault at Selonia
Showdown at Centerpoint

The *Cantina* Trilogy Edited by Kevin J. Anderson
Tales from the Mos Eisley Cantina
Tales from Jabba's Palace*
The Bounty Hunters*

Crystal Star
by Vonda McIntyre

and in hardcover

Children of the Jedi
by Barbara Hambly

The Illustrated Star Wars Universe*
by Kevin J. Anderson & Ralph McQuarrie

**Forthcoming*

SHOWDOWN AT CENTERPOINT

Book Three of the Corellian Trilogy

Roger MacBride Allen

BANTAM BOOKS

TORONTO · NEW YORK · LONDON · SYDNEY · AUCKLAND

SHOWDOWN AT CENTERPOINT
A BANTAM BOOK : 0 553 40883 6

First publication in Great Britain

PRINTING HISTORY
Bantam edition published 1995

Bantam Books are published by Transworld Publishers Ltd,
61–63 Uxbridge Road, Ealing, London W5 5SA,
in Australia by Transworld Publishers (Australia) Pty Ltd,
15–23 Helles Avenue, Moorebank, NSW 2170,
and in New Zealand by Transworld Publishers (NZ) Ltd,
3 William Pickering Drive, Albany, Auckland.

Printed and bound in Great Britain by
Cox & Wyman Ltd, Reading, Berks.

To Mandy Slater
who was there when it started

Author's Note

I would like to offer my thanks to Tom Dupree, to Jennifer Hershey, and to all the other good people at Bantam, who have demonstrated great confidence in me throughout this project. Thanks likewise to Eleanor Wood and Lucienne Diver for their support and for their efficient handling of the business side of things.

I would also like to thank my wife, Eleanore Fox, who had enough to put up with learning a new language and packing up for our move to Brazil. She certainly didn't need a novelist underfoot at the same time, but she got one, and she dealt with the situation. Clearly, the U.S. Foreign Service only hires the best. At least in the present case.

Thanks as well to Mandy Slater, friend and confidante, to whom this book is dedicated. She was there, at the kitchen table in Washington, when the call came in, summoning me to active duty as a *Star Wars* author. She helped convince me that I could pull this thing off. If it turns out I have, and you see her, please let her know she was right. Of course, *finding* her to tell her might be a problem. The last time I saw her was in New Orleans, and she had just flown in from Romania via London, and she was en route to Chicago. Before *that*, the last time I saw her was in Fresno, California, for my wedding, and the time before that was in London, and before London, Toronto, I think. After a while it's hard to keep track. But thanks, Mandy, all the same.

Speaking of travel, one of the grand traditions of a

good *Star Wars* story is that everything happens everywhere at once. I'm afraid the second book in this series was written almost completely in and around Washington, D.C., plus maybe a little on a trip to Philadelphia and New York. This third one got itself done not only in Arlington, Virginia; Bethesda, Maryland; and places of similar ilk, but also in New York, Miami, over the Caribbean and the Amazon, in Sao Paulo and in Brasilia. It was edited in Bethesda; Norfolk, Virginia; Atlanta; Montgomery, Alabama; and Biloxi, Mississippi. If that's not mobility enough for you, we're going to have to talk.

One final note, on the dangers of dedicating anything to an English teacher. I did indeed dedicate the second volume of this trilogy to Beth Zipser and her husband Mike. Beth taught me eleventh-grade English many moons ago, and she now plays a mean hand of poker. When she learned of the dedication, she was so moved she instantly sprang into action—and started searching the manuscript for grammatical errors. Let this serve as a warning always to do your best. After all, you never know when *your* high school English teacher might check up on *you*.

ROGER MACBRIDE ALLEN
April 1995
Brasilia, Brazil

What Has Gone Before

It is a time of uncertain peace in the galaxy. Fourteen years have passed since the defeat of the Empire and the death of Darth Vader.

Leia Organa Solo, her husband **Han Solo,** and their three children **Jaina, Jacen,** and **Anakin,** accompanied by **Chewbacca** the Wookiee, set off on a family trip to Corellia, Han's homeworld. Unbeknownst to them, the mysterious **Human League** has set in motion a plot to take over the Corellian Sector.

Leia engages a tutor for the children, a Drall named **Ebrihim,** who takes them on a tour of a large archaeological site. During the tour, the three children locate a huge and strange installation of unknown age and purpose.

Mara Jade arrives at Corellia with a coded message. The unknown senders of the message claim to have touched off a recent supernova, and intend to set off more, in populated star systems, if their unspecified demands are not met.

The Human League begins its long-planned revolt against the New Republic. Chewbacca, assisted by **Q9-X2,** Ebrihim's irascible droid, escapes with the children to Drall aboard the *Millennium Falcon.*

The Human League's leader reveals himself to be **Thrackan Sal-Solo,** Han's long-lost cousin, a man known for his guile and cruelty. A powerful jamming system comes on, cutting off virtually all communications in the Corellian planetary system.

Han helps New Republic Intelligence agent **Belindi Kalenda** steal an X-TIE Ugly fighter. She flies toward

Coruscant with news of the catastrophe, but Han is captured by the Human League.

Meanwhile, **Luke Skywalker** has agreed to accompany **Lando Calrissian** on his search for a suitable wife. Lando meets **Tendra Risant** of the planet **Sacorria**. Luke and Lando then set course for Corellia, where they plan to attend the trade conference. They fly into a huge interdiction field that surrounds all of the Corellian star system. The field, far larger than any in history, prevents travel through hyperspace anywhere in the Corellian system. Lando and Luke turn back for Coruscant to bring word.

Leia is captured, and locked up with Mara Jade. The two of them accomplish a daring escape to Mara's private ship, the *Jade's Fire*. Han, likewise imprisoned, is forced to fight the Selonian **Dracmus,** a fellow prisoner, for the amusement of the Human League's commanders. Thrackan, angered by Han's insolence, then throws him in the same cell with Dracmus. Before Han can attempt a foolhardy escape, Dracmus's fellow Selonians break them out of prison.

Luke, Lando, and Kalenda reach Coruscant, only to learn that the Republic is at a very lowered state of readiness. It is decided that they must go to see **Gaeriel Capistan** on the planet Bakura, in hopes that she can assemble a Bakuran fleet. She does so, and **Admiral Hortel Ossilege** is placed in command. A task force of four ships, equipped with special equipment to break through the interdiction field, heads for Corellia. The plan is to stage a diversionary raid at Selonia before moving toward the real target, the massive Centerpoint Station that seems to be the source of the jamming and the interdiction field.

The children, Chewbacca, Ebrihim, and Q9 arrive on Drall and meet with Ebrihim's **Aunt Marcha, the Duchess of Mastigophorous**. Aunt Marcha leads the group to an underground facility identical to the one on Corellia. The chamber is a huge and ancient planetary repulsor, capable of moving the planet itself through space. There is little doubt that there are similar repulsors on all the inhabited worlds of the Corellian system. They hide in the repulsor cavern, and try to learn more about it.

Meantime, Tendra Risant discovers a huge fleet assembling in the Sacorrian system. She flies toward Corellia, intent on warning Lando and Luke, unaware that they are not yet there. Forced out of hyperspace by the interdiction field, she flies on in normal space. Using an antique radionic communications system, she sends a signal to Lando—and despairs when he does not respond.

Back on Corellia, Dracmus puts Han aboard a most unreliable-looking spacecraft, a coneship. He is flown toward Selonia, for reasons he does not fully understand. Mara and Leia likewise decide to head for Selonia, and both craft are en route when the Bakuran task force arrives. A space battle ensues between the Bakuran ships and units from the various rebellions. Lando, aboard his ship, the *Lady Luck,* for the first time since arrival in the Selonian system, finally hears Tendra's warning message only seconds before he goes into battle. In the battle, one of the four Bakuran ships is smashed into rubble by a shot from the planetary repulsor on Selonia.

The Selonian coneship malfunctions and the *Jade's Fire* effects a rescue of Han and the Selonians. Han and Leia are reunited.

Meanwhile, far across space, in the system of the next star to be blown up, a frantic evacuation effort gets under way. Many are saved, but many are left behind in the chaos and panic. The star explodes. Thousands die.

The third star on the starbuster list has a population of millions. It will be impossible even to begin to evacuate everyone. Unless the puzzle of the starbuster plot can be solved in time, millions of innocent people will die . . .

CHAPTER ONE

Approach

Honored Solo, we are running out of time!" the voice squawked from the comm unit. "We will be entering atmosphere soonest if our approach is not controlled!" The intercom gave out a strangled squeal. Either the comm circuit up to the ship's control cabin was on the verge of giving out again, or else Han had just gotten lucky, and Dracmus was about to lose her voice. *That* would be a blessing.

Han slapped the answer switch and tried to stay focused on his work. "Keep your shirt on, Dracmus," he said, shouting just a bit. "The comm unit send-circuits needed work as well. Tell honored Pilot Salculd that I'm nearly done." Why did the universe require all shipboard repairs to be on the rush? *What I wouldn't give to have Chewbacca here,* Han thought.

"What shirt?" the voice asked worriedly. "Should shirts be worn? Is this for safety?"

Han sighed and pushed the answer button again. "It's an expression. It means 'be patient,' " he said, struggling to keep his own patience. Dracmus was a Selonian, and most Selonians did not like being in space. Understandable for a species that mostly lived underground, but having an agoraphobic being in command was enough to drive anyone crazy.

Han Solo made the last hookup, closed down the last of the inspection hatches, and crossed his fingers

1

for luck. *That ought to do the trick,* he told himself. It had better. It was about time that *something* worked properly. If the coneship he was aboard was a fair example of the breed, Selonian spacecraft weren't much for reliability. Han engaged the power switch and waited for the inverter system to energize.

Han was starting to question his own sanity in volunteering to help fly this particular coneship down out of free space to the surface of Selonia. He could have said so long and good luck and ridden down with Leia on the *Jade's Fire.* But when a job needed doing, and no one else could do it, volunteering was not really all that *voluntary.* He hadn't had much choice in the matter. He couldn't have left Dracmus high and dry. He had obligations to her, and to her people.

And Dracmus had made it clear they *had* to get this ship down. Her people couldn't afford to abandon any spacecraft, no matter what shape the craft was in. The nameless coneship might be a piece of space-going junk, but Dracmus had assured Han that it was better than anything else the Selonians had at the moment. Or, more accurately, it was better than anything that the Hunchuzuc Den and their Republicists had.

"Hurry, Honored Solo!" Dracmus called again.

Why couldn't that intercom break down the way everything else did on this ship? Han hit the answer button again. "Stand by, Dracmus. Pilot Salculd—watch your power settings!"

Knowing he was with the Hunchuzuc would have been a bit more useful if Han had had some clear idea about who or what the Hunchuzuc Den was. All he knew for sure about them was that the Den was part of an amorphous faction of Selonians who lived on Corellia, and that, so far as Dracmus knew, they were still allied to a pro-New Republic alliance of Selonian Dens called the Republicists, and that he was mixed up with them.

Dracmus was a member of the Hunchuzuc, and she had either kidnapped Han or rescued him from

Thrackan Sal-Solo—or both. Han was still not sure. The Hunchuzuc *seemed* to be having a fight with the Overden, the leadership on Selonia proper, a fight that was going on in parallel with the Republic's battle against the rebellions in the Corellia system, though the two fights did not seem to be directly related to each other. The Overden was on the Absolutist side, which wanted absolute independence for Selonia. But even if the Hunchuzuc were Republicist and the Overden were Absolutist, Han was coming to the conclusion that neither side much cared about principles, either way. Each was primarily against the other.

But Han did know a few things for sure. He knew that Dracmus had saved his life, and that she had taken risks to treat him well. He knew that a member of his own family—Thrackan Sal-Solo—had treated Dracmus's people with the utmost cruelty. By Selonian standards, that alone was enough to brand Han himself as a villain, a killer, a monster. Yet Dracmus had given Han every benefit of the doubt. She had treated him with decency and respect. If that was all Han knew, it was also all he had to know.

"When will it be working?" Dracmus called, her voice growing more strident. "The planet is getting closer!"

"That is the idea when you're trying to reenter," Han muttered to himself. Decency and respect to one side, there was no denying that Dracmus could be one major pain in the neck. Han pressed the answer stud again and spoke. "It's working now. Tell Salculd the inverter is back on-line. Have her power up the control circuits and let's see how it goes."

"We shall do so, Honored Solo," said the faint, worried-sounding voice from the comm unit. "Salculd says she is initiating control circuit power-up."

Han was kneeling down in front of the inspection hatch, and a low-powered hum made him think he might be just a bit too close to the inverter array. He stood up and backed away. The hum faded out after a moment, and the array's indicator lights came on, showing normal operation.

Han pressed down the answer button again. "Don't hold me to this," he shouted, "but I think it's working. The spare parts off Mara's ship did the trick. We ought to be able to get underway anytime you like."

"Good to hear, most Honorable Solo," Dracmus said, the relief in her voice almost painfully obvious. "Very good to hear indeed. We shall proceed at once."

The indicators flickered a bit to show the inverters were drawing more power. "Take it easy up there," Han said. "Throttle up nice and slow, all right?"

"We are doing so, Honored Solo. And we shall hold at one-third power. We have no desire to overload our systems again."

"That's very reassuring," Han said. "But I think I'd better head up there and keep an eye on you just the same."

Han crossed to the access ladder and climbed up to the nose cabin of the coneship.

The coneship was just that—a fat cone, with the engines at the base and the control cabin in the point. The nose itself was nearly all transparent transplex, affording a spectacular overhead view. The pilot, Salculd, lay flat on her back, looking up and out at the sky ahead. For a human pilot, it would not be the most comfortable way to work. Of course, Selonians were most decidedly not human.

Salculd looked over to the lower deck access hatch as Han climbed out of it. She gave him a toothy smile and then returned her attention to her work. *She* looked comfortable enough. Dracmus was pacing at the rear of the cabin, looking anything but calm or relaxed.

Though they were fairly standard bipeds, Selonians were taller but thinner than humans. Their arms and legs were shorter, and their bodies rather longer. They could manage equally well walking on two feet or four. Retractable claws in both their hand-paws and foot-paws made them impressive climbers and diggers. Their tails were only about half a meter long, but they packed a major wallop when used as a club—as Han had reason to know.

They had long, pointed faces, and their entire bodies were covered in sleek, short-haired fur. Dracmus was dark brown. Salculd was mostly black, but her belly fur was light brown. They both had bristly whiskers that were as expressive as human eyebrows, once you got a little practice in interpreting them. They also had mouths full of very sharp teeth. Han had been able to interpret the teeth with no practice at all. In short, they were elegant and impressive-looking creatures.

"How does all go?" Han asked Salculd the pilot, speaking in his rather labored Selonian. Salculd did not speak Basic.

"All is well, Honored Solo," Salculd replied. "At least until the next subsystem flips out."

"Wonderful," Han said to himself. "Everything be well, Honored Dracmus?" he asked in Selonian.

"Fine, fine, all is fine, until we crash and die," Dracmus replied.

"Glad we have a consensus," Han muttered to himself.

"It is *good* to plan ahead like that," Salculd said. "Here I was just going to land the ship the regular way. Now I am knowing that I will fail and we will crash. It is most comforting."

"That is enough, Pilot Salculd," Dracmus snapped. "Concentrate all attention on your duties."

"Yes, Honored Dracmus," Salculd said at once, her tone of voice most apologetic.

Salculd was a fairly experienced pilot, and knew her ship at least reasonably well, if not as well as Han would have preferred. Dracmus, on the other hand, was trained to deal with humans, and incompletely trained at that. When it came to ship handling, she had no experience, no knowledge, and no skill. Even so, she commanded the ship—not just in deciding where it would go, but down to the last detail of every maneuver. Salculd could not, or would not, overrule her. Dracmus was of higher status, or seniority, or something, relative to Salculd, and that was that, insofar as either of the Selonians was concerned. Neither seemed much concerned by the fact that Dracmus had only the slightest understanding of space operations, or by the fact that during the raid on Selonia she had repeatedly ordered the ship to do things it could not, and come alarmingly close to getting them all killed.

Salculd might have a smart mouth, and an irreverent attitude, but she followed all of Dracmus's orders—no matter how boneheaded—with alarming dispatch. It took some getting used to.

Han took his own place in the control seat next to Salculd. He had done his best to adjust the padding to fit a human frame, but the seat would never be comfortable. Han lay back and looked up.

The view out the transparent nose of the coneship was nothing less than spectacular. The planet Selonia hung big and bright in the sky, filling the middle third of the field of view. Selonia had smaller oceans than Corellia, and the land mass was broken up into thousands of medium-sized islands, more or less evenly spaced across the face of the planet.

Instead of two or three large oceans and four or five continental landmasses, Selonia's surface was a maze of water and land. Hundreds of seas and bays and inlets and straits and shoals separated the islands. Han remembered reading somewhere that no point on land anywhere on Selonia was more than one hundred fifty kilometers from open water, and no point on the water was more than two hundred kilometers from the nearest shoreline.

But there was more to the view than the spectacular planet. Mara Jade's personal ship, the *Jade's Fire,* hung in space a kilometer or two away, her bow hiding a bit of the planet's equatorial region. She was a long, low, streamlined ship, painted in a flame pattern of red and gold. The ship looked fast, sleek, strong, maneuverable—and Han knew she was all of those things. He wished, not for the first time, that he was aboard her, and not just because the *Fire* was a better ship. Leia was aboard the *Fire,* along with Mara Jade.

After Dracmus had managed to blow out nearly every system on board the coneship, the *Fire* had rescued them and provided Han with the spare parts he needed to repair the craft. Now the *Fire* was preparing to see the coneship to a safe landing.

Han did not like Leia being on one ship while he was on the other, but the arrangement made too much sense. Mara, not yet completely recovered from her leg injury, still needed some looking after, and she needed a copilot, at least until she recovered. Space knew the Selonians, Dracmus and Salculd, needed all the help *they* could get. Besides which, Leia spoke Selonian—spoke it better than Han, for that matter—and given recent events it made more than a little sense to have at least one speaker of the Selonian language aboard each ship, in case of difficulties at the landing field. The plan was for the two ships to fly toward Selonia in formation and land side by side.

But even if it all seemed perfectly reasonable and harmless for Leia to stay on Mara's ship while he flew in the coneship, Han didn't have to like it. He didn't need to ask what could go wrong. So many things had gone wrong already.

A bright light flashed on and off from the forward port of the *Fire.* Leia was using the landing lights on the *Jade's Fire* to send Mon Calamari blink code—combinations of long and short flashes to form the letters of the Basic alphabet. The technique was slow and clumsy, but the normal com channels were jammed and it beat not being able to talk at all.

READY TO BEGIN ENTRY, Han read. SIGNAL WHEN YOU ARE READY. "They say they are ready." He turned to Salculd. "Are we prepared?"

"Yes," said Salculd.

"Very well," Han said. "Honored Dracmus," he said in Basic, so that Salculd could not understand. "You will now do what I say. Stop pacing, take your seat, and instruct Salculd to accept orders from me. I would then ask you most kindly to shut up until we are on the ground. I want you to give no orders and say nothing. I just want you to sit quietly. Or else I tell the *Jade's Fire* that escorting us is a suicide run. I will instruct them to leave us here." It was all bluff, of course, but Dracmus was panicky enough that she wasn't likely to think it through.

"But—" she protested.

"But nothing. I know blink code and you don't. I can talk to the *Fire* and you can't. You nearly got us killed ordering this ship around before, and I'm not going to put up with that again."

"I must protest! This is robbery of the worst kind!"

Han grinned. "Actually, it's more like piracy. Or you could call it a pretty mild form of hijacking. And I might add that if you don't know robbery from piracy, you have no business running a ship."

Dracmus glared at Han, about to protest—but then she shook her head. "So be it. I must accede. Even to my eye, my ship orders were none too good, and I wish to live some more." She shifted to Selonian. "Pilot Salculd! You will obey the orders of Honored Han Solo as you would my own, and do so until such time as we reach the ground."

Salculd sat up in her seat and looked from one to the other before grinning even more widely than before. "Yes, Honored Dracmus!" she said. "I obey with pleasure!"

"See that you don't find *too* much pleasure in obeying, Salculd," Dracmus growled. "Honored Solo, if you would proceed."

"Take your seat," Han said to Dracmus in Selonian. "We all must strap in and prepare for acceleration. Salculd, you will fly a standard approach to the intended field of landing, starting on my command. Is that understood?"

"Yes, indeed," Salculd said. "Absolutely."

Han picked up the handlight placed next to his seat for the purpose, and signaled back to the *Fire*.

BEADY TO COMMENCE EMNTRY MANEUVERZ, he signaled, managing to spot every mistake just after he made it. "Someday I gotta take the time to brush up on this stuff," he muttered to himself.

WE ARE JUST ABOUT BEADY OURSELVES, Leia signaled back. TAKING POSITION TO YOUR STERN. WILL FOLLOW YOU IN.

"Ha, ha, ha," Han said. "Glad I married such a humorist." He shifted back to Selonian. "Very well, Salculd, take us in. With much care."

As he watched, the *Jade's Fire* came about on her long axis, putting her stern toward the coneship. Salculd edged the throttle upward, transferring minimum power to the engines. As the coneship began to accelerate toward the planet, the *Fire* drifted back, falling astern off the port side. As the faster, more maneuverable ship, and the one that was easier to control, it made sense for the *Fire* to go in second, where she could keep watch on the coneship. But even the spares on board the *Fire* had not been enough to patch up the coneship's stern detector grid. The coneship was, and would continue to be, all but completely blind astern. All she had was one wide-angle holocam set in the base of the cone, between two of the sublight engines. It would be useful during the final approach and landing, but even with the main engines off, its resolution was so poor that the *Jade's Fire* would be lost to view if she drifted only a few kilometers away. Once the engines came on, the stern holocam view could only get worse.

In other words, Han might—or might not—be able to see the *Fire*'s blink code signals if she signaled again. In theory, he could use the coneship's running lights to send blink code of his own, but he would not be able to see the lights himself, rendering it just that much harder to send accurate code. Han was hoping the question of signaling wouldn't come up.

The poor visibility to the stern made for another good reason to have the *Fire* go in second. Better to have a ship you trusted at your back.

At least a ship you more or less trusted. Han had managed to put to rest most—but not all—of his reservations regarding Mara. He could think of no reason, no motive, for her acting against Han and Leia and the Republic, and there was no hard evidence that she had done so. But she had never explained her actions to his satisfaction, either. She had been in the right places at the right times—and the wrong places at the wrong times—a bit too often in recent days.

On the other hand, if she had wanted to do real damage, Mara was too much of a pro to let things be bungled. And the opposition had certainly done some bungling, thank the stars. Not everything had gone their way. Say whatever else you might about the woman, but Mara was competent.

And that was a compelling argument. *No,* Han told himself as the *Jade's Fire* was lost completely to forward view. *Leave it be.* They really had no choice but to trust Jade. He watched as the *Fire* came into somewhat fuzzy view on the stern viewscreen. It was time to forget everything else and remember that the main thing was to get this crate down onto the surface. "Now, Salculd, it is your task," he said. "Do well."

"I will," Salculd said. "Don't worry about that." The ship chose that moment to lurch to one side, and Salculd grabbed frantically at the controls. "Sorry, sorry," Salculd said. "Stabilizer overcompensating. All right now."

"I can't tell you what a comfort that is," Han said. For a moment he considered the idea of shoving Salculd out of the pilot's station and taking over, but he knew better than that. The controls were set up for a Selonian, and the coneship had so many idiosyncrasies it made the *Millennium Falcon* look like a standard production ship. It might be an alarming thought, but unless things got really hairy, it was probably safest to trust Salculd.

Salculd edged the throttle up just a trifle more and the coneship moved just a bit faster in toward the planet. At least the coneship was not such a relic that it relied on ballistic reentry, using friction with the atmosphere to slow itself down. It could make a nice, civilized powered reentry. At least Han hoped so. Most spacecraft were designed to survive at least one ballistic reentry, but not this thing.

The planet moved closer. In another few minutes Salculd would have to turn the ship over and point its engines forward to slow the craft. That was the part that worried Han. Once they were decelerating, they would be at their most vulnerable. The coneship's fragility was far from the only source of danger. Someone on Selonia had sent a whole fleet of Light Attack Fighters up to meet the Bakuran ships.

The Bakurans had done a fair amount of damage to the LAFs, but Han had to assume that whoever commanded them would have the sense to hold some of them in reserve. And as Dracmus assured him that the Hunchuzuc had no such ships, it only made sense to assume that whoever it was who did have Light Attack Fighters might take a dim view of the coneship's arrival. Things could get sticky. Han had worked on the assumption that there would be trouble, and done his best to plan accordingly.

The *Jade's Fire* could provide a certain amount of covering fire, if push came to shove, but the other ship would be an uncertain protection at best. The coneship was completely unarmed, and had no shields at all. It didn't even have enough reserve power to hook up any weaponry—a moot point in any event, as there was no practical way to dismount any of the *Jade's* weapons or attach them to the coneship. Han had looked into it. Short of standing in the airlock and taking potshots at any attackers with his hand-blaster, there was not much he could do.

But Han was used to working with nothing. Even a ship as decrepit as this one could play a few tricks if need be. He had found a way to rig up a defense that might provide some measure of protection if things got hot.

Of course, sometimes, when you worked with nothing, nothing was exactly what you got. And sometimes, if you got into a fight with people who had better hardware, those other people won. Not a happy line of thought when you were on board a flying practice target headed into a war zone.

And his thoughts didn't get any happier a few minutes later when Leia sent that attack warning.

CHAPTER TWO

Landing

Leia Organa Solo, Chief of State of the New Republic, sat at the navigator's station aboard the *Jade's Fire*, watching the coneship drift in toward the planet Selonia. She had been a fool to let Han stay aboard that bucket of bolts. But she knew perfectly well that there had been no chance at all to get him off that ship, once he had decided he owed something to the Selonians on board.

But what, exactly, was he getting them into? Leia was forced to think not just like a wife but like a politician. She could not see any way of avoiding it, but there was no question that Han was being drawn in by these Selonians—and that Leia was being drawn in as well. It would be easy, all too easy, for the New Republic to find itself on one side or another of a fight it had no business in. It would be even easier to get tempted into bargains with these Hunchuzucs, bargains that had a few too many hidden strings attached . . .

"He'll be all right, Leia," Mara said. "We'll stay right with them, all the way down. The *Fire* can offer them more protection than you think."

"Hmmm? What? Oh, yes," Leia said, pointlessly embarrassed. It was somewhat mortifying to be reassured by Mara Jade, of all people. Somehow to have Mara assume that Leia was worrying about her husband's safety when she was really thinking about the politics of the situation made it even worse. Was she so callous that calculation of political advantage even pushed aside worries about her husband? So calculating that even Mara Jade was capable of more concern for Han?

But Leia told herself, rather firmly, that she had more sense than that. She had no choice but to think on more than one level. What good would it do Han if she got so tied up in sentimental worrying that she failed to foresee the dangers ahead?

"Han will be all right," Leia said again, trying to convince herself as much as her companion. "If anyone can get that tub down to the surface, he can."

"*If* anyone can," Mara agreed, none too reassuringly. Mara was at her usual post, at the pilot's station, guiding the *Jade's Fire* down toward the surface. She frowned and adjusted the thrust controls a bit, slowing them down again.

"Trouble?" Leia asked.

Mara shook her head without taking her eyes off the viewport. "Nothing we can't handle, but I don't like being behind the coneship. That Selonian pilot needs a flying lesson or two. If she hits the brakes like that too many times, she's going to get our nose assembly right up her stern."

"Can we back off a little?"

"Not if we want them to stay in visual contact with us. That stern holocam has no resolution at all. We might be too far back for it to see us as it is— Burning stars, she doesn't know how to fly!" Mara pulled her joystick violently up and to the right. "She's doing the pitchover maneuver way too early—and without shutting off her engines. Nearly clipped her."

Leia watched as the lumbering bulk of the coneship began its turnover, flipping end over end to direct its sublight engines toward the planet and slow its descent. It was painfully obvious that the pilot was not managing very well. The ship was lurching abruptly from one attitude to the next, pausing at intermediate stages of the maneuver instead of moving smoothly from a nose-to-planet attitude direct to stern-to-planet. It only made it worse—much worse—that the pilot was doing it under power. Leia was a pretty fair pilot, and she would have been very reluctant to try doing it that way.

Mara was forced to fly two more evasive patterns just to keep the *Fire* from crashing into the other ship. Finally she backed the *Fire* off by five kilometers. "They're going to be nose-on to us anyway," Mara said. "They'll be able to see us reasonably well."

"With a little luck," Leia said, a bit doubtfully. The *Fire* had first-rate detection systems, and could have tracked the coneship halfway across the Corellian system, but all the coneship had was straight visual. Leia peered out the *Fire*'s viewport and managed, with great difficulty, to spot the tiny dot that was the coneship. The bright bulk of the planet's dayside loomed up behind the ship, rendering it all but invisible. How easy would the *Fire* be to see, a little spot of red against the blackness of space?

Mara wasn't even using the main viewscreen anymore, but watching her detector displays. *She* wasn't relying on visual detection. Oh, well. As long as at least one ship could see the other, things should be all right—

"Trouble!" Mara announced. "Leia, weapons and shields to standby, fast!"

Leia ran the power-up routines as quickly as she could. She ran quick checks on the ship's turbolasers and shields. "All weapon and shield systems functional and on-line," she announced. "What's happened?"

"Power up the defense tracking systems and tell me," Mara said. "All the nav systems can tell me is that a bunch of blips just showed up out of nowhere."

"Light Attack Fighters," Leia announced as the defense trackers came on. "A double flight of them, twelve in all, coming in from right over our stern. Must have dropped out of a high polar orbit."

Mara shook her head as she stared down at the navigation display. "We can handle them, but it won't be easy. Not with the coneship to cover."

"We're too far off to extend our shields toward the coneship."

"And we're going to stay that way," Mara said sharply. "I'm not getting any closer to that pilot than I have to—especially in combat. She's already nearly rammed us twice. Get close enough to provide shield cover, and we'll all be dead. Covering fire is the best I'm going to be able to do. How soon until the LAFs get here?"

"Firing range in thirty seconds."

"Stand by for combat maneuvers."

"No! Wait! We have to blink-code to Han, warn them!"

"You've got twenty-five seconds," Mara said, steel in her voice. There was no point even trying to argue.

Leia reached for the landing light controls and flipped them back to blink-code mode. She forced herself to take a full five seconds to compose her message, and then sent it three times, in rapid succession. "Done," Leia said.

"Good," Mara said. "Hang on."

*   *   *

Han was almost too busy trying to keep from being flung out of his chair to notice the flashing lights visible in the overhead viewport. "Smooth and gentle, Salculd! Not sudden!" he shouted as he tried to concentrate on the blink code—not easy to do when the ship he was on was flailing about like a cornered bantha. The trouble was that Han was only marginally better at reading code than he was at sending it. Even under perfect conditions, he might have had problems. He struggled to catch it all. At least Leia used the special word-end signal between words. Otherwise, he'd have never gotten anywhere. *"B-A-N-D-I- something-*

something word ends," he muttered to himself.
"Bandi? Bandits! Oh, great!" He tried to concentrate
on the next word. *Missed something -R-O-M word ends.*
Burning suns, Leia, do you have to send so fast?
*Missed   something   -E-H-I-N-D   word   ends
J-A-D-E-S-F-I—*

Han missed the end of it as the coneship bobbled
about again, but he had read enough to know the
score. Bandits, enemy fighters, were headed this way,
coming from behind the *Jade's Fire.* And either by bad
luck or good timing they were heading in right as the
coneship was at its most vulnerable.

Han glanced over at the Selonians. You didn't have
to be an expert at reading Selonian expressions to
know that they were both scared silly, Salculd only
slightly less so than Dracmus. Han reminded himself
she did not speak Basic. There was no point at all to
telling Salculd about the bandits until she had the ship
under control. Han was sure she hadn't even seen the
blink-code message. Good. Let her work. Let her
work.

The coneship slowly lumbered around into braking
position, its fat stern pointed almost precisely straight
down at the planet, but canted just slightly into the
ship's direction of travel, so the braking run could kill
the craft's forward momentum as well.

Han checked his instruments, doing his best to make
sense out of the Selonian notation. By some miracle or
other, Salculd seemed to have gotten them into the
right position, and at the right attitude. "Good, good,"
he said as calmly as he could. Probably they had just a
few seconds left before the bandits jumped them. But
trying to rush Salculd would be worse than useless at
this point. If she got any more scared, she might freeze
completely. "Now then, Salculd, one other matter. Is
time to, ah, *test* our defense plan. You will bring the
ship to spin, please, of three spins per minute."

"Test?" Dracmus sputtered. "But you said it was a
one-time-only trick."

Han had been hoping no one would bring that up. At least Dracmus had spoken in Basic. There was still a million-to-one chance Salculd hadn't caught on. "Quiet," he said in Basic before switching back to Selonian. "Make the spins, please, Honored Salculd. Make sure all is well, in case needed."

It was clear that Salculd did not believe him—but it would seem she was willing to pretend she did, at least for a little while. "Yes, yes," she said, "of course. Commencing axial spin." The ship began to rotate around its conical axis, so the stars pinwheeled across the sky. Han studied the overhead view, as best he was able. He could just about spot the *Fire,* and the bandits were almost certainly smaller, and coming from behind. There was no way he could find them, especially with the ship spinning like a top. He gave it up. No point in worrying about things he could not change.

"Disable internal damping," Han said calmly, casually. The inertial dampers prevented anything more than a few percent of a ship's acceleration and motion from being felt by those aboard. Without them, the occupants of a ship accelerating to light speed could be squashed to jelly. No one liked turning them off—but sometimes you had to do what you didn't like.

"But if we cannot restart inertial damping—"

"Worry about such later!" Han snapped. He knew better than Salculd what it might mean if they couldn't get the dampers back on. But they would have to live long enough for the problem to come up. "We need to use centrifugal effect if plan is to work, and inertial damping cancels it out. End damping!"

Salculd inhaled nervously and reached out her hand to cut off the inertial damping system. All of a sudden, Han felt his weight double, then triple, as the dampers stopped compensating for the ship's deceleration. A moment later he felt the disorienting sensation of the ship spinning.

"Confirm all inner airlocks sealed," Han ordered.

"All inner airlock doors sealed. Pressure in locks," Salculd said. "Honored Solo, must we truly—"

"Quiet! We must. Be ready for next step! Maintain course, maintain thrust, unless I order otherwise!" Han struggled to concentrate on the spinning starfield overhead. If this was going to work, it would take exact timing. But how could he time anything if he couldn't see? Maybe he would get lucky and the *Jade's Fire* would signal the all clear.

And maybe he would wake up and discover the whole nightmare trip to Corellia had just been a dream. If only wishing could make it true. He had done his best. Now all they could do was hang on and see how it came out.

*   *   *

"Rear, ventral, and dorsal shields to full, forward shields to one quarter," Mara ordered. "Divert shields as needed for ship safety."

Leia worked the shield settings. "Shields configured as ordered."

"Good," Mara said. "Maintain turbolasers at standby. We are going to hold this course and speed. Act like they aren't there. They can't know how good or bad our detectors are. They've never seen this kind of ship before, but I know LAFs. They have the gear to detect turbos going on-line, but not shield activation. If we keep the guns off and stay on course, they might decide we can't see them."

"What good does that do us?" Leia asked.

"They might blow right past us and zero in on the coneship. My guess is that whoever is on those LAFs is targeting the Hunchuzuc, not us."

"But Han is—"

"Safer this way," Mara said, watching her displays. "We can handle seven or eight of them at once, but not twelve. Not in a direct engagement. But if the LAFs don't engage us, we'll have nice, clear forward view shots right up their stern plates while they're focused on the coneship. We can pick off three or four of them before the rest bring fire to bear on us. Set up the targeting system for tracking follow-fire. If they engage us directly, we return fire. If they go past us, commence fire when they are three kilometers past us. Understood?"

"Yes, but—"

"No buts," Mara said. "This ship fights my way, or not at all."

Leia gave in again. Mara had far more experience at this sort of fight than she did. "Very well," she said.

"Stand by. Here they come."

Leia watched the stern detector displays as the LAFs came in, directly behind the *Fire*'s stern, trying to hide in the detection shadow produced by the sublight engines. They *were* trying to sneak up. From that bearing they wouldn't even show up on most ships' detectors.

The LAFs swept in, their images in the detection screen breaking up just a bit due to interference from the sublight engines. Leia tensed up as they swept through the optimum firing range, and felt herself relax just a trifle as they swept on, past the *Fire*. But she didn't relax too far—not when they were passing her by to take a crack at her husband's ship.

The LAFs flashed past the *Fire*, zeroing in on the coneship. "The coneship!" she cried out. "It's spinning up. They must have got our warning."

"Let's hope Han's idea works better than it ought to," Mara said.

It wasn't the most tactful thing to say, even if Leia had been thinking the same thing herself. But there was no time. "Coming up on three kilometers distance," she said.

"Commence fire," Mara ordered.

"Not unless they fire first!" Leia said. "Maybe they're just here to throw a scare into us, or they might be on escort duty. No way to tell with communications jammed."

"All right," Mara said, the doubt plain in her voice. "You can make that—"

But the first flash of turbolaser fire from the lead LAF shut down the argument. Leia released the safeties on the *Fire*'s follow-fire circuits and started selecting targets, aiming first for the LAF that had opened fire.

*   *   *

"Here they come!" Han shouted in Basic, forgetting for a moment to speak in Selonian. Salculd got the message all the same. She looked up through the viewport at the tiny spots of light in the sky, and understood precisely what was going on. She let out a most undignified squawk. The whole slowly spinning coneship lurched to one side and came close to heeling over into a disastrous tumble.

"Calmness!" Han shouted. "Be calm, alert. Throttle down all engines. End all thrust. Stand by to open outer airlock doors on my command."

"Thrott—throttling down all engines," Salculd said. "Ready on the airlock doors."

"Wait for it," Han said, watching the LAFs come closer. Weight faded away as Salculd powered down the engines. With the inertial dampers off-line, and the engine thrust gone, Han found himself in zero gee for the first time in a long time. Han knew people who had spent half their lives in space without experiencing zero gravity—and with the flip-flops his stomach was doing all of a sudden, he could understand why.

But there was no time for that now. Not with a sky full of Light Attack Fighters heading in. "Be ready, ready," he told Salculd.

The lead LAF fired and caught them with a glancing blow to the starboard side, slamming into the hull like a giant fist. "It's all right!" Han shouted, having not the least idea if it was or not. "It's all right. Stand by on the airlock doors. Wait for it. Be ready—"

*   *   *

The *Jade's Fire*'s forward quad turbolaser blazed away, tracking the lead LAF across the sky. The LAF broke off its attack run, trying to fly an evasive pattern and escape. For a moment it managed to break out of the tracking pattern, but the *Jade's Fire* regained a positive lock and poured in fire again. The LAF's shields flared and blazed for a moment before giving way altogether. The fighter exploded, a blossom of fire that flared up and was gone.

Leia fed two new targets to the follow-fire system, and got busy herself with the manual guns, reading the detection screens for herself. But the rest of the LAFs were not going to be such easy pickings. They had their rear shields powered up to maximum, and did a better job of evasive maneuvers, good enough to completely bamboozle the follow-fire systems.

But not good enough to fool Leia. She settled in with the manual controls and began looking for targets. She concentrated her fire on the toughest shots, the LAFs closest to the coneship. She got a lock on one and fired, holding the guns on target long enough to burn through the shields and blow the fighter to bits.

Just then the coneship cut its engines, allowing it to drop straight for the planet's surface. It threw the LAFs off, if only for a moment or two.

Leia shook her head and sighed. Not much of an evasive maneuver, but probably the best Han could manage with that clunky piece of junk. But suddenly her detector displays showed a cloud of debris blooming out from the coneship in all directions.

Fear stabbed at her heart. That one hit on the coneship's hull couldn't have done that much damage, could it? Could the craft be breaking up before her eyes, with Han aboard? She had no desire to watch the death of her husband—but then something happened to one of the LAFs, and then another, and another. As they swooped in close to the coneship, they bounced and skittered and wobbled off course. Two of them lost power, and the third was rocked by a small explosion amidships. Leia got a target lock on one of the survivors and fired, catching a piece of him before he managed to get his shields up. Leia tried to track to a new target, but the LAFs had plainly decided to take the hint and accept the fact they weren't welcome. They scattered, hightailing out of there in all directions.

But how in the blazes had— Suddenly she understood. Of course. Of course. "Mara! His trick worked! Get us out from behind Han, fast! New course, five or six kilometers to one side of him, and try to overtake him if you can. It's not going to be so safe to be behind him for a while."

She smiled, relief flooding over her. She should have known Han wouldn't give up without a fight.

*   *   *

Han listened closely as the last of the junk went lumbering out of the airlocks, banging and clattering and thudding and reverberating through the ship. There was no air in the locks left to transmit noise, of course, but there was on the other side of the interior bulkheads—a fact that had made itself known with every bit of broken-down hardware that had slammed around the locks.

Han had spent half a day policing the ship, looking for every bit of surplus or broken hardware he could. Buckets of bolts, worn-out spare parts, garbage from the galley, unidentifiable bits of machinery that had been sitting in the hold for who knew how long—he had thrown all of it into the locks.

And all of it had tumbled out into space when the locks were opened, thrown clear by centrifugal force. Result—a cloud of slow-moving space junk left right in the path of the attacking LAFs. And the LAFs had quite sensibly configured their shields for maximum power aft, to defend against laser blasts from the *Jade's Fire*—leaving them with minimum power forward.

But plowing through a cloud of bits and pieces of broken metal and plastic at a closing speed of something like a thousand kilometers an hour was very far from a good idea.

However, piling a ship into a planet was an even worse one. "Good!" Han said. "They're gone! But we are not out of this yet. Reestablish inertial dampers and cut ship spin."

"At once, Honored Solo," Salculd replied. There was an odd shimmering sort of vibration as the inertial field came back on and weight returned.

The ship's ungainly spin slowed, and stopped—and then started up again in the opposite direction—and started to get faster.

"Salculd!" Han called out. "This is no time for the playing of games!"

"I am not doing so, Honored Solo. Failure in lateral attitude control system. I cannot shut it off!"

"Oh, for—" Han scrambled up out of his seat and dove for the main circuit breaker box. He yanked it open and tripped the lateral attitude control breaker by hand. That killed the thrusters that were producing the spin—but also killed the ones that fired in the opposite direction, and could bring it to a halt. He slapped the access door shut and returned to his seat.

"Hope everyone is liking to spin," Han announced in Selonian. "We are to do it for a while. Salculd! Restart to main sublight engines—and nice, slow throttle-up, please!"

"At once, Honored Solo," Salculd replied. She reached for the throttle controls and began adjusting them.

Nothing seemed to happen. "Not that slow, Salculd. We need to do some braking!"

Salculd looked at Han, and the panicked look that had seemed on the verge of fading away was there in full force, and no doubt. "No activation!" she announced. "Engine initiator not responding!"

"Horror!" cried Dracmus. "We incinerate for certain."

"Quiet, Dracmus, or I send you out the airlock. Salculd, try again!" Han said. "Firstly confirm you have power to all engine systems."

"Board shows all power systems fine and lovely," Salculd said. "Board says is working, but it not."

"Not helpful," Han said, jumping up. "Off I go again. Keep trying, and listen to the comm!"

Han rushed for the ladder to the lower decks and clambered down as fast as he could. As soon as he reached the lower deck, he smelled smoke. There was trouble, big trouble. That one hit from the LAF must have hit something in the transverse power coupling. Han jogged around the circumferential corridor until he reached the proper access hatch. It was sealed, praise be. The bad news was the smoke was coming off the painted metal on the hatch. Han checked the readouts. They showed there was still pressure in there, if the numbers were to be believed. The temperature gauge was pegged at the high end. He worked the hatch controls to pop the compartment's spill valves. They should have operated automatically once fire broke out. Obviously they hadn't.

But even if the automatics were out, at least the manual controls were still working. There was a sort of clank and a thud from behind the hatch, and then a roaring hiss that faded off into nothing as the air in the compartment vented into space. The ship lurched slightly to one side before the inertial dampers corrected for the off-center thrust.

Han resealed the spill valves. The hatch had a manual spill valve of its own that allowed pressure between the two sides of the hatch to equalize without opening it up. Han burned his fingers getting the safeties off, and then popped the hatch valve. The corridor was suddenly filled with a roaring, thundering rush of air that almost knocked Han over.

Han looked around, and, for a miracle, spotted a fire extinguisher within reach right where it was supposed to be. He peeled off his shirt and wrapped it around his left hand, then took the extinguisher in his right. He grabbed the manual hatch control with his left hand, and the shirt instantly began to smolder. He pulled the lever and swung the hatch open.

A blast of heat struck him in the face; he checked his grip on the extinguisher. If the renewed supply of oxygen started something burning, he wanted to be ready for it. But he did not want to try doing emergency repairs on equipment that was covered with spray foam if he could possibly avoid it.

Not that spray foam could have made things much worse. Han stood in the hatchway, stared at the compartment, and felt sick. The initiator was just not there anymore. There was no need for the extinguisher. Anything that could have burned already had. Han looked down at the blackened deck plates. The compartment was just under the outer hull. It looked as if the LAF's turbolaser hadn't quite burned through the hull, but it had clearly come close. The entire compartment was still hot, but was cooling rapidly now, the metal pinging and clinging as it gave up its heat to space.

But Han wasn't here to see what happened after an equipment bay fire. *Think,* Han told himself. *Think as fast as you ever have.* The coneship had a very awkward engine-start system, and one that had caused plenty of trouble already on this trip. More modern systems worked differently, but on this bucket, the initiators served as massive capacitors, storing up huge amounts of energy and slamming it all out at once to get the sublight engines over the power threshold where their energy reaction was self-sustaining.

With the initiators out, the sublight engines could not restart. And without those engines the coneship was going to drop like a stone, a shooting star aimed straight for the planet. They had to restart those engines. They *had* to. But there was no other system in the ship with anything like enough power to let the sublights reach their minimum start-up energy. Even if they overloaded every single—

Wait a second. That was it. It was unlikely it would work. But it definitely wouldn't work if he didn't give it a try.

And give it a try *fast*. They were in free fall, heading straight for a spot that was going to have a new crater in a few minutes. Han stepped back out of the initiator compartment and resealed the hatch. Where would the repulsor feedback dispersal system be on this tub? Useless to ask Salculd. She was so close to the edge she probably wouldn't remember where the pilot's station was. She had given him a tour of the ship when he had first come aboard—that was it! Just on the other side of the main power room. Perfect. Han rushed back down the circumferential corridor the way he had come and found the right access panel on the wall. He pulled it open and traced the connections. Good. Good. For a wonder, they were all standard hookups. He tripped the breaker by hand. Cable. He needed power cable. Stores room. They had all but cleaned it out to fill the airlocks with junk, but there had to be *something* left. He charged down the corridor and threw open the hatch to the stores room.

Nothing. Down to the bare walls. Utterly empty. Han started to swear to himself and at himself with impressive fluency, but there was no time for such indulgences. Think. *Think.* Life support. Main power to life support. No sense keeping it on. They were all going to be dead in about five minutes anyway if he didn't get some power cable.

Life support. Where could he kill power to life support? Right! Cut it right at main power and yank the cable from there. Han rushed back to the main power room, threw the hatch open, and went inside. Not everything was labeled, and what was labeled was in

Selonian, of course. He struggled to sort out what was
what. There! If he was reading the labels right, that
junction was MAIN DEVICE FOR THE BLOWING OF AIR
MEANT FOR BREATHING, and that one was CLEANSING OF
AIR FROM POLLUTANTS FOR PLEASANT BREATHING. A little verbose, perhaps, but clear enough. He found the
circuit breakers on the junctions and slammed them
off. Han could hear the fans and blowers dying all over
the ship. He yanked the power cables out of their sock-
ets and pulled them down off their cable guides. He
pulled the other ends of the cables, and then found a
label reading POWER INPUT HERE FROM THE POWERFUL
INITIATORS WHICH ARE IN ANOTHER COMPARTMENT. He
pulled the cables running from the destroyed initiators
and plugged in his borrowed life-support cables. He
snaked the cables out into the corridor, praying they
would reach, and gave thanks when they did. He made
sure the repulsors were off-line, then yanked the lines
running to the repulsor feedback dispersal unit and
plugged in his borrowed cables.

He stepped back and double-checked his work.
"Okay," he said to no one at all. "That ought to work.
I think." He turned and ran for the ladder up to the
command deck.

*   *   *

"Something's wrong," Leia said, watching her detector
screens. "The spin has reversed instead of stopping,
and they haven't restarted their main engines."

"Maybe they took some bad damage from that hit,"
Mara said.

"Can we dock with the ship and get them off?" Leia
asked.

"Not before they hit atmosphere," Mara said.
"There's nowhere near enough time. Besides, that
cloud of debris they threw out is still traveling with
them. We'd get hit the same way the LAFs were."

"A tractor beam, then," Leia said. "We could set that up and—"

"And what? That ship isn't all that much smaller than this one. The tractor on this ship doesn't have a tenth the power to hold that ship. If we tried it, more than likely they'd pull us down instead. I'm sorry, Leia. There's nothing at all we can do."

Deep in her heart, Leia knew Mara was right. But it felt *wrong* to give up without a fight. They had to do *something.* "Stay close," Leia said. "Get as close as you can without getting into the debris cloud and take up station keeping."

"Leia, there is nothing we can—"

"Suppose they get temporary control, or slow just enough that they can abandon ship?" Leia asked. "We need to be close enough to get in and help."

Mara hesitated a moment. "All right. But we won't be able to hold station keeping long. We're about five minutes from atmosphere right now, and once we hit it—well, that will be the end of things." Leia knew that. Without shielding, without braking from the engines, the coneship would turn into a meteorite, a streak of fire that burned across the sky before crashing in the planet. "I'll stay close as long as I can," Mara said. "But it won't be long."

"Do it," Leia said. But even as she urged Mara onward, she wondered why. What good would it do to watch from closer in as her husband was incinerated?

* * *

"Out!" Han shouted at Salculd as he came up out the hatch to the command deck. "Out of pilot chair now! I take over."

"But what are you—"

"No time!" he snapped. He sealed the hatch, just in case they lived long enough to worry about air leaks. "I must take over. No time to explain what to do. Out! Move!"

Salculd moved, undoing her seat restraints and bailing out of the pilot's station.

Han dove into the vacated seat and checked the status board. Good. Good. Repulsors showing full power in reserve. "Switching on repulsors!" he announced. He adjusted them for their tightest beam and maximum range.

"Honored Solo! The repulsors cannot work at this range!" Dracmus said in Basic. "They are only effective within two kilometers of surface!"

"I know that," Han said. "They need something to work against before they can set up a repulsion effect. But at these speeds, they'll encounter a fair amount of resistance from the top of the atmosphere. I know, I know, not enough to slow us down—but enough to start large power transfers through the feedback dispersal loop."

"But what good does that do?"

"I've taken the disperser *out* of the loop and run the cables through the initiator power intake on the engine power system. The feedback energy is just accumulating in the repulsor system. When the power level is high enough, I'll reset the feedback power breaker and dump the energy right into the initiator intake on the engine power systems."

"What?!"

"Jump-start it," Han said. "I'm going to jump-start it."

There was a moment of dead silence in the control cabin before Dracmus let out a strangled moan and covered her face with her hands.

"What is going on?" Salculd demanded in Selonian.

"I go to start engines by accumulating repulsor feedback power and dumping through initiator manifold," Han replied.

"But feedback buildup will destroy repulsors!"

"Get even more destroyed by crashing into Selonia," Han said in his awkward Selonian. "This not work and *you* have idea, *you* try yours. Hang on."

The idea was crazy. Han knew that. But not doing anything at all would be crazier still. Even a million-to-one shot was better than no chance at all.

He watched the feedback charge accumulator display as the excess energy built up in the repulsor system. The more power, the better the chance of restarting the engines—unless he accumulated so much power the repulsors simply blew out. The closer they got to the planet, the more resistance the repulsors encountered, and the faster the feedback accumulated. But of course, the farther they fell, the less time they would have to put on the brakes, if and when the engines did light.

Han knew that even the maximum power output he could hope for would be borderline minimum to get the sublight engines going—and he was going to get exactly one chance. Whether or not this stunt worked, it was going to blow out the repulsors and the feedback accumulator and half the other systems on the ship.

Han checked his estimated flight path meters. Twenty seconds from the average top of the sensible atmosphere—though the tops of atmospheres had a nasty habit of not being where they were supposed to be, raising and lowering depending on storms and tides and solar heating. But twenty seconds was the outside, the longest he could possibly wait. The repulsors were not likely to provide much more charging of the accumulator if they were being melted off.

It was going to be a tough call, a threading of the needle between competing disasters.

Han checked the altitude and acceleration displays. The coneship was gathering speed, terrifying speed, with every second. Even if he got the engines lit, there might not be time to slow the ship before piling it in.

"Honored Solo! Hull temperature suddenly increasing!" Salculd cried.

"Atmosphere's here a little early!" Han said. "Hang on! We're going to jump this thing and see what happens."

One chance, Han told himself. *Exactly one chance.* For a fleeting moment he thought of Leia, watching from the *Jade's Fire* and unable to do anything. He thought of his three children, off somewhere in the care of Chewbacca and Ebrihim the Drall. No. No. He could not die. Not when they all needed him. *One chance.* The ship bucked and shuddered as the atmospheric buffering shook it hard enough to get past the inertial dampers. *One chance.*

Han waited as long as he dared, then one moment longer, then one more. And then—

He slammed down the relay reset switch as hard as he could, dumping all of the feedback energy directly into the engine start manifold. He stabbed down on the engine start button—and felt a horrifying lurch, just as a low, rumbling explosion shook the ship from base to apex. That would have to be the repulsors blowing. For a long, sickening moment, nothing else happened. But then the ENGINES NOW CERTAINLY ARE INITIATED FULLY indicator came on, and Han had three good engines.

Three? Not four? One of them must have been blown out by that LAF fighter. Han had been afraid of that. But even if he had one less engine than he had hoped for, that was three more than he had expected.

Ignoring all his own advice on the subject, he brought the throttle up fast. There wasn't time to nurse the engines. There was a distant bang and sudden flurry of violent vibrations that faded almost before they started, but the engines were holding. At least for now. At least for now.

Han watched the acceleration meter, the velocity gauge, and the none-too-reliable altitude meter. For a wonder, the displays were all in standard units, and not some obscure Selonian format he had never seen before.

But what he was seeing was by no means reassuring. He had flown enough reentries to know at a glance that they were far from out of trouble. The best they

were going to manage was a controlled crash. Han
risked a glance out the viewport and saw that the
Jade's Fire was still staying close, somehow. Mara was
some kind of pilot.

Now if only he had a view that would show him the
direction he was going. Unfortunately, the ship was flying stern-first, and the stern holocam, which might
have shown him at least a vague idea of where he was
heading, had given up altogether at some point in the
proceedings.

On the bright side, air friction was slowing down the
ship's axial spin. Finally it stopped altogether, which at
least made piloting the coneship that much easier. It
was about time *something* got easier.

Han watched his velocity and altitude gauges, and
knew just how much trouble he was still in. He had to
shed some more speed. He had no choice in the matter. There was a way to do it, but it had its own draw-
backs. And making it work without maneuvering
thrusters was not going to be easier. He would have to
do all his steering by playing with the thrust of the
main engines—not simple when he was already jug-
gling their thrust vectors to compensate for the missing
engine. Still, it was doable. Maybe.

He eased back just a trifle on the thrust to number
three engine, and the coneship slowly pitched back, until it was flying at about a forty-five-degree angle of
attack. It was still falling straight down, but now its
nose was pointed an eighth of a turn away from the
vertical. If Han had it figured right, that ought to start
the coneship developing a bit of aerodynamic lift, in
effect causing it to work like an airfoil. The coneship
began to move sideways as well as down, and every
millimeter of lateral movement came straight from the
energy of their fall.

The ship began to bang and shudder violently, but
every crash and rattle was that much more excess energy expended.

"Honored Solo!" Dracmus protested above the

racket, "You have put us in lateral flight! Where are you taking us?"

"I haven't the faintest idea," Han said. "But we have to go lateral to shed some speed."

"But suppose we land outside the zone controlled by my Den?!"

"Then we have a problem," Han shouted back.

Dracmus did not reply to that, but she had a point. Landing completely at random on a planet in the midst of civil war was not exactly prudent.

Han pushed it from his mind. The job of the moment was getting this thing down in one piece. Down *where,* they could sort out later.

He checked his gauges. They were still falling like a rock—but like a slower rock, a gliding rock. And hull temperatures were actually falling, just a trifle. Maybe, maybe, they were going to make it.

Of course, landing on the sublight engines, rather than on the now-dead repulsors, and landing blind would be challenges in their own right. It would be at least another ninety seconds before he had to worry about such things.

He checked the gauges and shook his head. The lateral flight trick was slowing them down, but nowhere near enough. At this rate, they'd be lucky to drop below the speed of sound before they hit.

There was no way around it. He was going to have to get something more out of the engines. What about that fourth engine, the one that had refused to light? Maybe it was just its initiator link that had been blown off. Maybe the engine itself was still there, if he could just get it to come on. Maybe if he tried a parallel backfeed start. With the other engines up and running, he could borrow part of their energy output and back-flush it through the unlit engine. It *might* work. Han reset the power flow from the number two engine, routing five percent of it through the initiator lines to engine three. He stabbed down the button marked

PRESSING HERE WILL CAUSE ENGINE NUMBER FOUR TO
START.

A weird high-pitched squeal cut through the clamor-
ing roar that filled the command deck, and the coneship began to oscillate wildly as the engine lit and died
and lit and died. A display indicator came on, an-
nouncing ENGINE FOUR NOW OPERATING NICELY, but it
went out again, then popped on and faded one more
time before coming back on and staying that way.

Four engines. He had four good engines. He might
come out of this alive after all. But then he checked his
altitude, and found good reason to doubt it. They were
only three kilometers up. Han realized that he would
have to shed all of his lateral speed immediately if he
was going to set this thing down. He pitched the ship
around until it was flying flat on its side, the thrust axis
parallel to the ground. The planetary horizon swooped
into view and kept going right past, until Han was flying exactly upside down, his feet pointed at the sky and
his head pointed at the ground.

He throttled all the engines up to maximum, and
just a bit beyond, and held it there, until the ground
stopped rushing past from side to side and was simply
coming straight at him. Zero forward velocity, or close
enough.

But plenty of velocity in the direction of down. Han
pitched the coneship over again, until he was flat on
his back, looking at the sky, and made sure the engines
were cranked up to maximum power. There was nothing else he could do. "Hanging on!" he shouted in
Selonian. "Be strapped in and braced. We are going to
be hitting hard!"

Green lights started to flash all over the propulsion
status display. In most ships that would have been a
good thing, but not on this crate. To a Selonian, green
was the color of danger, disaster. The engines were
running full out, at or beyond the point of catastrophe.
Han wanted desperately to see if he could bully or
tempt just a little bit more out of them, but did not

dare. No point in coming this far just to have the ship detonate a half kilometer off the ground.

Maybe, maybe, they had slowed down enough to make this a survivable crash. Han cut power to all systems and diverted it all into the inertial dampers. There was no way the dampers could absorb all the energy of impact, but they would soak up some of it. Maybe if they were running at max power, it would be just enough.

And that was it. That was all. There were no tricks left. Nothing left to do but hold on and watch the numbers in the altimeter evaporate. Han had not the faintest idea where they were about to land. There had not been time, in his one quick glance at the ground, to do anything more than see that it was there. He had seen water, flat land, and some good-sized hills, but which of them he was about to hit, he had no idea.

One kilometer up. Eight hundred meters. Seven hundred. Five hundred. Four hundred. Three fifty. If only the repulsors were still working. Too bad he had been forced to fry them to a crisp starting the engines. Three hundred. How accurate was that altimeter, anyway? Two hundred. One fifty. One hundred meters up. Seventy-five. Fifty. Han braced for the impact and resisted the impulse to shut his eyes. Zero.

Negative ten meters. Not all that accurate. But every extra meter was another fraction of a second for the coneship's engines to slow them down. Neg twenty. Neg fifty—

SLAM!! A hundred crazed banthas jumped onto Han's chest all at once, driving him down into the padding of the pilot's flight station. Dracmus screamed, a startling, high-pitched ululation. A metal bulkhead tore itself apart somewhere in the ship with a terrible metallic shriek, and a dozen alarms started hooting at once. The overhead viewport held together, somehow, and Han could see the sky was filled with smoke and steam—and mud.

Huge gobs of sodden earth splattered down on the viewport, covering it all but completely.

Han hit the alarm cutoff, and was astonished by the sudden near-silence. But for Dracmus moaning in fright, and the plopping sounds of the last of the mud raining down on the ship's hull, all was quiet. They were down, and alive. A sudden flurry of water, falling in a single thin sheet of droplets, fell on the ship, washing some—but far from all—of the mud off the viewport.

Han got to his feet, feeling more than a little wobbly. "That one was close," he said in Basic, to himself as much as anything. "Come," he said in Selonian. "We must leave ship. Might be—" He stopped dead. Half his Selonian seemed to have faded away, at least for the moment. After that close a call, it was a wonder he was calm enough to remember his own name. But he couldn't think of the words for "chemical leak," or "fire," or "short circuits." "Bad things," he said at last. "Might be bad things on ship. Must leave *now*."

The two Selonians, both of them clearly shaken up, got to their feet and followed Han down the ladder to the lower deck and over to the main hatch. Han punched at the open button, and was not the least bit surprised when nothing at all happened. The ship they had risked their lives to land, the ship that the Hunchuzuc needed so badly, was a write-off. A complete loss. Han knelt down, fumbled with the access panel for the manual controls, got the cover off, and turned the hand crank. The hatch swung reluctantly open, and jammed up twice before it swung wide enough for them to get out. Han stuck his head out first and looked around.

It looked like they had landed square in the middle of a shallow pond—and splashed it dry on impact. The bottom of the pond was completely exposed, but for one or two puddles here and there. The mud was steaming here and there, letting off the heat produced by the ship's impact. It was a beautiful, perfect spring day. Somehow, the picturesque meadows and woodlands that surrounded the splashed-out pond made the mud and the mire and the mess of the landing seem just that much more out of place, just that much more absurd.

The coneship had buried itself at least a half meter into the soft mud of the pond bottom. What had been a meter and a half drop from the hatch to the ground was suddenly a lot shorter. Han sat down on the edge of the hatch and hopped down—only to sink in over his ankles in the thick mud. He lifted his left foot up out of the muck, nearly losing a boot in the process, and planted it as far away from the ship as possible before pulling his right foot out.

He squelched out of the pond basin toward dry land and saw a Selonian, an older-looking female with graying dark brown fur and a moody look in her eyes.

"That's a Hunchuzuc coneship, be it not?" the Selonian asked, watching Dracmus and Salculd stagger out of the craft.

"That's right," Han said, a bit distractedly as he slogged through the mud. That was the Selonians for you. A spaceship crash-lands in a pond in front of one, and what was the response? Not shock, or surprise, or fear. Not "hello," not "what an amazing escape," not "are you all right?" No. The first thing to worry about was what Den was involved.

"Hmmph," said the Selonian. "This is Chanzari land. We be Republicists, Hunchuzuc allies."

"Good," said Han, still struggling toward shore. "Glad to hear it." Han half climbed, half crawled out of the pond basin, and paused there a moment.

The old Selonian looked at the ship and shook her head. "Coneships," she said, her tone derisive. "The Hunchuzuc are foolhardy. Selonians do not belong in space."

Han looked at the Selonian for a long moment.

"You know," he said, "I'd just about worked that out for myself." He turned his back on the coneship and staggered off toward the other side of the clearing, where the *Jade's Fire* was settling in for a nice, calm, sedate landing.

CHAPTER THREE

At the Source

Tendra Risant sat in the pilot's station of the *Gentleman Caller,* and wondered if it was going to be all right, wondered how it could be all right. She had done her part, however little that might be. In purely objective terms, all was well. She had used the radionics transmitter to tell Lando of the fleet hidden in the Sacorrian system. His friends had gotten the news, and it might well prove vital to them. She knew Lando was alive, and well, and that he was glad she was in-system.

But none of that could change the fact that she was *stuck* out here, and no one could get to her. She looked through the forward viewport at the bright star of Corell, dead ahead. Unless that interdiction field went down, it was going to take her months to cross the distance from here to there. It was worth it, she knew that. She had more than likely saved lives, many lives—perhaps even Lando's life.

But the thought of more months alone on this ship was more than she could bear.

But the people Lando was with, the Bakurans, had asked her to send them more information. There was not much she could tell them that she had not said already—but she would tell them what she could. She switched on the radionics transmitter and set to work.

*   *   *

The Bakuran light cruiser *Intruder* fired her main forward turbolaser battery three times, and three times Pocket Patrol Boats exploded. "Very well," said Admiral Hortel Ossilege. "You may hold your fire. Bring the turbolasers to their stowed position and power them down. Make sure our friends can detect what you are doing. We have shown we can hurt them at will. Now we extend an invitation to leave. Let us see if our friends out there understand that we plan to play rough if they stay."

A reasonable tactic, Luke Skywalker thought, feeling none too happy about it. A show of overwhelming force *might* convince the surviving defenders to withdraw. After all, the odds of a handful of fighters defeating the *Intruder* and her sister ships, *Sentinel* and *Defender,* and all their fighters were almost zero.

On the other hand, the Rebels had faced such odds more than once in the war against the Empire, and had emerged victorious. Good training, strong motivation, good equipment, good intelligence—and plain good luck—could even up the odds quite a bit. There was no such thing as certainty in war.

Luke Skywalker stood next to Admiral Ossilege on the bridge of the *Intruder.* As always when he agreed with the man, he did not feel comfortable doing so. Luke glanced at Lando Calrissian, standing on the other side of Ossilege, and the look on his face told Luke that Lando shared his concerns. The tactics were sound, even conservative. The enemy forces consisted of little more than twenty or so PPBs. There was nothing much to be gained in wiping out such a small force. If Ossilege could convince them to withdraw without exposing his own forces to needless casualties, that would be all to the good.

Very sensible and cautious. Except that Ossilege was not a cautious commander. If it seemed he was trying something careful, Luke had a hunch that it was merely a cover for something madly audacious to follow. Ossilege had shown a tendency to dare too much rather than too little. When he played a conservative game, the odds were fair that what appeared to be caution was just an elaborate preparation for a very large gamble indeed. Or had losing the *Watchkeeper* to the Selonian planetary repulsor cost him his nerve? Ossilege was a small, wiry-looking man, who favored dress-white uniforms that set off his collection of medals and ribbons. He was a dried-up, self-important little man who seemed to have little patience for anyone or anything. He looked to be a comic-opera caricature of an admiral—but Luke had never met as hard-edged, as cold-blooded, a military commander. No one found it relaxing to spend time in the presence of Admiral Ossilege.

Of course, with the massive, overwhelming bulk of Centerpoint Station dominating the sky outside the viewports, Luke would have felt a little edgy even if the *Watchkeeper* hadn't been destroyed.

"There they go," Lando announced, pointing toward a cloud of tiny dots lifting away from one of the docking bays of Centerpoint. The defending fighters were withdrawing. "Decided they couldn't do any good against us, I guess."

"Or perhaps they decided we would be unable to do Centerpoint any harm," said Ossilege. "A wise tactician retreats from an indefensible position in order to preserve his forces. But a wise tactician will likewise avoid expending his forces needlessly in the defense of the impregnable."

"What are you saying?" asked Luke.

Ossilege gestured toward Centerpoint. "We are dismissing the enemy fighters because they are so small in comparison to us. But, proportionately, we are far smaller in comparison to Centerpoint. It is, somehow, the source of power that can impose an interdiction field over an entire planetary system. What other powers might it have?"

"No way to know," said Lando. "I figure the one

thing we can count on is being surprised. And I doubt that many of the surprises are going to be pleasant."

Just at that moment, a service droid wheeled up from behind them and came around to stop in front of Lando. "And here's a surprise now," Lando muttered. "Yes, what is it?" he asked the droid.

"Begging your pardon, sir, but Lieutenant Kalenda wishes to see both you and Master Skywalker, sir. A new message from Source T has come in."

Lando looked worriedly at Luke. "That ought to make me happy," he said. "But I have the feeling she's not calling in just to chat." He turned toward the service droid. "Lead the way."

*   *   *

Source T was Tendra Risant. Lando and Luke had met Tendra on her home world of Sacorria, one of the so-called "Outlier" worlds of the Corellian Sector. The local authorities had kicked Lando and Luke off Sacorria almost immediately after meeting Tendra.

As they followed the droid down to the cruiser's com section, it crossed Lando's mind, not for the first time, that Tendra would be vastly amused to learn that Bakuran military intelligence had given her a name as ridiculously pompous as Source T.

Lando had met Tendra while searching the galaxy for a rich wife. Tendra was certainly well off enough to qualify as rich, and it was certainly within the realm of possibility that she would make a good wife for Lando—if they could get together in the same place at the same time long enough to get to know each other.

But even if they had not had the time to fall madly, passionately in love with each other, the two of them had very definitely made a connection with each other, established a solid bond, something that they could build on, someday, if the universe gave them that chance.

As best he could piece together, Tendra had somehow managed to spot some sort of military buildup in the Sacorrian system. Connecting the buildup to the interdiction field, she had decided she had to get word to Lando. Toward that end, it would seem she had gotten her hands on a spaceship, bribed her way off Sacorria, and crashed it into the Corellian interdiction field.

None of that would have done anyone much good, but for one other fact—Lando had given her a radionics communications set. The radionics set did not use any of the standard comlink frequencies, but instead sent and received messages on a modulated carrier wave in the radio band of the electromagnetic spectrum. The radionics signals were completely immune to the system-wide jamming, and were likewise completely undetectable to anyone using comlink equipment. The downside was that like all other forms of electomagnetic radiation—infrared, visual light, ultraviolet, gamma ray, X ray, and so on—radio band radiation traveled at the speed of light. Tendra's messages to Lando, and his replies, therefore likewise crawled along at the speed of light, and were highly susceptible to interference.

She was still aboard her ship, the *Gentleman Caller*, at the outskirts of the Corellian system, ambling gradually in toward the inner system at speeds that were distinctly sublight. It took long hours for her messages to reach him—but it could well take long, weary months before her ship could cross the same distance.

Unless, of course, they could bring down the interdiction field. And that was what they were here to do.

They arrived at the com section. He and Luke waited as the service droid extended a data probe and plugged into the security port by the com section door. Lando's original radionics set was still aboard his ship, the *Lady Luck*, but the *Intruder*'s tech staff had had no trouble at all putting together their own radionics set from the plans and spec sheets the *Lady Luck* also carried, and had actually managed to make their transmitter more powerful, and their receiver more sensitive.

But it wasn't radionics Lando had on his mind. He was concerned with Tendra.

As if the situation with Tendra wasn't complicated enough, there was the small matter of the actual information she was broadcasting to Lando. It was enough to give the intelligence staff fits.

The security system beeped its clearance code, and the hatch to the com section slid open. Lando looked inside before entering and let out a small sigh. There she was, as if the mere thought of anxious intelligence officers was enough to summon one. Lieutenant Belindi Kalenda, of New Republic Intelligence, was waiting for them, and she did not look happy.

"Didn't anyone ever tell your lady friend how to *count*?" she demanded the moment the hatch slid shut. Kalenda had never been much for small talk, and she was just about at the end of her tether now.

"What's the problem now, Lieutenant Kalenda?" Lando asked wearily.

"The same as always. Numbers, that's the problem," Kalenda said. She was a somewhat odd-looking young woman. Her wide-spaced eyes were glassy, almost milky, and a bit off-kilter. She was almost, but not quite, cross-eyed. She was a bit darker-skinned than Lando, and her black hair was done up in a complicated sort of braid piled on top of her head. The scuttlebutt was that she had at least some small skill in the Force, or at least that her intuition was good, and her hunches tended to play out, that she seemed to see more than most people. In any event, she had an odd way of seeming to look past your shoulder at something behind you, even when she was glaring right at you—as she was right now. "Numbers. We still have no idea how many ships are waiting out there at Sacorria."

"We wouldn't know there were any ships at all there, if not for Lady Tendra," Lando said sharply. "Maybe your NRI operatives on Sacorria know more about ship spotting, but did any of them have the initiative to get into the Corellian system and let us know about them?"

Kalenda looked woodenly at Lando. "I never told you there were NRI agents on Sacorria," she said warily.

"And I never told you I used to be a smuggler, but you know it just the same," Lando snapped. "Don't treat me like a fool. If you didn't have agents there, someone wasn't doing their job."

"Let's try and get back on track here," Luke said, attempting to smooth things over a bit. "What's wrong with Lady Tendra's message?"

"We have sent three follow-up queries asking her to give further details of the types, sizes, and numbers of ships she saw. Her latest message seems longer and more detailed, but once you weed out all the qualifiers and caveats, we still have nothing but the vaguest sorts of estimates."

"She can't tell you what she doesn't know," Lando said, wondering how many times he would have to tell that to Kalenda before she would believe it. Or when he would stop being frustrated by the intelligence group reading messages intended for him—and reading them first.

"But we have to know more than we do!" Kalenda said. "Whose ships are those? How many are there, and how well armed are they? Who commands them, and what are their intentions? You'll have to transmit again, and ask for more information."

"I won't," Lando said sharply. "I don't care what your psych teams say about her responding best to me. She told you all she can, and I'm not going to help you harass her anymore."

"But we need more—"

"The trouble is, she doesn't have any more," he snapped. "You have all the details you're going to get. Did you expect Tendra to be able to tell you the fleet commander's middle name by looking at ships in orbit through macrobinoculars? She's given us a warning, and a very useful one. She's given you all the information she can, and there are limits on how far we can press her."

"And there are also limits to how many messages you can ask her to send," Luke put in. "Every time she sends us one, the odds of her being detected go up."

Kalenda looked at Luke sharply. "Detected? How? By whom?"

"Think about it," Lando said. *"You're* the intelligence officer. The *way* she's broadcasting is secret, but it's not hidden in any way. She's broadcasting in clear, without any coding or encryption. Anyone who had the right sort of gear for scanning radio-band frequencies could lock in on her radionics transmission in a heartbeat. *You* did it easily enough. Then they'd not only know that *we* know about the ships tucked away in orbit of Sacorria, they'd be able to triangulate back and zero in on her location, the same way we did."

"What difference would that make?" Kalenda asked.

"Plenty, if we're talking about the people who control the interdiction field. They'd want to silence her. Say they switched the field off for thirty seconds. With good targeting and good planning, that would be enough time for a ship to drop into hyperspace, pop out next to the *Gentleman Caller,* blow Tendra out of the sky, and then return to base before the field went back up."

"But she broadcasted constantly for days without anything happening to her," Kalenda objected.

"She didn't have any choice. She had to transmit until I responded. Now she doesn't have to take that chance. Your radionics broadcasts are much more powerful than hers, and they're closer to anyone listening in the inner system. If the opposition spots your transmissions, they'll know to look for her."

Kalenda's face was expressionless. Had she known all this, and elected to risk Tendra's life on the chance of getting more information? Or had it not occurred to her? That seemed unlikely enough in an officer as sharp as Kalenda seemed to be—though the last few days had been hard on all of them. Lando half expected her to offer excuses, to lie and say she hadn't thought it through.

But even if Kalenda played a cagey game, she didn't play a dishonest one. "It's never easy," she said, "figuring the balance. I knew the risk was there, but I had to weigh the danger to her against the consequences if she had some bit of data without knowing about it—something that could save dozens, or hundreds, or millions of lives. If I had her *here,* and I could do a proper debriefing, I'm sure she could tell us all sorts of useful things."

"But you don't have her here," Luke said.

"No, I don't," Kalenda agreed. "Even with a standard comlink I could get somewhere. But this business of waiting hours and hours for an answer, and then waiting hours and hours for her to hear the next question—it makes it impossible to get anywhere. If I had a comlink we could scramble so there was at least some chance of keeping it private—then we could get somewhere."

"That's a lot of ifs," Luke said. "Let's leave them all out. What are the odds on your being able to get anything more out of Tendra as things stand?"

Kalenda sighed and shook her head. "Just about zero," she said. "But the *stakes* are so high."

"So high you had to try," Luke said. "I understand. But if it can't be done, it can't be done."

Kalenda smiled humorlessly. "That doesn't sound like a Jedi attitude," she said.

"Even Jedi know their limits," said Luke.

Kalenda nodded reluctantly. "Very well," she said. "There are a large number of warships parked in orbit of Sacorria. That's all we're going to get out of Source T."

"All right then," Lando said. "Let's leave it there. We're coming up on Centerpoint Station. Figuring it out ought to be enough to keep us busy right there."

Kalenda looked toward Lando again, and this time her glance seemed to meet his. "That's an understatement, if ever I heard one," she said.

* * *

It didn't take Belindi Kalenda long to confirm that idea. Centerpoint was so absurdly big, so complex, and so unlike anything in her experience, that it was all but impossible to know where to start. Over the next day or so the Bakuran fleet moved in on Centerpoint, advancing very slowly. If Ossilege was merely pretending to be cautious, he was doing a good job of it. He moved his ships in carefully, pausing repeatedly in his approach to scan every bit of the station to the limits of the Bakuran detection systems. Not that Kalenda could blame him for caution. Not when Centerpoint could have swallowed the *Intruder* whole through the smallest of its sally ports.

But even from the closest range Ossilege was willing to risk, the scan results weren't good enough to satisfy Kalenda. She sat at a scan station in the *Intruder*'s intelligence section, sifting through the endless, inconclusive images of Centerpoint.

It *seemed* as if the place was deserted, but go try to prove a negative. The enemy could have hidden a whole fleet of Star Destroyer-type warships in there, and a whole army of stormtroopers. If the ships were properly powered down to standby, and if the enemy was using the right sort of shielding, there would be no way to detect them.

What made it even more worrisome was that the enemy had shown almost no large ships so far. They *had* to be hidden somewhere. That was part of why

Kalenda had wanted better numbers from Source T. If she had gotten good, hard data from Source T about the types of ships she had seen at Sacorria, she would have some idea of what might be lying in wait inside Centerpoint. For that matter, Centerpoint might not even need ships to defend itself. She had spotted fifty or sixty points on the exterior of the station that *might* be weapons ports. The station was an incredible amalgam of familiar and alien, modern and ancient. There was no way to know how long a given object had been there, or who had built it, or if it still operated.

She ran the images across her scan screen, one after the other. Armored portals and hemispherical blisters, long cylindrical objects on what looked like aiming platforms, attached to complicated plumbing and wiring. Some of them might be massive covered-over turbolaser sites. And those Phalanxes of dark circular openings. Some could be missile batteries. And some might be refueling stations or docking facilities for refreshment bars. There was no way to tell.

They would have to send in a team.

*　　*　　*

The *Lady Luck* launched itself out of the *Intruder*'s landing bay, and lifted off into the blackness of the sky and toward Centerpoint. "Why do I always get handed these jobs?" Lando asked no one in particular as he guided his ship toward the station.

"Maybe it has something to do with the way you volunteered," replied Gaeriel Captison from the seat behind the copilot's station. Lando didn't feel too happy about having her along, but she had insisted. The ex-Prime Minister of Bakura had been granted full rights to speak for her government by the present Prime Minister, and she had been determined to join the scouting party, so that the Bakuran government was properly represented. Much to Lando's regret,

Threepio was also along for the ride, in case any translation was needed.

"I *had* to volunteer," Lando growled. "Once Luke volunteered, I knew he was going to need his wingman." Luke had launched first, in his X-wing. He was flying about two kilometers ahead of Lando, just close enough for easy visual tracking.

Kalenda, in the copilot's seat of the *Lady Luck,* gave Lando an odd look. Of course, all of her looks were pretty odd, so maybe it didn't mean much of anything. Or maybe she was wondering why a man who had worked so hard to establish a reputation as a devil-may-care adventurer, the sort who only looked out for himself, was sticking his neck out. Again. "Somehow, I think a Jedi Master would be able to take care of himself," she said.

"Maybe," Lando said. "And maybe not. Let's just say that I owe him one."

"Who in the galaxy doesn't?" Gaeriel asked.

"Actually, Lady Captison," said Kalenda, "you're the one I most wish weren't here."

"Thanks for *that* compliment," Lando muttered.

Kalenda winced. "Sorry, that came out wrong. What I meant was that Captain Calrissian and Master Skywalker have military training. They're more likely to be ready for—for whatever we find. Not really the job for an ex-Prime Minister."

"There are other skills in the universe besides knowing how to shoot and fly and fight without getting killed," Gaeriel said. "If we get lucky, there might be someone reasonable on that station. Someone we can negotiate with. If so, having a trained negotiator with plenipotentiary powers on hand might be a good thing."

"We're going to have to get *really* lucky for that to happen," Lando said. "So far we haven't found many people who are particularly reasonable in this star system."

* * *

Luke Skywalker felt good. He was back at the controls of his X-wing, alone, except for R2-D2 riding in his socket in the aft of the fighter. Maybe Mon Mothma wanted to push him into a position of leadership. Maybe circumstances were pushing him that way—or maybe the whole *universe* was pushing him that way. But right now, at this very moment, it was just Luke, his droid, and his X-wing. Nearly all pilots loved the solitude, the distance, of flying, and Luke was no exception there. Flying was, in and of itself, a pleasure, an escape from his worries and cares and duties.

Not that the escape would last for long. There was, as always, a job to do.

Luke looked toward the massive station. Indeed, they were now close enough that he would have been hard-pressed not to look at it. It all but filled the X-wing's viewports.

Luke could scarcely believe his eyes. He had seen all the reports. He knew how big Centerpoint was, or at least he had read the numbers—but somehow, numbers did not express the *hugeness* of the object hanging in the sky.

Centerpoint Station consisted of a huge sphere, a hundred kilometers across, with a massive cylinder stuck to each pole of the sphere. The station was roughly three hundred kilometers from end to end, and rotated slowly around the axis defined by the two polar cylinders. To judge by looking at the entire exterior surface, it had been built almost at random over the millennia.

Boxy things the size of large buildings, pipes and cables and tubes of all sizes running in all directions, parabolic antennae and strange patterns of conical shapes sprouted everywhere. Luke spotted what seemed to be the remains of a spacecraft that had crashed into the exterior hull and then been welded in place and made into living quarters of some sort. At least it *looked* that way. It seemed like a rather ad hoc way to add living space—and adding living space seemed more than a bit redundant for something the size of Centerpoint.

And yet none of that spoke of the real *size* of the thing. It was, after all, the size of a small moon—by some standards, maybe even the size of a largish one. Luke had been on worlds smaller than this station. This station was large enough to *be* a world, large enough to contain all the myriad complexities, all the variety, all the mystery of a world. Large enough that it would take a long time indeed to get from one end of it to the other. Large enough that you could live your whole life there without seeing all of it. *That* was Luke's definition of a world: a place too large for one person to experience in a lifetime.

Luke had been to countless worlds, and yet he knew he had never seen all there was to see on any of them. People tended to label a world, and leave it at that, as if it could be all one thing. But that was wrong. Another part of Luke's definition was that a world *couldn't* be all one thing.

It was easy to say Coruscant was a city world, or that Mon Calamari was a water world, or that Kashyyyk was a jungle world, and leave it at that. But there could be infinite variety in the forms of a city, or an ocean, or a jungle—and it was rare for a world really to be all one thing. The meadow world would have a mountain or two; the volcano world would have its impact craters; the bird planet would have insects.

And Centerpoint Station was *big,* so big it was difficult to judge the scale of the place. Space provided few visual cues available on the ground to tell the eye how big things were.

Apart from the questions of size, the idea of a spinning space station was disconcerting. Spinning was something that planets did, and they did it slowly. Centerpoint Station was spinning at a slow and stately rate, but you could *see* it moving.

The techniques for producing artificial gravity on a

station or ship without spinning the object on its axis had been old at the founding of the Old Republic. Luke had never seen such a thing as a spinning space station. It seemed, somehow, not part of the natural order of things.

An absurd thought, of course. What was natural about starships and space stations?

But there was something else, something more fundamental than size or spin, bothering Luke about the station. The station was *old*. Old by any human standard, old by the standard of virtually any sentient being. So old that no one knew how long ago it had been built, or who had built it, or why.

And yet, it was not truly old at all. Not compared to the ages of planets, or stars, or the galaxy. Even ten million years was not so much as an eye blink to the four- or five- or six-billion-year-old planets and stars and moons that filled the universe.

But if what seemed ancient to humans was all but newly minted in the eyes of the universe, then surely all the endless generations of remembered galactic history *were* nothing more than an eye blink of time. The birth, the rise, the fall of the Old Republic, the emergence and collapse of the Empire, the dawn of the New Republic, all shrank down into a single brief moment, compared to the immensity of time on a truly galactic scale.

"-uke — -ou the—"

"I'm here, Lando, but your signal is breaking up badly."

"-our signa- —eaking up t—"

Luke sighed. Another nuisance. With normal communications still utterly jammed throughout the Corellian system, the Bakurans had done their best to improvise a laser com system that sent voice signals over low-power laser beams. It did not work well, but it did work. Maybe they would have done better to use a version of Lando's radionics system, but it was too late to think of that now. "Artoo, see if you can clean that up a little."

Artoo booped and bleeped, and Luke nodded. "Okay, Lando, try it again. How do you read me?"

"Much better, —anks, but I won't mind when we can go ba— to regular com systems."

"You and me both."

"Well, I'm not holding my breath. But never mind that now. Kalenda spotted something. Look at the base of the closest cylinder, -ight where it joins the sphere. There's a —inking light -ere. See it?"

Luke peered through the viewscreen and nodded. "I see it. Hold on a second while I get a magnified view." Luke activated the targeting computer and used it to get a lock on the blinking light, then slaved his long-range holocam to the targeting system. An image popped into being on the fighter's main viewscreen. There was the blinking light—next to a large outer air-lock door that was opening and shutting, over and over again. "If that's not an invitation to come on in, I don't know what is," Luke said.

"We all agree with that back —is end," Lando's voice replied. "Even Golden Boy understood what it meant, and he's incoherent in over six million forms of communication."

Luke grinned at that. There had never been a great deal of love lost between C-3PO and Lando, and the last few weeks had not done much to endear the droid to the human. "Glad it's unanimous," Luke said. "The question is, do we accept the invitation?"

CHAPTER FOUR

Child's Play

Anakin Solo stared at the featureless silver wall for a full minute, and then thumped twice, hard, at one particular spot on it. Sure enough, an access door popped open, revealing another purple-and-green control keypad with a five-by-five grid of keys. Anakin frowned at the keypad, as if trying to decide his next move.

The experimental droid Q9-X2 watched Anakin carefully—which was really the only prudent way to watch him, when one thought about it. Q9 found Anakin's skill with machinery, his seemingly instinctive ability to make devices work, even when he had no idea what the devices were, to be remarkably disconcerting. It seemed to have something to do with this Force business that was so important to this group of humans. The theory seemed to be that Anakin's talent in the Force had somehow given him the ability to see inside machines, to manipulate them from the outside, down to the microscopic level. Not that Anakin was infallible, by any means. He made mistakes—and sometimes he quite deliberately made machines do things that no one else would want them to do. But one could learn a lot about an unknown device by watching Anakin figure it out.

Thus, the droid had two purposes in watching the child—first was at least to attempt to prevent him from doing *too* much damage as he wandered from one piece of machinery to the other.

His other duty was simply to record what the child did when he started fiddling with the hardware he found.

It was a full-time job—a more than full-time job, really. Q9-X2 drew most of the duty, thanks to his built-in recording systems. But even a droid had to recharge once in a while, and besides, Q9-X2 did not *want* to spend all day every day preventing this most peculiar child from pushing the wrong button and melting the planet. If nothing else, the constant strain would be too much for his judgment circuits. At least it *might* be, and that came to much the same thing. Perhaps not the most straightforward thought process, just there, but it was enough of an argument to get him a break from Anakin-watching once in a while, and that was more than good enough.

Anakin punched a code into the access panel, and a low chime sounded. Past experience had taught Q9 that this sound was not a good sign. It seemed to be a sort of warning bell.

"That will do, Anakin," said Q9.

Anakin looked around in surprise, as if he hadn't known Q9 was there. "Q9!" Anakin shouted. "Oh!"

If the droid had been programmed to do so, he would have let out a sigh. Q9 had been with him for hours now, so it seemed unlikely the child could be surprised by his arrival. On the other manipulator, Anakin hadn't shown much sign of acting talent. Q9 had *heard* of the phenomenon known as absentmindedness, but he hadn't had any reason to believe it really existed until he met Anakin. "I think it would be best if you stopped examining that machine until Chewbacca or one of the others can take a look at it."

"But I've almost got it working!" Anakin protested.

"Do you know what it does? Do you have any *idea* what it does?"

"N-n-no," Anakin admitted, quite reluctantly.

"Do you remember what happened the last time you heard that chime and you kept going?"

"A trapdoor opened," Anakin said, suddenly finding reasons to look everywhere but at Q9.

"Yes. A trapdoor opened. Under me. And I fell into a waste disposal chute. If I had not managed to jump my repulsors to high power in time and bounce back up, what would I be right now?"

"Mashed down to a ten-centimeter cube. Unless the machine had melted you down by now."

"Quite right. But Chewbacca only found that out afterward, didn't he?"

"I helped him," Anakin protested.

"Yes, you did. And we need you around to help him more. So what would we do if the trapdoor was under you this time?"

Anakin's eyes grew wide with alarm. "Oh," he said. "Maybe I'd better stop and let Chewie look."

"Maybe you'd better," agreed Q9. "Come on, let's go find the others."

Anakin nodded. "Okay," he said, and turned back the way they had come.

Q9 followed after on his repulsors, relieved that Anakin had decided to be cooperative—this time. Q9-X2 had been designed with the capacity to learn new behaviors by trial and error, but he had never expected to use that capacity to learn practical child psychology. The skills required to handle Anakin with even marginal success were taking up an inordinate portion of system resources. Q9 decided he was going to have to perform a partial memory wipe on himself, and free up some capacity, when this was over.

If it ever *was* over. As they came out of the side passage and into the central chamber, Q9 reflected that this situation was starting to look rather permanent.

They were a motley crew, all of them holed up in

this huge and alien place. Anakin and Q9 paused at the exit from the side passage and looked around.

Seen from this vantage point, the repulsor chamber seemed too large and obvious for a hiding place, but, from the surface, Q9 knew just how difficult it would be for outsiders to find this place. It was shielded from every detection system that Q9 knew about—with the exception of Anakin Solo. *He* had found this chamber—and its identical twin on Corellia—with no trouble whatsoever.

And there were good reasons for hiding the chamber. It contained the planetary repulsor that had propelled Drall into its current orbit, unknown millennia ago. Likewise with Corellia and, no doubt, with the other inhabited worlds of the Corellia system—Selonia and the Double Worlds, Talus and Tralus. Each of them had a hidden chamber like this one. Each of them had a planetary repulsor like this one. And each of them had been transported into the Corellian system long, long ago, by some long-forgotten race for some long-forgotten reason.

But now the hunt for the repulsors was on. The party in the repulsor chamber had been cut off from outside contact for some time, but the last information they had was that the rebel forces on at least some and probably all of the inhabited worlds were actively searching for the repulsors. The reason was not entirely clear. While the repulsors would make powerful and effective weapons, they were not war-winners, not by any means. According to Ebrihim, a planetary repulsor could be used to knock out a ship in orbit—but it would be hard to aim and unwieldy to use. There would be the element of surprise, but only the first time the repulsor was used. There were other, simpler, cheaper, more reliable ways of shooting down enemy spacecraft, and many of them were available to the rebel groups. So why were they expending precious time and effort in the middle of a war in order to find weapons of marginal utility?

Q9 gave it up. He had come to that point in the analysis two hundred thirty-nine times before, and it didn't seem likely that an answer that did not spring to mind any of those times would do so on the two hundred fortieth attempt.

Instead, he admired the strange and massive forms that made up the main planetary repulsor chamber. The chamber itself was a huge vertical cone, just under a kilometer from top to bottom, the walls of which appeared to be gleaming, perfect metallic silver. At the base of the conical chamber were six smaller cones of the same silver material, each just over one hundred meters tall. They were spaced evenly around a circle centered on the axis of the pyramid. In the exact center of the chamber's base was a seventh, larger cone, twice as tall as the others, but with the same slender proportions. Passages to side chambers were spaced around the circumference of the chamber, and vertical shafts in the floor of the chamber led to a series of lower levels they hadn't even started to explore.

It was a huge, artificial, gleaming, impersonal alien place—and a ramshackle, improvised, crude, homey-looking campsite was sitting right in the middle of it, right by the base of the central cone. No doubt to human or Drallish—or even Wookiee—eyes, the camp looked incongruous enough. To the droid's eyes, it looked absurd.

The *Millennium Falcon* was there—and it had been a very close job flying it into the concealed topside entrance. The Duchess's hovercar was parked alongside it. A line with washing on it was strung between the *Falcon*'s topside parabolic antenna and a spike antenna on the roof of the hovercar. Chewbacca was trying to use as little power as possible, to reduce the chance of detection. Even the *Falcon*'s clothes drier was off for the duration. Folding chairs and tables were set up to one side of the two vehicles, and the children, tired of the close confines of the *Falcon,* had moved their sleeping pads outside and under the ship. As always, the children had arranged their beds so they could all sleep together—the twins' beds close together, with Anakin just a bit farther off.

Q9 could see all the rest of the party from here— Jacen and Jaina carrying some sort of gear out of the *Millennium Falcon;* Chewbacca the Wookiee, sitting at his camp chair, fiddling with some recalcitrant bit of hardware or other; and the two Drall, Ebrihim and his aunt, Marcha, the Duchess of Mastigophorous, at the other end of the table, hunched over their own work.

The two Drall, like all of their species, were rather short by human standards, Ebrihim being just about Jacen's height. They were short-limbed and thick-bodied—downright plump, in fact—and covered with thick brown fur. As Q9 had learned, to human eyes they tended to look like stuffed toy animals. Some humans found them hard to take seriously—but failing to take Drall seriously was always a huge mistake. They were sober, serious, levelheaded beings in general. Even if Ebrihim was found to be a bit flighty by Drallish standards, his aunt was one of the most commonsensical beings Q9 had ever met.

No doubt Anakin's latest somewhat unnerving discovery would give them something else to work on, give them another piece to the puzzle they were struggling to put together. They intended to develop a useful understanding of the repulsor's control system. All in all, Q9 felt, the two Drall had the hardest job of anyone in the camp.

The hardest job besides waiting, of course. And they were *all* doing that.

"Come on, Q9," said Anakin. "Quit *dawdling.*"

Another bit of child psychology to note down—no matter how slow they might be when one was waiting for them, no caregiver had ever moved fast enough when it was the child doing the waiting. "Coming, Anakin."

*   *   *

Jacen set down the crate he was lugging out of the *Falcon,* looked up, and saw Q9 and Anakin heading back to camp. "Finally," he said. "I thought they'd never get back. Now we can eat."

"Darn. We can? Maybe we can get them to stay away a little longer." Jaina set down her own crate and waved to Anakin. Her little brother waved back.

"Come on, the survival rations aren't that bad."

"They aren't that good, either. Especially the nine millionth time in a row. I think they call them survival rations because no one knows if you'll survive eating them."

"Ha ha. Very funny. I think you've told me that *joke* nine million times—and it wasn't so good the first time."

"Sorry," Jaina said, sitting down on her crate. "Not much new inspiration here."

"I know, I know," Jacen said. "Things here don't change much." He could have gone and checked the *Millennium Falcon*'s chronometer, but without that and Chewbacca's rigid insistence that they all eat and sleep at normal intervals, there was no clue at all to how much time had passed. The light in the chamber was unchangeably bright, coming from some diffuse and undefinable source in the upper reaches of the cavern. There was no sound at all from the massive cavern, except the sound of their own moving around and talking. But every sound anyone made produced a series of faint, distant echoes, whispering down from the top of the chamber for long seconds afterward. And the echoes of every sound mingled with all the others, Anakin's laughter blending with Chewbacca's growl or the whir of a machine, or the bang of a camp chair bumping into a table merging with the low, serious voices of the two Drall in conversation with each other.

Whenever the camp was busy and active, there was a constant whisper of background echoes reverberating down from above, just enough to make the chamber seem less foreboding and empty. But five or ten seconds after they stopped moving or talking, the chamber would fall silent again, and the stillness would seem to shout louder than any noise how strange this place was, how old its flawless gleaming silver walls, how alien and powerful its capabilities.

Night—or what they pretended was night—was the hardest. With the silver walls still gleaming in the unchanging light, they would go to bed—the children to their sleeping pads in the shadow of the *Falcon*, Chewbacca to his usual shipboard bunk, the two Drall to foldout beds in Aunt Marcha's hovercar, and Q9 plugged into a charge stand. Then, all would be so quiet that the slightest noise seemed to echo forever. A cough, a whisper, Ebrihim's muttering snore—or Anakin crying in his sleep—seemed to carry up to heaven and come down again and again.

It was not the best way to live, Jacen reflected. But in a sense, it was not a way of life at all. It was a way of waiting. All of them, even Anakin, seemed to know things could not last this way forever—or even for very long. There was a war being fought out there, and sooner or later, one side or the other would find this place, and after that—

After that, no one even pretended to know what would happen.

* * *

"Sit up properly, Anakin," said the Duchess Marcha, "and stop banging your foot against the table leg. The noise is bad enough, but the echoes will drive me to distraction." She shook her head and looked toward her nephew, Ebrihim. "Honestly, nephew, I do not understand these human children. What does Anakin gain by slouching over and making such irritating noises?"

"I have not dealt with them long enough to obtain a clear answer, dearest aunt. However, I might add that it would seem that even human parents do not understand the purpose behind much of what human children do—and that in spite of having once been children themselves."

"Somehow, that does not surprise me. I suppose our own young ones can be some trouble, but I must say I have no recollection at all of *your* misbehaving as badly as Anakin does."

"Don't talk like I'm not here!" Anakin shouted indignantly. These Drall grown-ups were worse than regular human grown-ups for pushing kids around. "I was just *thinking* about stuff."

"What kind of stuff?" Jaina asked.

All of them ganging up on him, even the other kids. "Just stuff," Anakin said, frowning fiercely.

"Well, Anakin, there is certainly nothing wrong with thinking," said Aunt Marcha. "I'm sure the universe would be a better place if we all indulged in the practice a bit more. If you could do your thinking without the banging, that would be a great help. All right?"

"All right," Anakin said, still feeling kind of grouchy. But he knew he was lucky they had stopped asking questions when they had. Because of all that Jedi stuff, he would have had to tell the truth if they asked more, or his brother and sister would catch him fibbing, and then he'd be in even more trouble. Sometimes Jacen and Jaina acted just like grown-ups.

If he had told them he had been thinking about that control panel Q9 had told him to stop fooling with, they all would have yelled at him. He knew he could get it to do something. Something big, and important. What, exactly, he wasn't sure. But *something.* He could feel that. It was like the control panel was calling to him, asking him to hurry back and set the machinery free, let it go out and do the work it was supposed to do.

But it didn't matter. They *hadn't* asked him about it. So he could think about it all he liked.

* * *

"Come, dearest aunt," said Ebrihim to the Duchess. "It is late. Everyone else is asleep. We have made great progress, but we can do no more with our researches tonight." The two Drall were sitting in the hovercar, reviewing their notes for the day. And Ebrihim was right. They could go no further for the moment.

"Whatever progress we have made is only the barest start toward understanding this place," the Duchess replied. "We have some idea of how the alien keypads are laid out, and what some of the button markings and color coding seem to mean. But going from there to *operating* this place, and shutting it down safely—a machine that has been operating for at least tens of thousands of years and perhaps much longer? We have no idea how the system draws its power. Suppose we do learn how to turn it off. Where does the power *go* once it is not coming here? If it is some sort of geologic energy tap, as I suspect, we might set off massive seismic disturbances. I think it most probable that this chamber is but one part of a much larger system. I suspect this is merely the nozzle, if you will, for a propulsion system woven into the very being of this world. We are dealing with a device that can move a planet. A device of that power could also destroy a planet, if it was not used properly. I do not see any way of learning all we need to know in any reasonable period of time."

Ebrihim smiled faintly and let out a short bark of a laugh. "Unless, of course, we simply instruct Anakin to find the main control panel and then set him loose on it."

Marcha's eyes widened in horror. "Do not say such a thing, nephew. Not even in jest. Jokes like that have a way of coming true."

* * *

Anakin's eyes snapped open so suddenly it startled him. He was, quite abruptly, wide awake and staring up at the under hull of the *Millennium Falcon.* He sat up quietly and looked around. Jacen and Jaina were still sound asleep. Chewbacca was a deep enough sleeper that Anakin didn't even worry about him. Ebrihim and Aunt Marcha were in the hovercar. Anakin turned and looked in that direction. All the car's lights were out, the windows darkened, and the hatch was shut.

That left Q9. The droid spent most nights in standby mode, partially powered down, plugged into a portable charging stand between the hovercar and the *Falcon,* with his back to the larger craft. Anakin also knew that the bulk of the *Falcon* would block nearly all of the droid's sensors. So long as he kept the ship between himself and Q9, he ought to be able to sneak away without any problems.

Moving as silently as he could, he pushed back his blanket and rolled over so he was on his hands and knees. He crawled out from under the *Falcon,* and into the endless bright light of the repulsor chamber.

Anakin blinked once or twice as he got to his feet. Strange to be sneaking around in light as bright as day. But there was no time to worry about that kind of stuff. Someone might wake up any second and notice he was gone.

Padding along in his bare feet, clad only in his underwear, Anakin moved straight out for the perimeter of the huge chamber, glancing over his shoulder now and then to make sure that he was keeping the *Falcon* between himself and Q9.

He reached the perimeter and trotted unhesitatingly into the closest tunnel entrance. The passage he wanted was almost on the other side of the chamber from here, but that did not worry him. The others might get lost in the side passages, but not Anakin. He could *feel* which way was the right way.

He moved unerringly through the complicated maze of passages, taking every turning and passage with absolute confidence. He could feel the panel getting closer. Closer.

And there it was, just as he had left it, the initial keypad open and waiting. He stared at it for a minute, then reached out his hand and held it, palm down, over the pad. He closed his eyes, reached out, and *felt* the interior of the pad, tracing the circuits, the logic paths, the potentials and safeties that were inside the machine. It had been asleep for so long, so very long, waiting for someone to wake it up.

And now. Now was the time. He knew, knew with absolute certainty, how to make it work. No Q9-X2 here to tease him, or make him worry about trapdoors and stuff. He *knew*. He was *sure*.

Anakin Solo reached out and pressed the center button of the five-by-five grid. The green button turned purple. Good. He paused for a moment, and then, stretching his fingers as far as they would go, he pressed all four of the corner buttons at once. They turned orange, not purple. He frowned. That wasn't *quite* what he had expected, but never mind. Move on. Starting at the top and moving counterclockwise, he pressed the center button of each outer row in turn. These did indeed turn purple. That made him feel a bit better. The keypad made the chiming noise again, but this time it wasn't just once. It kept going, over and over and over.

Anakin closed his eyes once more and held his palm over the keypad. Yes. Yes. That was it. Starting from the bottom right, and moving clockwise, he pressed each of the corner buttons in turn. Each turned from orange to a reassuring purple as he pressed it. He paused, only for a moment, just before he pushed in the last one. Was this such a good idea? He was going to get in trouble for this, he knew that much. But would it be so much trouble that it wouldn't be worth it?

No. He *had* to do it. There was no turning back now.

He pushed in the last orange button. It turned purple, and suddenly the chiming noise was louder and higher-pitched. There was a low-pitch hum from be-hind Anakin, and he turned around.

A section of the floor was sliding away. For a mo-ment he wondered if he had been wrong about trap-doors. But then a whole complicated console rose slowly up out of the floor, a strange-looking control panel, all in the same silver stuff as the chamber itself, in front of a stranger-looking little seat that looked as if it were intended for a being that bent in different places from a human.

Hopping with excitement, all doubts forgotten, Anakin sat down in the odd little chair and did not even notice that it was adapting itself to his body, re-forming itself, lifting him up and moving him forward so he would be able to reach the controls more com-fortably. He stared at the instruments for a full minute, then extended his arms and spread his fingers out as far as they would go. He shut his eyes and reached out into the intricately, beautifully complicated universe of switches and paths and controls and linkages behind the knobs and levers and dials that covered the control panel. Power ratings, capacitance stowage, vernier con-trol, targeting subsystems, safety overrides, shielding constraints, thrust balancing. What they all were, what they all meant, how they all worked, and worked to-gether—all of it flowed into him, as if the ancient ma-chines were speaking to him, telling him their story.

He knew it all. He knew it all now.

Anakin put his hands on the control panel and felt it all flow through him. Wake it up. He had to wake it up. The whole system had slept for so long. It *wanted* to come awake, to revive itself, to do its proper work. He moved as if *he* were asleep, in a dream, moving to what his ability in the Force told him he could do, not to do what needed doing, or what he ought to do. He knew, somehow, the compulsion, the desire to make the sys-tem come on, was within himself, that the machinery was nothing more than machinery. But it *felt* as if it were the machine whispering to him, not his own instincts and abilities urging him on. Pull that long lever to start the initiator process activator. Twist that dial to bring the geogravitic energy transfer system on-line. Tap in that command sequence at the standard five-by-five keypad to clear the safeties. Somewhere, deep below him, the ground shuddered slightly, and a low, powerful hum began to build. The chiming noise grew more and more intense, becoming louder and louder, the chiming coming faster and faster.

A flat spot on the control panel twisted and shimmered and then started to swell upward, to form itself into a handle like a spacecraft's joystick. Anakin reached out to it with his left hand, barely aware of what he was doing, not noticing that the handle was forming itself, reshaping itself, to fit itself to his hand. A graphic display appeared in the air over the handle, a hollow wireframe cube, made up of a grid of smaller cubes five high, five across, and five deep. All the smaller cubes were transparent, but, as Anakin watched, one cube, in the far lower left corner, turned green.

Slowly, carefully, he pulled back on the joystick. The solitary green cube turned purple, and suddenly the three transparent cubes it touched turned green. The corner cube turned orange, the second layer turned green, and a new layer of cubes turned purple. The colors spread out until the entire five-by-five-by-five grid shifted through green to purple to bright, glowing orange. The ground trembled again, and the hum of power grew deeper, and, somehow, more emphatic, more solid, the sound of massive energies waiting to be unleashed.

Anakin let go of the joystick. At the moment he did, the chiming stopped. The control chamber was suddenly silent as the power hum dropped away into lower and lower frequencies, until it was so deep a tone it was below the threshold of hearing.

The joystick melted away, flattened itself back down into the control panel. And there, in the blank space at the center of the panel, a new button created itself, flowing up out of the panel surface, shaping itself into a disk about six centimeters across and a centimeter high. As he watched, the button shifted its color, changed from silver to green, green to purple, purple to orange, plain orange to a throbbing, pulsating orange, pulsing from the color of molten iron to the dull near red of a dusky sunset.

The chamber was silent. Anakin stared in openmouthed fascination at the final button, his eyes wide, the light of the throbbing orange button throwing weird and shifting colors onto his clothes, his face, his eyes.

The button. The button was there. It called to him, or else his own compulsion, his compulsion to make machines *work,* to make machines *do,* called from deep inside himself.

He did not know. He did not care.

He reached out his left hand. He held it poised over the button for a moment.

And then he pushed it down.

* * *

Lightning flared out from the apex of the central cone in the great chamber, lancing out toward each of the lower cones, slamming into them with sparks and fire. Thunder, deafeningly loud, the sound of the earth cracking open and splitting itself apart, roared out through the great chamber. Blinding light exploded out from the lightning strike to reflect off every silver surface, flooding the chamber with brilliance.

The lesser cones answered back, sending their own thunderbolts back to strike at the top of the center cone, blasting it into incandescence. Then, as suddenly as it had been there, the lightning was gone, and the cones were as they had been, unaffected by the massive power that had played around them. The sound of the thunder echoed through the chamber, reverber-

ating back and forth like the angry war cry of some
long-forgotten god.

The chamber shuddered and shook with the thunder. Chewbacca, aboard the *Falcon,* was thrown from
his bunk as the ship bounced and lurched along with
the chamber. He was halfway to the ship's control
room before he came fully awake and realized the ship
was on the ground.

Not just on the ground, but *under* it, in a sealed
chamber, with no hope of escape.

Shields. The *Falcon*'s shields would provide at least
some protection. He had to get everyone aboard, and
fast. He turned and headed for the open access ramp.

The twins had gotten out from under the ship. They
were on their feet and struggling to stay that way as
the ground bucked and heaved under their feet.
Chewbacca shouted for them to get aboard, but the
echoes of the thunder were so loud that even his voice
did not carry. He waved his arms, gesturing for them to
get aboard. Jacen saw him and nodded vigorously. He
grabbed his sister's arm and pulled her toward the
ramp. The simple effort of trying to move at all was
enough to knock them both off their feet. But they
kept on moving, crawling toward the access ramp.

The shaking of the ground seemed to ease off, even
as the echoing roar faded away. But Chewbacca had no
illusions that things would stay quiet for long.

He rushed down the ramp even as the twins were
crawling up it. The others. He had to get to the others.
Moving as if he were on the deck of a storm-tossed
ship in the sea, he made his way to the far side of the
ship. The hovercar had toppled over on its side. As he
moved toward it the side hatch popped open and
Ebrihim came crawling out, half carrying, half dragging
his aunt Marcha. She seemed to have a bad cut on the
left side of her head. She looked half-stunned.

Somehow, without even knowing how he did it,
Chewbacca crossed the distance to the hovercar. He
reached out and lifted Marcha away from Ebrihim's

side, then tucked her under one arm and lifted
Ebrihim down to the ground with the other.

He shouted at Ebrihim to get aboard the *Falcon,* and
pointed toward the ship. Either Ebrihim could understand what Chewbacca was saying or else he understood the gesture. He nodded and started toward the
ship. The ground had all but stopped moving, and
Ebrihim was to walk more or less without being
knocked over.

Chewbacca looked toward the ship himself and saw
Q9, down and inert, slumped over next to his charging
stand. Still carrying Marcha, he moved to the charging
stand and examined the situation. The droid looked
completely dead and motionless. Chewbacca pulled at
the cable connecting the droid to the charger, but the
connection seemed to have gotten jammed somehow.
Chewbacca yanked harder, and the cable snapped. He
scooped the droid up in his free hand and headed for
the *Falcon.*

At that moment the lightning struck again, blasting
out from the central cone toward the six smaller cones
that surrounded it. Chewbacca looked up involuntarily
to see the dazzling bright display, but then realized his
mistake and looked away before he could be blinded
by the light.

The light he could look away from, but the sound,
the overwhelming sound—there was nothing he could
do to shut that out.

He hurried toward the ship as the lesser cones answered back to the master, sending their own bolts of
fire back toward the central cone. The noise redou-
bled, louder than ever, and the ground bucked harder,
nearly knocking Chewbacca over. The *Falcon* was
bouncing on its landing jacks, riding their shock absorbers.

Chewbacca staggered around to the far side of the
ship and got to the entry ramp. He had to time his rush
up the ramp between the buckings and surgings of the
silver surface of the ground. Judging the moment to be

right, he rushed aboard ship. He hit the switch to raise the ramp, then got to the lounge. He set the Duchess Marcha and Q9-X2 down on the deck as gently as he could. Ebrihim had already produced a first-aid kit from somewhere, and knelt down next to his aunt.

The two Drall, the droid, the twins—Chewbacca suddenly realized that Anakin wasn't there. He had half assumed the youngest child would be with the twins. He turned and headed toward the door.

"Anakin's safe!" Jacen shouted over the thundering din, clearly reading Chewbacca's thoughts from his action. "He's in some sheltered side tunnel. I can feel him in the Force. He's not hurt, and he's feeling more scared we'll be mad at him than scared he'll get hurt. I think he set this off."

Chewbacca just stood there and stared at Jacen for a moment, unsure what to do. He had sworn to protect the children above all else. If Anakin were indeed safe, then he could button up the ship and wait this thing out. But if—if—Anakin were in danger, then what could he do? Search all the endless side corridors for him during this massive disturbance? But if he did that, he would be exposing the ship, and those aboard her, to greater danger. He would have to get the shields raised and lowered so he could go in and out—and no one besides him knew the ship well enough to keep the shields up.

To keep the others safe, he would have to stay here. Very well. It was not certain, it was not perfect, but it was the best judgment, the best decision he could make under the circumstances. If he had judged wrong, and harm came to Anakin as a result, then, he knew, his own life would be forfeit, and rightly so.

It took him but a moment to think it all through. But thought was nothing without action. He rushed for the cockpit and activated the *Falcon*'s shields at full strength. The sound faded away somewhat as the shields engaged. Chewbacca tried to activate the ship's repulsors to raise her up off the heaving deck of the chamber, but they would not engage. He checked the propulsion readouts. Every propulsion system was off-line. He had no idea why. But there was no time to worry about that now. He needed to get the ship up off the deck before it was bounced apart. Even without the propulsion systems, there was a way to do that. Chewbacca worked the shield controls, shifting power away from the upper shields to the lower ones, extending the lower shields as far as they would go, and softening them, so they formed a gradual thickening membrane rather than a hard edge—if only the trick would work. The *Falcon* hesitated a moment, and then rose up off her landing jacks to rest on a cushion of softened lower-side shields. The bouncing and bucking and heaving of the deck was still there to be felt, but the shields smoothed it down and gave the ship a chance to ride it out. He set the shields to self-compensate and maintain their setting.

He could at least hope the shields would protect them against what was happening, but he would not be able to do more than hope until he knew what was going on. All he knew for sure was that it seemed to be happening above them all. He looked up, just as another spectacular cycle of lightning bursts flashed back and forth between the tops of the cones, and then another, and another. The cycle was clearly growing faster, and more powerful. There was no way of knowing what sorts of energy and radiation those bolts were putting out. Chewbacca could do little more than hope that the *Falcon*'s shields would protect those inside against it all.

The lightning transfers grew faster and faster, more and more powerful, until all the cone-tops were a constant blaze of light, joined together by spikes of fire.

Then, it seemed, the cone-tops drew the fire in, absorbing the energy that flowed around them. The roaring thunder of the lightning faded away as the cone-tops flared and flickered with energy, light of every color sparking and shimmering on their surfaces.

Just when Chewbacca thought the display had reached its climax, he realized the scintillating colors were flowing *down* the cones, toward the bottom of the chamber—toward the *Millennium Falcon.* Chewbacca tried frantically to activate one of the propulsion systems, any of the propulsion systems—but all of them stayed stubbornly off-line.

Suddenly the entire ship was bathed in lightning, a firestorm of sparks and flares that coursed around the shields, sparking and flaring everywhere. Every circuit breaker and safety cutoff in the ship tripped at once, and Chewbacca made no effort to reset any of them. He had no desire to have any active circuits running with that much power flowing around the ship.

As suddenly as it had flowed over the ship, the wave of power swept past it. Chewie craned his neck around to watch the energy wave moving, just in time to see it incinerate the hovercar, detonate Q9's charging stand, and set everything else left outside ablaze.

The blaze of energy swept on, swooping up the sides of the chamber's conical interior wall, rushing up toward the apex of the chamber, a ring of seething power that grew brighter, more powerful, more energetic as it moved higher up the cone.

The ring of fire merged into a single point of raging power at the apex of the cone and exploded outward in a torrent of light that streamed forth in all directions, blindingly bright. The walls of the cone seemed to shudder, shake, expand as the power burst rippled through them.

Another stream of scintillating power coursed down the big central cone and the six lesser ones, down over the base of the chamber, blanketing the *Falcon* in bolts of blazing glory as it swept past the ship, out and up and in toward the point of the conical chamber, racing toward the pinnacle, blasting out its energy, making the very walls of the cone shimmer and shake with its power. And again. And again. And again.

Until the power burst did not meet in a point, but

instead reached the top of an open cone, and exploded as a ring of light—with the blue skies of daylight visible above.

Chewbacca, still stunned and amazed, began to realize what was happening. The conical chamber of the planetary repulsor was transforming itself, opening itself out, opening out its apex point to give itself a clear shot at the sky.

Another power burst swept over the ship. Another. Another, another, another, each burst riding up to the top of the now-open cone and forcing it open wider and wider and wider. Chewbacca checked the shield displays and saw that, for a miracle, they were holding. That was, no doubt, less a testimony to the strength of the shields than it was to the characteristics of the energy sweeping past the ship. The power bursts were flowing over the shields, not attempting to penetrate them.

But Chewbacca was past worrying about such things. Whether or not they survived, or were burnt to a cinder, was out of his hands, of anyone's hands. This titanic machine would do whatever Anakin had ordered it to do, and nothing could stand in its way.

Chewbacca thought of the endless megatons of rock and stone and dirt the chamber had to be slamming out of the way, the massive shock waves that had to be reverberating throughout the whole vicinity. There had been a whole series of underground tunnels leading to the hidden entrance to this place. Surely all of them had collapsed, along with the Drallist building that sat atop them. The Drallists had been searching for the planetary repulsor. By now, beyond doubt, the planetary repulsor had found them, destroyed them as they had attempted to destroy the New Republic's government. Chewbacca found a rough justice in that thought, and smiled to himself.

Jacen came into the cockpit and slipped into the pilot's seat, his father's seat, straining to see what was happening. The boy seemed very small, and very frightened—and yet controlled, adult, serious. There was no time now to feel the terror of the moment. That could come later. That was what nightmares were for.

The boy looked up and saw what was happening, saw the job that the roiling, seething energies were doing. "It's opening," Jacen said, his voice full of wonder. "And it's getting higher."

Chewbacca looked up. He hadn't noticed that, but Jacen was right. The walls of the cone were getting taller, even as they spread wider. Perhaps that was to insure the stone and earth it shoved out of the way did not tumble down into the cavern. Perhaps it was for some other reason altogether. Who could know what the makers of this stupendous device had intended?

Chewbacca turned toward Jacen and pointed toward the outside of the ship, then held his hand out, palm down, at the height of a small child's head as he let out a worried growl.

"Anakin's still all right," said Jacen. "I can feel him. He's out *there*"—Jacen pointed toward one specific point in the perimeter of the chamber wall—"and he's scared—maybe even more scared than we are—I mean more scared than Jaina and me—but he's all right."

In the midst of his own fear, Chewbacca managed to find a little bit of a laugh. A clever recovery on Jacen's part. The child knew that Wookiees did not like admitting to fear, and had found a way to avoid offending a Wookiee who was downright terrified. Any rational being would be terrified by all this. Chewbacca pointed to the back of the Falcon and made another interrogatory-sounding noise.

"They're all okay back there," said Jacen. "Aunt Marcha woke up, and I think she'll be okay. Except Q9. He's still dead—or off, or shorted out, or whatever. He's not moving, anyway."

Chewbacca nodded. They were lucky any of them were alive. If Q9 could be repaired, Chewie would attend to it later. If not—well, one casualty seemed a very low price indeed for riding out this storm.

Another pulse of energy swept over the *Falcon,* a bit rougher ride than the last one. The ship bounced once or twice and spun about a few degrees to starboard. Chewbacca growled thoughtfully. A reminder, that was.

A reminder that they were nowhere near close enough to the end of this to talk about living through it.

CHAPTER FIVE

Down the Hatch

Thrackan Sal-Solo, self-proclaimed Diktat of the Corellian Sector, leader of the Human League, stared at the bottle in front of him and gave serious thought to the idea of getting himself good and drunk. There seemed precious little else he could do, besides wait.

Thrackan had never been much good at waiting—which was ironic, for he had spent much of his adult life waiting. Waiting for a superior to resign or retire or be arrested, waiting for a plot to mature, waiting for the time to be right, waiting for the long-awaited offer of the succession from Dupas Thomree, Diktat of Corellia—waiting until the day Thomree died, and that fool Gallamby had taken his place instead. Waiting for the Empire to wake up and understand the danger represented by the damnable Rebels, waiting for the Emperor to strike back from the hammer blows the Rebellion gave the Empire, waiting for Thrawn's conterstrike to succeed.

Waiting, all of it, in vain. Waiting for things that had never happened, waiting for sweet victories that had melted away into bitter, humiliating defeat.

Thrackan grabbed the bottle by the neck, like an enemy he was trying to strangle. He stood up and walked around his desk, out of his office, and out into the corridor of the dig headquarters. The dig HQ was not as large or as comfortable a place as the old headquarters, but at least it was secure. Thrackan would have preferred to keep his headquarters in the underground bunker in the countryside on the far side of the city— but the Human League had been forced to abandon that supposedly secret location. The blasted Selonians had yanked their compatriot, Dracmus, out of there, along with Thrackan's traitor cousin, Han Solo.

It hadn't taken much imagination to realize that a group that could take two prisoners out of an underground bunker could just as easily put one bomb in. So Thrackan had been forced to withdraw from there, and they were minus one headquarters. Call it another debt on the account Thrackan was drawing up against Han Solo. Sooner or later, Han Solo would pay for all of it.

Thrackan walked out of the building and out into the fading light of twilight. He watched the second-shift men coming on duty, headed for their work underground. A number of them saw him and cheered. Thrackan forced a smile onto his face, put his hand to his forehead, and gave the boys a small, informal sort of salute. He made no effort to hide his bottle. That was one nice thing about his boys. He didn't have to pretend he wasn't human, that he didn't like a drink now and again. Or even a drink more often than that.

Now if only his boys were good at finding things. They were still searching for the Corellian planetary repulsor. It had to be hidden in the tunnels somewhere beneath them. It *had* to be. Or things were going to get very sticky indeed.

Except things were already sticky. Solo had escaped. Leia Organa Solo had escaped. The Bakurans had busted through the interdiction field, somehow. They were loose in the system, and might have already seized control of Centerpoint. Things were not going according to plan. At least he had managed to accomplish a little bit of revenge, already. Leia Organa Solo might have escaped, but others never would. With any luck at all, history would record that Governor-General Micamberlecto had died of injuries he suffered during the initial attack. But even if the true story of the Frozian's demise came out, Thrackan wouldn't much mind. Terror could be a very useful tool.

But killing the Governor-General was incidental. The stakes were much higher than that—and Thrackan knew just how dangerous a game he was playing. He knew more of the real story than anyone else in this star system. *He* knew how much of a bluff it all was. *He* knew how many dangers surrounded him from all sides. He had claimed to control the starbuster plot. For the moment, at least, it suited the purposes of the starbuster's real masters to let him go on claiming it. It provided them with additional cover, an extra level of protective deception. Not that they could do anything about it at the moment, but more than likely they believed Thrackan would keep to his side of the bargain, and back off his claim when the proper moment came for them to reveal themselves.

They could believe what they wanted. Thrackan had no intention of doing any such thing. The starbuster's masters also believed that Thrackan would turn over the planetary repulsor on this world as soon as he found it, in return for granting Thrackan a free hand on the planet Corellia. They could go on believing that, too, if they wished. Thrackan had other plans. The masters of the starbuster had told all the rebel leaders that the planetary repulsors were superb defensive weapons, nothing more. Thrackan knew better. Thrackan knew it would suit the starbuster's controllers just fine if no one ever got the things working, so long as the controllers sat on top of them and kept anyone else from getting near them. But Thrackan knew the repulsors were weapons of denial, blackmail weapons, weapons of threat that worked best if they were aimed, but never fired.

Let the other rebel leaders, the dirt-grubbing Selonian Overden or those bumbling fools, the Drallists, think what they might. Let the scramble-brains on Talus and Tralus believe what they were told about the repulsors. Thrackan knew better. He knew the masters of the starbuster plot had double-crossed them all. And Thrackan also knew that a double cross was nothing more than the necessary first step toward a successful triple cross.

But none of it would do any good unless his people could find the repulsor and get it operational. If the dirt-digging Selonians could do it, surely humans could do at least as well.

"Diktat Sal-Solo! Diktat!"

Thrackan turned around to see General Brimon Yarar, the man in charge of the dig, jogging toward him. "What is it, General?"

"News, sir. Maybe big news. The Drall planetary repulsor just came alive."

"What?!"

"Just now, sir. The jamming is still in place, of course, so we can't get any more information. But our sensors just picked up a huge jolt of repulsor activity coming from Drall. Unfocused, uncontrolled, but it's there. The Drallists have got the thing working."

"I don't believe it," Thrackan said. "I *can't* believe it. The Selonians, maybe. They're good at underground work. The Overden has some good technicians. But the Drallists? They were never anything." In moments of honesty, Thrackan knew his own Human League forces were not exactly the cream of society. Thugs, most of them. Even with all the help he got from the starbuster's masters, he had not been able to recruit many high-quality people. He had learned to accept that, and view his troops as the best tools he could lay hands on, if not the best tools for the job.

But, thugs or not, compared to the Drallists, they were perfect gentlemen and leading scientists, every one of them. Thrackan had at least been able to buy himself a few disgruntled technicians, some ex-Imperial soldiers and administrators. Not the Drallists. Whatever else you could say against the Drallish species, the pompous little fools were relentlessly honest, upright, cautious people. There had actually been some sort of discontent on Corellia, and probably on Selonia and Talus and Tralus, around which to build a revolt. On Drall, the rebellion had been, out of necessity, completely artificial. Even the Human League wouldn't have taken on humans as low-down as the Drallists—and Drallist technical capability was no better than Drallist behavior.

The idea that they had been able to get a planetary repulsor up and running was simply incredible—

Wait a moment. Wait just a moment. Maybe the Drallists hadn't gotten it running. Maybe someone *else* had managed that little trick. Suddenly Thrackan had a shrewd idea who that might be—and if he was right, he might just pick up a nice little bonus from all this.

Because no matter who had gotten the repulsor running, Thrackan Sal-Solo was willing to bet they would not keep it long. He turned toward Yarar. "Get the best of the repulsor tech crews together, along with a strike platoon." He lifted the bottle to his lips and took a big swallow. A warm glow started to flow through his insides. "We're going to pay a little call on the Drallists."

*   *   *

Luke watched the blinking light over the huge airlock chamber, and wondered who was on the other side, asking them in. Or more accurately, wondered if it would be wise to head on in. He and Lando had been debating the point for five minutes now. Luke decided to turn the debate on its head. "Okay, just for the sake of argument," he said, "suppose we *don't* go in that airlock. What's the alternative?"

"I don't know," Lando replied. "If we landed on the other -ide of the sphere, or went in on the end of the farther cylinder, we -ight be able to explore f— weeks before anyone caught up with us. And that might -e a goo- idea."

"How so?" Luke asked.

"You know me, Luke. I think big."

"That's for sure." Lando had made something like a career out of building huge projects of one sort or another. Of course, the projects had a bad habit of going bust for reasons that were no fault of Lando's, but that was neither here nor there. "So this place is big. What do you think about it?"

"I think something is wrong. I thought so the first time I saw this place, and the closer -e get, the surer I am. I think big, but I also —ink in function. Big makes sense for some jobs, but this is too -uch. That station has a hundred, a —ousand times the volume it should for any job I can think of that it might do, and the underlying design is all wrong. The -ocals don't see —at something's wrong because the station has been here so -ong. They take it for granted, think of it as a natural object. But trust me. Something about that station feels wrong."

Feels wrong. Lando had no talent in the Force. Luke was sure of that. But that didn't mean his intuitions couldn't be right. Luke shut his eyes and reached out, probing with his Force ability, searching for the feel of the station, of the beings aboard it. He could detect exactly one sentient mind, a human. Only one? Perhaps there were others, their minds shielded from him in some manner. He reached out and touched the one mind he could sense, touched as gently as he could. He discovered no sense of evil or bad intent. What he did find was a powerful sense of fear and uncertainty.

He probed toward the blinking light, and the airlock door that was still opening and shutting. There was one mind there, a human one, a young woman. And that mind still seemed worried and afraid—but friendly enough, for all of that.

"I say we accept the invitation," Luke said. "You're right—we could spend weeks exploring on our own.

But I don't think we *have* weeks to spare. And I think the natives are friendly. At least, there's one friendly one."

There was a dead silence on the line that lasted long enough for Luke to start wondering if the laser com system had given out altogether. But then Lando finally spoke. "When you're right, you're right," he said. "We have to take the chance."

"All right," said Luke. He brought his throttle forward just a fraction and flew toward the airlock, the *Lady Luck* right behind him.

As they drew closer, the light stopped flashing and the airlock door swung open wide and stopped there. Luke had to do some tricky flying to line his fighter up with the airlock and match lateral velocity as it rotated. Doing so while flying inverted made it only slightly more difficult. Luke was used to flying in all sorts of attitudes relative to his target, and with the station spinning to simulate gravity, he had to make sure the X-wing's landing pads were pointed straight out at the sky as he made his way into the airlock.

The closer Luke got to the airlock entrance, the bigger he realized it was. From a distance, it had appeared of ordinary proportion, but in reality, the thing could have handled the *Intruder,* the *Defender,* and the *Sentinel* flying side by side. Luke's X-wing flew in with as much room to spare as an insect flying into Jabba the Hutt's wide-gaping mouth. Lando followed right behind in the *Lady Luck.*

*   *   *

Admiral Hortel Ossilege was less than happy when the *Intruder*'s detectors picked up the massive, off-the-scale repulsor burst from Drall. Surprises were rarely welcome in a military operation, but doubly so when one was this far behind enemy lines and dealing with forces of such *power.* Lando Calrissian had warned him that his tactics of audacious advance might get him in over his head. Well, so be it. There was no real going back. Caution would gain him nothing. He would have to investigate that repulsor burst. It was almost certainly another planetary repulsor. But the burst seemed to have fired at nothing at all—almost like a flare shot straight up in the air for no better purpose than to attract attention.

Ossilege frowned to himself as he stared at the detector screen. Perhaps—perhaps—that was exactly what it was. With all conventional communications shut down, how else to announce one had captured a repulsor? A signal flare. But the enemy, the opposition, had kept *their* repulsor at Selonia secret. That suggested the people holding this repulsor were on the other side. Perhaps warning the other side that they were not the only ones with such a mighty weapon. Not just a signal flare, but a warning shot, perhaps.

Clearly, Ossilege had no choice but to investigate. But the timing could not have been worse. His ships had just taken up their positions around Centerpoint Station. Gaeriel Captison and her party were now inside the station, completely cut off from any communication with the Bakuran forces.

He could not abandon his position at Centerpoint or leave his people behind. He would have no choice but to divide his forces. For the briefest of moments, he considered sending nothing more than a flight of fighters or an assault boat loaded with troops. But no. The opposition was likely to move on the Drall repulsor as well. The Bakuran forces would have to go in ready to fight, not just investigate.

Ossilege smiled, his lips forming into a thin line. Calrissian had, indeed, warned him against audacious action. But Ossilege had been extremely cautious as he moved in toward Centerpoint Station, and he had discovered something about caution: he did not like it. Ossilege turned toward the ensign standing next to him.

"My compliments to Captain Semmac," he said to

her, "and relay my order to set course for Drall. The *Intruder* is going to investigate that repulsion burst. *Sentinel* and *Defender* will remain at Centerpoint." Ossilege looked back toward the detector screen. "*Someone* has sent us an invitation. I think it is only common politeness that we accept."

*   *   *

Luke's X-wing and the *Lady Luck* floated fifteen meters off the deck, moving slowly forward into the airlock, their shields up and in formation so as to give each other cover. What good such precautions might be up against a space station the size of a small planet, neither of them asked.

Luke brought the X-wing into a hover over the center of the lock and swung the fighter around to cover the *Lady Luck* as she came in. The *Lady* moved forward slowly, easing her way into the interior. The airlock chamber was cavernously huge and profoundly dark. The *Lady Luck*'s landing lights came on and swiveled about, throwing a shifting spot of brightness on the interior wall of the lock, but Luke was not able to make much of what the spot revealed. The huge exterior airlock door lumbered shut, sealing them inside. Now they were trapped, if they wanted to think of it that way.

Then the lock's own interior lights bloomed into life, coming up slowly enough that Luke's eyes were not dazzled. The interior of the lock was a half cylinder on its side, with the flat wall of the half cylinder forming the deck.

The deck was littered with debris, odds and ends of all sorts. Bits of clothing, broken pieces of luggage, freight containers, abandoned machinery, even a small spacecraft with all its access ports open and its nose assembly removed. Obviously it had been cannibalized for parts.

"-ooks like -ome folks got out of here in a -urry," Lando said.

"Looks like," Luke said. What, exactly, had they been in such a hurry to get away from? And had they made a run for it last week, or a hundred years before? He didn't feel easy in his mind. "Listen, Lando, normally I'd say land the ship with the passengers first and let the fighter fly cover. But with that airlock door shut, there doesn't seem much point to it. I'll land first. Maybe if it's a trap, they'll spring it on me first and then—"

"Then what?"

"I don't know," Luke said. "But don't land until you're sure it's safe."

"If I wait *that* long, we're -oing to be sittin- here in hover mode for a long time," Lando replied.

There didn't seem to be any good answer for that, so Luke didn't try to offer one. "I'm headed down," he said. Luke eased back on the repulsors and brought the X-wing slowly down onto the deck.

He made a nice smooth landing and was getting ready to undo his canopy and get out when Artoo beeped furiously at him. "What? Oh!" Artoo was right—the airlock chamber hadn't been pressurized. That could be a problem. Luke hadn't worn a sealable flight suit, and he was not entirely clear on whether there were pressure suits for all aboard the *Lady Luck*. But what was the point of bringing them in here if they couldn't get out of their ships?

Luke looked around the airlock chamber again and noticed that the debris was all inside a fairly well-prescribed perimeter. Why had everyone crowded together like that in the midst of what seemed to have been a panicked departure? A burst of light suddenly flared to life in the center of the airlock chamber's roof. Four streaks of light split off from the center and slid down to the four corners of the chamber. The streaks faded to darkness, and then the light burst came to life again, before splitting up and sliding down to the corners, and then the pattern repeated. It was as clear a signal as the airlock door opening and shutting. *Go down, go down, go down.*

Now Luke understood. "Lando," he said, "bring her down. They're using a force bubble pressurization system in here. I don't think they want to activate the force field until you've landed." By using a force field system, they could avoid constantly pressurizing and depressurizing the chamber—no small issue in a chamber this size.

"But then we'd both be trapped insi— the force field," Lando objected.

"What's the difference? We're already trapped inside the airlock."

"There's a difference between being in a cage with a bantha and climbing into the bantha's gullet," Lando muttered. "But all right, here we come."

The *Lady Luck* eased down on her repulsors and set down ten meters in front of Luke's X-wing.

The moment she landed, there was a shimmering in the space over their heads. After a moment it settled down into a thin blue hazy blur that surrounded the two ships, forming a hemisphere over them. A tunnel formed of the same blue haze came into being just behind the *Lady Luck.* Peering down it, Luke could see that it led to a more conventional-sized inner airlock hatch.

"Leading us there every step of the way," Luke muttered to himself. He heard a far-off, high-pitched hissing noise, and the body of the X-wing creaked and groaned once or twice as it adjusted to the change in pressure. The hissing dropped in pitch down to a low roar of noise, and the incoming air was whipping up some of the smaller bits of debris and throwing them around, until the inside of the force field bubble was swirling with bits of paper and dust and torn-up packing material. The X-wing rocked back on its shock absorbers as the rush of air pushed at it.

Luke watched his exterior gauges as the roaring subsided. At least as far as his instruments were concerned, it was perfectly normal air at perfectly normal pressure. Of course, it *could* contain some deadly nerve gas the X-wing's detectors couldn't sense, but if whoever was running the show here had wanted to kill them, they could have done the job about a dozen times already.

Never mind. Time to get on with it. Luke popped the canopy of the X-wing and let it swing up out of the way. He pulled his flight helmet off and stashed it, then climbed up out of the pilot's compartment. He slid down the side of the fuselage and dropped lightly to the ground. Relatively light gravity here, he noticed. Of course, they were fairly close to the spin axis here. The apparent force of gravity would be a lot stronger close to the equator line of the sphere.

The hatches of the *Lady Luck* swung open, the egress ramp came down, and Lando, Gaeriel, and Kalenda walked down it, closely followed by a rather agitated-looking Threepio.

"I don't like this place," the protocol droid announced. "Not one little bit. I'm sure we are all in the most terrible danger here."

"Yeah, whatever," Lando muttered. "Besides, what was the last place you *did* like?"

Threepio hesitated a moment and cocked his head to one side. "A most interesting question," he said. "I can't recall one, offhand. I shall have to consult my onboard archives."

"Do it later, Threepio," said Luke. "We might need you for other things."

"Certainly, Master Luke."

Gaeriel and Kalenda looked around the airlock chamber, and it was easy to tell the diplomat from the intelligence officer. Kalenda knelt down to examine some of the broken-up debris and snatched at a few of the bits of paper that were fluttering, no doubt in hopes of reading some important clue. Gaeriel made sure Threepio, the protocol and translation droid, was close, and directed her attention to the force field tunnel and the hatch that would lead them to their host.

Luke heard a beeping and a blooping from the topside of his X-wing. "Don't worry, Artoo, I haven't forgotten you." Back at a base, the normal thing was to use a winch to get Artoo in and out of his socket in the stern of the X-wing. In the field, it was possible for Artoo to get himself out, but the process was not very graceful, and had ended with Artoo toppling over and landing with a crash on more than one occasion.

But when the pilot of the X-wing was a Jedi Master, such awkwardness was not necessary. Luke reached out with his ability in the Force and lifted Artoo gently into the air.

"Do be careful, Master Luke," said Threepio. "It makes me nervous just to see you do that."

Artoo let out a long, low moan that echoed his agreement with Threepio. "Relax, both of you," said Luke. "I could do this standing on my head." Artoo moaned again. "Sorry," said Luke. "It's not nice to tease." Luke moved Artoo clear of the X-wing and was just about to start bringing him down to the deck when the hatch at the end of the force field tunnel began to lumber open. Everyone stopped what they were doing and turned to look.

Luke felt his hand move toward his lightsaber, but then he pulled it away. No. All he knew for sure was that he had touched the mind of a human who seemed to bear them no ill will. Whoever was about to come through that door had not summoned them all here to engage in single combat. They would be dead many times over by now, if that was her intent. He saw Lando and Kalenda make the same reflex reach for their own sidearms, and then pull their hands back.

The doors rumbled open, and a tall, thin, nervous-looking, pale-skinned woman came in. She hesitated at the entrance for a moment, and then shrugged and walked toward them at a brisk clip that seemed to say less about her eagerness to get to the end of the tunnel and more about her rather agitated state.

Luke watched her as she came closer. She was an attractive-looking woman with a long, thin face, thick black curly hair that reached to her shoulders, and prominent, expressive eyebrows. She looked worried as she came toward them, her eyes moving from one member of the party to the next. But then the worried look faded away to be replaced by one of pure bafflement as she looked upward.

"How are you doing that?" she asked. "And why?"

"Huh?" Luke asked, and looked up himself. "Oh!" He had nearly forgotten that Artoo was still hanging in midair. If he had lost any more concentration, Artoo would have crashed to the deck. Distracted by the sight of their hostess's arrival, it would seem that Artoo had forgotten it himself. Luke willed Artoo to move down and landed him gently on the deck. "It's sort of a long story," he said.

"I'll bet," the young woman said, giving Luke a long, hard, quizzical look. "Well, anyway. I'm Jenica Sonsen, C-point COO Ad-Op."

"What?" Luke asked.

Sonsen sighed. "Sorry. Force of habit. Centerpoint Chief Operations Officer, Administration and Operations. Basically, I run the place, these days. The C-point CE declared a bug-out right after the first major flare incident, and the whole Exec Sec evaced along with practically all the C-point civpop. I wish *I* could get out of here, but I was OOD when the bug was called, so regs said I was stay-behind."

Luke was about to ask her what *that* meant when Threepio stepped forward. "Perhaps I might be of help, Master Skywalker," said the droid. "She is using many terms that are similar to the bureaucratic argot of Coruscant. I believe that what Administrative Officer Sonsen means is that Centerpoint's Chief Executive ordered a full evacuation after the first flare disaster, and the entire Executive Secretariat left along with most of the civilian populace. Although she wished to leave with everyone else, Administrative Officer Sonsen happened to be the Officer On Duty at the moment when the evacuation was declared, and under those circumstances, she was automatically designated the officer to stay behind and serve as a caretaker."

"She didn't say anything about a disaster," Lando said suspiciously.

"I beg your pardon," Threepio said, "but she did refer to a 'major incident.' That is a common bureaucratic euphemism for a major catastrophe."

"Hold it," Sonsen said, "the tin box got it all correct, but I *am* right here. You could ask *me* what I meant."

"Only if you promise to speak Basic like everyone else," Lando said. Luke had to smile. Lando never had had much use for bureaucratic double-talk.

For a moment it looked as if Sonsen were about to bite Lando's head off, but then backed down. "Maybe you've got a point. But I have to know what you're *doing* here. Your ships blew out of nowhere and then those fighters bugged out too."

"Were they your fighters?" Kalenda asked. "And what government do you represent?"

"The fighters you were shooting at? They weren't Fed-Dub."

"Fed-Dub?"

"Sorry. The Federation of the Double Worlds.'

Kalenda nodded and looked to Luke, her gaze seemingly somewhere over his left shoulder. "The Federation is the duly elected government of Talus and Tralus."

"You people still haven't told me who you are and what you're doing here," Sonsen said.

"Our apologies," Gaeriel said, speaking for the first time, "I am Gaeriel Captison, plenipotentiary of the planet Bakura. This is Captain Lando Calrissian, Jedi Master Luke Skywalker, and Lieutenant Belindi Kalenda, all of the planet Coruscant. We represent the

New Republic and the planet Bakura." She went on in a tone of voice that suggested she was expecting argument, but wasn't going to put up with it. "We are," she said, "taking possession of Centerpoint Station in the name of the New Republic."

"Well, *good,*" said Sonsen. "It's about time *somebody* did. Come this way and I'll show you where everything is." She turned around abruptly and starting walking down the tunnel toward the inner hatch.

Gaeriel looked at Luke, clearly taken aback. "She's not what we expected," she said.

"Most things aren't, around Luke," Lando said. "But if she's going to hand over the keys to us, I think we'd better not let her get too far ahead."

*   *   *

The four humans and two droids found Sonsen waiting for them on the other side of the inner hatch. "There you all are," she said. "Shall we start the tour?" Her tone was utterly matter-of-fact, as if handing over space stations to more or less allied forces was all part of the daily routine. "I can't show you all of the station, of course, unless you all want to die of old age before we're half done, but I can show you the basics. This way." She ushered them all into a waiting turbovator car on the opposite side of the lock chamber. They followed her in. Luke entered the car after everyone else, feeling quite bewildered. The turbovator car was huge and scruffy-looking. All the walls were covered with dings and scratches, as if the car had seen a lot of heavy use moving cargo. There was a meter-wide porthole in the back wall of the car, likewise a bit dinged-up, and another like it in the ceiling. However, there seemed to be nothing but blackness to see.

"Hang on just a second," she said. "We have to move the car through an airlock. Pressure difference. And, ah—well, something happened to the air where we're going." She worked the controls, and the car lurched forward a few meters. They heard a hatch seal behind them. There was the whir of air pumps and then, through the viewport, they saw another hatch open before them.

Sonsen pushed another button and the car started to move, not up or down, but sideways. Lights on the exterior of the car came on, showing the way forward. The tunnel they were in was circular in cross-section, and dark pink in color. The tunnel ahead trailed off into what seemed an infinity of darkness. Luke felt as if they had been swallowed by some huge creature and were rushing down its gullet, toward an appointment with the digestive system.

"We might as well start out with Hollowtown," Sonsen said. "It's what everyone always wants to see first."

"Hollowtown?" Lando asked.

There was a second's awkward pause before Sonsen spoke. "You're not all that well briefed, are you?" she asked.

"Things have happened kind of fast," Luke said. "There hasn't been a lot of time."

"I guess not. Well, let me start from scratch. Hollowtown is the open space in the exact center of the central sphere. It's a spherical hollow about sixty kilometers across. Where you docked was just about at the join between the North Pole—that's what the locals call the cylinders, the North and South Poles—and the central sphere. We're now moving parallel to the axis of rotation, sideways, in toward Hollowtown. We have to pass through about twenty kilometers of decks and shells first. A shell is what we call real high-ceilinged deck, anything over about twenty meters or so. There are about two thousand levels all told. We're accelerating pretty fast right now, faster than you think. We'll come up in Hollowtown in about five minutes, and then start moving downslope, toward the heavy-gravity areas. Farther out from the axis you go, the more of a spin, and the higher effective gravity, of course."

"The spin must get to be an awful nuisance,"

Kalenda said. "Why haven't you shifted over to standard artificial gravity?"

"We've thought about it. Cap Con Ops—sorry—the capital construction operations office—has done about a dozen studies on de-spinning the station and using standard artigrav."

Luke managed to translate that last as "artificial gravity" and tried to nod encouragingly. "So what do the studies come up with?"

"Too expensive, too complicated, too disruptive, and too many unknowns. The station's structure might or might not respond well to the shifted stresses. But it's your problem now. You can de-spin it all you want as far as I'm concerned."

"I take it you want out," Luke said.

"Do I ever. I was into real short-time when the first flare went whump. I was almost down to counting the days on one hand—and then, well, you know the rest."

"Lousy briefing, remember?" Lando said.

"Wait a second. You people don't know about the *flares*?"

"First we've heard of them," Luke said. "We just broke through the interdiction field into the system a few days ago."

Sonsen let out a low whistle. "Broke through the interdiction field? *That's* something, all right. I'll bet whoever is creating that field isn't real happy with you just now."

Kalenda frowned. "Hold it. *You're* generating the field."

"What? What are you talking about?"

"The field. The interdiction field is centered on this station. Centerpoint Station is generating the interdiction field. And the communications jamming, for that matter."

"Burning stars. It *is*?"

"You didn't know that," Lando said. It was not a question.

"Nope. None of us here did. Looks like my briefing wasn't so good either."

Luke was getting more confused by the minute. How could the people running the station not know the station was creating the field? And what were these flares Sonsen was talking about?

It was becoming plainer and plainer that things were not as they appeared. But it was also becoming progressively less clear *how* they appeared in the first place.

"I think we have a few things to talk about," said Luke.

The turbovator moved smoothly toward Hollowtown.

CHAPTER SIX

The View From Inside

"W hat you've got to understand about this place is that no one understands it," Sonsen said. "We just live here. It's here, so are we, and that's about it. No one thought much about why things were the way they were. We didn't know *why* Centerpoint did most of the things it did, but we knew what most of them were. At least we thought we knew, up until a while ago. Up until the terrorists started showing us a few tricks."

"We just got here," Lando said. "What terrorists?"

Sonsen shook her head. "I'd love to know the answer to that one. There have been attacks—nasty ones. But no one has claimed responsibility or made demands. Not so much as an anonymous tip. We have suspects—the TraTaLibbers, the Two Worlders, and so on, but they all denied having anything to do with it. Besides, if they could pull off the stuff that's happened here, they wouldn't waste time making threats. They'd just move in and take over. Of course, the station's been cut *off* from everybody since the jamming started up. The investigators on the ground could have wrapped up the case, solved it completely, and we wouldn't know about it."

Luke made a guess that TraTaLibbers meant the Tralus and Talus Liberation Party, or some such. Two Worlders probably meant some crowd that wanted separate governments for each planet. Guesses were good enough. He had an idea what Sonsen meant, and he had a hunch the groups in question were not worth worrying about. "Tell us about the attacks themselves."

Sonsen went to the turbovator car's viewport. "You'll be able to see for yourself in a minute or two. Hollowtown used to be quite a place. It grew enough food for the whole station, with a surplus. It had parks, and nice homes, and lakes and streams. Green and blue, cool and lovely. Then someone started messing with the Glowpoint."

"The Glowpoint being a sort of artificial sun?" Luke asked.

"That's right," said Sonsen. "And someone made it go crazy."

"Who normally controls the Glowpoint?" Lando asked.

"No one, of course," Sonsen replied, as if Lando had just asked where she kept the on-off switch for the galaxy's spin. "As I said, it's just there, the way the whole station is. We didn't build it. I guess it was here when we got here—whenever that was."

"The Glowpoint is just *there*," Lando repeated. "Anyone know how it works? How it gives off light?"

"There are theories of one sort or another. One idea is that the Glowpoint draws its power directly from the gravitational interflux between Talus and Tralus. But no one has been able to come up with an instrument to test the idea. There's nothing conclusive."

"You don't know how the power source for half your food production works?" Gaeriel asked.

"No," said Sonsen. "Do you know how the hyperdrive motors that got you here work?"

Luke had to smile to himself. Jenica Sonsen had a point. There was scarcely a human being alive who completely understood every bit of technology he or she used. The Centerpointers, it seemed, were just a bit more obvious about it.

"Anyway, we're coming up on Hollowtown, if you want to get a look at it." The other humans joined her at the viewport, leaving the two droids off by themselves in the back of the car. A spot of light began to gleam through the end of the tunnel up ahead. "That's the Glowpoint," Sonsen said. "It's back to normal, at least for the moment. That's what it used to be like all the time."

The turbovator car moved closer and closer to the tunnel, giving the illusion that it was moving faster and faster as it got closer to the light. The humans in the group shielded their eyes against the sudden brightness.

In a moment that seemed to take forever to arrive and then to happen all at once, the turbovator car burst out of the end of the tunnel and, with a stomach-dropping lurch, began to move straight downward. But no one in the car paid much notice to the violent change of direction. They were too busy looking at Hollowtown.

Or what was left of it.

The Glowpoint was just that, a glowing point of light suspended in midair, in the precise center of the huge spherical chamber. It looked like a miniature sun, warm, bright, comfortable, inviting. But there was nothing comfortable about the landscape below.

Hollowtown had been burnt to a crisp, charred down to a blackened land of ashes. Hazy clouds of dust floated everywhere. Luke could see the skeletal remains of burned-out buildings, what had once been neatly planted orchards that were now nothing but rows of incinerated tree stumps. A lake had boiled dry, and the lake bottom was exposed, the remains of ruined pleasure boats lying there like children's toys left behind when the water was drained from the tub.

It was a terrible place, a nightmare place, made all the worse because it had so plainly been lovely, well tended, not so very long before. "Normally I'd stop the car at one of the intermediate stops and let you get out and look around," Sonsen said. "But there's just about no free oxygen left in there. All of it got consumed in the fires. I don't know how we'll ever get breathable air in there again. For that matter, it took some doing to get breathable air in this turbovator car. It didn't use to have its own air source, just a compressor that pulled air in from the outside. The air in the tunnel and near the spin axis was always too thin to breathe. After the first flare, the techs installed a full air system so I could still use the car. It's the fastest, easiest way from the equator to the docking zone and the techsec, where I met you. The engineers yanked the compressor and hooked up some air tanks and a carbon dioxide scrubber."

"What happened, exactly?" Lando asked.

"The first flare was about thirty or forty standard days ago," Sonsen said, her voice suddenly sad and tired. "Up until then, everything you see here now was parkland, or farmland, or luxury estates. It was beautiful to see. The Glowpoint would shine down constantly. The farmers would use shadow-shields to block the light and simulate seasons. From the inside of the shields, it could be as light or as dark as you liked, just by twisting a dial. From the outside, the shield could look like shadows, or like silver bubbles, or squares of gold—however you wanted to set them. People decorated their shields all sorts of ways. There was a special feeling, knowing it was always day here—but that under every spot of gold was a secret little patch of night. All of it gone now. Gone. Gone when the flare hit."

"That was before the jamming started. I came into the system about that time," Kalenda objected. "I never heard anything about this. It should have been big news. The biggest."

"We tried to keep it as quiet as we could," Sonsen said. "The Fed-Dub government was weak enough as it was, and what terrorists want most is publicity. The

Feds were afraid that if this got out, it could spark a
panic or even a rebellion here. And I guess they were
right. We could keep news of this"—she gestured
toward the devastation out the window—"from getting
to the other worlds, but the refugees all had to go to
Talus and Tralus. The word spread, and we got our
rebellions, all right. One on Talus, two on Tralus. One
group or the other—I don't even know which—landed
a bunch of fighters somewhere on the South Pole a
while back, claimed the station for themselves." Sonsen shrugged. "What was I going to do? Fight them off
by myself? I left them alone, and they did the same to
me—until you chased them off."

"What do you mean, by yourself?" Gaeriel asked.
"Are you the only one still on the station?"

Sonsen shook her head. "Probably not. It's a big
place. We tried to evac everyone, but my guess is
someone got left behind. I haven't seen anybody, but
that doesn't mean anything."

"You keep talking about the first flare," Lando
asked. "How many more were there?"

"Just one more. Two in all. The second happened
just about a day or so before the interdiction field and
the communications jamming came on. And don't ask
me what the point of a terrorist attack is when there's
no one left to terrorize, and there's nothing left to
burn."

"Uh-huh," Lando said, a bit distractedly. "This station is exactly at the centerpoint, the barycenter between Talus and Tralus, right?"

"Right," Sonsen said, giving Lando another strange
look. "Were you people briefed at *all*?"

"I knew that much," Lando said. "I just wanted to
confirm it. The Glowpoint. It's at the exact center of
Hollowtown? And Hollowtown is at the exact center of
the station?"

"It might be off by a centimeter or two. Feel free to
get a measuring stick and check if you want."

Lando ignored Sonsen's sarcasm. He pointed out across the huge spherical space, toward the far side of the rotation axis, and then tilted his head back to look through the overhead viewport. "Those conical structures coming up out of the North and South Poles, right on the rotation axis. What can you tell me about them?"

Luke looked through the overhead viewport, and then through the forward view. Up until just a moment ago, they had been too close to one cluster of cones to see it clearly, and the other had been lost in the glare of the Glowpoint. But Lando seemed to have spotted them in the moment they became visible. Almost as if he had expected to see them. The two clusters seemed to be identical: a larger central cone surrounded by what looked to be six smaller cones, all with similar proportions of height to width.

Sonsen shrugged, a bit theatrically. "I can tell you that one set is called the South Conical Mountains, and the other is called the North Conicals. I'll let you figure out which is which. People try to climb them once in a while, but even in the near zero-gee zone at the spin axis, it isn't easy. Anything else of vital interest you need to know? Like the names of the boats in the bottom of the lake bed?"

"No," said Lando, his mind clearly somewhere else. "I think that's all I need to know."

"Great," said Sonsen. "Sometime I'll have to spend five minutes learning everything important about *your* homeworld."

"Hmmm? What? No, no. I'm sorry. I didn't mean it that way. I mean, I think I know enough to understand what's going on."

"After five minutes? No offense, but our ITA people have been trying for *just* a bit longer, and we haven't worked it out yet."

"ITA?" Luke asked.

"I believe in this context, the reference is to Intelligence and Technical Assessment," Threepio said in a helpful tone of voice.

"I'm sure you've got good people," Lando said, "and I didn't mean to sound rude or condescending. It's just a question of viewpoint. You've been seeing this thing from the inside out your whole life. I happen to be in a position to see it from the outside and—"

Just at that moment, Artoo let off a low, unsettled-sounding whistle. His view lens swiveled up to take in an overhead view, and then he turned to Threepio and let off a series of beeps and whistles that were too fast for Luke to follow.

"Very well, Artoo, I will inquire, though it is very rude of you to interrupt." Threepio turned toward Jenica Sonsen. "Pardon the intrusion, Administrator Sonsen, but my counterpart wishes to know, rather urgently, if the two previous Glowpoint flare events started suddenly, or if there was a gradual increase in the light source's brightness."

It was plain that Sonsen was less and less sure of this crowd of visitors with every moment that passed. "Interesting droids you've got," she said to no one in particular. "As best we're able to tell, the brightness came up gradually, over the course of about half an hour. We don't know for sure because no one who was in here to see it got out alive—and of course all the recording instruments were destroyed as well."

Artoo rocked back and forth on his roller legs and whistled urgently, his head whirling back and forth.

"Oh, dear!" Threepio said. "I quite agree. We must depart at once."

"What?" Lando asked. "Why? What's going on?"

Threepio turned stiffly toward Luke and stared at him in surprise. "You have not noticed? Oh! Of course. My apologies. Your eyes compensate so automatically that you are unaware of the change. An interesting demonstration of the difference in our perceptions."

Lando glared at the protocol droid. "Threepio," he said in an artificially, calm voice, "if the next words from you are not an explanation of the problem, I am going to power you down right now and permanently disable your speech center. What is the problem?"

Threepio seemed about to protest, then thought better of it. "It is, quite simply, Captain Calrissian, that the visible light output from the Glowpoint has increased six percent in the last five minutes."

*   *   *

"Anakin!" Jacen could *feel* his little brother nearby, and he knew perfectly well that Anakin could sense Jacen's presence. But all the knowing back and forth in the world, all the ability to zero in on each other's location, did not do much good in the current situation. For Jacen could also sense that Anakin was scared and feeling guilty, feeling sorry for what he had done.

It was a wonderful paradox, in a sense. If there was ever a kid in the history of the galaxy who *deserved* to be in trouble, it was Anakin Solo, now, today. After all, they had been trying to keep this place hidden. Anakin couldn't have made it more visible if he had tried.

But the sheer magnitude of what he had done made it all but impossible to hold him responsible. Anakin couldn't possibly have understood what he was doing, or he never would have done it. He was just a little boy who liked to play with machines. Jacen thought back to a few incidents in his own life when his parents had let him off easier than they might have. Nothing this big, of course, but the point was the same. Jacen had always thought those had been times he had gotten off easy, gotten lucky. Now he was not so sure. Maybe it hadn't been him being lucky, but his parents being understanding.

"Anakin! It's all right! Nobody's mad at you." Well, Chewbacca wasn't exactly *thrilled* with him, and Aunt Marcha wasn't all that pleased with him for getting her hovercar vaporized or getting her head cut open. If and when they ever got Q9-X2 working again, he was not likely to express his gratitude for what Anakin had done. But no one was *mad*. Not exactly. "Come on out." Jacen knew perfectly well it was no good chasing Anakin or going in after him. He would just run away, hide again. Jacen would have to get him to come out on his own.

"I wanna stay here!" Anakin called out.

That was, strangely enough, a good first step. Jacen knew his brother well enough to know he was asking to be talked out of what he had just said. "Come on, Anakin," Jacen said. "You can't stay there forever."

"Can so!"

"But it's getting dark." For reasons best known to the beings who had built this place, the steady, perfect illumination the chamber had produced from out of nowhere when it was cone-shaped wasn't there anymore now that it was open to the sky. And night was coming on. "What about food?" Jacen went on. "Aren't you hungry?"

"Well, maybe a little."

"Maybe a lot," Jacen said. "Tell you what. Why don't you come get something to eat, and then if you want to go back to hiding, you can." The suggestion made no sense at all, of course, but that was all right. It gave Anakin a way to save face, a way to back down.

There was a long silence—and that was a good sign too. Anakin was thinking about it. Jacen waited for a minute, and then gave it another try. "Anakin? Come on back to the camp—to the ship—and have some food." He couldn't really invite him to the camp. There wasn't much of a camp left. Everything that hadn't been inside the *Falcon* had been burned to a crisp.

"Can I really come back and hide later if I want to?" Anakin asked.

"All you want," Jacen promised, knowing how easy

it would be to keep that promise. After all, Anakin hadn't needed permission to run away and hide the first time. He wouldn't need it the next time, either, assuming they didn't put a round-the-clock guard on him or lock him up and weld the hatch shut. And Jacen wouldn't put it past Anakin to manage an escape even with a guard and a locked door.

"Well, all right. Wait a second." After a moment Anakin appeared at the entrance to the corridor. He paused there and looked toward his big brother.

"It's all right, Anakin, really." Of course, there was very little that *was* all right, but Anakin knew what Jacen meant. Anakin came forward, slowly at first, then suddenly he was running as fast as he could. He threw his arms around Jacen and Jacen hugged him back.

"I'm sorry, Jacen. I didn't mean to do anything bad. Honest."

"I know, I know. But what you mean to do really doesn't count so much, sometimes. It's what happens that matters." Jacen could almost hear his father telling him the same thing. Suddenly he found himself thinking not of what his father or mother would do— but *about* them. They were probably in trouble too, out there, somewhere. The last any of them knew about their parents was that they had remained behind, trapped in Corona House, when Chewbacca had gotten the three children, Q9, and Ebrihim out. Were they still there? Or had Dad's cousin Thrackan locked them up someplace else? Or had they gotten away, somehow? Jacen suddenly felt a wave of guilt pass over him. Why hadn't he worried about them more, thought about them more?

"I miss Mom and Dad," Anakin announced, with his face mashed up against Jacen's shoulder, his voice a little muffled and a little snuffly.

Jacen was surprised to hear his brother say that just then. It would seem Anakin's mind worked a bit more like Jacen's than Jacen had thought. "So do I," Jacen said. "So do I. Come on. Let's go back to the others."

* * *

The two boys walked hand in hand toward the center of the massive chamber. Anakin slowly settled down enough to take an interest in his surroundings. He looked up toward where the top of the conical chamber had been, toward where the sky was now.

"Boy," he said. "Things have really changed."

"Yeah," agreed Jacen. "They sure have." He looked up himself and was astonished all over again by the sight.

The sky was getting dark, and so was the interior of the chamber, but the silvery surface did a good job of reflecting what light there was. It was probably just about sunset, but there was no real way to know. All they could see was a perfectly circular patch of dark sky, exactly overhead, right at the zenith, with the gleaming shadows of the seven silver cones stabbing into the edge of that perfect circle of night. Jacen could see stars starting to peek through, here and there.

They walked on, toward the *Falcon,* moving a bit more carefully as they picked their way through the heaps of burnt-up belongings. Everything that had been outside the ship was reduced to melted puddles and to ashes. Jacen and Anakin paused again to get a look at the *Falcon.* "The ship's broken again," Anakin said. It was not a question.

"Uh-huh. It looks like all the propulsion systems blew out before Chewbacca could get the shields up."

Anakin nodded slowly. "That isn't good," he said.

Jacen looked straight up, at the top of the cylinder, something like a kilometer or two over their heads. Unless Chewbacca could get the ship running, or unless someone could figure a way to walk straight up the side of the smooth, slick, sheer, impenetrable walls, they were stuck down here. "It sure isn't," Jacen agreed. "Come on," he said. He almost told Anakin they were all waiting for him, but then it occurred to him that would not exactly encourage his brother to step lively. "Let's go in."

*   *   *

The Duchess Marcha of Mastigophorous sat in the lounge of the *Millennium Falcon,* feeling downright gloomy. The company was not enlivening. Her nephew, Ebrihim, was playing a dispirited game of sabacc with Jaina. The fact that Jaina had lost several hands showed just how low her spirits were. Q9, or what was left of him, was propped up against the far bulkhead of the compartment. He reminded Marcha all too closely of a mummified corpse no one had gotten around to burying.

She herself had a pounding headache, though she knew that she could count herself lucky to have no more serious complaints than that. It was a miracle that none of them had been killed. Well, maybe Q9 *had* been killed. At least Chewbacca had not been able to revive him.

Of course, it might not matter that much who was alive and who was dead right now. They were trapped here, and most of their rations had been outside the *Falcon,* either stored on the hovercar or else in storage crates that had been stacked outside the spacecraft to make room. The *Falcon*'s emergency stores would last for a while, but not forever. Marcha's best guess, which she had not shared with anyone, was that they had perhaps enough water for six days and enough food for ten.

And they might well be lucky if they were alive long enough to worry about such things. She agreed with Chewbacca that it was all but certain that the repulsor's violent awakening had wiped out the Drallists, and good riddance, but there was bound to be *someone* who had been far enough away to survive the disturbance and had noticed it.

She saw two possibilities. Perhaps Drall scientists would notice the seismic convulsions, or the electrical disturbances or whatever, and come take a look. However, that seemed a *trifle* improbable, as there was, after all, a war on, most public institutions had been shut down, and there were massive travel restrictions in effect. Unpleasant as it might be to concede the point, it seemed far more likely that a military group of some sort, equipped to detect repulsion activity, would have seen a burst of repulsor power bright enough to blow out their detector screens and come to investigate.

It seemed most unlikely that it would be anyone pleasant who arrived under those circumstances. And leaving behind the trifling problem of the sort of thing most of the military groups in the system were likely to do to captured enemy civilians, there was the question of what they could do with the planetary repulsor, once it was in their possession. Lots of unsavory people had been looking for the things for a long time. Marcha did not know what they hoped to do with the repulsor, but she doubted it would be anything good. All she knew was that the enemy regarded the repulsors as vitally, urgently important. It was not beyond the realm of possibility that by handing this one over to the enemy, Anakin had lost the entire war, single-handed.

But these opinions, too, she kept to herself. Things were bad enough already, and there was no sense making them worse right now, when they would no doubt deteriorate on their own in due course.

Their one hope seemed to be that Chewbacca could get the *Falcon*'s propulsion systems working again. The Wookiee was working on the problem now, rooting around in all the access panels, knee-deep in cables and burned-out parts. She could hear him from here, banging and thudding about. He was doing his best, no doubt, but Marcha had strong doubts that he would succeed. It seemed likely that what had knocked them out was the initial massive burst of repulsor power so strong that it had managed to jump across open circuits. In all likelihood, a similar electromagnetic pulse had blown out Q9.

No, the situation was not good. Not one little bit good. And it seemed unlikely to do anything but get worse.

She heard the sound of footsteps coming up the *Falcon*'s entry ramp and looked up in time to see Jacen and Anakin come into the lounge. Ebrihim and Jaina looked up as well. It would seem that Chewbacca heard them also, as he appeared in the door and stood there a moment or two after the two boys came in.

"Hi, everyone," Anakin said. "I'm back. I'm—I'm real sorry for what I did. I didn't *mean* to hurt anything—but I did. I'm sorry."

A miracle of understatement, that. What the child had done might well have condemned millions to a life under tyranny. Marcha could even at least imagine a scenario where loss of the repulsor meant loss of the war for the New Republic, so damaging the New Republic's prestige that it collapsed altogether. Quite a lot to put on one small child's shoulders.

"It'll be all right, Anakin," Jaina said. "We'll find a way to fix it all. Don't you worry."

Marcha exchanged a glance with her nephew, and then with the Wookiee. Clearly neither of them was in any more of a mood for empty platitudes than she was. But sometimes platitudes were all one had left. And there were times when a completely unreasoned, and unreasonable, expression of optimism was absolutely necessary. "Of *course* it will be all right," she heard herself saying as she stood up and moved a step or two toward him. "Come here, Anakin."

Suddenly the child burst into tears, rushed over to

her, and flung his arms around her. "There, there," she said, putting her arms around him. "There, there."

If she had known, exactly, what she meant by the comforting words, she might have found them comforting herself.

CHAPTER SEVEN

Seeing the Light

I suppose I won't like the answer if I ask you if this thing can go any faster," said Lando. The turbovator car continued its stately descent down to the equator line of Hollowtown and the nearest way out. The Glowpoint had started brightening when they were just about at the midpoint of their descent.

Jenica Sonsen shook her head. "No, you wouldn't like the answer," she said.

"I had a feeling you'd say that." Lando looked up through the turbovator car's overhead viewport. The Glowpoint was dazzlingly bright, but the question was, how *much* brighter and how fast was it brightening. Could he judge it any better by looking at the ground, at the reflected light, rather than at the source? He peered intently at the ground for a moment, then gave it up. Threepio, annoyingly enough, had been right for once. The human eye was just too good at adjusting for changes in brightness. There was no way he could make an eyeball estimate of how fast it was getting worse. He could ask Threepio, of course, but even in the midst of this crisis, there was a part of him that didn't want to give the droid the satisfaction. Besides, Golden Boy would probably just start giving a running report of brightness levels and drive them all crazy.

"I'd say we're up to a twenty percent brightness increase," Luke announced. Of course. With his Jedi control over his senses, he would be able to make that sort of estimate. "But the brightness isn't all of it. As we go lower, we're going to get into thicker air that can hold a lot of heat." Luke turned to Sonsen. "How high a temperature can this car take?" he asked.

Sonsen shrugged. "How should I know? I doubt if anyone ever bothered to figure it out. It's a glorified elevator, not a spacecraft. But it's definitely getting hot in here."

"There is indeed a significant temperature rise already," said Threepio. "If you wish, I could gladly provide you with a running account of—"

"No, we would *not* wish," Lando said. "There's nothing we can do about it anyway." He held the palm of his hand flat over the interior wall of the elevator car, and then, very gingerly, touched it with just the tip of his index finger. "The skin of this thing is getting warmer though, and the heat is percolating through. No doubt about it."

"How long until we're out of here?" Kalenda asked.

"Another five minutes or so," Sonsen said. "But there's a flaw."

"What flaw?" Lando asked. This place was clearly bad news.

"There's a pressure differential between the equatorial region of Hollowtown and Shell One, on the other side of the lock. No big deal, maybe an eight percent differential, but it's enough that you have to use an airlock. The main turbovator airlock jammed up during the second flare. It was never meant to do more than match the slight pressure differential between Hollowtown and Shell One. I managed to get it working again after the flare, but it wasn't easy, and I'm not so sure my repair is going to hold up."

"So we're stuck," Lando said.

"Heavens! We'll all be roasted alive," Threepio said.

"You speak when you're spoken to," Sonsen said, obviously starting to share Lando's opinion of the protocol droid. "We're not stuck," she said to the others.

"There's a personnel lock right next to the turbovator airlock. It's smaller and simpler, and it got a lot more use, so it's a real heavy-duty job. I'm sure it'll still be working. If we can't get the turbovator lock running, we'll have to make a run for the personnel lock."

"But you did happen to mention there's no oxygen left out there," Luke said.

"Even if there were any oxygen left, it would probably kill you to breathe out there. Very high CO_2 levels, plus all sorts of toxic burn products."

"Can we all make it into the lock at once?" Luke asked.

"Well, the lock is big enough," said Sonsen. "I don't think we should try all of us at once. The lock is normally set with this side closed. There's a control panel on this side of the lock and it has to be operated by hand. I'll have to open the turbovator door, run for the lock, and get it open. I don't think it would be so smart to have everyone waiting on me getting the door open. We should do it in two passes."

"This is going to be interesting," Lando said.

Sonsen smiled humorlessly. "So it will. But we might get lucky. Maybe the turbovator airlock will work."

"Maybe it will. But if it doesn't, and you have to run for the other airlock, I'll go with you. I used to run a place called Cloud City. I had to go in and out of toxic atmosphere a lot. If you run into trouble, it might be smart to have some help along."

"Lando, if anyone should go with her, it should be me," Luke said.

"No," Lando said. "Your Jedi powers give you the best endurance. We might all need your help. You'll have to watch everybody. All I want to have to worry about is Sonsen and that airlock."

Luke seemed about to protest, but then nodded reluctantly. "Maybe you're right," he said. "And the bad air won't bother the droids. That'll be some help."

"It's not as if Kalenda and I are helpless or anything," Gaeriel said.

"No, ma'am, and I didn't mean to imply that you were," Lando said. "But we don't have time to do this politely. The fact of the matter is Sonsen has to go because she knows the lock. Someone should go with her. I'm no hero, but someone who's had toxic air training is the best choice to go with her. That makes it me. And for what it is worth, next to Luke, we're *all* helpless. And I might add that Lieutenant Kalenda doesn't seem to be protesting the arrangement."

Gaeriel Captison looked from Lando to Kalenda's expressionless face. "All right," she said. "I was in politics long enough to know when it's time to back off."

"We're getting lower," Luke said. "And the heating is starting to move some serious air."

Lando looked out the window. Luke was right. The lower, thicker layers of air were heating at a different rate than the upper, thinner layers. Hot and cold air at different air pressures was a recipe for weather in any circumstance, but especially in a spinning, inside-out world with a gravity gradient. Dust devils were spinning up everywhere, miniature tornadoes, funnel clouds spewing dust and debris up into the air.

The wind began to howl as the car moved lower and lower, into the nightmare dust storms popping up everywhere. A wall of gritty dust enveloped the car, cutting off the view as the wind peppered the car with thousands of small impacts that clicked and clattered on its exterior.

It seemed as if the winds abruptly reversed direction, and the outside world reappeared as suddenly as it had vanished.

They seemed to have crossed under some sort of cloud deck. The car was moving along the inner wall of the spinning sphere, from the spin axis toward the equatorial regions in a long, swooping curve. By now the car was moving forward as much as it was down, and the increase in apparent weight was more and more noticeable with every moment. Lando realized his eyes had made a subconscious adjustment, deciding that the car was no longer proceeding down the side of a cliff, but down a long hill that was getting less and less steep with every moment. Some sort of tilt-table mechanism kept the floor even as the car moved down the track.

"Close now," Sonsen said. "We should start slowing in a minute." As if on cue, the car began to decelerate smoothly. Lando reached out a hand to steady himself against the wall of the car, but he thought better of it at the last moment. He held his hand a centimeter or two back from the wall, and felt plenty of heat that way.

The car slowed even further, until it was barely moving, maybe twenty-five centimeters a second. The swirling clouds cleared again for a moment and revealed a large two-story building directly ahead. "That's the main entrance complex for this sector," said Sonsen. The turbovator's track led to a large set of pressure doors, the sort that split down the middle, with the two halves sliding apart to either side. "So let's see what happens," she said. 'I'll let the automatics try it first."

The car eased to a complete halt a meter or two in front of the doors, and then nothing happened for a moment.

"Is it broken?" Gaeriel asked.

"It just takes a little time for the pumps to match pressure. Here we go." The pressure doors started to move apart smoothly enough—but then jammed up when they were only about a meter apart. "Blast it," Sonsen said. "Exactly what they did before. Let me try cycling them on manual and see if I get lucky."

She went to the panel by the car's door and twisted a dial that was pointed to AUTO over to MANUAL OVER-RIDE. She pressed another button marked OPEN HOL-LOWTOWN SIDE AIRLOCK DOORS. The doors strained a bit, but didn't move any farther apart. She pushed the CLOSE DOORS button—and the doors moved all of three centimeters back toward each other before grinding to a halt. Sonsen ran through the whole procedure again, but the doors refused to move more than that three centimeters back and forth. "That's that," she said. "They won't open far enough to get the car in, and they won't shut at all. The inner doors won't open at all unless the outers are shut."

"No emergency override on that?" Lando asked. "No way to force inner doors open if the outer ones are jammed?"

"Nope," Sonsen said. "Why bother, when there was supposed to be breathable air on both sides of the lock, and there's another airlock ten meters away? I keep telling you people. This is a fancy elevator, not a spacecraft system."

"All right, then," said Lando. "Looks like we get out and walk. Time to do a little getting ready."

He pulled his blouse off, pulled out his vibro-shiv, and started slicing the blouse into ribbons. He saved one larger wad of cloth and stuffed it in his pocket, along with the knife. "Wrap one of these around your mouth and nose," he said. "If you pass out, or your breathing reflex gets the better of you, a little cloth might filter out the worst of it. And if you *have* to breathe, if you can't stop yourself, do it through your nose. It does a much better job of cooling and filtering than your mouth."

"Let's hope the personnel airlock opens so fast that you've lost your shirt for nothing," Sonsen said.

Lando grinned. "It breaks my heart to mess up my wardrobe when I don't need to," he said, "but I think I could deal with it just this once." Lando wrapped a strip of cloth around his own mouth. "Where's the other airlock?" Lando asked, his voice a bit muffled by the cloth.

"You can't quite see it from here," Sonsen said. "The window is too small. But it's about ten meters to the left of the main airlock. It should be matched to pressure on the other side, but it shouldn't take long at all to match—" Sonsen stopped talking, and looked up at the ceiling of the car, where the air tanks were hanging. "Match pressure," she said. "Wait a second. I just got an idea. We've got air tanks up there. If we dumped the air into the car here, we could get air pressure higher than the outside. Then when we opened the door, our air would push out, instead of the bad air pushing in—"

"And we'd have a pressure curtain," said Lando. "Good idea! Then the second group could close the doors after we go, and maybe still have some air to breathe."

"Boost me up there," Sonsen said. Luke knelt down and made a stirrup out of his hands. Sonsen put her hands on his shoulders to balance herself and stepped into his hands. "Okay," she said, "up."

Luke stood up as easily as if there was no weight on him at all.

"Whoa," Sonsen said. "Captain Calrissian, your friend *is* strong. Steady now. A little to the right—no, *my* right, your *left*. Back a bit. Okay, good." Sonsen reached for the pressure regulator and touched it gingerly. "Definitely getting hot," she said, "but not quite hot enough to burn. Not yet."

"I would suggest hurrying," Threepio said. "The Glowpoint has now increased its brightness by thirty-five percent."

"How about we leave that droid behind when we go?" Sonsen said as she cranked the regulator up as high as it would go. A loud hissing started almost at once.

Lando worked his jaw and felt his ears pop. "You've got my vote," he said. "I've been trying to leave him behind for years."

"Forget it, both of you," Luke said. "I've been through a lot with Threepio."

"All right," said Sonsen. "That should do it. Let me down."

Luke lowered her to the ground.

"Okay," said Lando. "Administrator Sonsen—Jenica—what's the plan, exactly?"

"I'm going to open the door here," she said. "When I do, we should let a good-sized blast of our air out, and that'll at least slow down the bad air coming in. Lando and I will get out as fast as we can and run to the other lock. You"—she pointed at Gaeriel—"as soon as we are out the door, close it again, by pressing this button here. Okay?"

"Okay."

"Once the door is shut, the regulator will come back on and pump in clean canned air, but there is still going to be a lot of that junk out there in the mix. But no matter how bad the air gets in here, breathe it. It's only going to be worse outside. So breathe as best you can once that door is shut. Give us three minutes—no more, no less—and then pop the door again and come running. That will give us time to get through the lock ourselves, get to the other side, and then cycle the lock so the outer door is open. Get into the lock *fast*. If the droids can get there with you without slowing you up, great. If not, leave them on this side, and we'll cycle the lock again for them once you're through. They don't have to worry about breathing. Got it?"

"Got it," Luke said.

"We'll be left behind for sure!" Threepio said in his most theatrical tones, and even Artoo let out a sort of low moan.

Lando paid them no mind. Not when this whole Hollowtown place was about to get burned to another crisp. If only that were the worst of it. If the Glowpoint's flaring again meant what he thought it did, a little thing like five people and two droids being roasted alive wasn't going to matter much at all.

"Okay," Lando said, "tie your cloths over your mouth and nose, and then let's do one more thing that might help us get through this in one piece. We need to get as much oxygen into the bloodstream and lungs as possible before we go out there. The high pressure will help, but we need to do more. Everybody, start breathing in rapid, shallow breaths. It'll help you hold your breath a little bit longer when the time comes." Lando followed his own advice, and started to breathe in fast, shallow, panting breaths. Not the healthiest thing to do for long, but it would help get him through the next few minutes. He looked out the viewport at the swirling clouds of murky ash and soot and shook his head. "Don't breathe this stuff at all," he said, around his panting breaths. "Even if it had all the oxygen you needed, that crud would probably burn a hole in your lungs."

Lando started to follow and kept up his rapid, shallow breathing until he started to feel just this side of light-headed. He only hoped he was remembering all the procedures properly. "All right," he said. "Artoo, you time it. Come after us in three minutes. Let's do it."

Sonsen tied her own cloth over her mouth and nose, looked around to make sure everyone else had done the same, and then hit the DOOR OPEN button.

The air blew out of the turbovator car with terrifying speed, and then a blast-furnace wall of air rushed in, pulling a stream of noxious dust and smoke and soot with it. Sonsen dove through the door, and Lando followed after her, already half blinded by the stinging, burning fumes that were everywhere. There had been nothing they could do about eye protection. Where the devil was Sonsen? Had he lost her already?

The air—if you could call it air—screamed past in the howling wind and cleared the view for just a moment. He spotted her, through watering eyes, heading toward the building.

The heat was nearly as bad as the poisoned air and the dust. Already the sweat was streaming out of his body, dripping down his brow, getting into his eyes, making it that much harder to see. He resisted the urge to wipe his brow—and the urge to breathe. Amazing how fast you wanted to start again once you stopped.

Never mind. Sonsen—Jenica—was at the airlock, trying to work the very old-fashioned-looking controls—but the metal buttons and knobs were already too hot to touch. Lando pulled the torn-up piece of cloth out of his pocket—being careful to keep his vibro-shiv from falling out—and handed it to her.

She nodded gratefully, not wasting breath on words, and wrapped the cloth around her hand. She threw back the spill lever, equalizing pressure between the interior of the lock and the outside. It would seem the pressure was higher on the outside, judging by the column of smoke and soot that got sucked into the lock. Jenica threw back a big lever and the door swung out and open. She waved her arm vigorously, urging Lando in—and he needed no urging. It was a big lock compartment, capable of handling twenty or thirty people at once. That wasn't good. The bigger the lock, the more air there would be to move, and the longer it would take.

The dust and smoke swirled around in the wretched air as Lando stumbled into the oven-hot interior of the lock—and suddenly realized that Jenica was not with him. He turned around to find her slumped over by the lock entrance, face-down on the ground, coughing and retching.

His own lungs feeling as if they were about to burst, Lando forced himself to go back outside after her. He grabbed her under the arms and dragged her in, wishing mightily for enough breath to curse the too-high gravity here in the equatorial regions of Centerpoint Station.

Half blinded by the caustic chemicals burning his eyes, Lando hauled Jenica Sonsen into the lock. He was about to let her slump down onto the deck when he realized just how hot that metal deck had to be by now. He threw her left arm over his shoulder and held her up as he searched frantically for the inside lock controls. She managed to take a bit of her weight on her own feet. Coughing horribly, she pointed an unsteady finger over to one corner of the lock.

Lando looked in the direction she was pointing. There! He dragged himself over, Jenica still draped over him, and pulled the close-lock lever, burning his hand in the process. The metal was hot and getting hotter. It seemed to take forever for the door to swing back shut.

He had his finger jammed down on the air pump button almost before the door latches had closed, but the automatics cut in at once anyway—not pumping in good air, but dumping the bad stuff out into the other side of the lock. Shell One, Jenica had called it. The air pumps whirred busily, stirring the ashes and soot up into a new blinding cloud of dust.

Lando's lungs were screaming for air, demanding that he breathe immediately. He felt as if he were about to pass out, but he knew he did not dare. If he fainted, his reflexes would start him breathing again—and that would probably kill him.

The pressure equalized, and the far lock door opened. The air outside was far colder than the stuff in the lock, and the temperature difference was enough to make up a sharp little gust of wind as the hot bad air expanded out into Shell One—and good cool air swept into the lock chamber.

Lando let go of Jenica and dropped to his knees. He barely noticed the burning heat of the deck as he gasped for air, coughing, gagging, his lungs heaving. He pulled the cloth away from his mouth and coughed harder, spitting out the horrid slime that seemed to have gotten into his mouth, even if he hadn't been breathing that mess. "Out," he said, his voice little more than a weak creaking noise. "We need—get out—set lock for others."

Jenica had collapsed next to him. She nodded, unable to speak even that much. They helped each other to their feet and staggered out of the lock chamber.

The air here was a swirling mass of dreadful, sulfurous smoke—but there was air there too, good air. They could not breathe *easily* just yet, not until the dust and smoke dispersed. But at least they could breathe.

Jenica went to the Shell One side control panel and pulled the old-fashioned lever to swing the interior door shut.

"Hold it!" Lando shouted. He had spotted something. There was a rack of emergency equipment by the lock door—including two small tanks of oxygen with breathing masks. Lando grabbed one, twisted the valve to start the oxygen flowing, and threw it into the lock. Most—or maybe all—of the oxygen would go to waste, of course. But it didn't matter. Even at full flow, a bottle that size would last ten or fifteen minutes before it went empty. But maybe just enough oxy would blow around to do some good. Or maybe if they were all blinded by the fumes, someone would still hear the hissing noise, and someone would find the mask, and put it to his or her face.

The door swung to, Jenica pulled the lever to open the Hollowtown-side door, and that was that. She turned around and slumped down on the floor with her back to the wall. Lando grabbed the other oxy tank and sat down on the floor facing her. He opened the flow valve and handed her the tank.

Jenica put the breather mask to her face and breathed in deeply—and was subdued by another wave of wracking coughs. She tried it again, with better success. "Yuck," she said. "I didn't mean to breathe any of that stuff, but something must have gotten in." She handed the tank to Lando. He put the mask to his face and breathed in deeply. The cool, clean oxygen felt wonderfully pure and sweet. "Is there anything else we can do to help them in?" he asked.

She shook her head. "Not really. There's a viewport in the airlock here. The safeties won't let me open both doors at once, but I might be able to set things to pop open the hatch on this side before the chamber repressurizes. That might get 'em in here a little faster. That's about all."

It had taken all of ninety seconds to get them in here. Amazing how much longer than that it felt. But if there was company coming, they had best get ready. Lando took another deep breath off the oxy tank and handed it back to Jenica. "Come on," he said. "Let's get the lock set so you can pop the inner door early."

"Yeah. We'd better. I have a nasty feeling your friends might have it a little rougher than we did." Jenica stood up and rubbed her face. Her hand came away even dirtier than it had been. "Burning stars, but I must be a mess."

"You did look better before," Lando said with a smile. "Your face has about a centimeter of dust on it."

"Oh, a little soap and water will fix *that*," she said. "But I don't even want to *think* what this has done to my hair."

*   *   *

Luke Skywalker watched Artoo intently, waiting for the three minutes to be up. He forced himself to calmness, to clarity. Jedi were not impatient.

Except sometimes. This situation was getting out of hand. The temperature in the car had jumped dramatically when the outside air had come in. All of them were sweating profusely. And all of them—even the great Jedi Master himself—were having trouble breathing.

Kalenda coughed again and swore under her breath—what little breath she had. "How much longer?" she asked. Either the smoke or the cloth over her mouth made her voice seem a bit murky, a bit throaty.

"About another thirty seconds, I think," Luke said. "Let's get ready. Both of you out before me so I can keep an eye on you," he said.

Gaeriel seemed about to protest, but Luke cut her

off. "It's no time to be modest," he said. "My Jedi powers give me an edge you two won't have. If they didn't, I've wasted my time with all that training for all these years. Artoo, Threepio, you come after me. *You* watch *me.* Watch all of us. We might need your help—but maybe we can move faster than you two can. If we get there first, we're going to have to leave you on this side of the lock—but we'll cycle the lock again as soon as we're through. All right?"

Artoo whistled and beeped and swung his head back and forth. "I quite agree with Artoo," Threepio said. "We might be immune to the poisonous atmosphere, but the corrosive airborne chemicals and the rising temperatures could easily do us harm. Please do not delay in getting us."

"I won't," Luke said. "I promise."

Threepio nodded happily. "I am glad to hear it," he said. Apparently the word of a Jedi Master was good enough even for a protocol droid.

"Kalenda—Gaeriel—are you ready?"

"No, not really," said Gaeriel, coughing just a bit. "But I doubt I ever will be ready for this sort of thing. Let's go."

Kalenda nodded and let it go at that.

"Here we go," Luke said, and hit the button.

A new blast of burning-hot air struck at them as the door opened. The winds were blowing more and more fiercely as the Glowpoint dumped more and more energy into the system. Gaeriel stepped out into the storm and was nearly blown off her feet before Kalenda could grab at her. Luke stepped out into it and was nearly bowled over himself. The heat was incredible, and the noxious gases seemed to eat into his skin, his eyes. *For a Jedi there is no pain,* Luke told himself. *There is awareness. There is calm.* The three humans stepped around the side of the turbovator car—and discovered they had been in the lee of the wind. The full force of the corrosive gale blasted straight into their faces, utterly blinding them, forcing them to jam their eyes shut. The wind carried fine-grained sand, and that slammed into them as well.

Luke got one fleeting moment of good visibility before the roaring wall of dust and cinders enveloped them, one moment when he saw where the airlock hatch was—and saw that it was swinging open for them. That one moment would have to be enough. It would be worse than useless to open his eyes in this storm. Not only would he be unable to see—his eyes would be destroyed. He would have to do it by dead reckoning—and drag the others with him. He reached out with the Force and found Kalenda and Gaeriel hand-in-hand, just a meter or two ahead of him. They were headed in the wrong direction. They must have been turned around by the wind already.

Luke lunged forward into the wind and, using the Force to guide him, grabbed Kalenda by the hand and yanked hard in the proper direction. Kalenda came willingly enough, and Luke could feel Gaeriel in the Force, feel her hesitate a moment and then follow along as well.

Luke became aware of a burning sense in his chest. Air. He needed air. And if *he* felt the urgent need to breathe, the others must be in an agony to do so.

Closer. Closer. In his mind's eye, he could see the hatch. He knew, with all the power and precision of his Jedi senses, exactly where it was. But that did not get him there any faster, did not give him the power to move effortlessly against this deadly wind.

There. They were there. He still did not dare open his eyes, but he knew they were at the entrance to the lock. He pulled Kalenda forward, pushed her in ahead of him, and shoved Gaeriel in as well before stepping in himself—and running smack into something metal, something hard and angular and tall. He suddenly realized it was Threepio. "It would seem Artoo and I got here before you after all, Master Luke!" Threepio shouted over the howl of the sandstorm. A droid could speak in this mess without wasting air or getting sand in his mouth. Luke couldn't, and he settled for a nod instead.

Luke nodded and moved farther forward into the lock, out of the stinging wind. He wiped the worst of the dust from his eyes and risked opening them, just in time to see the lock swinging shut.

There was a sudden flare of orange from behind him. He turned around. Gaeriel and Kalenda were standing, eyes still shut, in about the midpoint of the lock chamber, holding to each other, coughing miserably.

And Gaeriel's long flowing white dress was on fire—and Gaeriel did not know it yet. Luke lunged for her and threw his body on the blossoming flames, trying to smother them. His flight suit was insulated and fireproof. He felt a brief bloom of heat on his chest, and that was all. The fire died. He stood back up and helped Gaeriel to her feet.

A red-hot bit of debris, blown from someplace where things were hotter still, must have gotten itself lodged in the fabric of Gaeriel's dress. But how could it burn, with no available oxygen?

Luke heard a hissing noise from behind him and looked around. An oxygen mask. Lando and Kalenda had thrown an oxygen mask into the lock chamber—and Gaeriel had been standing right on top of it. Her dress must have trapped the oxygen. A million-to-one shot, but one that had almost killed Gaeriel.

All of that flashed through his mind even as he was grabbing for the mask. He tore the cloth strip off her mouth and put the oxy mask over her mouth and nose. Still half blinded, and probably still unaware of why Luke had knocked her over, she jerked away from the mask at first, until she realized what it was. Then she grabbed for it greedily, opened her mouth, and took in a deep, urgent breath. She started coughing almost instantly. Luke handed the mask to Kalenda, who took two deep breaths herself before handing it back to Luke.

Luke pulled down his dust cloth, exhaled the last breath he had breathed in back in the turbovator car, and sucked in as much air as the mask had to give. He realized that he had been seeing spots before his eyes, there toward the end. *Even Jedi Masters have to breathe,* he told himself.

He was just handing the mask on to Gaeriel when the inner door swung violently open, and the air in the lock blasted out into the chamber beyond in a last choking, blinding—but now harmless—cloud of dust.

They had made it.

* * *

"I was on *fire?*" Gaeriel asked, looking down at the remains of her dress. Jenica had led them all to a small infirmary near the Shell One side of the airlock. Everyone had cuts and bruises and scrapes and minor burns that needed attention of one sort or another. They all needed baths and clean clothes as well, but those could wait just a bit. "I was on *fire* and I didn't know about it?"

"A claim not many can make," Luke said, laughing. "I apologize for knocking you over—"

"And *I* apologize for throwing that oxy mask in there," said Lando.

"Don't either of you apologize," Gaeriel said, a bit tartly. She went over to the sink and started scrubbing her hands. "The mask probably saved all our lives in there. I was near passing out, and if I had fainted and breathed in much more of that stuff than I did by accident—well, at best I'd have been in here with something a lot worse than a sore throat. And I'd much rather have a bruised dignity than third-degree burns."

"I think we were all pretty lucky in there," Kalenda said in more serious tones as she sprayed some quick-heal salve on Jenica's burned hand. "The way the temperatures were rising, I don't think we'd have gotten out another five minutes later."

"What's it like in there now, Artoo?" Luke asked as Lando sprayed antiseptic solution into the sand burns on his face. "Ow! That stuff stings."

"Hold still," Lando said, dabbing ointment onto the worst of the burns. "Almost done."

Artoo, who had plugged himself into a dataport in the infirmary wall, squeaked and whistled and buzzed and beeped in an agitated fashion.

"Dear me," said Threepio. "Things *are* rapidly getting worse in there."

"What did that Artoo thing say, for those of us who don't speak bird-whistle?" Jenica asked.

"Temperatures where we were ten minutes ago are up over the boiling point of water and headed higher," said Threepio. "The surviving detectors show hot spots closer to the Glowpoint well over five hundred degrees—and there are probably temperatures much higher than that, except the detectors are not there anymore to tell us."

"Not good," said Lando. "Not good at all."

Jenica Sonsen nodded her head. "And it's also no terrorist attack," she said. "Even twice didn't make a great deal of sense—but three times?"

"I think you're very wrong there," Lando said. "Very wrong indeed. But I'm afraid your people here weren't the intended victims. I think you were more like innocent bystanders who got in the way."

Jenica turned and looked sharply at Lando as she flexed the hand with the burn salve on it. "Captain Calrissian—Lando—you said a few things earlier that made it sound like you had an idea what this was all about. Maybe now would be the right time to explain yourself."

Lando let out a deep sigh. "I think maybe you're right," he said. "But no one's going to like it much. I might even be wrong—but on the other hand, it's all staring us in the face."

"What is?" Luke asked.

"Centerpoint," Lando said. "Centerpoint is right in

the middle of it all. Think about it. There are three big, impressive, inexplicable technologies at the middle of this crisis. The first, and the easiest to explain, is the system-wide jamming. Impressive, but all you really need for that is a whole lot of power. And where does the jamming come from?"

"Centerpoint," Jenica said. "Without Fed-Dub even knowing about it—and we ran the place."

"Or at least you thought you did," Lando said. "Second up is the interdiction field. Nothing incredible about it, beyond its size. But if you had a powerful enough gravitic generator, you could do it. Where does it come from?"

"Centerpoint," Jenica said again. "And from what you were asking about earlier, you thought it had something to do with the way we're right at the balance point of gravitic potential."

"Right. I have no idea how, but it seems to me that Centerpoint taps into the gravitic output of the Double Worlds. Now it seems someone has found a way to convert that power into an interdiction field."

"And the third unexplained technology?" Luke asked.

Lando looked straight at him. "The novamaker, of course. The starbuster. We all wondered how it was done. We all wondered where the starbuster was. I'm just about positive we're sitting in it right now. I think the Glowpoint flare means it's just about to go off again."

CHAPTER EIGHT

Meeting in Progress

It was a lovely morning. The star Corell was rising in the east. The lovely rolling hills and clean blue sky of Selonia were laid out before them. The Hunchuzuc Den had put them up in a splendid hilltop villa, clearly purpose-built for the use of visiting human dignitaries. They had been comfortable and well cared for from the moment Mara Jade had set the *Jade's Fire* down.

"I am tired of waiting, Dracmus," Han said.

"Patience, Honored Solo. Waiting is not yet tired of you."

"Whatever that means," Han growled. "Have you ever given a straight answer in your life?"

"What, exactly, are you meaning by straight answer?"

Han Solo turned to his wife, who was sitting placidly at the breakfast table. "You see what I've had to put up with?" he asked. Dracmus had come to pay her morning call, as she did every day. And as *he* did every day, Han found himself wondering what the point of the visit was. "Riddles. Incoherent riddles. That's all I ever got. It's all we ever get."

"Take it easy, Han," Leia said. "Patience is the hardest part of diplomacy."

"But mine has reached its limits," Han said.

"I'm afraid I agree with Han," Mara said. "Things are moving too fast everywhere else for me to put up with waiting here any longer."

"I'm still not even sure why we *are* here," Han said. "Right from the moment you yanked me out of that cell, I haven't known for sure if I was your partner or your prisoner. *Are* we prisoners? Hostages, maybe? Or are we here to negotiate something? And if so, what?"

"I'm afraid it is not that simple," Dracmus said. "To my people, these things—partner, prisoner, hostage, negotiator—are not so separate from each other as they are with your folk. To my people, one might be only one of these or all of them at once, or some of them changingly over time."

"So which is it?" Han asked, a very clear warning note in his voice. A note Dracmus plainly missed.

"It is not yet determined. You must understand that to my people consensus is being all. Ambiguity has much use for us. If the issue is uncertain, then the meeting can go on, for disagreement is more difficult if no one understands the problem fully."

"So is agreement," Han said. "There are people with guns and ships out there who are shooting at our people. There is not much ambiguity out there."

"Please! Please!" Dracmus said. "Understanding your impatience, but what you ask is not our way. For my people—"

"Traditions make for an awfully handy set of excuses," Mara said. "Every time I have ever dealt with a Selonian who didn't want to do something, she's explained to me how tradition made it impossible, or the ways of her people caused it to be difficult to decide, or whatever excuse seemed handy. And *my* people always had to be respectful of your ways, and accept the structure of your culture. No more. This isn't some trade deal for luxury goods where you can leave us hanging for six months on the off chance that your convenient traditions will get us so frustrated that we give up and offer a better price. This is *war*. This is survival. There is no time. It is time for you to accept the ways of *our* culture before we are all wiped out. It is our way to speak plain, to speak true, to choose a course, and to follow it."

"Please!" said Dracmus. "You *must* endure. Things are being complex. Take time to solve all."

"But *there is no time*," Mara said, putting a hard-edged emphasis on her words. "We cannot take what no longer exists, and we have run out of time. Or rather, you have. I may be many things, but I will not be your prisoner."

"What is the meaning of your words?" Dracmus asked.

"Inform whoever it is you should inform that I am leaving. In one hour, I am going to walk around to the landing pad on the other side of this villa. I am going to get aboard the *Jade's Fire* and I am going to fly away. My companions are welcome to join me if they wish, but I will be leaving in any event. I would also remind you that Leia and I escaped from the Human League and flew the *Jade's Fire* off Corellia, while we were facing much heavier opposition than anything I have seen here so far. Besides which, as my ship is the one that brought the Chief of State of the New Republic to this planet, the case could be made that an attack on it constitutes an attack on the New Republic that you claim to recognize and support. In short, I would not suggest trying to stop me. You will not succeed, and I will not be responsible for any damage from the attempt."

"But—but—"

"The *only* way to prevent my departure is to have our group meet with someone in authority, someone who will provide clear answers to our questions, someone with the power to make decisions before that hour is up. If such a person does not appear, I will leave—"

"And I'll be with her," said Han, and turned toward his wife.

Leia looked troubled and angry, but she nodded. "And so will I."

Dracmus looked from one of them to the other. "But—but—"

"But you have one hour," Mara said. "Vanish. Go make things happen."

Dracmus looked positively frantic. "I will be seeing what I can do. Please! Do not go."

"One hour," Mara said. "Go. Move."

Dracmus nodded, turned, dropped to all fours, and rushed away as fast as she could.

"If I didn't believe in the power of a united front, I would have refused to go along with you," Leia said, her voice testy. "You did some damage, but it would have been worse if I had refused to play along. I'm a diplomat, and you're not. You should have let me do the talking."

"I've *been* letting you do the talking, and all it's gotten us so far is an enforced vacation at this villa. I'm a businesswoman, a trader. Negotiation is my stock in trade."

"Do you call insulting our hosts negotiating?"

"Negotiating is the art of getting what you want," Mara said. "It's not the art of making the other side feel better."

"They aren't the 'other side.' They're our partners in this negotiation."

"If they were our partners, we wouldn't need to negotiate," Mara said smoothly.

Han noticed something. Mara's sharp tone, her apparent anger, her impatience, had all vanished at the same time Dracmus did. They had all been performance, posturing, for Dracmus's sake. Now she was calm, relaxed, as she spoke.

"Partners or opponents, I still don't think we'll get anywhere pushing them around like that," Leia said.

"We'll find out in about fifty-seven minutes," Mara

said as she poured herself another cup of tea. "I've dealt with the Selonians before. Have you or Han?"

"I speak the language, and I've dealt with them socially. But I haven't done any real negotiating," said Leia.

"I haven't really dealt with them at all," said Han. "Not since I was a kid back on Corellia."

"Then there is something you both have to understand," Mara said.

Leia seemed about to protest, but Han held up his hand, asking her not to do so. "Go on, Mara," he said.

"It's a little hard to explain." Mara paused for a moment. "Think—think about a sabacc game, where each player knows the other is bluffing, but they both keep shoving chips into the pot, just to save face. Neither of them can back down. Or two armies fighting each other, throwing endless troops into a vicious battle over a useless bit of land. There are cases when humans forget about the purpose of the competition, and the competition *itself* becomes absolutely vital. Sometimes it's irrational. Sometimes it makes sense. Sometimes it has survival value, or evolution wouldn't have given us the tendency. Maybe, sometimes, you're thinking about the next hand in the game, the next battle. Maybe if she knows you just won't quit, your opponent will decide the fight isn't worth the cost. She'll give up—and you'll win the next fight without even having to fight. Of course, most of the time, it's not even a conscious decision. We do that sort of thing without even thinking about it. It's a blind spot."

"None of that sounds much like Selonians," Han said.

"No, it doesn't," Mara agreed. "I was talking about a *human* blind spot. We're much more competitive and individualistic than the Selonians are. All that stuff about consensus isn't just talk. They really *are* that way. To oversimplify just a bit, they have a compulsion to reach agreement, whether or not it makes sense, just as we sometimes feel we have to win, whether or not it makes sense. It's something the Selonians can't *help* doing in a situation like this. It's a blind spot *they* have. If we just waited until they were ready for us, they could take weeks or months or years just to decide what they want to ask us for. I had to let them know they'd lose *everything* if they didn't ask for *something* right now."

"Are you sure that was wise?" Leia asked.

"No, I'm not. But sometimes the important thing is to make something happen. It almost doesn't matter what."

"That 'almost' can cover a lot of ground," Han said.

"I suppose so. But maybe it means we have the chance to choose our ground. Maybe if we can figure out what's going on around here, we can make some good decisions," Mara said. "There's something we need to consider. Dracmus told us that all these worlds have repulsors, and that someone from the outside was helping to organize the search for them. Fine and good. You can use one to shoot down a ship. Even better, from a military point of view. But you can shoot down a ship with a lot of things that are a lot easier to get at, easier to control, easier to aim and use. I don't think we have the whole reason behind the scramble to grab the repulsor on Corellia. And don't forget Dracmus said the rebels on the other worlds are searching for them—or else they've found them already, and they are putting them to use."

"Using them for what?" Han asked.

"I haven't the faintest idea," Mara said. "But you don't try that hard to grab something you don't need urgently. Not in the middle of a war where you're trying to save your strength for when you need it. We've seen all sorts of indications that the various rebellions regard the repulsors as being hugely valuable. I'm starting to think the repulsors are the whole reason there *are* rebels. In a sense, I don't think there are any rebels at all. They're a front, a smokescreen, for the real enemy."

"What do you mean?" Leia asked.

"I have a hunch that the repulsor searches aren't because of the revolts," said Mara. "My guess is that the *revolts* are happening as a cover for the repulsor searches. We're all fairly certain the revolts were organized from the outside. Dracmus said as much, for what that's worth. Besides, what are the odds against rebellions on five planets simultaneously just by coincidence? There *had* to be some coordination. We've all agreed on that. I'm saying the organizing principle was the need to get at the repulsors."

"That makes sense *if* it's someone from outside doing the organizing, an external force," said Leia. "I can't quite see our Human League acquaintances making a first approach to their close personal friends in the Selonian Overden to put this together. If some outside force did the organizing, they could approach a dissident group on each planet, supply it with money and expertise and so on. And we know the rebels are coordinating with each other, at least to a certain extent. All of them participated in that coordinated attack against the Bakuran ships."

"But *why* would the rebels cooperate with each other, and with this external force?" Han asked. "What's in it for them?"

Leia shook her head. "I can't say for sure, but if I were setting up the deal, I'd say something like, take our money and information, cooperate with us, use your local people to dig up the repulsor for us, hand it over to us, and when we kick the New Republic out, we'll give you a free hand on your own planet. But in exchange we get your help—and ultimate control over your planet's repulsor."

"Except then you run the risk of the rebels deciding that the repulsors are worth something," Han said.

"At a guess, something like that is what happened with the Human League," Mara said. "If this external force idea is right, then the externals would be the ones running the starbuster—not the Human League.

When the Human League started tossing threats around, the external force couldn't have been too happy about it."

"If they even knew about it," Mara said. "They may be completely external to this star system. They'd have some representatives, some observers, in-system, but once the jamming comes on, you can throw the observers in jail and say whatever you want without anyone outside hearing it. And once the interdiction field goes on, outsiders can't get at you to do anything about it. Sooner or later, the interdiction field and the jamming are turned off—but by then, Thrackan Sal-Solo is running the planet, maybe the whole star system, and the external forces can do what they like. And if he's managed to grab a few of the repulsors by then, maybe he's got some serious bargaining chips. Or maybe not. We don't even know what the repulsors can be used for, let alone why they are so important."

Leia thought for a moment. "If all this is true, then the rebels themselves aren't the problem. It's the repulsors, and the people who got the rebels searching for them, the external forces. It's obvious the externals don't care about the rebel causes—the rebels are all *against* each other. The Human League is mostly anti-Selonian and anti-Drall, as much as it is *for* anything. So the externals are supporting them for some other reason—as a way to get at the repulsors. Cut the links between the rebels and the external forces, gain control of the repulsors, figure out how to use them against the externals, and the rebellions ought to dry up and blow away."

"Fine," Han said. "Very nice and neat. But you've just given yourself a huge list of jobs there. I don't see how we could even start to accomplish any of them."

"But at least they're political jobs, intelligence jobs, not military jobs," Leia said. "Considering we have no military assets at all in system, that's good news. There's a military aspect, of course, but we're hoping to get some help on that angle from the Selonians."

She glanced at Mara. "Unless the Selonians call your bluff in another forty-five minutes."

"I wasn't bluffing," Mara said.

"Do you have any clear idea of how the Selonians fit into all this?" Han said. "Are the Overden and the Hunchuzuc even still fighting each other? I haven't seen any signs of battle, or any mention of it from Dracmus—and she's not so good at keeping secrets."

"It wouldn't surprise me if they had stopped fighting," Mara said, "but if they have, that's probably bad news for us. My impression is that the Overden has indeed seized control of the repulsor—and the repulsor is a very powerful weapon. Selonians aren't much for lost causes. A lot of times we humans fight on even when all hope is lost. Honor requires it, or we're hoping for a miracle, or we're praying that a million-to-one chance breaks our way. Not the Selonians. Typically, a fight between two groups ends when one side or the other demonstrates they have a massive advantage over the other. The Selonians on the losing side will then see there is no point in going on, and request a negotiated settlement. More than that. They will want to ally themselves with the winners."

"And you think our noble Hunchuzuc allies have decided that they've lost," Han said. "You think they're dickering with the Overden, and we're part of the deal?"

"Something like that. Maybe the Overden wants us as bargaining chips, maybe as hostages, maybe they want to negotiate directly with Leia. Of course we don't even know for sure that it's the Overden and not the Hunchuzuc who have the repulsor. Maybe our side won."

"It is most regrettable," said a new voice, "but I fear that is not the case. The inestimable Mara Jade has described the situation exactly." Han looked behind himself in surprise. The newcomer had arrived in utter silence from inside the villa. She was an older-looking Selonian, tall, but a little stooped over, her fur shot through with gray, but her eyes bright. "I am Kleyvits," she said, "and I speak for the Overden. We have won our Hunchuzuc sisters over to our cause." She paused, and then smiled, displaying an unpleasantly impressive collection of teeth. "And that means that we have also won all of *you*."

*   *   *

Tendra Risant had had just about enough of *waiting*. It was time for a little *doing*.

The *Gentleman Caller* would be stuck in normal space, moving in toward the first-distant inner planets of the Corellian star system for months yet, assuming the interdiction field stayed up.

But suppose it didn't stay up? The *Gentleman Caller* was not the fastest ship in the universe, but even a slow ship would need only a minute or two in hyperspace to cover the remaining distance to the inner system. Tendra knew better than anyone about that fleet waiting in orbit around Sacorria. It seemed quite likely they would be headed this way. They would need the field to come down for that to happen. They might or might not reactivate it once they were in. The field might be down for just a very brief period.

Therefore, it seemed likely there would be a moment, maybe only a few minutes, perhaps longer, when she could activate her hyperdrive and get to where she was going—if only she knew when that moment *was*.

The navicomputer had a gravitic field indicator, one that was very definitely showing the effects of the interdiction field. All she had to do was rig an alarm that would go off when the field went down. Then it would merely be a question of computing and making the jump before the field came on again.

There were dozens of things that could go wrong, any number of perhaps unwarranted assumptions. But if she did nothing for much longer, she would go mad. She knew she had to take charge of her own situation if she was going to hang on to her sanity. But for the most part, she didn't think of it in those terms.

She just wanted to do whatever would get her off the ship.

*   *   *

"Freen?! Zubbit! Norgch! Norgchal. Normal. Normal processing resumes. Resumes? Reset! Reset! Normal processing resumes! Wowser! Freen!" The stream of babble continued as Q9-X2's head spun around three times, and a perfect forest of probes and sensors and manipulator arms popped in and out of their compartments.

"Not quite," Anakin said, frowning a bit. He pushed the droid's main power button off. All of the manipulators abruptly retracted into their compartments, and his status lights went off. Anakin reached into Q9's interior and unplugged a cable. "This one was in backward," he said. He plugged the cable back in and turned the power back on.

This time the droid powered up a bit more sedately. His head spun around exactly once, his status lights came on, none of his probes or arms came out, and he simply beeped twice and announced, "Normal processing resumes."

"Well, I should hope so," said Ebrihim, "after all the trouble we have been to in order to get you fixed."

"Frixed? Flough wuz I broken?" Q9 asked. "Expuse me. Voder sybems not quite stablized. Once moment." About half of his status lights went out for a few seconds and then came back on again. "Let's try that again. Fixed? How was I broken?"

"Anakin turned the repulsor on, and there was some sort of power surge," said Ebrihim. "We were afraid we had lost you altogether—but Anakin and Chewbacca got you working again."

Ebrihim found himself wondering if Q9 had actually needed any substantial repair at all. It hadn't taken

Anakin more than an hour or two to do the job. Had Chewbacca left the work on Q9 for Anakin as a way of letting Anakin make amends for what he had done? Or was Anakin's instinctive, near-mystical ability with machines so great that he could do things Chewbacca, with his centuries of experience, could not? Chewbacca had only worked on Q9 for a few minutes at a time, when he was taking a break from his work on the propulsion systems. Ah, well. Life was full of minor mysteries that would never quite be solved, and Ebrihim's command of the Wookiee language was not good enough to question Chewbacca on such a subtle point. Not that it was ever wise to question the Wookiee *too* closely.

"I am grateful to both of you—all of you—for repairing me," said Q9. "But what is this about turning the repulsor on? That seems a most foolhardy act. Whose idea was it?"

"My idea," Anakin said, looking down at the deck of the lounge compartment. "I'm sorry. I didn't mean to cause so much trouble."

"I am relieved to hear it. I would be even more relieved to learn that you had caused no trouble at all. I gather this was not the case?"

"Oh, Anakin managed to do just a bit of damage," Ebrihim said breezily, "but we will discuss that later. Right now I would suggest that you run a full set of diagnostics on yourself. It might well be that you find that several corrective adjustments need to be made."

Q9 activated his repulsor pads and floated up into the air to his normal hover height. "I shall do so," he replied. "But I would suggest that someone else around here might want to run some diagnostics and make some adjustments." With that, he floated silently out of the compartment.

"What did he mean by that?" Anakin asked.

"I think he was suggesting that little boys should try and learn from their mistakes."

"That's not what he said," Anakin objected.

"No, my version was more polite. But the advice remains good."

Anakin looked from Chewbacca to Ebrihim. "You mean I should think more before I work on a machine?" Anakin asked.

"That is *precisely* what I mean," Ebrihim said. "Precisely. Now run along and play—with your toys, not with machinery." He watched the lad hurry off to find his brother and sister. "Of course," he said to Chewbacca, "the problem is that Anakin sees toys and machines as one and the same thing."

Chewbacca nodded grimly as he put away his tools.

"In any event," said Ebrihim, "it is good to have Q9 up and about again. Thank you for your help. And I think it is about time I relieved my aunt. My watch is about to start."

Chewbacca gave a yip and a hoot of polite dismissal and Ebrihim turned and left the lounge.

The two Drall had been taking turns on watch in the *Falcon*'s cockpit. The sensor displays there might well give them some sort of warning if trouble showed up.

By having the Drall take the watch, Chewbacca had time to keep up his work on his repairs to the *Falcon*. Wookiees in general, and Chewbacca in particular, were not given to bursts of optimism, but Chewbacca had made it sound as if he was close, very close, to getting at least *some* propulsion restored. Even if all they could do was fly high enough to get out of this enormous trap of a cylinder and back up to the surface that would be at least some help.

Ebrihim entered the cockpit and saw his aunt sitting at the pilot's station. She was using a pile of old clothes under her somewhat ample rump to boost her up high enough to see all the instruments. She looked around as he entered. "Greetings, nephew. Q9 floated in a moment or two ago and made several insulting remarks. It is good to see that he is operational again."

"It is indeed, dearest aunt. Is there anything to report?"

She shook her head. "No, there is not, and for that let us be profoundly grateful—" She stopped speaking and looked at the overhead detector display. She stared at it, stock-still, for all of five seconds. She shook her head. "It would appear I spoke too soon," she said and then slapped down the red-alert siren. It started hooting loudly, loudly enough for the children outside the ship to hear it and come running.

"Aunt! What is it?" Ebrihim asked.

"I should think that would be obvious," she said, studying the display. "It's a ship, of course, coming in right on top of us. But I am not so much interested in *what* it is. I would much rather know *who* it is."

CHAPTER NINE

If and When

"I t's amazing how much you can find when you know where to look," said Lando, studying the data that was flowing past, screenful after screenful. "And it doesn't hurt to have someone as good at data searches as Artoo. And, ah, well, even Threepio's language skills have been helpful."

Threepio turned his head rather briskly. "Helpful? I would say they have been essential. You wouldn't have been able to translate a tenth of that information without me."

"Don't push it," Lando said. "Yes, you were a great help, all right? There, I said it. But I was *about* to say that without Administrator Sonsen, we wouldn't have gotten anywhere at all."

Jenica Sonsen smiled broadly and gave Lando a jab in the ribs that was probably just a trifle harder than she had intended it to be. "Easy, all of you," she said. "All I did was show you the log files."

But the log files had told them a lot—and led them in a lot of profitable directions. It was all down there, very clear.

Looking from here, it was easy to spot signs of something going wrong. Station systems no one had even known about started coming to life. Power fluctuations. Spikes and drops in various forms of radiation, some of them significant enough to require the temporary evacuation of part of the station. The station re-pointing its spin axis, gradually reaiming its poles in new directions.

"The change in spin orientation. How did you peo-ple explain *that* away?" asked Lando.

"Centerpoint has always been self-correcting," Jen-ica said. "The barycenter point isn't absolutely stable. The station has always moved itself around a little to stay properly oriented and positioned. It wasn't like it hadn't ever happened before."

"That to one side," said Lando, "the main thing is that I've now pretty much confirmed what I suspected the second I saw those conical forms in the poles of Hollowtown. That form of six small cones around a larger one is the exact geometry you need for a partic-ular kind of old-style repulsor. Actually, if you get down and take a look on the microscopic level, you'll see exactly the same pattern, repeated over and over and over again, on the surface of modern repulsor sys-tems. Crudely put, we don't make one big repulsor ele-ment like that anymore, because the bigger the repulsor, the heavier the object has to be for the repul-sor to work efficiently." Lando brought up a wireframe diagram of Centerpoint and pointed to the image of the repulsors. "These are pretty big, but on the other hand, planets are pretty big too."

"But all the inhabited planets have their own repul-sors," Kalenda objected. "What did the builders of Corellia need this place for?"

"Because this isn't just a repulsor," he said. "This is a *hyperspace* repulsor. This station was designed to open up a—a gate, a tunnel—through hyperspace, grab a planet, and pull it back this way. It acts as more of a tractor beam than a repulsor, really, but that's the idea."

"How?" Luke asked. "How does it work?"

Lando shrugged. "I don't know. But as Administra-tor Sonsen has pointed out a time or two, knowing how it works isn't always that important. It's knowing that it *does* work. My guess is it serves as a 'lens' that can amplify and direct a massive burst of repulsor energy through hyperspace. I think it must tap into the gravitic potential of Talus and Tralus, but I don't know for sure."

"But why would they use a space station as a super tractor beam?" Jenica asked.

Lando shook his head. "That's not the question. The question is—why did your people use the hyperspace tractor-repulsor as a space station? The architects of this star system built Centerpoint, used it, finished with it, and left it alone. Then your ancestors—or at least somebody's ancestors—decided it would be a nice place to live. The structure you called Hollowtown was never intended as a place to live. It was a containment facility for the massive energies the tractor-repulsor put out as it was charging up."

"Charging up? Wait a second. Are you saying that Hollowtown is just a power storage battery?"

"Pretty much," Lando said.

"But people lived there!"

"Maybe so, but that's not what it was designed for."

"So why did the Glowpoint stay on all the time?" Jenica demanded. "It's been functioning, and putting out a very steady level of light and heat for thousands of years. There has to be a reason for it. *We* thought it was to provide Hollowtown with sunlight, but I guess we were wrong. I mean, if you're right."

Lando frowned. "I don't know. Maybe it's like some stoves and ovens on planets where they burn hydrogen or methane for cooking. You always leave a little tiny flame burning, so that you can reignite the main system easily when you want to do some cooking."

"You're saying that the Glowpoint that provided us with light and heat was a *pilot light*?"

"Maybe. But maybe the builders *did* leave it on when they were done, and it provided light and heat to Hollowtown. Maybe they *did* intend for the charging containment to be converted to living space. After all, *they* had no reason to turn the hyperspace tractor repulsor on again. They were finished building the Corellian star system.''

"We're getting a little off-point here," Kalenda said. "Can you show us why you think Centerpoint is the starbuster?"

"Well, first off, either you take my word for it, or I can show you the math to demonstrate that the form and level of power needed to pull a planet in through a hyperspace link can be converted into the power needed to induce a compression wave in a star's core. If the tractor-repulsor energy is directed at the core of a star, and concentrated in a burst, the burst will be sufficiently powerful to touch off a nova explosion.''

"We'll take your word for it," Jenica said hurriedly. "Math was never my strong point. What's the rest of it?"

"It would take a generation or two just to trace out circuits and systems we've found, but all you've got is me and a couple of droids, and no time. Even so, I do think I've got the broad outlines of the thing worked out. This is the pattern I can put together by sifting through the records here, and matching them up with events off the station. First off, Centerpoint Station suddenly reorients its spin axis drastically. Then there were a lot of reports of 'unexplained power surges' and 'unscheduled energy pulses' and 'transient events' and 'unplanned radiation releases' reported in the station log, along with a lot of other nice bureaucratic phrases that mean no one knew what was going on.

"I think all the transient events and so on were just Centerpoint getting ready to fire up the Glowpoint. But, in any event, the first Glowpoint flare happens, lots of people die, there's chaos and panic and the evacuation. Then, shortly thereafter, the first induced supernova happens. Then civil war breaks out. Just after the first supernova, Centerpoint shifts its spin axis *again*. It's also a more drastic shift than anything Centerpoint had ever done before. No one was here on the station to report all the events, but the automatic logging reports I've found indicate there was more of the same. Then there was a different sort of power flow shifts from the automatic recording instruments that have kept up right until the present moment—and they start at *exactly* the time the jamming and the interdiction field come on. Then we get the second Glowpoint flare, and, shortly thereafter, the second induced supernova."

"But how could it be we didn't feel any of that, or see anything?" Jenica asked. "You're talking about a hugely powerful pulse of energy being shot off from this station. No one saw anything. There wasn't any huge vibration or any burst of heat."

"This station is putting out a hugely powerful interdiction field and a powerful jamming field right now. Can you feel either of those?"

"The pointing," Kalenda said. "What does the repointing show?"

Lando brought up a holographic projector, and threw up an image of the stars near to Corellia. "The red spot at the center of the display is our position. This is the pointing of Centerpoint's South Pole relative to the starfield before things started happening." A blue line streaked out from the center of the display and pointed toward nothing at all. "This is the pointing after the first shift in spin orientation." A line of red lanced out and stabbed straight through the heart of a star. "That is TD-10036-EM-1271," Lando said. "The first star to go nova." Lando punched in another command, and a shaft of gold streaked out and touched another star.

"Thanta Zilbra," Lando said. "The second star on the list. A population in the tens of thousands. My guess is most of them are dead. I know logistics, and I don't see how they possibly could have gotten everyone out in time. And this," he said, "is where we're pointed now." A line of violet fire flashed out, and hit another star, square and true. "That is the third star on the hit list we got in the initial warning message. Bovo Yagen.

I looked it up. One source says one planet with eight million. Another says two planets with a total estimated system population of twelve million on the planets, and who knows how many stations and habitats and mining camps and so on. Centerpoint is the starbuster, and it is getting set to blast that star and those planets and all those people down to cinders and dust."

"When?" Kalenda asked.

Lando hit another control button and a countdown clock appeared. "Artoo ran the problem. We have to backtrack a little to account for how long the pulse will take to travel through hyperspace, and how long it will take for the chain reaction to take hold inside the star and build up to an explosion. Centerpoint is going to have to send a tractor-repulsor hyperspace burst in exactly one hundred twenty-three hours, ten minutes, and thirteen seconds from *now* in order to keep to the schedule in the original warning message. Twelve hours and twelve minutes after that, the chain reaction induced by the energy pulse will bloom out of the star's core, and up it will go."

"Burning stars. Centerpoint—my home—is a weapon," Jenica said, her voice full of shock.

"And whoever controls it is going to have the power to control the Corellian Sector—and maybe the whole galaxy," Gaeriel said. "Do what we say, or we blow up your star."

"Wait a second," Luke said. "There's a piece that doesn't fit. If Centerpoint is the starbuster, then it's the prize, the most important place in the Corellian system. Why the fuss over the planetary repulsors? Why didn't the plotters worry about Centerpoint?"

"Three reasons," Lando replied. "The first is that they didn't try to get it because they already had it—or at least had found a way to control it. I figure there is some well-shielded, well-hidden control room on this station. Someplace we wouldn't find it if we looked for a hundred years. Probably there isn't anyone in it, anyway. All of it automated, set to work off timers and remote control. Second reason might be plain old misdirection. If you get everyone worried about the repulsors, no one's going to have time to go looking for the starbuster. And the third reason—"

"Has been staring us right in the face," Kalenda said. "I think I just figured it out. I haven't really worked with repulsor field theory since school, but part of what makes repulsors work is that they can interfere and resonate with each other, right? And you can use that interference between two or more repulsor cells to provide steering and control. Power to a small side repulsor cell can deflect the beam from the main repulsor."

Lando nodded. "Exactly. The planetary repulsors can jam Centerpoint's hyperspace tractor-repulsor beam. They are the only repulsors strong enough to do it.

"But it goes deeper than that. The planetary repulsors can work as amplifiers, not just as jammers. In practice it would be the devil to manage, but, in theory, you could tune *all* the planetary repulsors into a single network slaved to Centerpoint. That would provide Centerpoint with even more power and range than it has now. Right now, Centerpoint gets its power by tapping a little bit of the gravitic potential of Talus and Tralus. Suppose it could tap into Selonia, and Corellia, and Drall? For that matter, I haven't quite worked out the geometry of it yet, but with all five planets and Centerpoint in the network, you could probably tap into the star Corell's gravitic potential. If I'd designed this system back whenever it was designed, I'd make sure that was possible. Just imagine Centerpoint with *that* much power. It would be able to strike at any point in the galaxy. The masters of Centerpoint could grab any planet they wanted and pull it into this system—or drop into a star, if they wanted. Centerpoint could blow up any star its masters chose. It could set up an interdiction field or communications jamming over the whole galaxy—or any part of it its masters wanted to isolate. It could probably do a lot of other things we haven't even *thought* of yet."

"A lot of things that didn't make sense are starting to make more sense than I'd like," said Luke. "But using the repulsors for jamming. How would that work?"

"That's a lot simpler," Lando said. "If any of the planetary repulsors fired a properly tuned beam at Centerpoint, it would disrupt the aim and the tuning of the tractor-repulsor beam."

"Could the planetary beams actually move Centerpoint itself?" Luke asked.

"Not enough to make any difference," said Lando. "Centerpoint's more powerful than any of the planetaries. If the planetaries pushed Centerpoint off its present position, Centerpoint could just push it back. But any one of the planetaries can shut Centerpoint down by sending out a jamming signal."

"All right," Kalenda said. "Now we know all this. What do we do about it?"

Lando turned his hands palms-up in a gesture of helplessness. "Not much. We don't know it's being controlled, or from where, or how. We've got a rough idea of what the system is, but we're nowhere near understanding how to *operate* the system."

"There must be some cable we can cut, some control system we can smash," Jenica said.

"I bet there is—but I don't know where it is. And we won't find out unless we search every deck and shell and compartment on this station. And even if we found the control system, I'm not so sure we could smash it. Remember this system is robust enough that it's been up and running since before the Old Republic."

"Then we could blow up the whole station," Gaeriel said.

"With what?" Kalenda asked. "We have one light cruiser and two destroyers. None of them are carrying any bomb powerful enough to destroy something three hundred kilometers from end to end. Maybe, if you gave the Bakuran engineers enough time, they might be able to rig fixed-point detonators powerful enough to wreck the interior pretty thoroughly. *With enough time.* But not with only one hundred twenty-odd hours to do it."

"Well, there's one thing we can do," Luke said. "Get the word out. Tell our people what we've found out. If we can find Han and Leia and Chewbacca, if we can find our allies on the worlds here, and let them know what we know, that's a start. If they can get to a planetary repulsor in time, and if they can figure out how to run it, and if they can jam that hyperspace tractor-repulsor beam, then maybe we can save some lives."

Lando shook his head. "That's a lot of ifs, Luke," he said, the doubt heavy in his voice.

"I know," said Luke. He looked up at the countdown clock, the clock that showed how long Bovo Yagen had to live. The seconds were melting away. "And it's going to take all the ifs we have to beat that *when* up there."

*   *   *

The ship dove down into the repulsor chamber, moving fast and aggressively, but not so fast that Ebrihim wasn't able to see the insignia painted on the underside of its fuselage as he looked up at it. A stylized human skull with a knife in its teeth. "Human League!" he cried out. "Can we get the shields up?"

"No!" Aunt Marcha shouted. "The children are still outside. We have to wait for them to get aboard."

Ebrihim hopped up into the copilot's chair and turned toward the weapons controls as the enemy ship dropped down to a fast, assault-style landing. Burly figures in combat gear were tumbling out of the attack boat's hatches even before it had stopped bouncing on its landing legs.

Weapons. Ebrihim did not know much about such things, but he had to try. There had to be some sort of auto-system to let the turbolasers—

Suddenly huge hands were scooping him up out of the seat, tossing him out of the way. Chewbacca scrambled into the copilot's chair and started powering up the defense systems. Power began to surge through the *Falcon*'s weapons.

"The children are aboard!" Marcha shouted. "Raise the access ramp. Activate the shields!"

Chewbacca hit the ramp close button and reached for the shield controls—but it was too late. A trooper with a very powerful-looking blaster was looking *up* at Chewbacca from below the cockpit. The *Falcon* was surrounded by troops standing *inside* the shield perimeter. Chewbacca tried the shields anyway. The lights in the cockpit surged for a moment as power went to the shield generators, but nothing else happened. Chewbacca roared in frustration. Shield jammers. They must have attached shield jammers to the hull, preventing the shields from forming.

A tall, heavyset, bearded figure stepped out of the assault boat and walked toward them, a most unpleasant smile on his face.

"Sal-Solo," Ebrihim said. "It's him."

"That's our dad's cousin?" Anakin asked. Ebrihim turned around and realized for the first time that the children had crowded their way in. All of them, the entire party, were there, in the cockpit.

"That is his cousin and yours, child," said Marcha. "But I doubt you will gain much joy from knowing him."

Ebrihim tried not to listen. There was something that had just flitted across his mind, at the thought of their all being together. Wait a moment. That wasn't true. They *weren't* all together. But if he, Ebrihim, assumed they all were here, then surely their friends outside might make the same mistake. Ebrihim had an idea. Not even a plan, just an idea that would give them options, advantages. Maybe enough so that there would still be a way out of this. It was a long shot, but still it was a chance that could turn this thing around. That was the good news.

The bad news was in two parts. First, they only had a few seconds to put it in motion. And two, his idea relied completely and entirely upon Q9-X2.

* * *

Thrackan Sal-Solo could not have been happier. It was a gift from the gods, an absolute gift from the gods. He strode about his new possession, admiring it, thinking of all it could do—and do for him. At last he had his hands on a planetary repulsor. He had gambled everything that he would get to one in time. He had thought it would be the one on Corellia. That he ended up grabbing the one here on Drall was but a slight irony. He had one. That was all that mattered. He had one in time to control the situation. He looked up, admiring the view straight to the surface, that sharp-edge circle of blue, kilometers above his head. He looked down a bit, at the massive, graceful cluster of cones that made up the repulsor array itself. All his. All his.

His eyes strayed lower, to the *Millennium Falcon.* What a bonus, what a magnificent and glittering extra prize it was. Grabbing the *Falcon* by itself would have been enough to humiliate Han Solo, to pay him back for the crime of escape. But to find Han's Wookiee and his children aboard as well—what could be better? There were two absurd Drall as well, but they were no prize at all compared to the children. The children represented not just a chance for personal vengeance, but something else, something more—an opportunity. If he handled it right, a war winner. Now, suddenly, he could control, could manipulate, Leia Organa Solo herself. Now she would have to come to the bargaining table, because she had no choice.

And once she came to that table, Thrackan was certain she would leave with nothing at all. He would force her into a bargain that would leave the New Republic with its heart torn out, so badly injured, so utterly discredited, that it could not survive.

Of course, the recent destruction of Thanta Zilbra and the coming destruction of Bovo Yagen might well accomplish that on their own. A galaxy that saw that the New Republic could not prevent such a disaster would be a galaxy that lost faith in the New Republic. It would be a galaxy that realized revolt against the New Republic was possible. That would be all to the good, of course. But better, far better, if the galaxy saw Thrackan Sal-Solo as a central figure in bringing the New Republic down. The man who dared to grab the Chief of State's children and hold them hostage—that would be a man to fear, a man to reckon with. Now he would be that man.

But holding them would do no good unless Han Solo and Leia Organa Solo knew about it. The communications jamming would have to come down. That was easy to accomplish. An encoded radionics command to the hidden control station on Centerpoint would shut down the com jamming in short order. No doubt the people who had built the hidden control center took a dim view of Thrackan controlling it in their stead—but they should have thought of that before sending in operatives who could be bribed, operatives who would betray their masters.

But now, now, the last piece of the puzzle had dropped into place. He had a planetary disrupter, and alone of all the rebel leaders in the Corellian system, he knew what a planetary repulsor could do. Being able to smash a ship was trivial compared to the ability to hold the starbuster plot hostage.

Thrackan knew it would take time—perhaps a long time—before his technicians would be able to operate the repulsor, but even that did not matter. For now he was in a position to bluff things out, to *pretend* he controlled the repulsor. That ought to be more than enough to get what he wanted.

More than enough.

*   *   *

Admiral Hortel Ossilege watched on the long-range scanners as the Human League assault boat dove down the mouth of the repulsor. The image was grainy and blurry; the scanners were working at maximum range, which meant the assault boat was far beyond the maximum range of the *Intruder*'s weaponry. It was galling to be beaten to the punch. Frustrating. Infuriating. But it would not do to show it. It would not do at all. And one had to admire the nerve, the *audacity,* of the assault boat's commander, quite literally diving his whole ship down the barrel of a weapon that could have reduced his craft to dust and rubble in milliseconds. Even if the *Intruder* had been capable of atmospheric operation or planetary landing, he could not have risked it with a move like that. Not when the *Intruder* represented such a huge fraction of the firepower on the Republic's side of the equation. Ossilege envied his opponent's freedom to take chances.

But, speaking of taking chances, he faced a repulsor precisely like the one that had smashed the *Watchkeeper* down to nothing at all. He had to assume this repulsor would be just as powerful within a short period of time—if it was not so already. After all, *someone* had turned it on. More than likely, that someone knew how to aim it and fire it as well.

And, it occurred to him, more than likely that someone was an ally of the Human League. If that was so, then the assault boat hadn't been taking chances, but had flown in to take possession of a planetary repulsor that had been located and activated by Human League agents.

And yet. And yet. That was a fast, hard assault landing, not a slower, safer arrival at a secured base. Almost as if the other side had been as surprised as Ossilege himself. Almost as if they had been trying to do what he had been trying to do—take advantage of an unexpected opportunity. Ossilege had the feeling the story was not over. Something *else* was going to happen here, something more was going to change. And change could usually be exploited.

Besides, it was just one small assault boat. There could not be more than twenty or thirty people aboard it, at most. Surely the *Intruder* ought to be able to take on a force that small, no matter how powerful the weapon they controlled. Ossilege had always been a great believer in the idea that weapons mattered far less than the people who used them. The *Intruder* carried a small force of assault troops, and she carried her own assault boats. Perhaps the *Intruder* would not be able to attack the repulsor in a frontal assault, but there were other forms of attack. Forms that took a bit more time, and a bit more finesse, but could work just as well, if one was audacious.

Ossilege turned to the ensign at his side. "My compliments to Captain Semmac. The *Intruder* will move into an orbit synchronous with the planet's rotation, well out of line-of-sight from the repulsor site. We will await developments here while we commence preparations for a ground assault."

The ensign saluted and scurried away. Ossilege stared at the image of the planetary repulsor in the scanner screen. He raised his hand and offered up a small, mocking salute to the commander of the assault boat. "You have won the first round," he said to the screen. "But let us not forget the main event is still to come."

CHAPTER TEN

Casting the Stone

L uke stepped out into the huge airlock where the *Lady Luck* and his X-wing were waiting, and breathed a sigh of relief.

Jenica had taken them on a roundabout route, but they had gotten here faster than he had thought possible. And with that clock counting down toward the death of Bovo Yagen, there was no time at all to waste.

He thought he knew what he had to do next, but he had to be sure. He had to check. The others watched as Luke found a packing crate that had been abandoned on the airlock deck and sat down on it. He shut his eyes and concentrated, forcing himself to take it slow, to be sure, to extend his senses as far as possible.

"Leia is on Selonia," he said at last as he opened his eyes. "No doubt about it. I can *feel* her there. My guess is that Han is with her, and probably Mara Jade as well. The three children are on Drall, and if what Kalenda told us is right about how they all escaped from Corellia, that probably means Chewbacca and the *Falcon* are there with them. I can get a sense of a mind that's *probably* Chewbacca, but I can't be sure. Not at this range. And I might add that all of them seem worried. It's hard to explain, but—but I get the sense, the feeling, that all of them—Leia and the kids, and the people with them—are all prisoners of one sort or another."

"Then we'd better get cracking and bust them out," Lando said briskly. "You go to Leia," Lando said. "Take Artoo and the X-wing. Figure out the coordinates for the kids' location on Drall and give them to me. I'll fly Gaeriel and Jenica back to the Bakuran fleet, where they can inform Admiral Ossilege of what we have learned. Gaeriel should get back to her post on the ship, and Jenica is our expert on Centerpoint. She ought to be of some help if things get rough. After I've dropped them off, Lieutenant Kalenda and I will fly on to Drall and see what we can do about getting to Chewbacca and the kids."

Jenica looked toward Lando. "You're not very optimistic, are you?"

"We don't know how to find the Drall repulsor," Lando replied. "I don't care how good an engineer Chewbacca is, there isn't going to be any way for him to work on a repulsor he can't get to. We have to rescue them, of course, but unless they're sitting right on top of a repulsor, I don't see how finding Chewbacca is going to help us get one." He turned back to Luke. "Leia is by far the better chance. She's on a planet where they've got a working repulsor, and it's probably controlled by the people holding her. All you have to do is let her know what's going on, and then hope she can talk her captors into jamming Centerpoint."

Luke smiled faintly. "Yeah. Easy. Should be a piece of cake."

Jenica rubbed her chin. "It all *nearly* makes sense," she said thoughtfully. "But I don't like the fact that we're leaving Centerpoint unguarded."

"I don't think the loss of the overwhelming force represented by two small ships, two droids, and five people is going to matter that much," Lando said. "What are we going to be able to do, anyway? Wait for someone to land and then sneak up and kick them in the shins?"

Jenica cocked her head a bit to one side and nodded. "Point taken. I guess I don't know what more we can do."

Luke stood up and nodded. "In that case," he said, "I suggest we do what we can, right now."

*   *   *

"We have you, but we'll not keep you long," said Kleyvits, speaker for the Overden. She sat at a table opposite Mara, Leia, and Han. Dracmus sat at Kleyvits's side, demonstrating simply by her presence that her clan had submitted to the victors. She did not look happy to be there. "We need merely come to certain straightforward agreements, and then all may be on their way."

"We're not going to come to your agreements," Leia said wearily. The morning had lengthened into late afternoon, and they were in the sumptuous interior of the prison villa. For prison it had proved to be. The Overden had thrown a force field around the *Jade's Fire,* and guards around the force field. Leia could see the ship on the landing pad, just outside the door, but there would be no escape aboard her this time. "Even if we did wish to reach agreement, we could not do so while you were detaining us. Even if we did, it would be pointless. My government would never ratify any agreement made under duress."

"How can you be under duress when you will be free to go as soon as we are agreeing?"

"We are under duress *now,*" Leia said, her voice and manner calm, imperious. "And we will not agree in any event. Therefore, the point is moot."

"I ask you again to be reconsidering," Kleyvits said. "All we ask is that you are acknowledging reality. We are free. We are no longer of the New Republic. We have thrown you off. We are our own place, our own planet. We ask merely that you are recognizing this fact."

"You are no freer now than you were under the New Republic," Mara said, her voice cold. "There was no dictator over you, no one telling you how to think and feel and act. You have thrown off no tyranny. It is not freedom for Selonia you ask her to recognize. It is the dominance of the Overden."

"Hey, I'll tell you what," Han said. "Let's give them what they want. Complete freedom. Complete freedom from trade, from interstellar commerce, from imports. Complete freedom from travel off-planet. Total embargo. How does that sound?"

"It sounds quite pleasant to us of the Overden, who wish to be free of anti-Selonian influence. Is that not so, my dear friend? Speak for the Hunchuzuc. Do you not agree that complete isolation would be the greatest of blessings?"

"Oh yes, eminent Kleyvits," Dracmus said in a mournful tone, clearly feeling miserable and humiliated. "There could be no doubt that all the people of Selonia long to be isolated from the outside universe."

"What about all your friends and relations on Corellia, where you lived all your life?" Han asked.

"They will rejoice with me in knowing we are free of all outside influence," Dracmus said, staring down at the table.

"I'm afraid you're no good at lying, Honored Dracmus," Han said. "I've seen dead people who were more convincing."

Dracmus looked up worriedly, and risked a quick look over at Kleyvits. "Please be in no doubt at all about my sincerity, Honored Solo."

"Don't worry on that score," said Han. "I have no doubts at all."

"I insist that we return to the main point," Kleyvits said, clearly a bit put off by Dracmus's performance.

"Recognize the freedom of Selonia under the guidance of the Overden or never leave this planet alive."

"You've got yourself a deal," Leia said.

Kleyvits looked toward her eagerly. "Then we have persuaded you?"

"Absolutely," said Leia. "We pick the second choice, the one about not leaving alive. Go ahead and kill us all right now."

Kleyvits sighed wearily, and extended her claws to drum them on the tabletop, making a rather unsettling clicking noise. It was hard to miss just how sharp those claws were. "I can see," said Kleyvits, "that we are going to be here for a while."

*   *   *

Thrackan Sal-Solo sat in the copilot's seat and watched intently as the pilot brought the assault boat up to the rim of the huge cylinder that was the planetary repulsor. Slowly, slowly, slowly up and over. The assault boat hung motionless in the air for a moment, then spun slowly about, until its nose was pointed directly at the two bright spots of light on the evening horizon. Talus and Tralus. Thrackan could not spot it with the naked eye from this distance, but he knew that, with just the slightest of magnification, he would be able to see Centerpoint there as well.

All was in readiness. All he had to do was press the button, command the radionics system to send its signal, and then order the pilot to bring them back down into the repulsor. Then it would simply be a matter of waiting for the radionics signal to cross the distance between here and Centerpoint to reach the control center. The automatic control center would shut off the jamming, and that would be that. He would not even have to come up here again to transmit the broadcast over com channels. The com signal wouldn't be blocked by the repulsor or require line of sight. Most convenient.

Simple, really. Thrackan was not generally of a poetic turn of mind, but it occurred to him that what he was about to do was to cast a stone into a pond, square into the middle. The ripples would move out from where the stone struck, out in all directions. Some of the consequences he could predict, but he knew, if anyone did, just how risky a game he was playing. The ripples might well spread out in directions he had not considered, touch on shores he did not expect. He wanted to turn off the communications jamming because it served his own purposes, but being able to communicate would serve many other purposes beyond his own.

Some consequences he could predict. Once the jamming was down, the original controllers of the starbuster plot would immediately use the primary com system to send the command shutting down the interdiction field. They would move into the Corellian system and run right up against the Bakuran ships. That suited Thrackan fine. Let the two sides battle it out. Let one side defeat the other. The winner, whoever it was, would be weakened by the fight, and Thrackan's own forces would have an easier time of it in the final confrontation.

He was also just about certain that the system's original controllers would lock out the subsystem Thrackan had been using, preventing him from manipulating the system any further. *They* would not want the jamming back on. So be it. That meant Thrackan's enemies here in the Corellian system would suddenly be able to communicate with each other, exchange information. They would learn things about each other, and about Thrackan—but they would learn them too late. He was not worried about that.

But what of the consequences he had not imagined? What unknown risks was he about to take? There was, clearly, no way to know.

But there was one thing he did know. Shutting off the communications jamming would allow Thrackan

Sal-Solo to tell the whole Corellian system that he had Han Solo's children. Han Solo would hear it, and know it, and be helpless to do anything about it.

What sweeter revenge could there be?

Thrackan pushed the button. The command signal went out.

* * *

Ossilege watched on the *Intruder*'s long-range scanners as the assault boat hovered just barely into view over the top of the repulsor, turned itself slightly, and then floated back down out of sight. He looked toward the *Intruder*'s chief gunner and saw the man shake his head. "I'm sorry, sir. There just wasn't time to set up a shot. Not at this range. Especially with atmosphere in the way. If he had stayed there another thirty seconds—"

The chief gunner left the thought unfinished, but Ossilege understood. He sighed. If that assault boat had stayed there long enough for the *Intruder* to set up the shot, then this war might be over right now.

* * *

"Boy, you get out of touch for five minutes and everything changes," said Lando as the *Lady Luck* flew clear of the mammoth Centerpoint airlock. "Where's the *Intruder*?"

"What's the *Intruder*?" Jenica asked.

"Biggish sort of thing. A ship. A Bakuran light cruiser. It should not be hard to miss, but I can't spot it."

"Have you looked in the last place you had it?" she asked.

Lando smiled. "I did, just now, and it wasn't there. But I bet I find it in the last place I look."

"So where is it?"

"At a guess, something has happened, and Admiral

Ossilege has charged off as bravely as possible to do something about it, whether it needs doing or not."

"I'm not sure I appreciate your tone, Lando," said Gaeriel.

"I'm not sure I appreciate the way Ossilege takes chances," said Lando. "But the question is, what do we do now?"

"I'm not sure," Gaeriel said. "Life is going to be a lot easier if and when we get communications back." She thought a moment. "Can we get a laser comlink with either of the two destroyers?"

"Not easily," Lando said. "It'd probably be easier and faster just to fly over to the closest ship, dock, open the hatch, and ask what's going on."

"Then let's do that," Gaeriel said. "We can decide what to do when we know more."

"A very sensible attitude, that," said Lando. "We're on our way."

*   *   *

Jaina let out a sad sigh. Things were very bad. The prisoners sat, sad and forlorn—and rather crowded— in the mobile stockade, unable to do anything but watch as the Human League troopers and technicians unpacked their gear, obviously getting ready to settle in for a long stay.

The mobile stockade was really nothing more than a force field generator designed to stay outside the force field itself, so that those held in the field could not get at the generating machinery. The force field was transparent, however, and those inside could *see* the generator, plain as day, straight in front of them.

This did not sit well with Anakin, to put it mildly. The idea that he could *see* but could not *touch* the device that was holding them prisoner seemed to upset him far more than the fact that he was a prisoner.

The other two children tried to keep him as distracted as possible, but it was not easy. On the bright side, struggling to keep Anakin cheered up distracted them from their own worries. The two Drall, Ebrihim and Marcha, seemed to have decided that being locked up gave them a chance to catch up on a decade or so of family gossip—and they clearly had an enormous family. They sat there, for hour after hour, discussing the doings of this cousin, the money problems of that uncle, the scandalous failure to divorce of that great-aunt twice-removed and her fifth husband.

Chewbacca paced back and forth, from one side of the hemispherical force field containment to the other. He was forced to watch the Human League techs poking around the *Millennium Falcon,* wandering around on the upper hull, opening the access panels, and studying the interiors. Once or twice, a League tech would open a panel and laugh out loud at what he saw. It was difficult to restrain Chewbacca at those moments. He would pound his fists on the force field and roar his frustration, but doing so gained him nothing more than slightly singed fur on his hands and upper arms.

Perhaps only the two Drall were calm and settled enough to deal with the situation rationally when Thrackan Sal-Solo marched over from the assault boat. Jaina certainly wasn't in any mood to be reasonable. A Human League tech was by his side, carrying a holographic recorder.

"Good afternoon to all of you," said Thrackan in that voice that was so close to her father's, and yet so far away. Cousin Thrackan—strange and unpleasant to think of him that way, Jaina told herself, but that was what he was.

"Hello," said Jaina, and Jacen muttered a hello as well. Anakin took one look at his father's cousin and burst into tears—and Jaina couldn't blame him. It was upsetting just to look at—at Thrackan. He looked so *much* like their father—just a little darker, a little heavier, the hair a different shade. The beard helped make him seem at least a *little* different from Dad, but somehow that only made the similarities more upsetting. It was like looking at—at a dark side version of her father, the way *he* could have been, if anger and resentment and suspicion had taken hold of him.

"Make that child stop crying," Thrackan said, as if Jaina could make Anakin quiet with a wave of her hand.

"I can't," she said. "He might calm down in a minute, but he's scared of you."

"There's no reason to be scared of me," said Thrackan. "Not yet." *That* was less than comforting.

Jaina knelt down and gave her little brother a hug. "It'll be all right, Anakin, honest," she whispered to him, hoping that she was telling the truth.

"Why are you here?" Jacen asked, glaring at Thrackan. "What do you want?"

"Not much at all, not much at all," Thrackan said. "I merely need some pictures of all of us together."

Chewbacca roared, growled, and bared his teeth, then gestured for Thrackan to come into the stockade containment.

Thrackan smiled. "I don't speak your barbaric language, Wookiee, but I understood *that.* No, thank you. I can get quite close enough to you for my purposes from *outside* the force field."

"Why do you want holos of us?" Aunt Marcha demanded.

Thrackan smiled. "I should think that would be obvious, even to a member of your species. I am in the process of turning off the jamming of communications. When the jamming is off, I will broadcast the holos to demonstrate that you are my prisoners. While I doubt anyone will much care what happens to a pair of rotund Drall or a psychotic Wookiee, I would expect that the children's parents will be inspired to more reasonable behavior if they knew I had their children— and a planetary repulsor."

Marcha, Duchess of Mastigophorous, drew herself

up to her full height and glared at their jailkeeper. "You are on the verge of a most serious error," she said. "For your own safety, I urge you to reconsider this act."

Thrackan laughed out loud. "You are scarcely in a position to make threats, Drall. Save your breath."

"Very well. May the consequences be on your head alone. Honor required me to say what I did. But a wise being can tell a warning from a threat."

For the briefest of moments, the bland smile flickered off Thrackan's face, but then it was back, as calm and meaningless as ever. "I need say no more to any of you on this subject," he said. "Now I want the three children on this side of the stockade, closest to me, and you three aliens on the far side."

"Why—" Ebrihim began.

"Because I wish it!" Thrackan snapped. "Because if you do not obey, I can manipulate the force field to make the stockade half the size it is. Because I can shoot you all dead if I so choose." Thrackan paused, and smiled. "Because I can and will harm the children if you do not," he said. "Now go to the other side."

The two Drall and the Wookiee exchanged looks with each other. It was clear they had no real choice. They moved to the opposite side of the stockade.

Anakin had more or less settled down by this time, and Jaina urged him to his feet. There was always one sure way to distract Anakin, and that was to have him watch someone use a machine. And of course there might be other benefits to watching the procedure. "Look, Anakin," she said. "Watch what the man does."

Anakin nodded and wiped his nose. The three children stood as close as they could to the edge of the field and watched intently as the technician knelt down by the stockade's force field generator. He pulled a very old-fashioned metal key out of his pocket, shoved it into a slot on the generator, and turned it a quarter turn to the left. Then he changed several of the settings on the device. A new force field, a vertical wall running across the middle of the stockade field, and separating the adults from the children, came into being. He turned the key back a quarter turn to the right and pulled it back out. "Ah, Diktat, sir, it might also be wise to intensify the fields somewhat, so that they are more plainly visible on the holographic recording."

"Will it make the prisoners themselves harder to see?"

"Very slightly, sir, but they will be quite recognizable, and the sight of the force field will make a very clear visual statement that they are prisoners. It will make your words stronger."

"Very well," Thrackan said. "Make the adjustment."

The technician turned a dial, and the force field turned a trifle darker.

"Very good," said Thrackan. "Very good indeed. "Now, then. Take your holo recorder and shoot," he said. "Get a nice long sequence of each face in turn, and then a wide shot of all of us together. I don't want there to be any chance of someone not being sure I have the children, or of someone thinking that it's been faked in some way."

The technician lifted his holographic recorder to his face and set to work, recording the image of each unsmiling face in turn, then taking a wide shot of Thrackan with all the prisoners. At last he was done. "That should do it, Diktat Sal-Solo," the tech said.

"Very good," said Thrackan. "Let's go get the transmitter set up and get ready to send that out."

"What about setting the force field back, sir?"

Thrackan looked at the stockade for a moment. "Leave it," he said. "It might be wise to keep the children separate from the aliens. It might make it harder for them to scheme together." With that, he turned and walked away, the technician following behind.

Jaina watched as the two of them walked away. "Did you see enough of what the tech did?" she asked Jacen.

"Not really," he said. "I don't think I could manipulate the controls with the Force, anyway. I don't have that kind of fine control. And besides, the tech had that key."

"Anakin, what about you?"

"I could do *something* if I could *get* at it," he said. "Change some stuff. But you need that key to turn a field on or off, or cut all power. *You* saw him. Have to have that *key* to turn it off."

"No hope there, then," Jaina said.

"Hush, child," said the Duchess Marcha from the other side of the vertical force field wall. "There is always hope—particularly against an opponent who believes everything can be won with bullying."

Jaina went over to the vertical wall, the other children trailing after. "Has he really made a mistake, Aunt Marcha?" she asked, wanting comfort and reassurance as much as information.

"Oh, yes," she said, "very much so, child."

Chewbacca laughed gently, a small growly noise, and then let out a yip and a hoot. The Wookiee looked around to make sure no Human League trooper was close enough to watch. Then he moved up as close as he could to the vertical wall and opened the palm of his hand.

He had a pocket comlink.

Jaina looked up at Chewbacca with a wild grin. "I should have known," she said. "With all that long fur, you could hide practically *anything* on your body. And besides, who's going to frisk a Wookiee?" Chewbacca chuckled again at that question.

"But what good does that do us?" Jacen asked. "That thing doesn't have any range at all. Not more than a few kilometers."

"You're forgetting someone who is quite nearby," Ebrihim said. "Someone who has built-in communications equipment." Ebrihim smiled to himself. "Someone who is probably getting most tired of waiting."

*   *   *

Q9-X2 was most definitely tired of waiting—in itself a remarkable accomplishment in a droid. Any other droid would have simply turned itself off after setting an implanted timed wake-up command in its standby circuits. Not Q9. He was afraid of missing something. Not that there could be much to miss when stuffed upside down into one of the *Falcon*'s hidden smuggling compartments. Q9 found that he was more bothered by being confined than by being inverted. It would have been more pleasant to have been right-side up, but time had been exceedingly short, and this had been the first place they had found where he could fit at all, in any orientation.

Ebrihim's instructions had been simple enough, and did not require Q9 to stay turned on. *Wait at least fourteen hours. Do not emerge until it is safe to do so. At that time, examine the ship and the situation as best you can. Determine the best method for coming to our aid, and carry out that method.* Rather on the vague side, but the intent was straightforward. The execution would be tricky, as most of Q9's sensors had to be extended out of his body before he could use them, which meant they were less than helpful while he was upside down in a tight-fitting storage bin.

He *could* have stayed powered down, but he was simply too agitated for that. Q9 had run some diagnostics and analyzed his on-board service log. He knew exactly how close he had come to being destroyed by Anakin's activation of the repulsor. Droids were rarely reminded of their own mortality in quite that way. Now, shortly thereafter, Q9 had ample time to consider the notion of his own destruction. It had nearly happened in the recent past, and the odds seemed fairly high that it would happen in the near future. Under the circumstances, deliberately shutting oneself off seemed the height of folly. Suppose one component had failed, or was on the verge of failing, and his diagnostics had missed it? Suppose he loaded a timed wake-up event, went into standby, and then the wake-up command was never implemented? In short, he had no desire to turn himself off when he was not confident he could turn himself back on again.

Clearly, it was an absurd state of affairs, but there it was. Q9 was afraid to go to sleep.

He settled in to wait some more.

*   *   *

Gaeriel Captison stood on the hangar deck of the *Sentinel*, next to the *Lady Luck*. "I don't think there's any argument about what we should do," she said. "We go on to Drall, and rendezvous with the *Intruder*."

"Absolutely," said Lando. "If someone has already found a repulsor there, that is the place to be."

"Not for me it isn't," said Jenica. "*Sentinel* and *Defender* are keeping watch on Centerpoint Station, and I'm the closest thing to an expert on Centerpoint they're going to get. I stay here."

Lando nodded. "You're right," he said. "Lieutenant Kalenda, what about you?"

Kalenda cocked her left eyebrow up a bit and shook her head slightly. "A tough call," she said. "But at this point, I'd say my place is with Admiral Ossilege."

So you can keep an eye on him? Lando wondered. "Good enough," he said. "Get aboard, then."

"What about me?" Threepio asked. "Shall I continue on with you? It is more likely that my language skills will be more useful on a trip to Drall than here."

Lando was sorely tempted to refuse and leave Threepio behind. But the irritating thing was that the droid might be right. Suppose they got to the repulsor and encountered Drall who didn't speak Basic? "Get aboard," he growled. Threepio trotted up the access ramp.

Gaeriel and Kalenda said their farewells to Jenica and boarded the *Lady Luck*. Lando waited just a moment before going aboard. There was something more he wanted to say to Jenica Sonsen, something he might not get the chance to say again. And by the amused look on her face, it seemed as if she was expecting *him* to say something. In fact, she said it first. "Is this the part where you tell me how you never met anyone like me, and how you want to get to know me better? That sort of thing? Maybe something about how we've been through a lot together, we've made a connection, and we shouldn't just let it drift away? Some nice, smooth line a lady couldn't help but fall for?"

Lando couldn't quite tell if she was mocking him or daring him, warning him off or urging him on. The strange thing was it didn't matter. He had been shot down in romance plenty of times before, but there was a little piece of him that felt quite sure this would not have been one of those times. But this time, there wasn't going to be a this time.

Lando sighed and shook his head. "There was a time, not very long ago, when I would have said those words, and meant every one of them—at least, while I was saying them, even if I sort of forgot them later. The problem is, I did say something very like them to another lady, very recently, and I *did* mean it at the time. The funny thing is, for the first time in my life, I'm catching myself *still* meaning it. I might even mean it for a long, long time. So I'm afraid I'm going to have to back off."

Jenica looked surprised—though not half as surprised as Lando felt. "You know," she said, "that might be the classiest speech of its kind on record. I think you've got yourself a very lucky lady out there, and I don't mean the *Lady Luck*." She stuck out her hand to shake, and Lando took it. "Take care of yourself, Lando. I must admit I almost wish you *had* made a play for me—just so I could know for sure what I would have done about it. Now I guess I'll never know."

Lando smiled back, his broadest, most charming grin that showed every tooth in his head. "Neither will I," he said. "You take care of yourself too." He let go of her hand, boarded the *Lady Luck*, and made his way to the pilot's station.

Gaeriel was waiting in the starboard observer's seat, and Kalenda was at the copilot's station. "So," said Kalenda as she ran the preflight check, "is she going to let you call her?" Her eyes never left the instruments, but there was just the hint of a smile at the corner of her mouth. Lando wasn't sure, but he thought he heard a very un-ex-Prime-Ministerial giggle from behind him as he sat down.

"Excuse me?" he asked.

"Call her. You asked if you could look her up after this was all over. Did she say yes or no?"

Lando felt himself blushing. Had it been that obvious? Was his reputation that bad? "Um, ah, well—if you *have* to know, she asked if I was going to ask, and I said I couldn't. Promises made elsewhere."

This time Kalenda did turn away from the instruments, to look straight at him. "You're kidding," she said, that disconcerting over-her-shoulder gaze of hers throwing him more than a little off.

"Ah, no," said Lando. "I'm not. I don't know why I should tell you any of this at all, but that's what happened. Trader's Honor."

Kalenda let out a low whistle and shook her head. "Well then, Madame Prime Minister. It looks like our little bet is off. Captain Calrissian, why don't you get us out of here?"

"Uh, um—right, yes," said Lando. He finished his own preflight check and gently lifted the *Lady* up onto her repulsors. There were definitely times and places when he realized that he still had a lot to learn about women.

The *Lady Luck* left the hangar deck, gathered speed, and headed for Drall—and for the *Intruder*.

*   *   *

Luke Skywalker eased the X-wing's throttle up to maximum thrust and kept it there. The dance of the orbits had put Selonia just about as close to Centerpoint and the Double Worlds as it ever got, but the distances were still great—and he was in a hurry. He, too, had wondered what the absence of the *Intruder* had meant, but he had no time to worry about it. He had a job and a duty. Bovo Yagen, and its millions of people. Now, at last, they had at least a hope of saving them. And if—if—they could stop the destruction of Bovo Yagen, it might well mark the beginning of the end for the starbuster plot and the rebellions on the worlds of the Corellian system.

But the galaxy had little interest in *ifs*. The universe concerned itself with what *did* happen, not with what *might*. They had a slender chance here, but that was all. And the survival of those twelve million people might well depend on how fast he got to Selonia, and Leia.

Twelve million people. Luke remembered thinking, not so long ago, that in the galactic time scale, what happened here scarcely mattered at all. All of recorded history, all the days of myth and legend before that time, were a blink in the cosmic eye. But twelve million people, twelve million lives. That many hopes, that many dreams and pasts, that many families, that many memories and histories that would vanish as well, as if they had never been. All the unborn generations that would never be born, all the promise, all the potential, that would be gone, stolen from the galaxy's future.

Surely it was wrong to destroy a star, something that old, that big, that powerful and complex and beautiful, just for the sake of some transient political advantage.

Luke smiled. No one was going to use supernovas as weapons. Not during *his* eye blink of history. Not if he could help it.

Artoo beeped and whirred in tones of warning, and Luke checked his display screens. "Oh, boy," he said, "company." A flight of eight Light Attack Fighters was climbing out of orbit to meet him. It was not the sort of trouble Luke needed just now. Maybe he could scare them off without getting too involved.

Luke eased back the throttle of the X-wing and zeroed out his shields completely, shunting all the surplus engine and shield energy to his weapons system.

Artoo let out a twittering squeal of protest. "Take it easy, Artoo. I'll have the shields back up before we're in range of their weapons." Luke had flown against LAFs not so long ago. He knew what they could do— and what they could not. The LAFs were overmatched by the basic X-wing, but not to the point where he cared to take his chances against eight LAFs singlehanded. The best way for Luke to win this fight was to avoid it altogether.

The trick now would be to convince them that Luke and his enhanced X-wing fighter put together were unbeatable rather than just very good.

Luke reached out with the Force, extending his senses as far as he could, touching the minds of the Selonian fighter pilots, seeking not to manipulate their emotional state but to judge it. The Selonian temperament, with its desire for group consensus, was not one much given over to the strains of battle. They did better when fighting alone, on behalf of a group, rather than as part of a group fighting side by side.

He felt at once that the Selonian pilots were nervous, jumpy, unsure. From two or three of their minds he detected the sensation of returning to a place of doom and fear. At a guess, those were veterans of the recent fight against the Bakurans, veterans who had just barely come back.

It was enough. If Luke did this right, then everyone would come back from this one. They might not enjoy it, but they'd be alive.

Luke checked his power displays. Weapons power was at maximum. Luke shifted all his shield generation power and weapons-charging power into the propulsion system, and throttled up to a hundred twenty percent of maximum rated thrust. The X-wing leapt toward the LAFs at terrifying speed. Two of the LAFs fired at him, panicky unaimed shots that went completely wild. One of them nearly shot his own wingman.

Luke knew the chance he was taking, flying without shields. If one of those random shots turned lucky and managed to connect—well, that would be too bad.

Best to try to get this over with before anything like that could happen. This one would require all his skill, all his ability in the Force—and a fair amount of luck as well. Luke disengaged the firing computer, shut his eyes, and aimed the X-wing by feel, by instinct, through the Force. Once, twice, three times, he fired. Three turbolaser bursts leapt out. One, two, three, the bursts hit the LAFs, catching each of them square on the ventral weapons pod. Suddenly three of the LAFs could fly, but could not fight.

It was flying, and shooting, intended to send a message. *I am faster than you, bigger than you, have better weapons than you, and can shoot from farther away. I could destroy you all if I chose to do so. I do not so choose. Do not make me change my mind.*

The three veterans got the message right away, it seemed, reversing course immediately and heading for home. Two of the other LAFs hesitated for a moment, then followed the others.

That left three to deal with, and three was a lot better than eight. On the other hand, it left him facing the three pilots who were hardest to scare. The three of them were headed for him in a face-on triangle, one fighter at each angle of the triangle. They were rapidly closing to firing range. Luke throttled back enough to let him put his forward shields back on, but he didn't switch power back to weapons charging. One way or another, this engagement would be over before his weapons systems ran out of stored power.

Suddenly Artoo began to whistle excitedly, and a

text message began to scroll past Luke's display screen, much too fast for Luke to follow. "Artoo, what is it?"

The droid's half-frantic beeping and whistling sounded in Luke's headphones. Luke checked his detector display, saw the three LAFs closing fast, and made a quick, easy decision about priorities. "Artoo, later," Luke said. "I've got another problem right now. Whatever it is, it's going to have to wait."

These three pilots weren't easy to scare, but they weren't the best tacticians, either. They were bunched up too close, too tight. A shot that missed one of them was almost bound to hit one of the others. Maybe he could use that. But he would have to do it before he got in under their firing range.

Still unwilling to kill without need, Luke thought fast. Suddenly he thought he saw a way. He switched the fire control selector from LASER to TORPEDO, and rapidly punched in a series of commands, reprogramming one proton torpedo for distant proximity fusing.

Suddenly all three LAFs fired at once, concentrated volley fire. It would seem the LAF pilots were managing to coordinate their fire in spite of the communications jamming. Maybe these pilots knew their business better than he thought.

The laser blasts slammed into the X-wing, and Luke gave thanks that he had thought to reactivate the shields when he did. The X-wing's forward shields handled the multiple hits, but just barely.

Luke knew he had to get out of here, and fast, if he was going to live through this. One last trick. He fired the reprogrammed proton torpedo square into the center of the LAF formation. The X-wing shuddered slightly as the torpedo leapt away.

Part of what Luke was counting on was the element of surprise. No one used proton torpedoes in fighter-to-fighter encounters. They were slower and less accurate—but more powerful—than turbolasers, intended for use against bigger targets.

The three LAFs fired in volley again, the incoming

laser blasts streaking past the outgoing torpedo. Luke's X-wing shuddered from stem to stern as the second laser volley slammed into it. Luke checked his shields and shook his head. The next volley would punch through his shield for sure.

Luke cut his engines, letting the X-wing move on its own forward momentum alone. Let them think he had lost engine power. It might make him that much harder to find when—

The proton torpedo exploded precisely in the middle of the LAF formation, lighting up the sky, no doubt blinding the pilots, at least for a second or two, and, with any luck, scrambling half their instruments as well. Luke reengaged his engines, accelerating at maximum power, right into the blast of the proton torpedo, right through the middle of the opposing fighter formation.

The X-wing bucked and slammed and shuddered as it flew straight into the explosion's shock wave, its weakened shields offering just barely enough protection.

Luke flew into the blast of the torpedo, hanging on for dear life as he rode the maelstrom. Then, suddenly, it was over. He was through, clear, safe. Luke checked his detector screens. Two of the LAFs were tumbling, clearly disabled, at least for the moment, while the third seemed to be in only marginal control. One of the disabled fighters seemed to be starting to recover as he watched, but Luke knew better than to stick around to see how it all came out. He came about on a new heading, straight for Selonia.

Luke breathed a sigh of relief. That one had been just a bit *too* close. There were times when the advantages of being a Jedi Master could turn around and bite you, no doubt about it. A regular fighter pilot without the power to use the Force wouldn't have felt any moral obligation to risk his own life while using the Force to spare his enemies. Luke smiled faintly to himself. One of these old days, his moral obligations to spare life were going to get him killed.

Artoo whistled again for his attention. Luke reconfigured his power levels back to normal distribution and leaned back in his pilot's seat. "All right, Artoo," he said. "What is it?"

Artoo took control of the main status display screen and showed him. The display paged to communications status, and Luke saw it there for himself. "The communications jamming is down!" he said. "But why—"

But Artoo answered Luke's question before Luke could finish asking it. The screen cleared again, and Artoo began playing back a message he had recorded even as Luke was chasing off the LAFs.

A grinning, stylized human skull with a knife between its teeth appeared on the screen, with a blaring shout of triumphal music behind it. Luke recognized the skull. The symbol of the Human League. The skull faded out, to be replaced by the only somewhat more pleasant features of a smiling Thrackan Sal-Solo.

But Luke was not smiling as he listened to what the man had to say.

CHAPTER ELEVEN

The Ripples Spread

It was evening, and Kleyvits and Dracmus were just on the point of leaving. Han had lost count of the number of times they had come to call, asking if Leia had changed her mind yet. This had to be the third or fourth visit already today. Clearly, they did not know when to give up.

Leia, Han, Mara, and the Selonians were all in the living room of the prison villa, standing up, saying their pointless diplomatic good-byes, when suddenly the com system in the corner came to life, all on its own. A blare of static filled the room.

Han was startled enough to jump half a meter in the air, but the others took it all a bit more calmly. "Relax, Han," said Mara. "Someone out there has just used the auto-on system, that's all." It was possible to turn most com systems on by remote control, so that the authorities could make an emergency announcement.

The flat-field screen came on, showing a crazy-quilt of shifting, scrambling color. Then the image settled down to show a grainy image of a huge grinning skull. It appeared to a thunderously loud and distorted musical accompaniment. The graininess and distortion told Han that the signal was being broadcast by a transmitter that wasn't quite up to the job, some piece of equipment that was being pressed into service.

Even as he judged the technical quality of the broadcast as a matter of reflex, it took Han a moment to realize the full implications of the system's power-on. "Hey, wait a second!" he said. "This means the jamming is down! Now we can—"

"Shhh! Quiet," Leia said. "If it's worth it to Thrackan to shut off the jamming just to make an announcement, it has to be important. I want to hear it." She hit a button on the com system's control panel, setting it to record the message, then sat down in front of the com screen.

"How are you knowing it is Sal-Solo who—" began Dracmus, when the skull image faded away and, sure enough, there was Sal-Solo himself, seated in what looked like the control room of a small military craft of some sort, smiling with every bit of the warmth and kindness of the skull his image replaced. There was something awkward, a bit clumsy about the setup, as if it had been improvised. The image wobbled a bit, as if it was coming from a handheld holographic recorder.

"Greetings to all of you throughout the Corellian system," Thrackan said as a bit of static scrambled his image for a second. "I am Thrackan Sal-Solo, Diktat of Corellia. I have ordered that all communications jamming be turned off, so that I might inform all those in the Corellian system—our friends and enemies alike— of two very important new prizes that Human League troops, acting under my command, have won. First, let it be known that we have gained control of Drall's planetary repulsor. The New Republic kept even the existence of this extremely powerful device secret from you, the people of the Corellian system—"

"Because we didn't know it existed," Han muttered.

"Shhhh!" hissed Leia.

"—but now it is our possession. Soon we will control the repulsor on the planet Corellia as well. I understand that these devices are unknown to all of you.

Suffice it to say that with these powerful weapons we shall be able to protect ourselves from all our enemies, whoever they may be."

Dracmus turned to Kleyvits. "The League now has the Drall repulsor?" she demanded. "What will this mean?"

"The second prize that we have won is of a more personal nature," Thrackan went on. "We have rescued the three children of Leia Organa Solo, Chief of State of that same New Republic."

Han felt the blood drain from his face, felt his heart turn to ice. He looked to Leia and saw the same horror there.

"We have saved them from the aliens who held them prisoner," Thrackan went on. "They are safe, here, with me now. I look forward to my chance to return them to their mother. First, of course, she must make her whereabouts known to us. She herself must come out of hiding and confirm her recognition of the Corellian Sector's freedom. I offer this video imagery to prove that I have the repulsor, and have the children safe."

"Of all the low-down, dirty, rotten—" Han growled. "The *lies* that man tells!"

The screen went dark again, and then showed a vast, silver cylindrical interior space, as seen from the bottom. The image was a bit wobbly still, and the resolution was not all it could be, but the picture was clear enough for all of that. The holocam panned about to show an assault boat—and the *Millennium Falcon*—sitting at the bottom of the cylinder. Men in uniforms walked purposefully about the two ships. The holocam panned up, to show six huge cones rising from the floor, and a seventh, larger than the others, in the center of the chamber, with the sky visible through the top of the chamber.

"It is at least most certainly identical-ish to our own repulsor—" said Dracmus, before Kleyvits cut her off with a warning glare.

The holocam view swung back down to the floor of the chamber and zoomed in to a group of forlorn-look-ing figures sitting and standing in a confined space.

The view faded away, and then the image brightened to show a closer view of the sad-looking group.

It was the children, held inside a force field contain-ment, with Chewbacca, Ebrihim, and a Drall Leia did not know held in an adjacent containment. The cam moved from face to face, showed a close-up of each of them. Jacen, looking sad but determined; Jaina wor-ried, her gaze straying to Anakin; Anakin glaring straight at the cam. His face was streaked with tears, and he looked snuffly, as if he had just calmed down after crying. The cam moved along to show Thrackan, smiling coldly.

Leia choked back a sob, and Han felt a lump in his own throat. Thrackan had them. Thrackan had stolen *children*, Han's children. Thrackan had kidnapped his own flesh and blood. But then Han felt his sickness at heart, his fear, his horror, turn to cold, hard anger, clear-sighted anger. Thrackan *wanted* them scared, and shocked. But already Han was determined not to give Thrackan what he wanted.

The holocam panned to the second Drall, and then, at last, to Chewbacca. There was something in Chewbacca's stance, in Chewbacca's expression, that gave Han hope. Chewbacca stood tall, he looked at the holocam, bared his fangs at it. He didn't look or act remotely beaten. Han knew Chewie—and that was not a Chewbacca who thought he was beaten. In that in-stant Han knew, knew beyond doubt, that Chewbacca still had a trick or two up his sleeve. Or at least he would have, if he wore clothes.

The image faded away and returned to the original shot of Thrackan in the ship's control room. "That —ould be proof enough f— all that I speak the truth," Thrackan said, as another ripple of static whipped through the broadcast. "I await the answer of the Chief of State, and as Diktat of the Independent

Sector of Corellia, I call upon all Corellians to grant me their true allegiance."

The skull-and-dagger image came back up, there was another blare of martial music, and the screen went dead.

"Han—Han—he's got our children. He's got our children, and we—we *can't* do what he says. We *can't.*" Leia looked to her husband, her eyes full of tears.

"I know," said Han, the words tearing at his insides. "It wouldn't do any good, even if we tried." What good would it do, even if Leia said the words, even if she confirmed Corellian independence? At the very least, she would be driven from office, more than likely arrested on a charge of treason, and the agreement repudiated—and that would be nothing more than simple justice. It was plainly obvious that Corellia could not be allowed to break away, or else the whole New Republic might well collapse. Even a failed attempt, a failure that managed to seem noble and heroic, that looked like patriots struggling to throw off tyranny, would badly weaken the New Republic. Perhaps weaken it fatally. And how many would die in a new round of wars and rebellions? How many children of other parents would be murdered in those battles? "I know we can't," Han said, the words ashes in his mouth. "But how can we let him *have* them?"

"This is most horrifying, and most bad!" said Dracmus. "Thrackan turns even more deeply against his own blood, his own Den and clan."

Kleyvits turned toward Dracmus. "What is it you are saying, Hunchuzuc?" It was plain that "Hunchuzuc" was not meant as a compliment when it came from Kleyvits.

"Know you not, eminent Kleyvits? Thrackan Sal-Solo is of the blood of Han Solo, of Leia Organa Solo's children! Close as two clans of the same Den! He threatens his own!"

"Impossible!" Kleyvits said. "How could any being do such a thing? I am astonished! Astonished by so many things. Thrackan asks that you confirm your recognition of Corellian independence! Have you indeed recognized his claim? I do not understand, and I must."

"Thrackan Sal-Solo lied," Dracmus said, the disgust plain in her voice. "He said things that were not true, for his own gain. Half of what he said was false, or else truth phrased to make lies seem true."

"Impossible again! He said that—"

"Quiet! Both of you!" Mara shouted. "It is possible, and he has done it." She gestured with her arm to indicate Han and Leia. "He has done it to *this* man, and *this* woman, and their children. Respect their shock and sorrow. Be gone! Give them time for shock, for grief, and take your foolish debates elsewhere!"

"No!" shouted Han. All his anger at his cousin, his blazing hot fury at the villainy of his own relation, suddenly found a new target, one closer to home, one that he could strike at and do some good. Suddenly he found words that were weapons, weapons that could strike at the bumbling, seemingly reasonable, manipulative, dissembling enemy who stood before him. "Stay where you are! You, Kleyvits. How dare you sneer at Thrackan Sal-Solo, because he holds those of his blood hostage for gain? You do the same! You hold us!"

"But—but—you are not of my family, not of my blood!"

Han stabbed his finger at Dracmus and spoke. "She is of your blood, and you hold her spirit hostage by holding us, by forcing her to collaborate with you in goading us, harassing us.

"She has saved my life, and I hers. She has risked her life for mine, and I have risked mine for hers. She has vouched for me with your folk. She has granted me her protection. We have lived and fought together. No, it is not blood—but *it is family*. We have claims on each other, of duty and respect. We were allies against *you* and your Overden. Now you force her to spit on her allies, against her will, for your own amusement."

"Honored Solo, please—no more!" Dracmus said.

"There is much more, much more," Han said to Dracmus. "Your people speak the truth and have no skill in lies. Can you say, with honesty, that anything of what I say is wrong?"

Dracmus suddenly seemed smaller, sadder, pushed down. "No," she said, "I cannot."

Suddenly Han was inspired. Suddenly he had an idea, a hunch, an instinct. It might be wrong—but if it was right—if it was right, and he understood the Selonians properly . . . Yes. Yes. "Then let us have more truth," Han said. "You, Kleyvits. Speak now of your repulsor. Who operates it? Whose hand-paws are on the controls?"

Kleyvits looked suspiciously at Han. "Why, those of good Selonians, of course."

"But *whose* Selonians?" Han demanded. "Are they yours? Are they of the Overden?"

There was a moment's deadly silence, and Kleyvits stood stock-still, only her eyes moving, back and forth from Han to Dracmus. Then her whiskers twitched once, involuntarily, and the claws of her hand-paws extended just a hairbreadth before retracting. "I must say no more about that," she replied.

Han felt an angry jubilation, a moment's brutal glee. He had won. He knew it. But he could not play the next card in this hand of sabacc. Only Dracmus could turn it over. This was the crucial moment. Dracmus could choose not to hear what she had heard, or else—

"You are wrong, eminent Kleyvits," Dracmus hissed from behind clenched, fully exposed, needle-sharp teeth. "You are wrong down to the depths of your dishonored soul. You must, indeed, say more about it. You must say a great deal more."

"I—I must say no more—"

"Who?" Dracmus demanded. "Who controls the repulsor? We capitulated because you had shown your power. But the power was not yours! It is dishonor! *Who?"*

"I must say no more—"

"I will be *ANSWERED*!" bellowed Dracmus, a Dracmus who suddenly seemed the size and spirit of an enraged Wookiee. Her eyes blazed, her fur bristled. Her claws were out, her teeth were bared, and her tail-stump lashed with anger. "WHO?"

"It is—they are—they are—the—the Cast-outs. The Sacorrians. The Selonians of the Triad."

"Sweet burning stars," Mara whispered. "The Sacorrians. The Triad. I don't believe it."

The room was silent again, but the silence seemed to echo from every corner, to shout at them all, to fill the room with its deadly emptiness. "If an outworlder, a human skilled in lies, had told me such a thing, I would join with the honored Jade and refuse to believe it," Dracmus said, speaking at last, speaking in a voice as low, as quiet, as threatening and ominous as far-off thunder. "But you, a Selonian, speak the words, Kleyvits, and I am forced to believe. The words sicken me. The truth fills me with revulsion."

Kleyvits dropped to all fours and cringed at Dracmus's feet. Plainly, it was no empty ritual. It was Kleyvits submitting to Dracmus and begging for mercy. "Rise up," snarled Dracmus. "Rise up and come with me. Others must be sickened by the truth. Others must hear. And then the days of the Overden will be over."

Kleyvits got up on her hind legs and bowed deeply to Dracmus. Dracmus did not acknowledge the bow, but turned and left the room, her head held high, the humans forgotten. Kleyvits followed after her, head down, shoulders slumped, the roles of victor and vanquished utterly reversed.

And, suddenly, the humans were alone.

"I don't understand," said Han, drastically understating the case. "I had a hunch there had to be some ringers brought in. I figured it had to be outsiders who had researched its operation that were actually running the repulsor. I figured that would make Kleyvits look a little bad—but nothing like *that*. What happened?"

"I'll explain later," Mara said. "Right now, see to Leia."

Han turned toward his wife, who had sat back down in one of the splendid, luxurious chairs that filled this splendid, luxurious prison of a villa. She was sobbing quietly to herself, the tears falling quietly. "Oh, Han. Our children. That man has our children."

"I know," said Han. "I know. But he is not going to keep them. I promise you that we will get them—"

But suddenly Leia was on her feet, looking up, an eager, faraway look in her eyes, the change in her demeanor bewilderingly fast. Han exchanged a glance with Mara, and it was plain they were both wondering, for a fleeting moment, if Leia had suddenly become unhinged. But Han should have known better. Leia was made of sterner stuff than that.

"It's Luke!" she said. "Luke is coming this way. I can feel him, reaching out with the Force to me. He's homing in on me."

"How soon is he coming?" Han asked. "How fast will he—"

Han's question was answered even as it was drowned out by the roaring thunder of a fast, low-flying aircraft. The tremendous noise filled the room, rattled the windows, and knocked several knickknacks off side tables. The sound receded as suddenly as it had arrived, as Luke's X-wing buzzed the villa.

Han rushed out the open doors and saw the X-wing flying off into the distance before swinging around to make another pass.

The X-wing came in low and slow this time, circling the villa. Leia and Mara had joined Han outside, and all of them were frantically waving their arms, as if there was some mad chance that Luke would miss them, after flying in directly on top of them with pinpoint accuracy. The X-wing made one long, slow circuit around the perimeter of the villa, firing one or two bursts of turbolaser fire to encourage the guards to be on their way. The guards took very little convincing. By

the time the X-wing set down next to the *Jade's Fire,*
they were all headed straight for the nearest spot on
the horizon.

The canopy of the X-wing swung open, and Luke
climbed out as fast as he could and jumped to the
ground. He threw his arms around his sister, and then
around Han. Mara hung back from these more effusive
greetings, but at least managed a sincere-looking smile
for Luke.

"Oh, Luke, it's been so long, and so much has happened!" said Leia, giving him yet another hug.

"That it has, Leia, that it has," said Luke.

"I don't know that it's been all that much *time,*" said
Han, "but I'll go along with the part about a lot happening." The last time they had seen Luke, he was bidding them all farewell on their way to a nice, quiet
family vacation on Corellia. Han hadn't expected to
encounter anything more exciting than a walk down
memory lane, or anything more deadly than an exces-
sively dull diplomatic reception. Things had not turned
out as expected. It did *seem* a lifetime ago since they
had seen Luke, but how long had it really been? A few
weeks? A month or two, at most? The constant
changes from planet to planet, the differences in
length of day and time zone, all made it hard to keep
track. All he knew for sure was that it seemed as if
everything had been happening at once for a long, long
time.

Luke looked up from his embrace with Han and
Leia, and nodded to the other party present. "Hello,
Mara," he said. "It's good to see you."

"Good to see you too, Luke," she said, and it
seemed to Han as if the hard edge of her voice was just
a trifle softer than usual.

"I wish the occasion could be happier," Luke replied. "I saw Thrackan's broadcast. I don't know what
to say, except I'm sorry. We'll get them back, Leia. I
promise we will."

"I know we will, Luke," said Leia. "I know. But thank you."

"Look," said Mara, "no offense to anybody, but Luke's chased off all the guards. I'll bet we can crack open the force field around the *Jade's Fire* pretty quick if we tried. Shouldn't we be escaping along about now?"

Luke shook his head. "Let's get your ship clear, by all means. But I think it might be smart if you stayed right here for now. If I've got this worked out right, we're going to need a lot of help from the people who were holding you, and we'd better stay where they can find us."

"Why? What?" asked Han. "What's happened?"

"A lot," said Luke. "Most of it bad. Though *maybe* there's some good news, as well, buried underneath it all. And that's where our Selonian friends come in."

Han looked at Luke, and sighed wearily. "It never is simple, is it? Come on, kid. Let's head inside. I think it's just about time we all sat down and compared notes."

*   *   *

"Q9! Q9! Come in! Q9! Are you there?"

"Of course I am here," Q9 replied. "I'm here, right where you left me, upside down in a storage bin. Where else would I be?" The droid had grown quite tired of his hiding place, and become quite irritable as a result.

"An interesting rhetorical question," said Ebrihim, his whispered voice coming in via the droid's comlink system. "But never mind. Suffice to say that we would like you to come over here, now, if you would."

"With pleasure," replied Q9. "Or more accurately, I will take great pleasure in getting *out* of this smuggling compartment. However, I will come to you, assuming I can get to wherever it is you are being held."

"We are quite nearby, within sight of the ship."

"Very good. But let us discuss a point or two before I come. My built-in surveillance gear detected the cessation of jamming quite some time ago. It is two hours since I monitored Thrackan Sal-Solo's broadcast. Parenthetically, I must add that none of you were looking your best in that. But in any event, why have you waited until now to call me?"

"We have been waiting for the Human League troopers to go to sleep. The last of them turned in about an hour ago. It would seem they are now all quite soundly asleep, on board the assault boat."

"Why have they not posted a guard? Why are they so lax?"

Ebrihim laughed. "We are at the bottom of a sheer-sided, kilometers-deep pit; we are being held inside a force field; and of the two ships available, one is non-functional, and the other is full of enemy troops. I expect they simply felt rather secure in their situation."

"It could be a trap," said Q9. "They could be trying to lull you into a false sense of security."

"They are the ones with a false sense of security. They do not know we have a comlink, and they are unaware of your existence."

"Where did you get the comlink?" Q9 asked suspiciously. "I did not know that you had one. How do I know you are Ebrihim? How do I know you aren't a Human League agent posing as Ebrihim? How do I know this is not a trap to lure me out of my hiding place?"

Q9 could hear the sound of Ebrihim sighing wearily. "Q9, I do believe that you have developed a paranoid streak."

"You would develop one too, if your main circuits were shorted out by a maniac child, and you were barely given a chance to double-check your repairs before you were stuck in a dark hole for a day. I have been in an inverted position for all that time, wondering what could happen to me next. I have come up with quite a number of alarming possibilities."

"I see," said Ebrihim, a note of impatience creeping into his voice. "That is most unfortunate. Let me see if I can put your mind somewhat at ease. We did not tell you we had a comlink because we were somewhat pressed for time when we were captured. I myself did not learn that Chewbacca had concealed the comlink on his person until long after we were off the ship. As for the other matter, I am indeed Ebrihim. The receipt of sale shows that I paid twelve hundred and fifty Drallish crowns for you. However, in reality, at the last minute I managed to talk your owners into a discount for cash of a hundred crowns, a detail which I forgot. When I inadvertently reported the higher amount as a deduction on my taxes, you pointed out the discrepancy to me and threatened to turn me in if I did not correct it. At the time I seriously considered selling you for the eight extra crowns I was forced to pay in taxes as a result. There have been many times when I have regretted my decision to keep you instead. Does that satisfy you?"

"I suppose so," Q9 said doubtfully.

"Very good then. Now stop acting like a mentally unbalanced victim of paranoid dementia and get the blazes over here as quickly and quietly as you can. Ebrihim out!"

"No need to be so irritable about it," Q9 said to himself, knowing full well Ebrihim had shut down his comlink. "I see nothing demented in my effort to insure my own self-preservation." He paused for a moment. "On the other hand, there *is* something distinctly peculiar about a droid that has started talking to itself. Master Ebrihim may well have a point concerning my mental state. Ah, well."

Q9 gently activated his repulsors, so they pushed the camouflaged cover up off the smuggling compartment. He let the cover get about a third of a meter high, and then lowered power to the port side repulsor, causing the lid to slide down to that direction and fall to the deck with a loud clunk. It was more noise than Q9 would have preferred to have made, but he had little choice in the matter.

Q9 extruded a pair of manipulator arms and slowly pushed himself straight up out of the compartment, until his body was completely out of the hole. He rotated his body around on the ball-and-socket joints of the arms until his base was pointed straight down. Then he activated his repulsors again and drew the two arms back into his body. It was a distinct relief to be right side up again, and out of that hole.

Q9 floated around the *Falcon*'s circumferential corridor until he came to the access ramp. The ramp was open and down, which saved him the trouble of opening it himself, and saved that much more noise as well. However it did represent lax enough security that Q9 could not help but worry anew that it was all an elaborate trap.

But if it was, he had already revealed his position, and he was as good as caught, anyway. He might as well press on. He moved down the ramp and out onto the wide expanses of the repulsor chamber's interior.

It was dark, the chamber lit only by the dimmest of starlight. Q9 switched over to infrared, and suddenly the chamber was ablaze with illumination. He moved forward about thirty meters from the *Falcon*, and then stopped. He spun his upper dome in a complete circle, scanning the interior. As Ebrihim had promised, the prisoners were indeed easy to spot. Six warm bodies inside a force field were a fairly obvious target. Obvious enough that Q9 was not exactly thrilled to be moving toward it. He consoled himself with the notion that he himself was probably a first-rate target in infrared anyway. He completed his scan, and got a good range and bearing on the assault boat as well. Just as well to keep a sensor pointed in that direction.

Q9 floated briskly toward the force field containment and came to a stop precisely one meter from its perimeter. "I'm here," he said. "Now what do you want?"

It was not easy to judge Drallish expressions in infra-red, but it would seem that Ebrihim was glaring at him. "Most beings would find that obvious," he said. "I want you to get us out of here!"

"Of course," said Q9. "To pose a rhetorical question, what else would you want?" Q9 rotated his view dome left and then right. "Any suggestions on how I might accomplish that?"

"Around the other side," Ebrihim said. "The control panel for the containment is on the children's side of the dome."

"Ah. So it is," Q9 said, realizing that he was suddenly feeling quite cheerful. He floated briskly around to the other side of the containment, and saw the control panel on the outside, and the children on the inside, watching him. "Good evening, children," he said, in a most lighhearted tone of voice. "How are all of you this evening?" He bobbled up and down on his repulsor, in rough imitation of a little bow.

Anakin regarded him gravely for a moment or two, and then turned to his brother and sister. "Q9 is acting weird," he announced.

"Am I?" Q9 asked. "A moment please, while I run a behavioral diagnostic." Q9 activated the appropriate routines and ran them against his action log for the past hour. "You're quite right, young Anakin. I *am* behaving somewhat erratically. It might well have something to do with being roasted alive and being stuck in a storage bin for hours on end, but that's all as may be. We're all friends here. In any event, rest assured that my actions and reactions are still within acceptable limits. Quite so."

"It is one of the flaws of the Q9-series design," Ebrihim said, speaking to the children in a quiet voice from the far side of the vertical wall that divided the containment. "At times, they do not respond well to periods of extended stress."

"But then, who does?" Q9 asked.

"He may exhibit fairly drastic mood swings for a

time, but he should settle down after a while," Ebrihim said. "We'll just have to deal with him as he is for the time being."

"Great," said Jacen. "We're counting on a manic-depressive droid to break us out of here."

"And break you out I shall," said Q9. "Just tell me how." He spun his view dome about to check again on the assault boat, and then spun it back, a bit abruptly. "But be quick about it, before the guards have a chance to awaken."

"Yeah," said Jacen. "Right. Anakin is the one to ask."

"Ah, yes," Q9 said. "Anakin, master of all machines. Just tell me what to do, and I shall do it. So long as pushing the wrong button doesn't drop the planet into the sun, or any such trivial inconvenience."

"Q9," said Ebrihim. "You must control yourself. Settle down. It is most important."

"My apologies," said Q9. Strange how they were all fussing over him now, when most of the time they barely gave him a moment's notice. That is, when they weren't actively *against* him. "Interesting," he said. "I already seem to be slipping back into a depressive paranoid phase."

"Just—just try and keep your thoughts ordered and balanced," Ebrihim said soothingly. "Anakin, get him started."

"Ah, okay," Anakin said. "The control panel's turned away from us, but I think there's a big slot for a sort of metal key right in the middle of it. Can you see it?"

"How did you know that was there if you can't see it?" Q9 asked suspiciously.

"I saw the other guy using it," Anakin said, glancing toward Jacen a little doubtfully. "It's there, right?"

"Yes, it is."

"Ebrihim said that sometimes you can use your manipulator arms to pick locks and stuff. Do you think you could pick that one?"

Q9 extruded a close-up view cam on the end of a flexible arm. It carried a small illuminator light at its end, right next to the cable. He switched on the illuminator and brought the cam to bear on the lock. He examined it carefully, from several angles, then turned off the illuminator and retracted the close-up cam. "No," he said.

"Oh," Anakin said. "That's not good."

"Is that it?" Q9 asked. "Can I go now?"

"No!" Anakin said. He shut his eyes and extended his hand out toward the control panel. "I can *almost* do it, but I can't *see* the controls the way I can see the inside." He shook his head and opened his eyes. "Read me what the labels say. Read me all the buttons and switches."

Q9 extruded the close-up cam again and turned on the illuminator to examine the display. "It is a most archaic system of controls," he said. "The first dial is labeled MAIN POWER SELECT—that's the one with the lock on it. The selector can be set to OFF, SINGLE CONTAINMENT, DOUBLE CONTAINMENT, or QUAD CONTAINMENT. It is set to DOUBLE. Below that is a dial marked OVERALL INTENSITY. It is marked off from one to eleven, and is set to eight point five."

"Twist that one down as far as it will go," Anakin said.

Q9 extruded a manipulator arm and twisted the dial to the left as far as he could. "It will not turn any lower than the point marked two. I would conjecture that it cannot be turned lower without the key."

"Right, right," said Anakin. The boy reached out his hand and probed cautiously at the force field. He seemed to be able to push his hand slowly into it, but only by a few centimeters. "No, no," said Anakin. "Still too strong. Read me the other controls," he said.

"There are three dials. The first is lit up. It reads DOUBLE CONTAINMENT LEFT SIDE RELATIVE INTENSITY. The dial is marked from one to eleven, with the dial set at the center point, six. The other two dials appear to control quad mode settings. As we are clearly in double mode, the quad settings are not of any consequence."

"Twist the double level to one side as far as it will go."

Q9 did so, and the force field forming the children's containment promptly darkened, so much that the effect was plainly visible even in the near darkness of the repulsor chamber.

"Turn it the other way," Anakin said.

Q9 did so, and the field faded away again, until it was completely invisible, even in infrared. Anakin pushed at the field again, and it gave a bit more this time—but even pushing as hard as he could, he could not get out.

"Any more controls on that thing?" Anakin asked.

"That is all," Q9 replied.

"Thought so," Anakin said. "Couldn't feel anything else."

"Then why did you ask me?"

"Because I wanted to be sure!" Anakin said. "Don't act so weird, okay?"

"Am I still behaving strangely?" Q9 asked. "Or do you just want me to *think* I'm behaving strangely? Is *that* your plan?"

"Q9, we don't have time for this," said Jacen. "Later. Whatever it is you're doing, do it later. All right?"

Q9 looked at him suspiciously. "I am not 'doing' anything besides following orders."

"Never mind," Anakin said. "Q9—is it all as low as it can go? So it makes the field as weak this side as it can be?"

"As low as it can go without the key, yes."

"All right," said Anakin. "Hope it's good enough. Here goes." He extended his arms in front of him and spread out his stubby fingers as far as they would go. He shut his eyes and stepped forward, until his hands were in contact with the force field. "Gotta move slowly," he reminded himself.

Pushing slowly, gently, he thrust his hand deeper and deeper into the weakened force field. The field around his hands began to shimmer and spark, brightly at first, but then fading away, until Anakin was standing in a pushed-out bubble of the force field, a bubble that was marked by dim, shimmering flickers of power. Anakin pushed farther on, but seemed unable to make further progress. "Help me," he said to his brother and sister.

Jacen and Jaina stepped cautiously forward into the extruded bubble of the force field. Jacen shut his eyes and stretched out his hands. He frowned and shook his head. "I don't see what you are— Oh, I get it." He pushed out his hands farther, and Jaina did the same. The bubble lit up again with shimmers and sparks that did not light up quite as much as they did the first time, and that faded away more quickly and more completely.

"Try again, Anakin," said Jaina.

Anakin pushed on the force field with just his left hand this time, with slow, steady pressure that stretched the field farther and farther. And then, moving quite slowly and gently, he bunched up his fingers into a fist and extended just his index finger. He pushed forward with his finger, stretching the field farther and farther until, at some gradual and indefinable moment, the tip of his finger was through and outside the field, on the other side. "Jacen, take my hand," said Anakin. "Jaina, take his."

Jacen grabbed his brother's right hand in his left, and Jaina took Jacen's right in her own left hand. Anakin pressed onward, until his whole finger, his whole arm, his shoulder, his head, his chest, were through. He leaned forward, pushing slowly, steadily forward. He lifted his left leg up, forcing it gently up and through the field. The field sparked and shimmered for a moment as his leg slipped clear of it and he set it down on the outside. His right leg seemed to move through more easily.

And then, but for his right arm, he was through, and on the outside. He kept moving forward, very slowly, leaning forward as he pulled, dragging his brother's arm out through the field. The field sparked and shimmered with greater violence when Jacen's hand touched it. Jacen winced, and almost flinched backward. There was the crackle and spark of static electricity as his hand moved forward through the field. It was as if the field was resisting him more than his brother, and it was plain to see from the expression on his face that it was far from a pleasant sensation. The field seemed reluctant to let his head come through, and sparks and fire flickered about his face. His head broke through quite abruptly, and he let out a little grunt of pain as it did. His hair sprang straight out from his head, alive with static electricity, something that had not happened to Anakin. The sparks flared and flickered about him as he forced one leg and then the other through the field.

Jacen gasped with relief as his body broke free of the field. Anakin still held his left hand, and the two boys moved slowly out from the field as Jacen pulled Jaina's hand through the field. Sparks shimmered again, but in a deeper, duller, angry color. "Ow!" Jaina said. "It's—it's like fire."

"Just keep coming," Jacen said. "Your hand is free of the field. Keep your eyes shut. It's easier that way, believe me. Keep coming. Keep coming. There's your arm free. Here comes your head. Hang on! Hang on! Almost free. All right, your face is clear. That's the worst part. You should see your hair! No, don't open your eyes yet, but it's sticking straight up from your head. Good. Good. Now push your leg through. Steady. Easy does it. Good. Good. Now the other one. Up, over, through. Good. Just the foot to come—whoops!"

Jaina tumbled down onto her brother as she broke free of the field, and Jacen went down, taking Anakin with him. The stretched-out part of the force field shimmered and sparked one last time, and then retracted, shrank, pulled back, merging smoothly back into the rest of the field, as if there had never been such a thing as a distortion in the field's surface.

"Boy, that hurt," Jaina said. "Like getting a shock all over my body."

"I think it was worse for you than me," Jacen said as the three children disentangled themselves from each other and helped each other up. "Did it hurt you at all, Anakin?" he asked his brother.

Anakin shook his head. "Nope. It sort of *tickled* a little bit. Well, it didn't feel nice like tickling, but sort of like that."

"That was impossible, of course," said Q9. "What you just did was quite impossible. No one can walk through a force field that way."

"We didn't go through it, really," Anakin said. "It was more like we went *between* it. Stretched it out until there was room *between* the field, sort of. Then I just pushed the parts apart, and went through. That's all."

"Ah. That's all. Thank you. That makes it all *quite* clear, I assure you."

"Anakin—what about Chewbacca and Ebrihim and Aunt Marcha?" asked Jaina.

Anakin shook his head. "I don't think I can do it from this side," he said. "Not to pull people through. It's harder to do, the bigger and heavier you are."

"Can you do anything with the control panel?" Jaina asked.

Anakin went over and looked at the panel, put his hand over it, and shut his eyes. He concentrated, focusing his attention deep inside the device. At last he took his hand off and opened his eyes. "No," he said.

"But you can make all sorts of machines do whatever you want," Jaina protested.

"Yeah, but that's easy," Anakin said. "Real *little* stuff I can move around. I can make stuff do what it's supposed to do. But the lock insides are too big. And the lock's *doing* what it's supposed to do. It's already working."

"I couldn't ask for a clearer explanation," said Q9. "But I take it you can't get the others out?"

"No," said Anakin. "Not without the key."

"I see you had this all carefully planned out in advance," Q9 observed.

"The plan was that *you* would be able to pick the lock," Ebrihim said, rather severely. "But that is all to one side. If we indeed cannot get out, obviously the children must attempt to escape on their own. With your help, of course, Q9."

"What?" Q9 asked. "How? How are we supposed to get away?"

"By flying away in the *Millennium Falcon,* of course."

"Wait a second," said Jacen. "You want *us* to fly the *Falcon*?"

Chewbacca looked at Ebrihim, made a yawping sound, and then bared his teeth and shook his head.

"I agree that it is foolhardy and dangerous," Ebrihim said to Chewbacca. He turned to the three children. "But it is nonetheless the best of many bad choices. Chewbacca, you yourself said the repairs to the *Falcon* were all but complete. I feel quite certain that you would have no trouble explaining to the children what still needs to be done. And I have no doubt at all they could perform the repairs.

"As for the rest of it, we three in here have far, far less value as hostages, and Thrackan knows it. The three jewels are already outside this force field stockade. Anakin, Jacen, Jaina—the danger would be great if you tried to escape on your own. But I sincerely believe that the danger to you, and to ourselves, and to others, would be much less than if you stayed.

Thrackan is a cruel and heartless man, and I do not wish you in his clutches. As I see it, there are only two possibilities. The first is that your mother goes along with what he tells her to do."

"She'd never do that," Jacen said.

"I quite agree. But if she did, I believe your uncle would decide you were too valuable to give up. He would keep you, in hopes of extracting further concessions. And every time she gave in, he would have more reason to hold on to you. I believe you would be permanent prisoners."

"And if Mom did give in to him because of us, a lot of other people would get hurt," said Jaina.

"And killed," added Jacen.

"Precisely. The second, more likely possibility is that your mother would refuse his demands. She would do so fully knowing the consequences, and it would break her heart. But she would refuse him, all the same. Sooner or later, your cousin Thrackan would either become so angry and frustrated that he would take it all out on you—or else he would threaten to torture you, or actually do so, in order to get what he wanted out of your mother."

"Torture?" Jaina said. "I hadn't thought of that."

"Would he really?" Jacen asked.

"I think it quite possible. Even likely."

Q9 looked from his master to the children, and back again. There was something unstated here, something he nearly said himself, before thinking better of it. No one was saying that it would be better for the children to have a clean, quick death in a crash rather than be the unwilling pawns in a cruel game. A cruel game where many others would suffer, a game that could only end with the pawns being destroyed at the exact moment it suited their master. How noble, how brave of them all to say nothing at all about it. How odd that he, Q9, was having such peculiar and emotional reactions to everything. Just that moment a new and terrifying thought crossed his mind. "Half a moment," he said. "What about me?"

Ebrihim looked toward Q9 and chuckled to himself. "Oh, you'll go with them, of course. What else could you do? What, exactly, do you expect Thrackan Sal-Solo would do to you if he woke up in the morning to find the chidren gone and you here?"

Q9 thought that one through, and did not care one little bit for the conclusions he reached. "I might have known," he said. "It's clear now that it's *all* been a plot against me."

"It seems to me there are other beings worse off than you in all this," Ebrihim said. "But never mind that. Go, and go now. The longer you delay, the greater the dangers will be."

"But we don't know what's wrong with the ship, and we don't know how to fix it," Jaina protested.

Ebrihim held up his hand with the comlink in it. "We have this comlink in here, and you children can use Q9's built-in comlink to communicate with us until you re-establish the link to the *Falcon*'s comm system. I'll have the comlink. Chewbacca can tell me what to do, and I'll tell you. We'll walk you through it. You can do it."

Chewbacca nodded his agreement, and made an encouraging little burbling snarl.

"It's nice for you to say," said Jaina to Ebrihim, "but that doesn't mean you're right."

"I'm sure you can do it. Now you must go," said Ebrihim. "The guards could awaken at any moment. We have no choice in the matter. Go!"

The three children looked at each other for a moment, and then, moving as one, they turned and headed for the ship, leaving so suddenly and quietly that Q9 was taken by surprise. He hovered, motionless for a moment, before he swiveled his view dome about and realized they were gone.

He raised himself up on his repulsors and took off after them.

* * *

Admiral Ossilege himself met the *Lady Luck* when she landed on the hangar deck of the *Intruder*. He waited, resplendent in his customary dress-white uniform, and watched as the *Lady*'s hatch swung open. "Greetings to you all," he said as Lando, Gaeriel, and Kalenda disembarked, Threepio following behind. "I trust your information is as interesting as you promise. I find it most ironic that the moment we are at long last able to speak over the comlinks, we must worry about being overheard."

"I think you'll agree that it's all worth hearing—and that it's worth being sure we keep it to ourselves," Lando said. "Let's get to someplace where we can talk."

"Of course," said the admiral. "We shall go to my private quarters. He glared at Threepio. "*That* can stay aboard your ship, I think," he said to Lando."

"Well, really, how inconsiderate—" Threepio began, but Ossilege frowned fiercely enough to silence him.

"The rest of you, come this way." Lando glanced toward Kalenda, but she just shook her head. No doubt the same thought had crossed her mind. The admiral spent so much of his time on the bridge, it had never occurred to either of them that he even *had* quarters.

But he did have them, and he led the group to them in short order. Lando had always prided himself on a sense of design, a knack for knowing what looked right. It was instantly plain to his practiced eye that Ossilege's stateroom suite was a jarring display of opposites—the opulent up against the spartan, the huge and magnificent against the small and thrifty.

The room itself was spectacular—the cream-colored walls and deep blue carpets, the sheer size of it, twice the size of any other stateroom on the ship. A huge circular viewport, two meters across, took up most of one bulkhead, and out of it Lando could see a breathtaking view of Drall framed against the night sky. The indirect lighting was warm and even, coming from every side so that it was impossible to cast a shadow in the room.

The personal appointments to the room, on the other hand, were barely there at all. A camp cot sat in one corner, with a fold-up night table by its side. The cot was made up with sharp-edged precision, the pillow plumped up and set precisely in the centerline of the bed, exactly over the point where the covers and sheet were perfectly folded back. Somehow, the perfection of it all told Lando that Hortel Ossilege made his own bed in the morning, despite any number of valet droids and human servants. He was not the sort of person who would trust anyone else to make his bed properly. There was an alarm clock, a portable comm unit, and a reading light on the night table, and a single, largish book as well. Whether the volume was a novel of some sort, a weighty historical tome, a Bakuran religious text, or the Bakuran Navy regulation book, Lando could not tell.

There were absolutely no other personal items at all in the room. Whatever else he did own was presumably hidden away behind the closet doors. In the far corner near the door was a spartan, utilitarian desk with a small, neat stack of work waiting for the admiral on one side, and a much larger, but equally neat stack of work already done on the other. There were a few writing instruments lined up neatly to one side of the desk, a desk lamp, a datapad, and another comm set. Nothing else. The desk was positioned so that when the admiral sat behind it, as he did now, the splendid viewport was behind him. That was the sum total of furnishings in the room. Indeed, there were no other chairs in the room beside the one behind the desk, but even as Lando was noticing this, a gunmetal-gray service droid trundled into the room, carrying three folding chairs on its back. It set the chairs in front of the desk with surprising speed and efficiency, and then was gone.

The three visitors sat down facing the desk, and Ossilege stared at them expectantly. "Tell me," he said, "all about Centerpoint."

Lieutenant Kalenda cleared her throat and spoke, a bit nervously. "The long and the short of it is that Centerpoint is the starbuster. It is the device used to make stars go nova."

"I see," said Ossilege, in about the same tone of voice he would have taken if Kalenda had just told him the evening dinner menu.

"And we also are pretty sure that the planetary repulsors are the way to shut Centerpoint down."

"Indeed?" he asked in the same calm tone. "Most interesting. Perhaps," he said, "you could provide me with a few details."

CHAPTER TWELVE

Incoming

The alarm buzzer squawked wildly in the tiny sleeping cabin of the *Gentleman Caller.* Tendra Risant leapt up out of bed, her heart pounding. She scrambled to her feet, getting herself entangled in the sheets and nearly falling flat on her face before she got herself sorted out and headed for the control room.

She didn't recognize the alarm. What in the burning suns had broken down this time? She reached the control room and checked all the displays, but saw nothing but a green board.

Then she woke up the rest of the way and remembered. She had installed this alarm herself. The one that went off when the *Gentleman Caller*'s navicomputer detected the interdiction field going down.

The interdiction field going down! Suddenly her mind was racing. One part of her was suddenly afraid. The field coming down could mean any number of things, many of them not good. But all that was beyond her control. Later she could let her imagination run wild, let herself speculate about what it all meant. Right now the field coming down meant exactly one thing. She could get moving at last. She scrambled into the pilot's seat and set to work.

Tendra had had very little practice with navicomputers before boarding the *Gentleman Caller,* but she certainly had plenty of time to practice with the one on the ship since then. Working as fast as she could, she set up the problem, getting a fix on her present location and a precise grid reference on her intended target point, letting the navicomputer massage the numbers and come up with the proper values for the jump in and out of hyperspace that would get her there.

She knew where she was well enough—she had had plenty of time to practice finding that out too—but the question of where to go she had never quite decided. It had seemed simpler to keep the navicomputer updated with all the potential destinations, so that she could decide at the last minute if there was a change in the situation. Except, now, it was time to make a decision, and she was far from decided.

But she had to move fast. Whoever controlled the interdiction field might well be able to bring it back up again at any time. She dithered for a moment longer, and then made up her mind. Centerpoint. She would go to Centerpoint. The last she had heard from Lando, it had seemed he was heading that way. She suspected that meant very little when dealing with Lando, or in time of war, let alone both, but she had to choose someplace. She punched in the proper settings and flipped the navicomputer over to automatic operation. The display came on, showing a thirty-second countdown clock. The clock started moving, and the seconds melted away.

For half a moment Tendra considered the idea of getting set to jump to hyperspace on manual if the automatics failed. That was the way the heroes always did it in the holovids, after all. But no. The holovid heroes were always seasoned pilots of the spaceways, or else they were the most naturally gifted pilots the galaxy had ever seen. Besides, they were always backed up by that most powerful of allies—cooperative scriptwriters. Life didn't work that way. She couldn't count on it all turning out right by the last scene.

Besides, this was exactly the second time she had ever flown a hyperspace jump. If something went wrong with the automatics, and they decided to shut down rather than proceed, it would be prudent of her to take their word for it. Better to sit out here for another month or two, going half mad with boredom, rather than have the hyperspace motors blow up under her or kick her out into the far side of the galaxy.

She checked the countdown clock. Fifteen seconds. It had been a hell of a long ride so far, and even if this worked, and she got into the Corellian system, even if her navicomputer was dead-on and she arrived right at Centerpoint's main docking collar, there were no guarantees that this ride was over quite yet.

Ten seconds. And what about Lando? Was he all right? Was he anywhere remotely near Centerpoint? Would she even be able to find him? It was the middle of a war, after all. Things were not likely to be all that well organized.

Five seconds. What was she doing here, anyway? Why had she climbed into an overpriced secondhand starship to go chasing after some smooth-talking ladies' man she had met exactly once? She had always thought of herself as a levelheaded sort of person. Right now the evidence was strictly to the contrary.

Three seconds. This was crazy. She was about to jump into a war zone. She ought to abort the jump to light speed, reverse course, and head back home to Sacorria, where it was safe.

Two seconds. No. Too late for that. If she did, she would spend the rest of her life wondering what if.

One second. Instead, she was about to find out.

Zero. The cockpit viewport exploded into life as the sky filled with starlines, and the *Gentleman Caller* made the big jump to light speed.

Suddenly Tendra Risant didn't have the time to worry about anything at all.

*   *   *

Ossilege stood up from behind his desk, turned, and paced the room thoughtfully. He paused in front of the viewport, and now gave a long, hard look at the planet Drall.

He had no interest when it was just a lovely sight, thought Lando. *Now that it has great military significance, though—now he wants to take a look at it.*

"So if I understand you correctly," he said, turning to face the others, "the planetary repulsors are of far greater significance than we thought. If we possessed one in time to deflect the hyperspace tractor-repulsor shot from Centerpoint—then that would save all the good people of Bovo Yagen—and perhaps, just incidentally, win us the war. Do I have that about right?"

"Just about right, sir," said Lieutenant Kalenda. "However, it is more than a question of possessing the repulsor. It is knowing how to use it. And I'm not entirely sure Thrackan Sal-Solo is able to control it."

"But they fired it already."

"Not really, sir. It was an—an uncontrolled start-up. There was a massive burst of unregulated repulsor radiation, that's all. The Selonian repulsor shot was much more controlled. And there's another reason. Remember his assault boat went into the repulsor after it was fired. We're only *assuming* it was his techs who fired it."

"After seeing that broadcast he made, I'll tell you who I think set it off," said Lando.

"And who might that be?" Ossilege said, smiling coldly, indulgently. An expression that said he had already rejected whatever Lando was about to say.

"The children," Lando said. "I think they managed to turn it on by accident. The repulsor burst attracted Thrackan's attention, the same as it did yours, and he got there first."

"Don't be absurd," Ossilege said, all but openly sneering. "How could children activate a planetary repulsor?"

"I don't know. It's possible Chewbacca did, but I doubt he would be so careless as to allow an uncontrolled burst like that. Maybe the two Drall did it. But someone in that group is the one who pushed the button."

"I doubt it. I believe it was some of Sal-Solo's people who activated the repulsor, an advance team if you will. I believe they somehow captured the children whilst in the process of searching for the repulsor. But all this is beside the point. Sal-Solo has the repulsor now. And I have a marine assault force preparing to go in and take it from him. It is just before local dawn at the repulsor site now. The marines plan to go in just after sunset tonight—though I may push that forward if circumstances merit. They are holding tactical exercises and running simulations right now."

"Why not go in now?" Lando asked.

"I asked Commander Putney, the assault troops' commanding officer, that same question, some hours ago. I assure you Putney is feeling as much anxiety as you to go at once, but it's not that simple. The main problem is that, as per my orders, their assault boats were combat-loaded for a prolonged exploratory sortie onto Centerpoint, in case that proved necessary. That is a wholly different mission than a quick-strike attack against a small force in a fixed position. It simply takes time to unload the boats from one mission profile and repack for another. There are other factors. The marine commander believes that going in during darkness will be to their advantage. He has also worked out the relative time zones, and the effects of changes in local time and duration of day. He calculates that the Corellians in the repulsor will be at their most tired, their most sleep-deprived, just about at local sunset this evening. Suffice to say that although you and I are actually in agreement on this point, and wish the attack to happen sooner, there are cogent reasons for the delay. The risks are obvious—but I believe that once all the factors are weighed, our best chance for success is to wait."

"And you're either right, or you're wrong, with no way to know for sure until it's too late. Then you're a genius for guessing right, or a monster and a fool for guessing wrong. I don't envy you that sort of decision, Admiral. They stuck me with a generalship once, a long time ago," said Lando. "I didn't care for it. Mostly because of decisions just like this one. You have my sympathy."

"Thank you, Captain Calrissian. Given our past differences, that was most generous of you to say."

"Believe me, every word was sincere. But we haven't touched the main question. Do any of you believe that our friend down there, the very high and mighty Thrackan Sal-Solo, is now able to operate that repulsor? Or, if not, will he be able to soon?"

"Hard to tell, really," said Kalenda. "My working theory is that the outside force running this thing sent in technical teams, intending to have their own people control the repulsors and not trusting to the locals. Sal-Solo would have been given enough techs to cover one repulsor. Has he kept those techs home, or has he brought them along? How good are they? Do they know what they are doing? What sort of shape is the repulsor in? Was it damaged by the uncontrolled start-up?" Kalenda shook her head. "There are too many variables."

"Hmmph. Someday, an intelligence officer will answer a question with an answer, instead of a new collection of questions. The Selonian repulsor is up and running. The Drall repulsor is a question mark. What about the Corellian one, or the units on Talus and Tralus?"

Kalenda shook her head. "We have no indication that they are functional. But that doesn't mean a thing. That they haven't been used might mean they haven't been found yet, or that the technicians have their finger on the button, just waiting for their big moment."

"Murk and muddle," Ossilege said. "All of it murk and muddle. Nothing clear, nothing absolute, no one clear enemy you can point your finger at and say it's him! Attack! What do you make of it, Madame Prime Minister? You have sat there, quite silent, for a while now."

Gaeriel leaned back in her seat and crossed her arms thoughtfully. "You have pointed your finger square at the chief difficulty. There are too many enemies, and they are too vague, too uncertain, too diffuse. I think that is part of a deliberate tactic. It is meant to confuse us, distract us, get us looking in all the wrong directions. And, I am afraid, it has worked. We have heard so many conflicting stories, dealt with so many contradictory claims, that we no longer know what is real. All I know for sure is that we have not met the real enemy yet. I no longer believe the rebellions have any reality. The rebel groups are essentially fakes, all of them. Some are wholly artificial, and some are tiny little splinter groups, fringe organizations that the real outside force has pumped up with money and support. The partial exception is the Human League. It was a real organization— but it got financed by the same outsiders as the rest of the rebels. And I feel quite confident that the Human League is now as much in rebellion against its paymasters as it is against us. The outsiders, the external enemy, set all this in motion in order to grab the Corellian Sector and damage the New Republic. But the Human League and Thrackan Sal-Solo have decided to grab Corellia for themselves.

"We haven't seen the real enemy yet. We've only seen their frontmen, their stooges, their stand-ins. But I think that the end of the communications blackout means that we are going to meet the real enemy, and very soon."

There was a discreet bleep from the intercom set on the desk. Ossilege turned and walked back to the desk. "Yes, what is it?" he asked.

"Sir," said a voice on the comm unit, "we've just

detected the interdiction field coming down. It is fading away very rapidly, and is already below the threshold to permit hyperspace travel."

"Is it indeed? Then I think we can assume someone or other is about to do some hyperspace travel. All stations on all ships to standby alert. I want the detection officers sharp."

"Yes, sir. Sir, there is another matter. The moment the field came down, we received another communication from Source A. He is on the—"

"One moment." Ossilege stabbed a button down on the comm, cutting off the speaker. He picked up the comm's handset. *Rare to see a handset,* thought Lando. *Even rarer to see one used.* Most people were glad to talk to the empty air with their hands free, rather than holding a hunk of plastic to the side of their head and talking into it. But handsets had the great advantage of keeping those nearby from hearing the conversation. And Ossilege had clearly never been one for letting anyone know anything unless they needed to know it. "All right, go ahead." Ossilege listened. "Is he indeed? By all means, put him through. No, no, voice only is fine. But one moment please." Ossilege put his hand over the handset's speaker. "My apologies to you all. If I had not promised otherwise, I would gladly include you all in this. But I gave my word to keep discussions with—ah—this source—private."

Gaeriel stood up, and Lando and Kalenda took their cue from her. "Of course, Admiral. We understand. Your word must be your bond."

"Thank you for your understanding, Madame Prime Minister. Lieutenant Kalenda, Captain Calrissian. We will continue this discussion later."

* * *

"I wish I could head up to the bridge and watch the show," said Lando as the three of them stepped out into the corridor.

"Why can't you? In fact, I think I'll go myself," said Gaeriel.

"Well, uh, yeah, but you're an ex-Prime Minister and the plenipotentiary and all that," said Lando, a bit hurriedly. "You're a very official person. I'm just some guy who's along for the ride."

"Lieutenant Kalenda?" Gaeriel asked. "Are you coming?"

"No, ma'am. Not just now."

"I see," said Gaeriel, though it was clear she did not. "I seem to be missing something. I should think you'd both be most eager to get up there and see what's going on."

"Well, yes, we are," Lando admitted. "But the last thing a bridge crew needs during a crisis is off-duty personnel playing tourist," *or uninvited high-ranking guests breathing down their necks and jiggling their elbows,* he thought, though he never would dare say such a thing to her out loud.

"I see," said Gaeriel. "I expect that military etiquette would preclude my going as well, wouldn't it?"

The woman was sharp. You had to give her that much. "Ah, well, yes, ma'am."

"In that case, to hell with military etiquette. I will go to the flag deck, which is designed with the purpose of letting those in it observe without interfering. I will not bother anyone. I will not get it into my head to start issuing freelance orders. But I am going up there to see what is going on."

"My, my apologies, Gaeriel—ma'am, Madame Prime Minister. I meant no offense," Lando said. *At least not so much that you need to bite my head off.*

Gaeriel Captison sighed wearily. "And none taken," she said. "My apologies to you. That was uncalled for on my part. But, by all that's sacred, this is my mission. I'm the reason this ship is here. Luke Skywalker came to me and asked me for help, and I got it for him. And my government named me as plenipotentiary, empowered to make all decisions in its name. I am entitled, I am honor-bound, to see everything, know everything, before I make those decisions. But they all coddle me here, insulate me, keep all the awkward facts and unimportant details away from me. It was a relief to go to Centerpoint and nearly die of smoke inhalation. At least I was doing something. And now Centerpoint is going to incinerate another star in three days time, and the interdiction field has just dropped, and the devils of dark space alone know what that means, and I'm supposed to just go to my cabin and sit quietly in polite ignorance because going to the flag deck isn't the done thing?"

"You've got a point," said Lando.

"And you two should see it all too, but you're not going to, because it would be rude?"

"Yes, ma'am. It sounds ridiculous, but—"

"It sounds ridiculous because it is ridiculous," Gaeriel said. She looked from Lando to Kalenda and back again. "I order you to accompany me to the flag deck, right now."

Lando glanced at Kalenda. He was just about certain that Gaeriel Captison had no legal authority under any interpretation of space law at all, to issue him an order, and he was only slightly less sure that she had no right to issue orders to Kalenda, either. But who was going to tell that to an ex-Prime Minister and plenipotentiary? "Very well, Madame Prime Minister," he said. "If you insist."

Gaeriel grinned. "Oh, I do, I do," she said. "So let's get going," she said, and led the way.

Kalenda and Lando followed, and they let her get a few steps ahead, and then a few steps more. Once she was safely out of earshot, Lando leaned over toward Kalenda and spoke in a low voice. "Well, I put my foot in it that time," he said.

"That you did," Kalenda said, her voice just as low. "But on the bright side, at least we get to see what in blazes is going on out there."

"Sounds good to me."

"On another subject," Kalenda whispered, "do you have any idea what that Source A business is about?"

What indeed, Lando thought. There was something about the idea of a casual question from an intelligence officer that didn't quite ring true with Lando. She was not the sort of person who ever asked questions without a reason. Was it a trick question? Was she trying to see if he knew more than he should? Or did she just see him as a good analyst, a good guesser, a good source for informed speculation? Or was she just making conversation while he was getting paranoid?

Not that it mattered what she was or was not after— Lando had no information. He had a guess or two, but that didn't count. The second he had heard the words "Source A," he had immediately thought of the brilliantly original idea of calling Tendra Risant Source T. That brought an immediate idea to mind as to who Source A might be. But he knew better than to stick his neck out. "You're the intell officer," he said, "your guess is as good as mine. Probably better."

"Oh, come on. You can do better than that."

"Okay, okay, I do have a guess or two, I admit it. I just think I'd like to keep them to myself. Even I don't quite believe them."

Kalenda laughed. "Fair enough," she said. "But I've got a feeling I have the same idea you do. Come on, let's hurry and catch her up, before she has us thrown in the brig for disobeying a direct order."

*   *   *

Tendra Risant figured she had to be the first one in. She had to be. It didn't take much of a guess to figure that whoever had dropped the field had done it to jump their own ships in, or that the ships would be at the ready. But even so, she would get there first. The *Gentleman Caller* was old and slow, to be sure, but how many other inbound ships were there likely to be inside the interdiction field?

It was not until after the automatics activated the hyperspace drive that it dawned on her that being first might not be the best idea when jumping into a war zone. After all, she knew for a fact that there were warships waiting in-system, at least some of them in the vicinity of Centerpoint—the spot she was headed for. The crews of those ships would be able to detect the interdiction field going down every bit as well as Tendra could—better, in fact. And they would know that meant ships—warships, enemy warships—coming in. So the incoming ships would be on alert, because the Bakuran ships would be on alert, with their weapons at the ready—in short, a fearful muddle of everyone on alert.

And she would get there first. All of a sudden, that didn't feel like anything to be quite so pleased about.

For fleeting seconds Tendra considered aborting the run and bailing out of hyperspace early. But if she knew two things for sure, one was that she was not a particularly skilled or practiced pilot, and the second was that, lacking skill or practice, the odds on surviving an uncalculated jump out of hyperspace were near zero.

Besides, she didn't have much more than fleeting seconds to think about it. The hop she was making was not long at all. In fact, the navicomputer was already counting down the final few seconds before the drop back into real space. There was little Tendra could do besides check her seat restraint and instrument display, and hang on for the end of the ride.

The navicomputer counted down to zero, and suddenly the viewport was a blaze of light once again, the starlines flaring down into the all-but-unchanged stars of the Corellian system.

The stars were the same, but not the rest of the sky. There, dead ahead, was the heart-stoppingly lovely sight of the Double Worlds, two blue, white, and green globes seen in quarter phase, their cloud tops and oceans and continents bright and clear and beautiful.

And there, directly and exactly between them, the strange shape of Centerpoint, a white-gray sphere with a fat cylinder stuck on each end. Her destination was in sight.

Tendra all but sobbed in relief. She had made it. She had made it. After all the endless days and weeks, time that seemed as long as months or years, she was no longer alone, cut off from the outside universe. She was here. And soon she would be able to get off this damned ship, stretch her legs a bit on something besides one little bit of ship corridor, eat something besides—

"Unidentified ship! This is the Bakuran destroyer *Sentinel*. Respond at once or be fired upon!"

Tendra would have jumped right through the viewport if her seat restraints hadn't held her down. It had been so long since the com system had been of any use that she almost forgot how to use it. But that "almost" had best not come true if she wanted to live through the situation. She concentrated for a moment, remembered what button to push, and spoke. "Ah, um, hello, *Sentinel*. This is, ah, Tendra Risant aboard the *Gentleman Caller*!"

"Stand by, *Gentleman Caller*. Please activate your standard identity code transponder."

"What? Oh!" Tendra reached over and flipped the appropriate switch. The transponder would transmit the *Gentleman*'s identity whenever queried by a standard traffic control system. "I forgot that thing was off. Hasn't been much use for a while."

"True enough, *Gentleman Caller*. You are cleared to proceed, but are cautioned not to approach within one hundred thousand kilometers of Centerpoint Station. There will be no warnings if you approach closer. *Sentinel* out."

That sounded ominous, and it definitely put a crimp in her travel plans. But it didn't take much thought to realize there was not much point in arguing with a destroyer. Nor did it seem the moment to call them back and ask if they knew where Lando was.

But then how was she going to find Lando? And where should she go, if not to Centerpoint?

But, at that moment, the *Gentleman Caller*'s detection system chimed for her attention. Tendra paged her main display to the appropriate screen to see what was up.

And suddenly where to go was the least of her problems.

Getting away from where she was, in any direction at all, had just become a top priority.

All of a sudden she had company out here. Lots of it.

* * *

The view from the flag bridge was certainly informative. There was no doubt about that, but what he could see from there did not exactly make Lando happy. The main screen was showing the tactical schematic display from the *Sentinel,* relayed back to the *Intruder.* It showed the *Sentinel,* the *Defender,* the relative positions of Talus, Tralus, and Centerpoint—and at least fifty unidentified ships, with more appearing at every moment. "The Sacorrian fleet," Lando said to Kalenda. "The Triad fleet that Tendra warned us about."

"But what are they doing here?" Kalenda demanded. "Whose side are they on?"

"I think a better question might be, 'Who is on their side?' " said Admiral Ossilege, who seemed to have appeared from nowhere at all. "I expect they will change their minds in a hurry, but right at the moment, that fleet is in search of the people who have caused them the most trouble in this system—and I'm afraid our little squadron does not meet that qualification."

"But who's caused them more trouble than we have?" Gaeriel demanded.

"The Human League," Kalenda answered. "The Human League hijacked their whole operation—or at least tried to."

"Exactly," said Ossilege. "The Sacorrians, or at least the Triad who rule that world, they were the ones behind it all."

"The Triad?" Gaeriel asked.

"That is the name given to the oligarchy, or joint dictatorship, that rules Sacorria, so-called because there are three of them. One human, one Drall, one Selonian. No one knows anything about the three dictators—not even their names.

"In any event, they discovered the secret of Centerpoint, and the existence of the repulsors. I expect it was the Drall who found it, buried in records in some ancient archive. The Drall keep excellent records. But that is not important. They recruited malcontents on the various worlds to front revolutions for them, with the intent of creating chaos and confusion —something they could hide behind while digging up the repulsors. They timed the revolts to coincide with the trade summit on Corellia, with the hopes of catching as many big fish as possible in-system. That part of the plan certainly worked. I expect the other revolts were set to go off at the first report of trouble on Corellia."

"How do you know all this?" Kalenda asked.

"I know almost none of it," Ossilege said, "if you require a person to have proof, evidence, witnesses, documents before they know a thing. I am guessing. But if my guesses are wrong, I, frankly, would be astonished."

"But you're saying that something went wrong with the plan," said Lando.

"Has there ever been a plan more complicated than crossing the street where something didn't go wrong?" Ossilege asked. "But yes, something did go wrong. And the something was named Thrackan Sal-Solo. Somehow or another, he inveigled his way into the inner reaches of the starbuster plot, and he betrayed it. I expect the Triad sent him technicians, and he either bribed or tortured them, or perhaps both, until they agreed to work for him. Those technicians were able to put him in control of Centerpoint's jamming capabilities, and the interdiction system, but not its starbuster mode."

Lando thought for a moment and nodded. "That makes sense. The starbuster seems to be running on automatic pilot right now, anyway. Somebody—this Triad, I guess—worked out a whole detailed program for it, with stars to shoot at and the times to do it, and so on. Then they just set it running, and it hasn't stopped yet. There must be some way to transmit a stop code, once they got what they wanted. I don't suppose you've figured out how that is transmitted, have you?"

Ossilege smiled coldly. "Not as yet," he said. "But, in any event, getting back to Sal-Solo. In the first public message regarding the starbuster, he declared that he, not the Triad, controlled the device. He laid claim to the Corellian system—indeed, the Corellian Sector—in his own name, not in the name of the Triad, and made impossible demands for no better reason than to throw everyone into confusion. Then he activated the interdiction field and the communication jamming."

"But what was the point of it all?" Lando asked. "He had to know that sooner or later all those ships out there would show up, one way or the other."

"I'm starting to pile guesses on guesses here, but my hunch is that he understood the real power of the planetary repulsors, something none of the other rebel leaders did. Controlling one gives him tremendous bargaining power with the Triad. He can shut down their whole starbuster operation any time he wants to. I think he was planning to be in control of one before he let in the Sacorrian ships. And, in point of fact, he is in control of one."

"But where did all those ships come from?" Kalenda demanded. "Sacorria's a pretty small planet to be able to throw that big a fleet around."

"Quite right," said Ossilege, "but I expect you'd be able to answer your own question, if you gave it a bit more thought."

Kalenda frowned, and then her eyes widened. "From here," she said. "They come from here. That's why none of the Corellian rebels were able to throw anything but LAFs and PPBs at us. The Sacorrians had the rest of their ships."

"But how did the Sacorrians get hold of them?" Lando asked. "And how were they able to find crews for that many ships?"

"My guess is that the plain old-fashioned answer is that this is the Corellian Sector," said Ossilege. "Practically everything is for sale—or for rent—in these parts. Probably the Sacorrians bought or leased ships, and hired crews, from the rebel groups they created, the rebel groups having stolen them from wherever they could. Easy for them to arrange, when you recall that the Sacorrian Triad owns the rebellions."

"But probably the majority of the ships and crews out there are ex-Corellian Defense Forces sold out to the highest bidder," Kalenda said. "The spaceside CDF betrayed Governor-General Micamberlecto wholesale, the first chance they got—after they shot up my ship and threw a scare into Han Solo. And most of the CDF ships used to be Imperial ships. Probably a fair fraction of the crew too. They're older ships, but that doesn't mean they aren't good."

"And what are you going to do about them?" Gaeriel asked Ossilege. "They've been continuing to arrive while we've been talking here. There must be seventy-five of them out there. Shouldn't we be getting back to Centerpoint to help out *Defender* and *Sentinel*?"

"No," said Ossilege. "We will do no such thing."

"What?" Gaeriel said. "What do you mean?"

"The *Intruder* must complete her mission here before rejoining the other ships. The assault on the repulsor is still our top priority."

"But *Defender* and *Sentinel* are outnumbered seventy-five to two!"

"And no one is shooting. Yet. Moving this ship toward the fleet could be seen as an aggressive act. And if it comes down to a shooting war, I doubt that seventy-five to three gives us much better odds. Frankly, seventy-five ships is a lower number than I expected. Either our friend Tendra Risant miscounted, or the Sacorrians have left a substantial reserve of ships back home."

"But if those ships move on Centerpoint—"

"Two ships, or three, it will be impossible to stop them. Please try to understand. If we lose all our ships, and control a repulsor, we win. But if we completely wipe out the enemy fleet, and Thrackan Sal-Solo still controls this repulsor, we have lost. And then the eight million people, or twelve million people, of Bovo Yagen, on their one planet or two, depending on what report you believe, will all die."

Gaeriel seemed about to protest further, but she said nothing. Lando understood how she felt. It seemed as if there should have been some way to answer Ossilege.

Unfortunately, of course, there wasn't.

CHAPTER THIRTEEN

Evasive Maneuvers

Han Solo paced the ground, back and forth, back and forth, the gravel crunching underfoot. He almost tripped over Artoo once or twice, until he managed to shoo the droid out of the way. "Go over this one more time," he said, turning to Dracmus.

The Selonian had joined Han, Leia, Luke, and Mara for dinner on the grounds of the villa. By all rights, they should have been lounging about the table, relaxing in the gentle breezes of perfect twilight, after a first-rate dinner.

But Han just couldn't do it. It seemed utterly criminal just to be hanging around, lolling in the lap of luxury, while the whole star system was falling to pieces.

Everyone kept telling him that there was nothing they could do but wait, but Han had had enough of waiting about five minutes after Luke had told them about Centerpoint.

"I know I need to understand the situation," said Han, "but I *also* know I'm completely lost. So please. Explain to me why it's in our best interest to just sit here and wait. Explain to me what it accomplishes."

"Yes," said Luke. "Please do. I'd like to hear this."

"Very wellness," said Dracmus, "let me be trying it

again. You have to start with knowing the idea that the three things that matter most to Selonians are honor, consensus, and the Den. All else comes behind those three. Everything, and far behind."

"All right, that much I get," said Han. "But what's that got to do with why having the Triad Selonians on repulsor duty was such a big deal?"

"Merely everything, that's all," said Dracmus. "The Triad Selonians on Sacorria descend from despised offshoot of a bloodline discredited long ago. I will not be going into the whole history, but suffice to be saying that the ancestors of the Triad Selonians disputed a just settlement in a matter of vitalness, centuries ago. Some of them tried to lie and cheat their way into a position of advantage over other members of their own Den. As a consequence, the Den was split up into two groups—the victims of the fraud and the nasty perpetrators. The perpetrators were kicked off Corellia by my ancestors, the ancestors of the Hunchuzuc, and also removed from Selonia by the Overden. So bad was the scandal that the victims formed a new Den under a new name, because the old name was utterly dishonored. Even now I must not speak it. It is obscenity, only to be used when time is right for splendidly rotten insult. This name-losing had never happened to any other Den ever before, and it has never happened again since."

"It doesn't seem quite fair to blame people for what their ancestors did," said Luke.

"Is muchly more fair for Selonians than humans, I am believing. Remember that the Den is all. The Den lives on while the individuals die. Also recall that the new individuals are virtual clones of the old ones. You humans tend to think of a Den as collection of individuals. But we are not like humans. In many ways, we are more like highly intelligent social insects. We are individuals, but the individual is completely in service of the Den. Well, nearly complete. We are something closer than your families, but not *quite* as close as the cells in the body."

"That's going a bit far, isn't it?" asked Mara.

"And it still doesn't seem fair to kick everyone out for the sins of the ancestors," said Luke. "Leia and I would be in very big trouble if humans did that."

Dracmus bowed very slightly to Mara, an almost imperceptible movement. "Maybe analogy is too far. Maybe yes and maybe no. But, Master Skywalker, when you bleed, do you worry how blood cells that go out of you feel about leaving? If some of your blood cells are diseased, do you think about what is fair to cells that are still healthy when you treat the illness— or do you get your blood changed completely, just to be on the safe side, just to make sure illness cannot come back?"

Han resisted the urge to start pacing again. "It's the story of my life with you, Dracmus, but we've wandered off the point again."

"Thought we were talking about how humans different from us," Dracmus said.

Han paused a moment, resisting the temptation to lose his temper again. He collected himself and then spoke. "I've got a feeling we're not going to get anywhere until we're all agreed on this, so okay. I'll tell you my reaction, and then maybe we can move on. I grew up with Selonians, and I never knew any of this. I admit it's embarrassing, but—"

"Be not muchly embarrassed, Honored Solo," Dracmus said in a soothing voice. "Don't be forgetting the Selonians you met were trained—and bred—for sole purpose of dealing with humans. Is our *job* to make you feel comfy with us."

"I know, I know. And they did a good job. I grew up thinking that Selonians were just funny-looking humans with a few quaint customs left over from the old days. But just to round this out, I should have found out how it worked, even if your people didn't want me to know. Back in my smuggling days, I made a career out of knowing what the other side's worldview was like—and yet I grew up knowing nothing about the people next door. It makes me wonder about the rest of my life, growing up on Corellia. How much else did I not see?"

"Probably quite a bit," said Leia. "None of us ever really sees our own culture all that well."

Han rolled his eyes. "Gee, there's an original thought. But even all this is off the point. What I was going to say was that it was embarrassing to find out how little I knew about you, but that right now I don't care about being embarrassed. Treat me like a complete idiot, but make me understand what's going on. If I've got this straight, now that Kleyvits has admitted to being in the pay of the Triad, and admitted to smuggling some of them back onto the planet, that changes everything, right?"

"Right," said Dracmus. "Excellent!"

"Great. I'm glad. But how?"

"Begging pardon?"

"How. *How* does Kleyvits confessing change everything?"

"Because it means my Hunchuzuc were tricked. We gave in under false pretenses. The Overden made us be thinking that the Overden ran the repulsor, and had smashed the Bakuran destroyer all by themselves. All was fraud," she said, her voice growing genuinely angry. "The Overden achieved a consensus favorable to themselves by trickery and deception, and by involving themselves with a dishonored and nameless Den. This is depth of crime. Even worse, the nameless Den was linked to Triad, and Triad linked to Sal-Solo, who kidnaps his own, steals children."

"Guilt by association," Han said. "How advanced and sophisticated."

Mara looked up at Han. "Think it through. In a group society run by consensus, guilt by association makes some sense."

"Anyway," said Dracmus, "Overden in bad. No way

could it be worse for them. You *saw* how Kleyvits caved in once the truth came out. That will be happening every time Hunchuzuc demands the truth of Overden Selonian. Overden will be losing so much face you'll be able to be seeing the back of their heads from the front. Hunchuzuc will take over. Take over consensus, take over much property—take over possession of the repulsor."

"But the Sacorrian Selonians are still the ones *running* the repulsor," Luke objected.

"Yes! And so we must wait. I know that human way—at least one human way—to deal with such problem would be to give the Sacorrian Selonians one chance to give up. If they didn't, in you go with all guns blazing nicely. But maybe everyone gets killed. You seize the repulsor, but have no idea where ON switch is." Dracmus shook her head. "This is not Selonian way. We will talk with Sacorrian scums, nasty though job will be. We are talking with them, right now. And we will talk to them. And talk to them. Finally, pressure—peer pressure on Sacorrians to give up—will be too much, and they will give up. And do more than giving up. They will cooperate with Hunchuzuc, tell us how to run machinery, as part of their penance for being on the losing side. This is how it will be. We just have to sit back and wait."

"Sounds terrific," said Han. "So what's the catch?"

"The catch is all takes time. Everything I tell of will happen. Is inevitable. The trouble is like in old Selonian saying. 'The agreed-to we do at once. The inevitable can take a little while.' "

"How *big* a little while?" asked Luke.

Dracmus shook her head. "An hour. A day. A month. A year."

Luke frowned. "An hour we have. Maybe even a day. But not much longer. Centerpoint Station is going to fire at Bovo Yagen in just over eighty-four hours. Unless we fire a planetary repulsor beam at Centerpoint at just the right moment, a whole solar system dies."

"And a whole Sector starts to panic and wonder who's next, and a whole galaxy starts to wonder what the point is of a New Republic that can't protect them," said Leia.

"And I hate to say it," said Han, "but they'd be absolutely right to start wondering."

* * *

"Should I reset the breaker now?" Jacen asked.

"Not yet. Just a sec," said Anakin, a bit absently. "One more of them to stick in." He was lying on his stomach, propped up on one elbow, leaning over the open underfloor access panel. He stared down into the morass of wires and cables and circuit boards for a minute or two, then reached in and pulled another of the fist-sized power-shunt transpacitors. It took a good solid yank to pull the thing out of its socket. He held it up and stared at it for a moment, almost as if he could see through it, into it. "Boy, did *this* get all melty inside." He set it to one side. "Jaina, gimme the one from the hyperdrive."

Jaina handed him the last of the transpacitors they had gotten by cannibalizing the *Falcon*'s faster-than-light drive. Anakin plugged it into the socket, then reconnected the power shunt board to the main sublight engine circuit. "All right," he said to Jacen. "Push the reset."

Jacen was sitting by the next access panel over, where the circuit breaker board was. He held his breath and threw the switch back to the ON position. There was the slightest of pauses, and then the green status light came on. Jacen breathed a sigh of relief, then turned to Q9. "It worked, Chewbacca. We ought to have repulsors and sublight engines now."

Chewbacca's voice—an anxious yelp and a growl—answered, sounding as if it came from a little bit out of

the comlink mike's normal range. There was something more than a bit incongruous about a Wookiee
voice coming from Q9's speaker. "Chewbacca says to
hurry," Ebrihim said, quite needlessly.

"Okay, okay, we're hurrying," Jacen said, getting to
his feet. He closed the panel over the breaker box
while Anakin closed up the one over the circuit board.
"We're on our way to the cockpit now."

The muffled sound of a comlink being fumbled
about came from Q9's speaker, and then a hoot from
Chewbacca and Ebrihim's slightly exasperated voice.
"Give it back," he said, apparently to the Wookiee.
"I'll tell them."

There was a slight pause, and then Ebrihim's voice
again, a bit louder and clearer. "Get moving as fast as
you can," he said. The sun will be rising soon, and I'm
sure our friend will be getting up as well."

"All right, all right," muttered Jacen. "Nag, nag,
nag, all the time. Come on, Q9, let's go."

"I still don't see why you couldn't have taken the
time to go get another comlink out of stores," said Q9,
speaking in his own voice. "I don't enjoy being used as
an intercom."

Jacen smiled as he headed for the cockpit. "It saved
us the five minutes of finding one and getting it tuned
and matched to the one Chewbacca's using. Believe
me, we needed the five minutes. Don't worry. We'll
switch over to the ship's main com system in a minute."

Jacen paused at the entrance to the cockpit of the
Millennium Falcon. He had been in the cockpit many
times before, of course—but this was different, very
different. No one was keeping an eye on him this time,
or making sure he didn't press any buttons, or shooing
him away. No. This time, he was here to *fly* the ship.
Fly her. The very idea terrified him.

"Want to have a contest to see which one of us is
more scared?" Jaina asked.

Jacen turned around and smiled. His twin sister and

his little brother were behind him, all three of them standing right at the threshold of the cockpit. "I don't know," he said. "How close do you think it will be?"

"Not close at all. I bet I'm a zillion times more scared than you."

"Don't be so sure about that," said Jacen. "*I* bet it's a tie."

"*I'm* not scared," said Anakin. "I'll fly her, if you want."

"I might take you up on that one if you weren't too short to reach the controls properly," said Jacen.

"Might I remind all of you of the need for haste at this point?" asked Q9. "I believe I have gotten over my recent bout with paranoia, but let us not forget that there really is someone out to get us."

"He's got a point," Jacen said. He turned to Jaina. "Which seat do you want? Pilot or copilot?"

Jaina paused for a moment, and then smiled. "Like father, like son. You take Dad's seat at pilot. He'd like it that way. I bet Mom would too."

Jacen smiled back at her, then climbed in and took his place at the pilot's station, adjusting the seat up as high and as far forward as it would go. Jaina did the same.

"All right, Chewie," said Jacen, "we're switching over to the ship's main comm system—now." He reached over to the com panel and threw the appropriate switch.

"*That's* a relief," said Q9.

"Can you still read us?" Jacen asked.

An answering roar came from the overhead speaker, and Jacen hastily turned down the volume.

"Good," said Jaina. "All right, Jacen. Seat restraint fastened?"

"Definitely," said Jacen. He glanced behind him and made sure that Anakin, seated in the observer's seat behind Jaina, also had his belt on. Q9 had clamped himself to a stanchion. "Everyone set?"

"Not quite," said Jaina. "Those Human League guys

are going to come after us the moment we take off.
Maybe we should sort of slow down good old cousin
Thrackan a little bit before we leave."

"Wait a second," protested Jacen, but Jaina had already activated the fire controls for the *Falcon*'s ventral
laser cannon. Jacen could hear the whir of the motors
as the cannon came out of the hull.

"I figure one aimed shot at the force field generator,
and then I re-aim as fast as I can and take a crack at
the assault boat."

"The force field generator? Suppose you miss and
hit Chewie and the Drall?"

"I *can't* hit them. They're behind the force field, remember? You just be ready to get us moving straight
up on the repulsors the split second I tell you to. I
don't think we should try anything with the sublight
engines until we have a little room to maneuver."

Jacen shook his head doubtfully. "All right," he said.
"But be sure you remember whose idea it was to start
shooting. Hold on a second." He studied his control
boards for a moment, and then flicked a series of
power switches on. The ship gave a sort of eager little
shudder, and Jacen felt a low hum of power flow
through the ship. "There we go," he said. "Repulsors
and sublight engines at standby."

"Chewie—get as close to the center of the containment as you can and shield your eyes, and tell the others to do the same."

A howl of protest came over the intercom.

"Will you relax?" Jaina said. "This will work, trust
me. You guys just get ready to run and hide as soon as
the force field goes down. Here we go." Jaina stared
down at the gunnery display, making minute adjustments to the ventral laser's aim. "One aimed shot," she
said again. "Either it works or it doesn't. Chewie—
Ebrihim—Aunt Marcha—get ready!"

"And *they* all think *I've* been acting strangely," said
Q9.

"One shot, on the count of three, then I re-aim on

the assault boat and shoot it up as best I can. Jacen, don't boost till I tell you to, all right?"

"All right, fine! I heard you the first time!"

"Here we go," Jaina said again.   "One—"

Jacen boosted himself up on his seat a bit to see what was about to happen.

"Two—"

Should he try harder to stop her? Jaina was going too far, but there really wasn't time to argue.

"THREE!"

A blast of fire roared from the ventral laser cannon, catching the force field generator square in the center of the control panel. It exploded in a gout of fire that seemed to light up the entire repulsor chamber. The force field winked out of existence.

The blaze of light dazzled Jacen, but Jaina had been watching her targeting screen. She swung the laser cannon around in the general direction of the assault boat and fired again. The first shot missed the boat completely, the blast of light bouncing off the reflective walls of the chamber to ricochet around a dozen times before it dissipated. She fired again, and hit the left rear landing skid of the boat, kicking the body of the boat up a half meter or so before it slammed down to the decks with a tremendous crash. She tried one more shot and missed completely again. The blast bounced back and forth off the walls and floors of the chamber.

Jacen could see three figures, one large and two small, running for the nearest entrance to the side caverns. Good. At least his sister hadn't killed them outright when she blew up that generator. "Jaina, the way those shots are ricocheting, you're more likely to hit Chewie than Thrackan."

She shook her head. "You're right," she said. "Go. Let's get out of here."

"Everyone hang on to something," said Jacen. "I've never done this before." He pulled back on the repulsor power control, and the *Millennium Falcon* lumbered up into the sky.

*   *   *

Thrackan Sal-Solo went sailing out of bed and crashed to the floor of his cabin. He lay there, half stunned for a moment, and then scrambled to his feet. The room was pitch-dark for a moment, but then the emergency lighting cut in.

Thrackan had taken over the captain's cabin in the assault boat, putting him in the only private space on board. Even so, the cabin was small enough that it took him a minute to realize that the deck was canted badly downward to the right and rear of the boat. What had happened? He could hear shouting, panicking voices in the corridor. He pulled on a robe and stepped out of his cabin.

Thrackan stepped out into a milling, chaotic throng, a tangled knot of frightened, confused men. He spotted the boat's captain, struggling to get forward to the control room. Thrackan grabbed the man by the shoulder. "Captain Thrag—what in blazes is going on?" he demanded.

"I don't know, sir," Thrag shouted back. He was short, fat, and bald, and not the most appealing person to see in his underwear this late at night, so long since his last shave. But there was a clear-eyed, hard-headed sort of integrity about the man. He took orders from Thrackan without being afraid of him. A rarity, that. "Some shots, and then some explosions, at least two of them. One pretty far off, and the other right under us. I think we lost one of the landing skids."

"That can't be. Let's get forward."

The two of them shoved their way forward to the control cabin. The captain hit the button and the hatch slid open, offering a clear view out the forward viewport.

"Burning stars," gasped Thrackan.

"Look at that," said Thrag. "I don't believe it."

The force field generator was a pillar of fire, the reflection of the flame glittering and gleaming from every corner of the silver walls of the repulsor chamber. The force field itself was gone, and the prisoners had vanished. There seemed little doubt about where they had gone, either. There was the *Millennium Falcon,* rising straight up off the ground, headed for the sky.

"After them!"

"But the ship was hit by laser fire!" Thrag protested. "We have damage! We have to check it first."

"No! If the ship is damaged, we fly with damage! Fly! Go!"

"That would put the life of every man aboard at risk."

"Every man aboard is at risk of execution right now anyway, for dereliction of duty," Thrackan snarled. "What about the man on watch? He should have been here. He should have raised the alert. Where is he?"

The captain laughed bitterly and hooked his thumb toward the rear of the boat. "With the rest of the sleepy drunks back there, would be my guess."

"What are you saying?"

"I'm saying look at the crew your people sent me. Dregs and scum, all of them. By the time men get posted to low-life duty like tending an assault boat, a lot of other people have turned them down. What do you expect when you recruit thugs?"

"Well, if they've all been rejected, then they won't be much missed when they all get killed. Launch this boat now!"

Thrag looked Thrackan straight in the eye, and then saluted. "Very well, sir. But on your head be it," he said, and sat down in the pilot's chair.

*   *   *

Ebrihim had a very nasty feeling that he had a large patch of singed fur somewhere in the small of his back. In any event, there was the acrid smell of burnt hair, and there was definitely a tender spot back there. However, this was not exactly the time or the place to worry about such things. Besides, his lungs were about to burst, and he was much more interested in catching his breath than in a lot of idle chitchat about whether or not his back had caught fire. The three of them—Chewbacca, Marcha, and Ebrihim—were hiding at the base of the cone nearest where the *Falcon* had been.

Had been. Ebrihim watched the *Falcon* rising straight up into the freedom of the night sky, her way illuminated by the glow of its repulsor pads, and fires lit by Jaina's marksmanship.

Where the ship *had been.* That was the key point. Nothing else mattered. Not really. It was cold and hard to say it, but even if the *Falcon* crashed, even if Thrackan Sal-Solo shot it down with the loss of all hands, this moment was a great victory. For Thrackan Sal-Solo had been denied even the hope of influencing Leia Organa Solo's decisions.

But he had paid a price even *trying* to use her kidnapped children against her. Ebrihim knew the Drall, and he thought he even knew the Selonians and humans fairly well. His attempt at blackmail had no doubt sickened and disgusted thousands, millions of people throughout the Corellian system. It must have turned millions against him, turned passive dislike into active resistance. It must have gained sympathy for Leia—and for the New Republic.

All that would have been worth it for Thrackan, if he had succeeded in manipulating her, forcing her to recognize Corellian independence. Even if she had been forced into a public rejection of his demands, that would have done her tremendous damage. A mother turning her back on her children—yes, Thrackan Sal-Solo could have done a great deal with that.

He hoped deeply, profoundly, with all his heart, that the children survived. But even if they did not, they had defeated their father's cousin, their enemy, simply by getting away.

"Good-bye," he said into the comlink, though they were almost certainly out of range already. "Good-bye, and good luck. May—may the Force be with you."

As he watched, the assault boat lifted off and lurched up toward the sky. There was no way to be sure, of course, but as best he could tell, the assault boat had lifted with all hands aboard. That left the three of them down here alone, even more stranded than they had been before. Of course, Ebrihim had no doubt they would have plenty of company in the near future.

The question was—who would that company be?

*   *   *

Jacen held the controls in a death grip as the *Falcon* rode her repulsors up into the early-morning sky. They came up out of the repulsor shaft, still moving straight up, but Jacen knew better than to try to fly too high and too long on repulsor power alone. He would have to make the transition to sublight engines—and make it quickly. The repulsors were not intended for indefinite boost in the first place—and Jacen knew just how much this ship had been through recently. He put his hand on the sublight engine throttles, and pulled back on them as slightly, and as gently, as he could.

The *Millennium Falcon* took off like a lightning bolt, streaking across the sky. Jacen pulled the *Falcon*'s nose up, trying to gain some altitude—or at least trying to avoid diving into the ground. He swallowed hard and eased the sublights back just a trifle, and then shut off the repulsors. The *Falcon* shuddered for a moment, but then settled down to smooth flight—at least for a moment or two. Then she was suddenly diving in toward the ground far below. Jacen pulled back up on the stick, forcing her nose up, fighting to keep her from fishtailing all over the sky. At last she seemed to stabilize as he got the feel of the controls. But he kept his tight grip on the joystick and kept his eyes constantly flitting back and forth between the viewports and the controls.

"Well, we're out," Jaina asked. "Now where do we go?"

"I don't know," Jacen said. "We never talked about that part, but—"

"Behind us!" Anakin shouted. "Look at the detector screen!"

Jacen had to look for a moment before he could even find the detector screen. But once he did, he had not the slightest trouble reading it.

There was cousin Thrackan's assault boat, hot on their heels. A blast of laser flared past the *Falcon*'s starboard side, and Jacen flinched involuntarily—jerking the ship's controls, and heeling the *Falcon* up and flipping her over on her roll axis until the topside of the ship was pointed down. The *Falcon* was suddenly climbing at about a forty-five-degree angle of attack, but with the cockpit pointed down instead of up. The artificial gravity system held them in their seats, but Jacen could look *up* and *back* and see the ground where a piece of sky should have been.

The accidental maneuver seemed to have shaken Thrackan off their tail, at least for the moment, but he would be back, no doubt about it. And he'd start shooting at them again.

"Shields up!" Jacen shouted.

"Where—where are the shield controls?" Jaina asked.

"Chewie moved 'em when he rewired the cockpit," Anakin said from the observer seat. "Under your left hand, sort of. The panel with the big *red* buttons."

"Where? Where?" Jaina said. "I don't see it."

"I'll get it," Anakin said. He undid his seat restraint, hopped out of his seat, and wriggled in between the two pilot stations. He reached in and flicked the safeties off a row of red switches, stabbed his chubby finger down on a big red button, and twisted two dials. "All right, *now* shields up! Top, bottom, and forward shields at—um—twenty percent. Rear shields at full."

A dull crash and a shudder that ran through the

whole ship told Jacen that Anakin had gotten the shields up just in time—and that cousin Thrackan's aim was getting better.

Was he trying to shoot them down? Were those warning shots? Or was he trying to disable them? So far, as best Jacen could tell, Thrackan had just used the assault boat's chin guns, low-caliber lasers intended more for antipersonnel work than ship-to-ship fighting. But what did it *mean*? Jacen knew his dad would have been able to interpret the shots, know just what Thrackan intended, and what to do about it. But his father was not here, however devoutly Jacen might wish that he were. Probably—probably—Thrackan was trying to disable the *Falcon*, not kill them. The thought was not much comfort.

Thirty seconds before, he had been worrying about figuring out where to go. Suddenly he wasn't all that interested in getting to anyplace at all.

All he wanted to do was get away from here, right now.

*   *   *

"Shoot!" Thrackan shouted. "Shoot, damn your eyes!"

"I can't shoot them if I can't get a lock on them," Thrag growled. "The chin guns don't have any sort of automatic target tracking. I can't fly a pursuit and try for a pinpoint disabling shot at the same time. Maybe *you're* that good, but I'm not."

"We'll see how good I am," Thrackan said, climbing into the copilot's chair. "Switch gunnery control to this station."

"But it's your own blood relatives!" Thrag protested.

"I ordered you to shoot at them, and I'm going to shoot at them myself. I'm not hypocrite enough to pretend there's a difference there."

Thrag turned his attention from his flying long enough to look Thrackan up and down. "Do your own dirty work, then, and welcome to it," he said, and switched over gunnery control. "But I never thought I'd meet a man who thought it a special point of pride to shoot down his own flesh and blood."

*   *   *

Ossilege's ensign rushed onto the flag deck, almost stumbling over his own feet in his hurry. "Sir, something's happened!"

Ossilege turned, raised one eyebrow, and regarded the young man with a withering stare. "Thank you for that cogent and highly detailed report," he said.

"Ah, yes, sir. I'm sorry. At the repulsor. Something's happened there. We detected several energy pulses that read like laser fire and explosions, and then—then two ships came out of the repulsor, one in pursuit of the other. They've just gained enough altitude for us to see them over the limb of the planet. Both are being flown very badly, and one of them seems to be damaged."

"Two ships?" Kalenda said. "That's all there were down there, unless someone is playing a very cagey game."

Ossilege stabbed a button on the flag deck's main console.

"Putney here," said a slightly high-pitched and nasal voice.

"Commander Putney, this is Ossilege. It looks like everyone has cleared out of the repulsor. Both ships have taken off."

"Why?" Putney asked.

"We're not sure, but one ship seems to be pursuing the other. We need to take advantage of the situation. They may or may not have left troops behind, but even if they have, some of their troopers and most of their firepower just headed off toward orbit. We are going to seize this chance with both hands. I don't care if your assault boat is only half loaded and your troops don't have their pants on. I want them headed toward an assault-speed landing in the repulsor *now.*"

"Yes, sir!" Putney replied. "Our heavy weapons aren't aboard, but if we're lucky, we won't need them. We can launch in five minutes."

"Do it in four," Ossilege said, and cut the connection. He turned and gestured toward Kalenda. "Get me visual and tactical on the two ships *now,*" he ordered.

Kalenda worked the controls with lightning speed and brought up the imagery from the long-range visual scanner and the tactical. The images of two ships appeared. Both were clawing for altitude, the one in the lead flying erratically—and upside down. "That's the *Falcon,*" Lando said. "That's the *Millennium Falcon,* Han Solo's personal ship. It's flying upside down, and I think the pilot must be drunk, but I'd know that ship anywhere."

"That's the assault boat behind it," Ossilege said eagerly. "And it looks to have taken some damage."

"Who the devil is flying the *Falcon*?" Kalenda asked.

"It's not Chewbacca, I can tell you that much," said Lando. "He could fly her better than that blindfolded and with one arm in a sling—and I'm not speaking poetically."

"Then who is it?"

"I have an idea, but none of you would believe me anyway," said Lando. "You didn't last time."

Ossilege looked at him sharply. "You're saying one of the *children* is flying that ship?"

"You said it, I didn't," Lando replied.

"The assault boat is firing again!" Kalenda cried out.

"Direct hit—but they're still flying," Lando said. "They must have gotten the shields up, somehow."

Ossilege peered intently at the tactical screen, trying to make sense out of the course projection, but the *Falcon* was flying so wildly all over the map it was impossible to know for sure. "Where are they going?" he demanded. "Where are they headed? Whatever course they're trying to keep doesn't lead even remotely toward anything. Where do they *think* they're going?"

"Nowhere," Lando said. "Away. Out."

"Do they know we're here?" Ossilege demanded.

Lando shook his head. "If they did, they'd be heading toward us, or hailing us, or something. They're just flying in whatever direction they happened to be heading in when the pilot managed to get control of the ship."

Ossilege was plainly excited, agitated—and just as plainly trying not to show it. "Can we get a tractor beam on either ship? Or both?"

Kalenda checked. "Not quite. But even if they are not moving straight toward us, they're moving in our general direction. We ought to have the *Falcon* within tractor range in twenty seconds, and the assault boat in range ten seconds after that."

"Wait until they're both in range, and then get tractor beams on both of them. Pull the *Falcon* in, but just hold the assault boat where it is, at least for the moment."

"Yes, sir," Kalenda said, and set to work relaying the orders.

"If we work this right," said Ossilege, "we can grab the repulsor and Thrackan Sal-Solo, all at the same time." He looked up to the main screen, still showing the Triad fleet forming up, getting ready to do whatever it was here for. "Except for the trifling fact of an enemy fleet massing for the attack, I think we might be in very good shape indeed."

*   *   *

The *Falcon* lurched wildly to one side as the assault boat managed another hit. "Shields didn't like that one," Anakin said, watching the defense display.

"That's it," said Jaina. "I've had it. Let's give them some of their own back. Powering up ventral laser cannon and setting for aft-aim."

"What?!" Jacen cried. "Are you out of your mind?"

"I think you're *all* out of your minds," Q9 said.

"Quiet, Q9. Jacen, he's already shooting at us! How could shooting back make things any worse?"

"I don't know," said Jacen, "but I bet we find a way."

"Ventral laser on auto target seek. I've got a target lock!" Jaina squeezed the trigger and the laser cannon blazed away. "Hit him!" she said. "Shields absorbed the shot, but I made him back off a little."

* * *

"Shields down five percent!" Thrag said. "A nice clean shot, and no mistake. If that had had any power behind it, we'd be a hulk in space right now."

"Shoot at me?" Thrackan said. "Those miserable whelps have the gall to shoot at *me*? Activating main armament!"

"But you'll blow them out of the sky!" Thrag protested. "You need them alive!"

"But I *want* them dead," said Thrackan Sal-Solo. "Main armament powered up and ready to fire."

* * *

Jacen risked a peek at the detector screen. "Jaina, he's not backing off, he's bringing his main turret cannon to bear! We've got to get out of here. Hang on!"

Jacen pulled back up on the stick, pulling the nose of the *Falcon* up. The *Falcon* climbed over its nose, into an inside loop, up and over before pulling out of the loop, right on Thrackan's tail.

"Anakin! Forward shields to full!" Jacen shouted, and his little brother scrambled to reset the switches, just in time to deflect a near miss from the assault boat's turret gun. The *Falcon* bucked and shuddered, but her shields held.

"We're in behind their shields! I have a shot! Hang

on!" Jaina called. She fired twice. The first caught the
turret gun right at the join with the assault boat's upper hull, blowing the gun clean off the hull. The second
caught the sublight engine array, smashing the sublight
emitters down to nothing.

The assault boat was dead in space.

Jacen had to stop cheering long enough to keep
from ramming the *Falcon* right into her stern.

And then a giant, invisible hand reached out and
yanked the *Millennium Falcon* by the scruff of the
neck.

*   *   *

"Assault boat has lost main propulsion. Tractor beam
on!" Kalenda announced. "Positive lock on assault
boat. Provisional lock on *Falcon*. *Falcon* attempting to
break free. We can't hold *Falcon* for too long without
damage to her."

Lando went to the flag deck com panel and punched
in a comm access code he had not used in a while.
"Let's hope Han didn't go and change codes on me,"
he muttered, then pushed the transmit key. "Lando
Calrissian to *Millennium Falcon*. This is Lando Calrissian calling *Millennium Falcon*. Shut down your engines
and do not resist the tractor beam. We are taking you
aboard a Bakuran vessel, allied with the New Republic.
Do you copy?"

"Lando?" came a young, eager voice over the com
line. "Is that you? Is that you?"

"That you, Jaina?" Lando asked.

"No, I'm Jacen," came the rather irritated reply.
"But Jaina and Anakin are here too. And so is Q9."

"Who or what is Q9?" Admiral Ossilege asked irri-
tably.

"I haven't the faintest idea," said Lando. "But it
looks like we'll get the chance to find out." He pressed
the transmit key again. "Where are Chewbacca and the
Drall?"

"Still in the repulsor chamber on the planet," Jacen answered. "We'll have to send someone to get them."

Lando glanced at the flag deck's hangar status board. "We've just launched our own assault boat to them," Lando said. "They'll be all right."

"Good," said Jacen. "We'll be really glad to see you, Lando."

"And I'll be glad to see you too," he said. "Oh—and one more thing. Nice flying—and nice shooting. Your father will be proud."

"Thanks, Lando!"

"Don't mention it," Lando said, and cut the connection. He looked up at the main tactical display, where the fleet of the Sacorrian Triad was moving in, slowly and carefully in toward Centerpoint Station, and the two lonely destroyers that stood guard on it. From there, his eye shifted to a countdown clock, showing the eighty-two hours remaining until Centerpoint would fire at Bovo Yagen. "At least," said Lando to the dead microphone, "he'll be proud of you if we all live long enough for him to hear about it."

And it occurred to Lando that he ought to make it his business to tell Han. Now. Before it was too late.

* * *

Captain Thrag sat in the smoky control cabin of his assault boat, and laughed, but there was little joy or happiness in the angry sound. "How have the mighty fallen, O mighty Diktat," he said. "They have beaten you, beaten you completely. Shot down by children. Children so young they probably had trouble seeing over the control panel."

"Shut up, Thrag," said Thrackan. "Shut up or I'll kill you on the spot."

Thrag let out one last chuckle and looked out through the assault boat's viewport. The enemy ship's tractor beam was pulling them in. They would be aboard in a few seconds' time. "The horrible thing is

that you might even do it," he said. "And why not? If
there has ever been a man with nothing left to lose,
you are that man now. They have you, *Diktat* Sal-
Solo." He nodded to the ship in the viewport, the ship
that was getting closer with every second. "Now they
have you, body and spirit."

*   *   *

The *Millennium Falcon* set down in the hangar deck of
the *Intruder,* the tractor-beam operator setting the ship
neatly down. The three children powered down the
ship's systems as best they could, and made their way
to the access ramp. Anakin worked the controls, and
the ramp came down. The three of them filed down
the ramp—and stopped dead at the foot of it. They
had brought the assault boat in first, and already the
Bakurans were taking the Human League troopers
into custody. One by one, they were led out of the
boat, hands on their heads, and hustled out toward the
detention block.

The next-to-last man out was a short, grubby-looking
man, dressed only in his underwear and a thin under-
shirt. All the other prisoners had looked scared or angry, but this man was laughing. Laughing out loud.

But the last man out, the last one of all, was not
laughing. Thrackan Sal-Solo came out of the assault
boat, walking straight and tall, hands at his side. He
paused for a moment as he stepped down onto the
hangar deck, and looked around himself.

He spotted the three children by the *Millennium Falcon,* and the smooth, arrogant look on his face melted
away. A look of pure hatred, pure anger and malice,
took its place. The three children backed away a step
or two, and Thrackan actually took a step or two
toward them before the guards grabbed him by the
arms and led him away.

Anakin stood between his brother and his sister,
holding each of them by the hand. He stared, wide-

eyed and solemn, as they led Thrackan Sal-Solo, Diktat of Corellia, away. "Our cousin is a very bad man," he said.

Neither of the other children could think of anything more to say.

*   *   *

"This is doing no good, Dracmus," Han said. "You come. You tell us there might be progress. You go away. You come back. You say it again. Around and around. There are people at war out there. A whole star system could die while you go back and forth."

"I am knowing, I am knowing, I am knowing," said Dracmus. "But believe me, there is nothing more we can be doing. We Hunchuzuc know the deadline. We are trying. But it is a very delicate situation. Push the Sacorrians of the nameless clan too hard, and they might commit suicide. Or die of shame. And die of shame not expression, like with you people." Dracmus seemed ready to offer an explanation of that statement, but then she caught Han's eye and got back to the point. "The best thing you humans can do to hurry us along is just to *be* here, looking impatient, checking the time, *reminding* us to hurry. I go tell negotiators you impatient, time growing short, and they work faster."

Just then, there was an odd, muted sort of beeping noise coming from Mara's pocket. At exactly the same moment Artoo suddenly kicked up a fuss, whistling and chirping and spinning his view dome back and forth.

Mara looked confused for a minute, and then seemed to remember something. She stood up, shoved her hand in the pocket of her coveralls, and pulled out a comlink. "It's been so long since these things worked I forgot it was there," she said. She pressed a stud on the side of the comlink, and the beeping stopped.

"That's a call from the ship's monitoring systems. A high priority message just came in."

"Artoo," asked Luke, "are you getting it too? The same message?"

Artoo let off an affirmative-sounding trill.

"Gotta be the same one," Mara said. "I've got to go over to the *Jade's Fire* to read my copy. Anyone care to tag along and see what it is?"

*   *   *

Artoo confirmed it was the same message the moment he plugged into the dataport on the cockpit of the *Jade's Fire*. That saved having to decode it twice. The decryption system on board the *Jade's Fire* was good, very good. It unbuttoned the message in only a few seconds—a job that would have taken Artoo a good many minutes. Mara, sitting at the ship's command station, hit the play button, and a hologram shimmered into life a meter or so above the floor.

It was a full-length view of Lando, shown at about half life size. "Hello," he said in a very solemn voice. "I don't know exactly what your situation is, so I will send duplicate copies of this to all of you. A lot has happened. The bad news is that the real enemy has finally shown up. It's the fleet from the Sacorrian Triad. Luke knows about it. They are the real enemy. Everything else—all the rebellions—are not much more than diversions. The fleet has a total of about eighty ships of all sizes, and they are closing—very slowly—on Centerpoint. They seem to be timing it so they will get to Centerpoint just as the Bovo Yagen shot goes off. We haven't interfered with them—yet—and they haven't made any hostile gesture toward our ships. I doubt that's going to last long, though.

"That's the bad news, and it's bad." The image of Lando paused for a moment, and then broke into a broad smile. "The *good* news is very good indeed. Don't ask me how, because we haven't had time to sort it all out yet, but the children have escaped from Thrackan—and they did it aboard the *Millennium Falcon*. They flew the ship. And before you can turn blue, Han, the *Falcon* doesn't have so much as a scratch on her. But the punch line is—they captured Thrackan. Han, you should have seen it. The kids flew a classic inside loop and put two disabling shots right into Thrackan's stern. The Bakurans have taken Thrackan prisoner. Anyway, I know you won't believe it, but the kids did it all—"

"I don't believe it," Han said.

"Sssh!" said Leia.

"—and they are all safe and sound aboard the *Intruder*. Chewbacca and two Drall who got mixed up in all this are being picked up from the repulsor right now. They're okay too, as best we can tell.

"But the real reason I sent this message is to ask you to come here. Gaeriel Captison has called a council of war for eighteen hours from now. We need you all there. Madame Captison wants a Selonian representative as well. Please arrange that if you possibly can. Also, to be blunt about it, the odds are good we're going to need every scrap of firepower we can get before the end of this. We need all of you, we need the *Jade's Fire,* and we need Luke's X-wing. Send a return message as soon as possible, reporting your intentions. But whatever you do, please hurry. We are almost out of time."

CHAPTER FOURTEEN

The Last Good-bye

Leia Organa Solo, Chief of State of the New Republic, ran full-tilt down the access ramp of the *Jade's Fire*, onto the hangar deck of the *Intruder*, and nearly knocked over two of the honor guard as she rushed forward to her children, flinging her arms around the twins. Anakin escaped her first swooping hug simply because he was hopping too fast and too high with excitement to be an easy target. But Han Solo was hard on the heels of his wife, and he scooped Anakin clear up off the ground. Luke joined the happy little knot of chaos, hugging the children, greeting them, tousling Jacen's hair, tickling Jaina, lifting Anakin out of Han's arms to hold him in his own. Threepio tottered around, offering his own greetings—and generally getting in the way.

"Anakin! Jacen! Jaina!" said Leia. "Oh, let me look at you all." But then she threw her arms around all three of them, and held them so tight it didn't seem likely she could see much of anything at all.

Lando Calrissian joined the tangle of welcome, throwing his arm around Han, shouting a friendly insult in his ear, pounding him on the back, giving Leia a kiss, teasing the children. The other new arrivals, Mara

Jade and the Selonian representative, Dracmus, followed.

Admiral Ossilege allowed himself a thin, wintry smile as he watched the proceedings. "Not the most dignified of entrances, eh, Madame Prime Minister? I would have expected more poise from the Chief of State."

Gaeriel probably could have managed some commonplace comment about ceremony giving way to family, or that there were other considerations besides dignity in the universe, but somehow she couldn't bring herself to do it. She thought of her own little daughter, Malinza, back home on Bakura. She looked to Luke Skywalker, lifting his niece up onto his shoulders, and thought of how good he was with children, and of all the things that might have been, but never could be now. But still, the admiral seemed to be expecting some kind of reply. So she decided to speak, and somehow, the truth slipped out. "I think it's beautiful," she said.

Admiral Hortel Ossilege turned toward her and regarded her with frank surprise. "Indeed?" he said. "Clearly, then, standards of beauty vary greatly. Mine do not include noisy and unruly children."

"Then I pity you," said Gaeriel, quite surprised with herself for being so blunt. "I know of nothing else that brings more beauty into *my* life."

Gaeriel Captison stepped forward, leaving a stunned Admiral Ossilege in her wake. She moved toward the newcomers and offered them a simple, graceful bow. "Madame Chief of State," she said. "Captain Solo. I bid you welcome to the *Intruder,* and wish you much joy of this wonderful reunion." And with that, she knelt down in her very official ministerial robes and gave each of the children a kiss.

Let the old sourpuss chew on that *for a while,* she told herself. Gaeriel had had something of a wild streak in her youth. It was good to know it had not completely abandoned her.

*   *   *

"The situation is, in one sense, complicated and, in another, quite simple," said Belindi Kalenda, addressing the council of war gathered on the flag deck of the *Intruder. And a motley crew this council is,* she told herself. To her immediate left was Ossilege in his perfect dress-white uniform and his chestful of medals, Gaeriel Captison in her ministerial robes, Lando Calrissian with a rather swell-looking purple cape thrown over one shoulder of his burgundy blouse, and Han Solo in a rather rumpled light brown shirt, with a utility vest worn over it. That vest had obviously seen a lot of use over the years. Then came Solo's wife, Leia Organa Solo, the Chief of State, in a plain blue shirt and dark slacks borrowed from Mara Jade. All of the Chief of State's own clothes had of course been lost, destroyed, or abandoned along the way in the last few weeks.

Next to Leia was her brother, Luke Skywalker, in his neatly pressed and insignia-free flight suit. Behind him, against the wall, his two droids, R2-D2 and C-3PO, stood by in case they were called on. Both of the two Drall, Ebrihim and Marcha, wore nothing but plain brown fur—though both seemed to have gotten bits of their fur cooked off in the last two days. Then came the Wookiee Chewbacca, who seemed either moody or thoughtful—she didn't have much luck reading Wookiee expression. Jenica Sonsen had managed to find herself wedged in next to Chewbacca on one side and a nervous-looking Selonian named Dracmus on the other. Sonsen did not look too thrilled about her seating position. By her expression, she expected the Wookiee and the Selonian to start arguing over light meat or dark at any second.

On the other side of Dracmus the Selonian was Mara Jade, looking cool and elegant in a well-tailored but otherwise quite ordinary ship's coverall.

And, Kalenda reminded herself, she was there too, of course. The last few days and hours had been so chaotic that it would have been easy enough to forget her own existence. "To cover the simple side of it first," she went on, "the enemy is closing in on Centerpoint. They need to keep us from interfering with the next starburster burst—which, of course, we must interfere with, no matter what the cost. Considering the number of lives at stake if we fail, I do not think anyone will disagree with me when I suggest that the destruction of our entire force would indeed be a low enough price for victory.

"And we must face the fact that we run such a risk. We have three major combatant ships carrying a total of thirty-two flight-worthy fighters. The enemy has at least eighty larger spacecraft. If all of them carried a full complement of fighters—though I very much doubt they do—the number of fighters on their side would be well up in the hundreds."

The numbers were daunting enough to cause a flurry of whispers and mutters around the table.

Kalenda waited for the murmuring to settle down, and then continued. "We do have a few advantages I can tell you about. We have managed some fairly good long-range scans of the enemy fleet. We've gotten some good imagery of some ships. Most are not that large or that well armed. I can tell you that many of those ships are old, some predating the Imperial period. I doubt that any of them are of post-war construction. They are probably both dated and in relatively poor repair. Parts for many of those ships are going to be hard to come by. They are all but certainly relying on nonstandard and jury-rigged repairs. I would also expect the qualities of their crews to be below average. Their pool of potential recruits could not have been the best. Probably most are flying with a minimum of previous training and experience. However, don't count too much on that. *Some* of those crews are probably going to be as good as ours. We just don't know which ones."

"In short," said Admiral Ossilege, "we have better ships, but the numbers are most definitely against us.

However, we do have a plan for dealing with the situation. We will come to that a bit later." He looked over and nodded at Kalenda. "Continue," he said.

"The complicated side of the situation is that we almost, but not quite, control two of the repulsors. To the best of our knowledge, none of the various front groups—I don't think 'rebel groups' quite suits the case anymore—none of the various front groups controls one at this time. I believe that was a major miscalculation on the part of the Triad. They assumed that locating and activating a repulsor would take much less time than it did."

"Unless they got the estimates exactly right," said Mara Jade, "and the Triad's people are sitting on the Talusian and Tralusian and Corellian repulsors, just waiting for the signals to push the button."

"Exactly right," said Kalenda. "Obviously, the Double World Talus and Tralus repulsors are the most worrisome ones. If the enemy controls those, he has the ability to crush our ships down to rubble in any millisecond he chooses."

"But we don't *think* they have that capability," Ossilege said. "Their fleet is moving in with a great deal of caution. Their behavior is consistent with fears that we control one or more repulsors, while they control none. In my considered opinion, it is *not* consistent with their controlling any of the repulsors. It is not even consistent with a bluff. If the enemy had the Talus or Tralus repulsors operational, this battle would be over already."

"That caution might also explain why they haven't reactivated the interdiction field," said Mara. "They might want to be sure they have a way out of here."

"That's possible," said Jenica Sonsen, "but we don't think that's why it's still down. We've run some numbers on how Centerpoint must operate, what it can do, that sort of thing. The short form is that we don't think they *can* reactivate it while Centerpoint is at this stage of powering itself up for a starbuster shot. Too much power being diverted, too many systems busy. You can turn on an interdiction field while the system is in standby. You can turn one off at any time. You can leave it on while the system is powering up. But you can't initiate an interdiction field while the Glowpoint is charging. At least we think that's the case."

"It damned well better be the case," said Ossilege. "Our plans with Source A depend on it."

"Excuse please," said Dracmus. "What or who is a Source A?"

"We'll come to that a bit later," Ossilege said, a slight smile on his lips.

"What about Centerpoint itself?" Han asked. "Is there any weak spot that we know about? Someplace where we might pile in a lot of firepower and get lucky? Blow the place up?"

"No, sorry," said Sonsen. "It doesn't work that way. Don't forget that the Glowpoint is a containment vessel for an extremely powerful reaction. It's very strong, and it's very good at absorbing and dispersing energy, and well insulated. The figures we worked up show that the energy levels in there at the moment are the equivalent of setting off a proton torpedo at least once a second, and Centerpoint has been putting up with that for days on end. And the rest of the structure is very strong, and very old, and so well sealed and shielded that we've never been able to map most of the interior. I'm told the *Sentinel* has landed search parties that are doing their best to find the control system and shut the system down, but that control system has kept itself pretty well hidden for at least a thousand generations. I doubt they'll find it in just a day or two of looking."

"So the repulsors are our only hope," said Luke. "But then why worry about the Triad fleet at all? Why confront it? Why not just withdraw, get our ships out of harm's way, and concentrate all our effort into activating the repulsors?"

"Because the repulsors are not the only game in

town," said Ossilege. "That *is* an eighty-ship fleet out there, after all. They could dominate this star system indefinitely, if they chose to do so, and we left them alone. Or suppose, for example, they got to the repulsors on Drall and Selonia and grabbed them from us before we were ready to use them?"

"Let's talk about the repulsors for a minute," said Luke. "Where are we with them? How about the Selonian repulsor? Dracmus?"

The Selonian shook her head mournfully. "There is no changing. I have been checking with our people just before this fine meeting. The Sacorrian Selonians, the Triad Selonians of the nameless Den, are weakening. They see the force of our arguments. But they are not with us yet."

"Is there any realistic chance of their being persuaded before the next starbuster shot?" Ossilege asked.

Dracmus looked miserable. "A small one," she admitted at last. "Only a small one. Our best people are working on the Triad Selonians. But we now think perhaps they have received indoctrination in just such a circumstance. We have tried everything, I assure you."

"Have you tried cash?" Mara asked.

"I am begging your pardon?"

"Cash. Money. A travel case full of credit notes. You know. A bribe. Or make it sound nice. Call it a consulting fee. Tell them you want to hire them, and will pay well."

Dracmus looked absolutely amazed. "This had never been occurring to us. We will try it at once."

"Good," said Mara. "And don't be cheap about it. Whatever you offer has got to be cheaper than letting the Triad win."

"What about our repulsor?" asked the Drall, Ebrihim. "Have you made any progress with it?"

"Our tech staff has only had a few hours to work on it," said Ossilege. "It's early to expect results. But rest assured, we have every person with pertinent experience down there working right now."

"That is not the case," said a new voice, a stern female voice that was used to being heard and obeyed. It was the other Drall. Marcha, the Duchess of Mastigophorous. "It is not the case, Admiral, and you know it not to be the case."

"Duchess, might I ask what you are talking about?" asked Ossilege.

"The children," she said. "Anakin in particular, but he works best when the other two are there to help him, guide him."

"Don't be absurd," said Ossilege. "What possible use could they be? How could they possibly have any expertise? I would urge you not to mistake a series of lucky accidents for ability. We do not have time to waste on such nonsense. Move on, Lieutenant."

Kalenda hesitated a moment. It was not her place to contradict her superior officer. But on the other hand, it was not *his* place to be a damned pigheaded fool. And Gaeriel Captison had reminded her, not so long ago, that there was more to life than adhering to military etiquette. "Sir, my apologies for discussing this in front of others, but there may not be another chance, and the stakes are too high. I believe you are making a mistake."

"What!?"

"Sir, it is my job to analyze events and come to conclusions. I have analyzed the events surrounding the children, and I have come to the conclusion that their abilities are—are remarkable. They have been constantly underestimated, their achievements constantly dismissed as exaggerated, or lucky accidents, or remarkable coincidences. That is simply not true. It is not credible." She pointed at Drall, plainly visible through the main bridge viewports. "The plain fact of the matter is that you have a repulsor down there because a seven-and-a-half-year-old boy found it for you, and turned it on. It is no longer in the hands of our enemy—and our enemy is in the brig—because that boy and his siblings managed to walk through a working force field, repair a disabled starship, fly that ship into space, and shoot down a pursuing spacecraft flown by a professional military pilot. I could go on for half an hour, describing all the things that they could not possibly have done, but the point will remain the same."

Ossilege looked up at Kalenda, his expression utterly unreadable. Was there anger seething under there? Was he simply considering her words? Was he infuriated at the assault on his authority, or simply wondering if she might be right? It was impossible to tell. The man was completely inscrutable. "You argue most effectively, Lieutenant Kalenda. You marshal your facts well. You will either go far as an intelligence officer or end your career in the brig for insubordination. I had intended to disembark all noncombatants on Drall in any event, and it occurs to me that the shielded side chambers of the repulsor are probably the safest place to be right now. Madame Chief of State, Captain Solo—if, as Lieutenant Kalenda claims, your children might be of help, would you consent to their being put to work?"

"Absolutely," said Han. "Not that it matters what we think. Get them within a hundred kilometers of trouble, and they'll find it all on their own."

"Madame Chief of State?"

"We need all the help we can get," said Leia. "Let them do their part."

Ossilege raised his eyebrows and looked hard at both of them. "Very well," he said. "Then let us move on. Lieutenant?"

"Well, sir, to sum up, we have two objectives, neither of them very easy. First is to defeat the Triad fleet and prevent it from dominating this star system. Second is to do whatever we can to prevent Centerpoint from firing again. I believe that covers everything we were going to discuss, except for Source A—and I believe you wanted to cover that yourself."

Ossilege smiled broadly—and it was unusual to see any smile at all on his face. He stood up and looked about at all the faces around the table. "Source A," he said. "Source A, if I am not mistaken, is known to several of you already. But let me tell the rest of you about him."

* * *

If the day had started with joyous reunions, it ended with tearful good-byes. "Do you really have to go, Mommy?" asked Anakin, his voice a little snuffly, his chin quivering just a bit. They were in the *Intruder*'s hangar deck again, the last load of noncombatants boarding the shuttle that would take them down to the safety of the repulsor's shielded side caverns.

"Yes I do, dearest," Leia said, kneeling down in front of him, forcing a reassuring smile onto her face. "And so do you. Everyone has a job today. I have to help Daddy and Chewbacca fly the *Falcon*. You and your brother and sister have to go down to the repulsor again, and see if you can make it work the way we need it to."

"I bet we can," said Anakin.

"I'll bet you can too, sport," said Han, tousling his son's hair. He was smiling too, but even Anakin must have been able to see the pain in his eyes. And even Anakin knew that everyone had to pretend that everything was fine.

Leia looked up at Jaina and Jacen. "You two take care of each other, and of Anakin, all right? And do what Threepio and Ebrihim and the Duchess tell you to do. And be sure to—be sure to—"

Suddenly Leia stopped, her voice choked up. It was all too ridiculous. She was going into battle, she was sending her children to operate a machine that could move a planet around, sending them off to face more responsibility than most intelligent beings ever dreamed of, she might be killed and never see them again, and yet she was left with nothing to tell them but the age-old motherly admonitions to behave themselves and brush their teeth.

"We will, Mom," said Jaina, her voice gentle and low. "Don't worry, we'll do all the things we're supposed to do."

"Fear not, Madame Chief of State," said Threepio. "I shall take good care of them all—assuming the Drall permit me."

Leia threw her arms about her children, shut her eyes, and squeezed them as tight as she could. "I love you all," she managed to say, before her voice choked up altogether.

She held them for as long as she could, and a little bit longer besides, until Han knelt down beside her and gently pulled her arms back. "It's time to go," he said. "The ship has to leave."

Leia nodded, unable to speak. She kissed each of them one last time, and Han did the same. The three children and Threepio walked aboard the shuttle transport, and the shuttle transport lifted off.

And they were gone.

*   *   *

There were plenty of other good-byes, of course, and none of them were easy. Luke, Lando, Mara, Kalenda, Gaeriel, all of the others. They all knew the odds were very much against everyone making it back. They all knew some of these good-byes might be for more than a day or two. They might be forever. And yet, they all understood that sort of good-bye. They all had been there before, said good-bye to a comrade for an hour or a day, and then never seen the comrade again. There was a code, a ritual, a sort of a ceremony to it all, that made such good-byes, if not easier, at least far more manageable, more understandable.

But there was one other leave-taking that had a different set of emotions behind it. There was one more person Han had to see before he went into battle. And that person was in the brig.

Maybe it was curiosity. Maybe it was the last frayed thread of the family ties. Or maybe those family threads were stronger than he thought. Maybe blood was stronger even than betrayal.

Or maybe—though Han doubted it—he just wanted to gloat. It didn't feel that way, but you never knew. You never knew.

Whatever the reasons, he had come. The guard activated the door control, and Han stepped into the detention cell. Thrackan was sitting on a low bench set against the far wall of the room.

"Hello, Thrackan," he said.

"Hello, Han. Come to see the rare specimen in his cage?"

"I'm not sure why I came," said Han. "For some reason I wanted to see you. So here I am."

"And here *I* am," Thrackan said, a cruel smile on his face. He lifted his head up, threw his arms out wide, and stuck his chest out. "Here I am," he said again. "Get a good look."

"You shouldn't have done it, Thrackan," said Han.

"Oh, there are lots of things I shouldn't have done," Thrackan said. "I certainly shouldn't have gone off in pursuit of those miserable, freakish children. That was a fatal mistake. Fatal. But what specific act did you have in mind?"

"The children," Han said. "My children. You should not have kidnapped the children. *Never involve the innocent. Always protect your family.* Two of the oldest traditions of Corellia. I remember your sneering at those ideas, saying it was no great sin in breaking them. But that was just words. You didn't just talk about breaking those laws. You did it. You *did* it. Thrackan, how could you?"

"Easily," Thrackan said. "Far too easily. They just

fell into my hand. How could I *not* keep them? Why shouldn't I have kept them?"

"Because it was wrong, Thrackan."

Thrackan sighed wearily and leaned back against the wall. "Han. Please. I'm locked away in a cell. By all rights, the longest part of my trial will be the reading of the charges against me. The jury shouldn't even leave the box. There isn't even any point to a jury or a trial at all. The sensible thing would be just to have me taken out and shot. But I'm sure they will give me all the relentlessly fair justice they can find to throw at me—and then lock me away forever. I'll probably never have any freedom of action ever again. So there's not much point in teaching me right from wrong. Not at this late date."

"You're beaten, Thrackan," said Han. "You've lost, and lost everything."

Thrackan chuckled. "True enough, Han. True enough. But I do have one consolation."

"What's that, Thrackan?"

Thrackan Sal-Solo, would-be Diktat of Corellia, gestured vaguely toward the outside of the cell, toward the universe beyond. "The Triad fleet out there," he said. "Maybe I've lost, Han, but it does me a world of good to know that *you* haven't won yet." He smiled in a chillingly close imitation of Han's own lopsided grin, an imitation turned cold and hard and cruel. "And I don't think you're going to, either."

Han stared at his cousin. Then, without saying another word, he turned and knocked on the cell door. It slid open, and Han walked away.

He still didn't know why he had come.

CHAPTER FIFTEEN

Showdown at Centerpoint

At last, at long last, it was time to board ship, launch, and head out into space. But getting to that point was not easy.

The Bakurans needed all the firepower of the newly repaired *Millennium Falcon,* and no one could argue that the *Falcon* needed a crew of at least three—a pilot, a copilot, and a gunner—in order to provide the maximum firepower. There was, of course, never even the slightest debate over who the pilot and copilot should be. Han and Chewbacca belonged in those seats, and there was no doubt about it.

But more than a few people tried to talk Leia out of sitting in the quad laser turret. It was not proper for a Chief of State to go flying around taking potshots at enemy ships. But Leia was adamant. She had had enough of being pushed around in recent weeks. It was high time she paid a little of that back. The harder people tried to talk her out of going on the mission, the more determined she became. Even Ossilege tried to talk her out of it. But even Ossilege realized, eventually, that he had to back down.

But now she was aboard, Chewbacca was aboard, and the *Millennium Falcon* was ready. Now was the moment. Han checked his status boards one last time, confirmed his departure instructions, brought the repulsors on, and flew out into the sky.

Once well clear of the *Intruder,* he eased back on the sublight engines and waited for the others to form up on him. They were going into battle together—Han, Chewie, and Leia aboard the *Millennium Falcon,* Mara Jade alone aboard the *Jade's Fire,* Lando aboard the *Lady Luck,* and Luke in his X-wing. It made a certain amount of sense to put all the non-Bakuran ships in one formation. It saved forcing the Bakuran fighter pilots to learn how to deal with nonstandard ships in their formations. Han had been aboard all of the other ships, and their pilots had been aboard his. Perhaps more importantly, all four of the pilots knew each other, trusted each other's skill.

Han watched as the *Lady Luck* flew out of the hangar doors and toward him. Suddenly Han felt good. They were flying into danger, into battle, but what of that? He had done it before. He was behind the controls of his own ship, in space, surrounded by friends. What was to feel bad about? He saw the *Lady Luck* do a double barrel roll just as Luke's X-wing launched. Han laughed out loud. He wasn't the only one feeling good. He keyed on the com system. *"Falcon* to *Lady Luck.* Lando, you old pirate, the idea is to fly in a straight line just at the moment. I think you just wobbled off course a bit."

"Aw, can't a guy have a little fun now and then?"

"Relax, both of you," said Luke as he pulled into position off Lando's starboard wing. "We're going to get a chance to do all the fancy flying we want today."

The *Jade's Fire* launched, and Mara came on the line. "I don't know about the rest of you," she said, "but I'd be just as happy if this stayed nice and simple."

Chewbacca cut off the ship-to-ship link, hooted loudly, and bared his fangs.

Han laughed. "All right," he said, "so she's a spoilsport. Any spoilsport who can fly the way she does can be my wingman any day of the week."

* * *

"How far have you gotten?" asked Anakin as he looked over the gleaming silver control panel. It looked just the way he had left it, after pushing one button too many a few days before.

The technician's name was Antone, and he was a thin, wiry-looking fellow, dark-skinned with shoulder-length, shiny black hair that hung straight down on either side of his face. He didn't answer at first, but instead gave Anakin a strange look, a look Anakin had seen before. It was the look Anakin got from grown-ups who had heard he was weirdly good with machines, but didn't quite believe it yet. Antone glanced at Jaina and Jacen, and got an encouraging nod from both of them. "I assure you, young Master Anakin is remarkably talented," Threepio volunteered.

Antone seemed unwilling to take the droid's word, but Ebrihim and Marcha and Q9 were there too, and somehow the presence of the Drall seemed to convince Technician Antone to take things seriously and cooperate. "I'd say we're stuck," he said, "except that might be saying too much. It makes it sound like we'd been making progress and then stopped. But we never got anywhere in the first place."

"Not at *all*?" Anakin asked.

"Not at all. The system won't respond to any commands we give it."

"Sure it will," said Anakin. He sat down at the control panel and pushed his hand down onto a flat, featureless spot on the console. He pulled his hand away, and the surface of the console started to shift and rise up, forming itself into a joysticklike shape—but one perfectly shaped to Anakin's hand. Anakin touched the joystick, just touched it, and a hollow wireframe five-by-five-by-five of cubes appeared in the air over the control panel. Anakin let go of the joystick. It remained in place for a moment, then melted back down into the console as the cube display vanished.

"How did you do that?" Antone demanded. He scooted Anakin out of the chair and pressed his own hand down on exactly the same place on the panel. Nothing happened. Nothing at all. Antone gave Anakin another strange look, and then comprehension dawned in his face. "Burning stars," he said. "Burning stars. It must have imprinted itself on your personal characteristics the first time you used it."

"Huh?" Anakin said.

"What do you mean?" demanded Jacen.

"It imprinted on him, somehow. It locked in on his fingerprints, or his DNA, or his brain waves, or something, and locked them into its memory. It'll only work for him."

Anakin's eyes lit up with a wild gleam. "Only for *me*?" he asked. "It's all *mine*?"

"There must be a way to let other users use it," Jacen objected.

"Yeah, probably," said Antone, "but we don't have time to look for them. We have to work with what we've got."

"Wait a moment," Ebrihim objected. "Are you saying what I think you're saying?"

Antone nodded solemnly. "Your little friend here is the only person who is going to be able to operate this control panel. And from what I've seen, and what you've told me, even if he can make it *work,* I'm not sure he really understands what it *does.*"

"I believe," said Threepio, "that you have just offered an *excellent* summing-up."

*   *   *

Gaeriel Captison watched Admiral Ossilege pace the floor of the flag deck, and could not help but feel sympathy for the man. They were, for the moment, alone on the flag deck, and that fact spoke volumes. He had told everyone to go off and do his bidding, and now they were gone. Later, perhaps, this place would be chaos, with aides rushing in and out, mountains of message forms covering every flat surface, klaxons blaring and orders bellowing out from the overhead speakers. But now it was quiet, empty, a lonely place.

And Ossilege must be an especially lonely man right now. There would be decisions yet to make, orders to give, but now, for the most part, his job was over. He had deployed his forces, issued his instructions, laid his plans. Now all he could do was wait.

"It isn't easy, is it?" she asked. "You send them out to do your bidding, and off they go, following your instructions, living or dying, winning or losing, because of what you ordered."

"No," he said, "it isn't easy. Everyone else knows what to do, because I have told them. But who tells me?"

For Ossilege, that was a remarkable bit of introspection, bordering on self-pity. He himself seemed to realize that had given too much away, for he stopped his pacing and sat down in the admiral's chair.

A chime sounded, and a deep, melodic robotic voice spoke from the overhead speaker. "All outbound craft launched and clear," it said. "*Intruder* getting under way in thirty seconds. All hands to assigned battle stations."

Ossilege sat motionless throughout the announcement, not moving or speaking. Gaeriel could not tell if he was listening to it intently or not even aware that the voice had spoken. The chime sounded again, there was a change in the vibrations of the ship, and the flag deck instruments started reporting forward movement. They were on their way.

"Tell me," Ossilege said at last, speaking after such a long silence that Gaeriel jumped ten centimeters in the air. "The plan. Do you think it will work?"

                         *   *   *

The irony was almost too obvious. After endless weeks
of being trapped aboard the *Gentleman Caller,* wishing
above all else to move faster, get to where she was
going sooner, Tendra Risant now had not the slightest
desire for her ship to go anywhere at all. The *Gent*
floated quietly in the darkness of space, in a stable free
orbit of Corell—an orbit that put her squarely between
the Triad fleet and the two Bakuran destroyers. She
had not the slightest doubt that both sides were tracking her, watching her go by. Probably both of them
recognized her ship for what she was—a civilian non-
combatant, accidentally caught between the two fleets.
As long as she floated, unpowered, through space, she
represented no particular danger. But she also had no
doubt at all that both sides would fire immediately if
they felt in the slightest way threatened by the *Gentleman Caller.*

   And the *Gentleman Caller* was surrounded. There
was no direction at all she could find that wouldn't
take her close to the path of one ship or another. She
did not dare maneuver, for fear of one side or the
other deciding she was a booby trap, a bomb or a
weapon disguised as a civilian ship.

   All she could do was sit here, and pray to whatever
gods she could think of that no one decided she was
getting in the way.

   No one knew exactly what was going to happen next,
Tendra least of all. But whatever did happen, she was
going to have a ring-side seat for it.

                         *   *   *

It has been said, by more than a few observers, who
have put it more than a few different ways, that war-
fare consists of long stretches of boredom, interspersed
with short, sharp bursts of chaos and terror. Lando had
been through battles enough in his day to realize the
truth of that description. Or, to put it another way, it

was a long, long flight from Drall to Centerpoint. Long enough that Luke, aboard the X-wing, returned to the *Intruder* twice for brief rest periods as they traveled. Luke, Jedi Master that he was, certainly could have toughed it out, but Luke was not a fool. And only fools deliberately went into combat worn and unrested. The others—Han and his crew, Mara, and Lando—could all get up and stretch, set the autopilot, and sneak off for a nap. Not Luke.

They could have used a very brief jump through hyperspace to shorten the trip substantially, but there were reasons they did not want the Triad fleet thinking too much about hyperspace. And they also wanted the Triads to have their attention focused on the *Intruder*, the three trading ships, and the *Intruder*'s fighter escort. The more they looked there, the less they would look in other directions.

Lando punched up his own detector system and tried to get an idea of how the Triad fleet was reacting. So far, they didn't seem to be in the least bit distracted by the *Intruder*. The whole fleet was still moving in toward Centerpoint at a slow, steady pace of its own. Nothing substantially different from the last time he checked, or the time before that. Soon, though. Soon. They were getting close enough to start picking targets, planning their attack—

Wait a second. Lando frowned at his display. Had that been there before, or had he just missed it? A tiny ship, civilian by the looks of what the detectors could tell him, right smack in between Centerpoint and the Triad fleet.

And wait another second. Where could that ship have come from? Lando sent a signal querying the *Intruder*'s position board database for the last few days. He went back to the time just before the interdiction field went down, and played it forward from there. The tiny ship winked into existence *before* the Triad ships. But how could anybody get here before the Triad, unless—

Lando sat bolt upright. Unless they were closer than the Triad ships, coming from much closer in. From inside the interdiction field, for example.

Lando finally had the sense to try it the easy way. He sent the standard ship-ID query signal. Fifteen seconds later he had his answer back. Twenty seconds after *that* he had changed course and accelerated to his top sublight speed in order to intercept. It was a full minute later before he realized he should have asked permission, a realization he came to mostly because his com board started lighting up. He punched the transmit button. "*Lady Luck* to *Intruder*," he said. "I've, ah, just spotted something. I'm just heading over to investigate it. I'll be back with the fleet in good time for the main event."

"*Intruder* to *Lady Luck*," replied a rather fussy-sounding voice. "The object you are on intercept for is an identified and uninvolved civilian spacecraft. No need to investigate."

"Well, I'm going to anyway," Lando said. "She might not be as uninvolved as you think." *Or at least,* he thought, *she's not going to be uninvolved for long.*

* * *

To Ebrihim's eye, the control room of Drall's planetary repulsor looked as if a bomb had hit it. It was knee deep in crumpled bits of paper and discarded food containers. Little knots of technicians were huddled in every corner of the room, arguing over readings, debating what various arrangements of purple and orange and green cubes and bars of light might mean. Handwritten labels were stuck over about half the controls on the console. As the other half of the controls seemed to appear and disappear and change shape and size almost at whim, it was a trifle more difficult to label them.

Jaina and Jacen were asleep on cots in the next room over. Ebrihim and Marcha were still on the go, in the thick of it, helping the techs order their readings, sketching out the various transmutations of the control panel. Q9 usually seemed to have two or three remote sensors out as he traced this signal or that through the interior of the control system and took power readings, and he and Threepio had found any number of things to bicker about.

But all the rest of them could work as hard and as much as they wanted. Anakin was still in the center of it all, still going strong, working the controls as he was asked, shifting the system from one mode to another, helping the grown-ups understand what all the buttons meant. He had that wild-eyed look in his eyes that human children sometimes seemed to get when they had been up too long or had been too stimulated for too long. Sooner or later it would all be too much for him, and the poor child would simply keel over from exhaustion. Ordinarily, it would already be time, and past time, to get the child to bed, but under the circumstances they had to get as much out of him as possible before—

"Newses! I have good newses!" an excited voice shouted. Everyone stopped what they were doing and looked up as Dracmus rushed into the room. "The Sacorrian Selonians! What a splendid idea this bribing was! Must congratulate honored Jade on fine suggestion!"

"They've agreed to cooperate?" Ebrihim asked eagerly.

"No, Honored Ebrihim!" said Dracmus in the same gleeful voice. "They refuse! They delay! Maybe later they come around, but not yet."

"Then why are you so happy?" Marcha demanded.

"Because bribe suggestion gives *them* idea." She held up a datapad and waved it in the air. "They still not willing to help with *their* repulsor—but they willing to sell instruction manual!"

"Lemme see that," Antone said, and grabbed at the datapad. He turned it on and paged through it, grinning more and more widely as he did so. He nodded enthusiastically. "This is it," he said. "With what Anakin has shown us, and what this tells us about the notation—I think—I'm not sure but at least I *think*, we can run this place."

"You mean," said Ebrihim, "you think that *Anakin* can run this place for—" He stopped in midsentence.

"Oh, dear," said Threepio. "He's done it again. It often happens when he stays up too late." Anakin was still sitting in the control panel's chair, but his head was resting on the panel itself, and he was sound asleep. Ebrihim nodded in wonder. Human children. Bizarre creatures. Anakin had been wide awake and busily working not thirty seconds before. "Ah, well," Ebrihim said. "The rest of us can keep working, but I suppose a child has to get a good night's sleep if he's expected to save two or three star systems in the morning."

* * *

Tendra Risant was asleep when it happened. The first she knew that there was anything going on was when a large booming noise echoed through the hull of the *Gentleman Caller.* To say she found it a startling way to wake up would be a massive understatement. She nearly jumped out of her skin. She sat up in bed, listening fearfully. What was it? Had a meteor crashed into the ship? Had something in the engine room blown up? Then she heard the whirring noise of doors sliding open and air pumps working. The airlock! Someone had docked with the *Gentleman Caller*!

She scrambled out of bed and pulled her robe on. Who was it? What did they want? A weapon. She needed a weapon. Was there even a blaster on board the ship? She stepped out into the corridor—and froze in her tracks. There he was, right in front of her, grinning from ear to ear. "I tried to call ahead," he said, "but there wasn't any answer."

"Lando?" she asked. He was the first human being she had seen in a month.

"Tendra."

And suddenly they were in each other's arms, holding each other tight. "Oh, Lando. Lando. You shouldn't have come. You shouldn't have. There are ships on all sides of us, and sooner or later the shooting is going to start and—"

"Hey, hey," said Lando. "Shh. Take it easy," he said. "Take it easy. My ship is plenty fast enough to get us out of here. We'll be all right."

"But it's too dangerous!" she insisted. "It was too risky."

"Come on," Lando said, stroking her chin and giving her a big, warm smile. "I had to think of my image. How could I possibly turn down the chance to rescue the damsel in distress?"

*   *   *

The hours crawled past. The Triad ships moved toward Centerpoint, the *Sentinel* and the *Defender* kept up their guard over Centerpoint, and the *Intruder*'s little fleet of armed trading ships and fighters moved in toward the Triad ships.

Ossilege watched it all on his status boards, hour after weary hour, alone on the flag deck. No one needed to come here. Not until the battle began. Time was the enemy now, and time was the ally. They had to thread this needle carefully, oh, so carefully. Too soon, and they would give the game away, and all of Source A's efforts would be in vain. Too late, and the other side would jump first, attack the Bakuran ships and be done with it.

And then there was the whole vexed question of the repulsor. Would they have it, or wouldn't they? Would it work, or wouldn't it? Were Calrissian's figures for the timing of Centerpoint's next shot even accurate? They had checked over the figures a dozen times, and they *seemed* correct. But what of the error no one saw, the bad assumption that everyone agreed to without even realizing it?

They were the sort of questions that had plagued military commanders from the beginning of time, and they were likely to keep on doing so for quite some time to come.

Time. *That* was the question. What was the proper time? There was no way of knowing for sure. No way of reading intentions off a display grid, no way of judging enemy morale and fighting prowess from a remote infrared image.

The ships moved closer to each other. Closer. Closer.

At last Admiral Hortel Ossilege stood up, walked over to the main display grid, and inspected it carefully, studying each ship, each status report in turn. Satisfied, or at least as satisfied as he was going to get, he returned to the admiral's chair, sat down, and pressed the com button. "This is Ossilege. Advise all ships via prearranged signal. Commence Operation Sidestep exactly on the hour, thirty-five minutes from now." One hour after Sidestep, it would be time for Source A. One hour, five minutes, and fifteen seconds after Sidestep, Centerpoint would fire. Either they would manage to deflect the shot, or they would not.

One hour. They would have to hold for one hour. He let go of the com button, and wondered if he had gotten the timing right.

*　　*　　*

"All right, Chewie," said Han, half an hour later. "Jump off in five minutes. Let's look sharp. Leia—time for you to get up to the turret and strap in."

Leia stood up from the observer's seat and nodded. "I know," she said. But she didn't leave. Not immediately. First she stepped forward, pulled Han's head toward hers, and gave Han a kiss. A warm, lingering kiss that did not so much end as fade gently away. "I love you," she said.

"I know," said Han. "And you know I love you."

Leia smiled. "You're right," she said. "I do." She stood up straight, reached over, and ruffled the fur on top of Chewbacca's head. "So long, Chewie," she said. "See you on the other side." And with that, she turned and left the cockpit.

Han turned and watched her go, then looked over to Chewbacca. "You know, Chewie," he told the Wookiee, "there's a lot to be said for this being married business."

Chewbacca let out a low, rumbling laugh and went back to double-checking the shield settings.

Han checked the time. Four minutes to go.

*　　*　　*

Luke Skywalker sat in the cockpit of his X-wing and felt the old tingle of fear and excitement starting to build. He reminded himself that he was a Jedi, that Jedi were calm in battle, that there was no fear. But Luke, better than any human being alive, knew that Jedi did not live in a world of absolutes and abstracts, any more than other people did. It would be just as bad to force all emotion from his life as to wallow endlessly in all his feelings.

It was time to fight. He was ready to do so. His Jedi abilities made him more ready.

That should have been enough. And it was.

Luke glanced at his chronometer. Three minutes.

*　　*　　*

Mara Jade sat alone in the command center of her ship. Alone. She had come to this star system with a pilot and a navigator, Tralkpha and Nesdin. They had vanished, along with so many others, in the first days of the war. Mara did not know if they were dead, or captured by one group or another, or hiding under some pile of rubble until it was safe to come out. Mara knew war as well as anyone. She knew full well that it was most likely that they were dead. They had been good at their jobs, and good, honest people, both of them. And now they weren't there anymore, more than likely executed for the simple crime of getting in the way of someone's bloody ambition. If nothing else had happened to inspire her to fight, that would have been enough.

But, of course, plenty more had happened. And she was going to start giving it back in about two minutes' time.

*   *   *

"I'm not so sure I did you any favor by rescuing you," Lando said, strapping himself in. "Where you were, you might have been killed by accident. Now if you get killed, it'll be because someone did it on purpose."

Tendra shook her head and smiled. "Trust me, Lando. If there is one thing I learned on board the *Gentleman Caller,* it's that I don't want to die alone. I've had enough being alone for a lifetime."

Lando reached out a hand to Tendra, riding in the copilot's seat. She took it, and held it tight.

Neither of them said anything more, but the silence in the cabin said more than enough.

But then the countdown alert beeped the one-minute warning, and there was no time.

*   *   *

Belindi Kalenda was already there, along with the rest of the flag staff, but Gaeriel Captison just got back to the flag deck in time to strap herself in. "I was in my cabin," she said, though Ossilege hadn't asked. "Meditating." *And thinking about my daughter. My daughter,*

Malinza, who has already lost her father. Is this the day she stops having a mother as well?

"A good time for it," Ossilege said. "There will not be much leisure for thought, starting in another thirty seconds."

Gaeriel dug her fingers into the arms of her acceleration seat, and stared out through the flag deck's main viewport, out over the *Intruder*'s main bridge level, and through the bridge's forward viewport. *The stars,* she thought. *The warm and inviting stars.* Was one of the ones she saw Bakura? Probably her home's star was nowhere near bright enough to be visible at this range. Home. She thought of home, and longed to be there.

"Ten seconds," the main speaker announced. "All hands, prepare for the jump to light speed. Five seconds. Four. Three. Two. One. Zero."

And the stars lanced out into spikes of fire, starlines that filled the viewport with a blaze of light—and then the starlines flared away, and were gone, and the familiar stars of Corellia's sky were right back where they had been.

But now there were more than stars in the sky. Ships. Ships of all sizes and descriptions had suddenly popped into existence. The *Intruder,* the *Sentinel,* the *Defender,* and all the lesser ships had made simultaneous, precision minimum-distance hyperspace jumps straight into the thick of the enemy fleet. Ossilege had hoped it would give them the benefit of surprise, and it would appear that it had.

The *Intruder*'s main laser cannon opened up at once, stabbing out at the ship nearest her, a boxy, ramshackle old troop transport that had no business in the middle of a combat fleet.

The transport exploded in a bloom of fire, but by then the main lasers had already found another target, a modern-looking corvette about the size of the *Jade's Fire.* The corvette got her shields up in time, but they were not intended to hold off intense short-range fire from a light cruiser's gun. Her shields failed and she went up as well, another blaze of hellfire glory.

The *Intruder*'s fighter screen winked into existence around her, fifteen General Purpose Attack fighters that immediately went over to the attack, blazing away at the smaller, lighter craft in this part of the fleet.

The *Intruder*'s secondary battery began to speak, blasting away at some target out of Gaeriel's view. A Triad ship fired and caught a GPA coming out of a loop low over the *Intruder*'s main bridge. The fighter exploded, a blinding bright flash of light that heaved a torrent of debris at the cruiser. The shields deflected most of it, and slowed the rest of it. Loud crashes echoed throughout the bridge as debris banged into the outer hull, but there did not seem to be any real damage. Except, of course, to the GPA and its pilot. The surviving fighters whirled and dashed about, blasting the X-TIE Uglies and B-wing chop jobs out of the sky.

At last an opponent worthy of the *Intruder* hove into view, an old, tough-looking ex-Imperial destroyer of a class Gaeriel did not recognize. The ship was smaller than the *Intruder,* but quite possibly her match in firepower. The *Intruder* opened up on her, directing all-guns fire directly at the destroyer's forward laser turret. The destroyer returned fire from her forward and rear turrets, but failed to concentrate her fire with any effectiveness. The destroyer's forward battery blew up, and the *Intruder* instantly redirected fire to her rear battery. The destroyer's overall shields must have been damaged in the first explosion, for they gave way completely after only a few seconds of concentrated fire on the rear turret. The turret went up in a dramatic sheet of flame, and the destroyer was disarmed.

Gaeriel glanced over at Ossilege, and was astonished to see that he was paying no mind at all to the fire and chaos outside. His eyes were glued to the tactical display in front of him as he watched the overall progress of the fight. He was letting the *Intruder*'s Captain Semmac fight her ship, while he attended to the larger battle.

"It's going well," Ossilege announced to no one in particular.

At least, thought Gaeriel, *it's starting well.*

* * *

"Hang on, Artoo!" Luke cried out as he flipped his X-wing over onto its back and then pulled its nose up, pursuing the X-TIE Ugly that was making a run in on the *Lady Luck* up ahead and above. "Lando, break starboard and down, hard, on my mark. Three, two, one, MARK!" Luke broke the X-wing down and to starboard a fraction of a second before the *Lady Luck* did. The X-TIE Ugly, a monstrosity of a ship slapped together out of the combined wreckage of an X-wing and a TIE fighter, was nowhere as maneuverable as an X-wing. The Ugly fell into the trap, making a longer, shallower dive in pursuit of the *Lady Luck*—and setting itself up for a perfect shot from Luke. Luke fired, and the starboard TIE wing blew clean off the Ugly, sending it tumbling out of control and out of the fight. It took Luke a moment to find the *Lady,* and he was not surprised to see her already in trouble again, trying to fight off a pair of what looked like Light Attack Fighters with beefed-up engines and weapons. Heavy Light Attack Fighters.

It was nearly always a mistake to hang overpowered weapons and propulsion on a design that wasn't meant to support them. That sort of beefed-up compromise was usually nothing more than a collection of weaknesses held together with wrap-wire and optimism. Luke decided to test the theory by experiment. He poured fire into the closest HLAF from extreme range, and caught it in the port-side engine, setting the fighter tumbling out of control before the pilot could kill the starboard engine. The engine flared over and started spewing thick clouds of vapor that enveloped the

HLAF. The vapor dissipated instantly in the vacuum of space, and the HLAF was hidden inside a strange, fast-moving cloud tumbling across space. Luke checked Lando, and saw he had dispatched the other HLAF himself. For the moment their little patch of sky was clear. That meant it was time to move elsewhere.

"Lando!" Luke called. "I'm tracking a slow-moving destroyer toward the rear of the formation. You have it?"

"I was just about to call it in to you, Luke," said Lando. "Let's go for it. Just what we're looking for." The plan was for the attacking craft to move through the Triad formation toward its rear, picking off targets of opportunity and trying to get the Triad ships to reverse course and pursue.

And never mind the obvious flaw in trying to encourage eighty major armed vessels and all their auxiliaries to chase you with all guns blazing. Sometimes you just had to take your chances. "Off we go," Luke agreed.

*   *   *

Anakin sat in the control chair, listening intently to Technician Antone as he ran down the checklist. "All right," said Antone, "that clears out the targeting sequence. We should be locked on to the South Pole of Centerpoint. Ready for the power initiation sequence?"

"Don't *think* so," Anakin said, a little doubtfully. "Something doesn't *feel* right."

Antone shoved his long black hair out of his eyes for about the zillionth time and looked nervously at Anakin. "*Feel* right?" he asked. "What do you mean it doesn't *feel* right?"

"He does it all by feel," Jacen said. "He knows by instinct and intuition. You've got an instruction manual. *You're* the one who said you didn't think he understood what it did."

"Do so!" Anakin protested angrily, glaring at his brother.

"Do you, Anakin?" Jaina asked. She was plainly getting as fed up as Antone. "Do you *really* understand or are you just showing off?"

Anakin frowned deeply and crossed his arms. "Stop being mean to me, or I won't help you anymore." And with that, he hopped down off the chair and stalked away.

"Oh, boy," said Jaina.

"I suspect that young Master Anakin is overtired," Threepio said. "He was up too late last night. He is often rather cranky the next day on such occasions."

Antone's eyes bugged out, and his jaw dropped open. It was at least a full five seconds before he was able to speak. "He's *cranky*? He's the—he's the only one who can—who can—" Antone gestured frantically at the control panel. "The starbuster is going to fire in an hour, and you tell me he's *cranky*?"

"Take it easy," Ebrihim said.

"But he's gone!" Antone said. "He's the only one who can run the machine!"

"You've been up all night," Ebrihim said. "You're overwrought. We'll get him back."

"Yeah. Up all night," said Technician Antone, nodding manically as he paced. "Maybe *I'm* just cranky too." He turned and stopped his pacing to face the twins. "Except that's not quite it. Actually, I think I'm in full-blown panic! I've got *relatives* on Bovo Yagen," Antone went on, half raving. "If I get her planet incinerated, my aunt is going to *kill* me."

"Settle down," Ebrihim said in a sterner tone of voice. "He can't have gone far. We need both of you to make this work. Jacen, go and get your brother back. Calm him down. And try to remember that the lives of twelve million people are riding on one cranky seven-year-old saving them in an hour's time. So *please*. When he comes back, let's everyone be nice to him."

"All right," Jaina said, her own voice turning a bit sulky. "But only for an hour."

*   *   *

"Concentrate volley fire on the forward airlock hatch!" Mara's voice called out from the ship-to-ship link. "Those welds look nice and sloppy!" Fire poured from the *Jade's Fire* into the lumbering, old, much-repaired Mon Calamari frigate that had ended up fighting for the other side.

"Copy that," said Han. "Leia, hang on. I'm going to pitch over a bit to give you a clean shot."

"I'm in the clear already," Leia said. "Commencing fire."

The quad laser turret started shooting. The outer door of the airlock had gotten jammed open somehow in the fighting. It began to glow red, then orange, then fire-white—and then the inner hatch blew off, the ship's atmosphere streaming away into space. The airflow cut off suddenly as a hatch slammed shut somewhere on the ship.

The frigate fired back, heavy volley fire straight into the *Millennium Falcon*. The shield alarms went on almost at once, and then cut off just as quickly as the *Jade's Fire* blew the frigate's main laser turret clean off with a mini-torpedo.

Disarmed and damaged, the frigate seemed to decide she had had enough. She came about and boosted away for all she was worth.

"Let her go," Han said to Mara. "She's out of the fight, and that's all that matters."

"How long has it been?" Leia asked over the intercom.

"About forty minutes," Han said. "Watch out, a pair of B-wing Uglies coming in from above."

"I'm on them," Leia said, the strain in her voice plain to hear. Fire lanced out of the quad laser turret.

An explosion broke up one B-wing, and the other decided that discretion was the better part of valor. If only the *Falcon* could have the luxury of reaching that conclusion. Sooner or later, one of those attacks was going to get through.

"Mara!" Han called out. "Let's keep moving through them." He reached over and cut out the ship-to-ship comm link. "Another twenty minutes," Han said to Leia and Chewie, "another twenty minutes, and it'll be over."

And so it would. One way or the other.

* * *

"*Defender* reports damage to main armament, but secondary weapons fully functional," said Kalenda. "Numerous minor hits, no major damage so far."

But a hundred minor hits could serve to weaken the ship enough for the hundred and first to destroy it. Ossilege shook his head. That was no way to think. Not for an admiral in the midst of running a battle. "What of *Sentinel*?" he asked.

"*Sentinel* has partial loss of propulsion. Explosive decompression of unspecified aft section, reported as contained. All weapons functional, reports numerous successful engagements."

"Very well," Ossilege said as he studied his tactical display. *Intruder* had taken a similar amount of damage. *It was working,* he thought. They were paying a high price indeed, but it was working. Ossilege had assigned a lane through the enemy formation to each big ship, and to each pair of smaller craft. The idea was to drive through the enemy ships toward the rear, keeping up a series of running engagements, intended to cause disruption as much as damage. And it was working. The tidy enemy formations were unraveling, and it seemed that half of them had reversed course to head off in pursuit of their tormentors.

"Sir! Captain Semmac reports four frigates closing on *Intruder*. It appears to be a coordinated attack."

"Does it indeed? I was wondering how long it would take them to mount one. Very well. Now we will see Captain Semmac's skills as a defender."

Ossilege watched his tactical displays. Four identical bulbous-nosed frigates were closing in from four different directions, lasers blazing. The *Intruder*'s shields held, at least under the initial onslaught. Captain Semmac brought the nose of the *Intruder* up and accelerated, trying to get out of the crossfire. The *Intruder*'s main guns began to return fire, concentrating on the closest of the four frigates. The ship's nose came down hard as Semmac attempted to break free, but the frigates adjusted course to stay with the *Intruder*, matching her move for move.

Ossilege frowned. Something was wrong. The frigates were pouring laser fire into the *Intruder*, but it was having no effect. There should have been local burn-throughs, the shields should have been weakened here and there. Ossilege checked the power levels from the frigate's lasers. Why were they so low? Unless—unless the lasers were just there as a deception, a distraction. And come to think of it, how were the frigates able to absorb so much fire from the *Intruder*?

He brought up a close-up view of the nearest frigate on his tactical display and felt his blood run cold.

Its windows were painted on. Painted on over what looked like solid durasteel.

He slapped down his comlink. "Captain Semmac! Those frigates are camouflaged robot ramships! Their guns are harmless. They are merely trying to get in close enough to—"

But it was too late. The first of the ramships fired its high-boost engine and accelerated at terrifying speed, directly at the *Intruder*, a multimegaton battering ram headed straight in at them.

It struck just forward of the bridge.

*   *   *

"Okay!" Jacen said. "I have him back."

"*Good,*" said Technician Antone. "Great. Let's get back to it."

Anakin came back into the compartment and looked long and hard at each of them before he took his seat again. "Okay," he said. "Ready."

"Good, good," said Antone, forcing a smile onto his face. "Then let's start the power initiation sequence."

"No," said Anakin.

The sweat was standing straight out on Antone's forehead. "Anakin, please. Try to understand. This isn't a game. Lots of people—lots and *lots* of people—are going to, to *die* unless we fire this repulsor at exactly the right time in exactly the right direction."

"I *know* that," said Anakin. "But it *isn't* aimed just right. It's too heavy. Too *heavy* somehow."

"What do you mean, too heavy?" Antone asked.

"Gravity!" Jacen shouted. "He means gravity! Those instructions you got are for the repulsor on Selonia! The gravity is different there."

"Right!" said Anakin. "*Too heavy.*"

Antone thought for a minute, muttering frantically. "Sweet stars in the sky. He's right! He's right!" He checked the countdown clock. "And we've got ten minutes to recalculate the aim from scratch." Antone grabbed one of the other techs by the shoulder and shoved him at Anakin. "Run him through the power initiation sequence and the rest of it, and we'll retarget just before we fire."

And with that, Technician Antone raced frantically away to find a desk and a datapad.

*   *   *

The second and the third robot ramships slammed into the *Intruder,* sending the ruined hulk pinwheeling across the sky. The fourth ram missed, but that did not matter. The ship was dead already.

Ossilege picked himself up off the deck and staggered back over to his chair. Gaeriel had managed to stay in hers. Belindi Kalenda climbed to her feet and looked around in shock. They were the only ones left. Everyone else on the flag deck was dead. Ossilege didn't even bother looking down to see if anyone had survived on the bridge. Most of it wasn't there anymore.

"ABANDON SHIP!" the overhead speaker shouted. "ALL HANDS, ABANDON SHIP!"

"I can't feel my legs," Gaeriel announced. "I can see they're bleeding, but I can't feel them, and I can't move them."

Ossilege nodded, not really knowing why. *Spinal damage,* he thought. *She must have been slammed around hard by those impacts.* Admiral Hortel Ossilege realized that he was holding his left hand over his stomach. He lifted his hand away for a moment and saw the red, open wound. Astonishing that he wouldn't feel something like that.

"ABANDON SHIP!" the automatic voice called again.

Ossilege looked from himself to Gaeriel Captison, to Kalenda. "Go!" he shouted at Kalenda. "We can't make it. You can. Go!" Suddenly he felt very weak.

"But—" Kalenda began.

"But I have a gut wound and the Prime Minister cannot walk. We would not survive the trip to the escape capsule, and if we did we would not survive until pickup. Go. Now. That is an order. You—you have been a good officer, Lieutenant Kalenda. Do not waste yourself now over a pointless gesture. Go."

Kalenda looked as if she were about to say something more, but then she stopped. She saluted Ossilege, bowed to Gaeriel, and then turned and ran.

"Good," said Ossilege. "I hope she makes it."

"We have to blow the ship," Gaeriel said, her voice barely more than a whisper. "Don't let her be captured."

Ossilege nodded to her. "Yes," he said. "You are right. But we must wait. Give the survivors time to escape. Wait until we are in deep among the enemy ships. Take them with us. Wait—wait for Source A."

"Source A?" Gaeriel asked, her voice vague and weak.

"Source A," said Ossilege. "We have to wait for Admiral Ackbar."

* * *

"One hour, Luke!" Lando shouted. "Let's get out of here while we're still in one piece each!"

"Copy that, Lando," said Luke. "Back the way we came, and *fast*!"

"What's going on?" Tendra asked. "Why are we retreating?"

"We're not retreating," said Lando as he heeled the *Lady Luck* around. "We're following Ossilege's plan. A plan so simple that even we could follow it. Get in, do as much damage as you can for one hour, and then get out of the way."

"Get out of the way for what?"

"For Source A, my dear Source T."

"What are you talking about?"

Lando laughed out loud. "It's not much of a code name system, but there it is. Source T for Tendra, Source A for Admiral Ackbar. Ossilege started getting coded hyperwave messages from him the minute the jamming field went down. Ackbar had spent every waking moment since we left Coruscant trying to put some sort of task force together. It sounds like he wasn't able to get that big a fleet together, but twenty-five modern ships with modern weapons—well, that ought to do some good out here. Especially if the opposing force is already pretty banged up and disoriented and out of formation and pointed in the wrong direction." Lando dodged the *Lady Luck* around the shot-up wreck of a modified B-wing, and ran at top speed, straight for Centerpoint Station. "I think we'll head for the north end of Centerpoint, thank you very much. The end that doesn't fire interstellar death rays."

"But what about Admiral Ackbar? What's the rest of the plan?"

"Well, that's pretty simple too. When Admiral Ackbar does his precision hyperspace jump, he'll land right on top of them, and they'll never know what hit them. And our ships don't want to be sitting in the shooting gallery."

"When does he show up?"

Lando checked the ship's navicomputer and the chronometer. "Uh-oh," he said. "Right here. And right now."

The piece of empty space in front of them was suddenly ablaze with the flaring light of starships coming in out of hyperspace, ships that were streaks of blazing white, flashing into existence and screaming past the *Lady Luck* to either side, over her, under her, so close that they could almost hear the nonexistent winds of space rushing past them as the ships roared by. It was an incredible sight, a beautiful sight—and a terrifying one. Lando clenched his teeth and wrapped his hands around the flight stick. He held on for dear life, forcing himself by sheer strength of will not to try to dodge the oncoming ships, for fear of flying smack into one he did not see.

And then they were past, and then they were gone. And then Lando slowed the *Lady* to a reasonable speed, and breathed.

And then the war was over, for Lando, and for Tendra.

*   *   *

Gaeriel Captison was starting to feel the pain. Not in her legs, of course, but everywhere else. Admiral Ossilege sat beside her, barely conscious himself, bleeding badly. Gaeriel thought she could smell something burning behind her. Not that such things mattered anymore, of course.

In spite of everything, somehow Ossilege had managed to open up the control panel set into the side of his chair, the ship's self-destruct. He had flicked up all of the safeties and pushed down all of the buttons. All but the last. He was waiting, still waiting, still watching his tactical displays. They were barely working, but they would not have to work well at all to show him what he needed to see.

"There!" he said. "There! Ships coming in! They're here."

"It's time, then," said Gaeriel. "You're a good man, Admiral Ossilege. You did your duty. You held them. You stopped them. Well done."

"Thank you, ma'am. I was—I was proud to serve with you."

"And I with you," she said. "But now it's time to go." She thought of her daughter, Malinza, left all alone in the universe. She would be cared for, of that Gaeriel had no fear. Perhaps—perhaps the universe would compensate for all the sorrow of her young life, and bring her nothing but good as she grew older. It was a comforting thought, Gaeriel decided. A good thought to go out on.

"I can't—I can't move my arm," said Ossilege. "I can't push the button."

"Here," said Gaeriel. She looked up and saw at least three Triad ships were near. She smiled and reached over. "Here," she said again. "Let me."

*   *   *

The explosion lit the sky, tore a hole across the Triad fleet. For a few glorious seconds a new light blazed up, a pillar of fire brighter than all the stars in the sky.

"Oh, sweet stars in the sky," said Tendra. "That was the *Intruder*. They're gone. They're all gone. It's over."

Lando looked down at the ship chronometer again,

then to Centerpoint Station, and then toward the distant dot of light that was Drall.

"No it isn't," he said. "But in one minute and twenty seconds, it will be. Maybe for a lot of people."

*   *   *

"Antone!" Jaina shouted. "Now! Now! We have to do it now!"

Technician Antone came rushing back in, his eyes bulging out of his head. "I can't," he said, and held up the datapad. "It's still running. The last part of the problem is still running. It won't be done for another five minutes at least. Twelve million people. Twelve million people." Antone sat down on the floor and covered his head with his hands.

"We're doomed!" Threepio moaned. "If they control the starbuster, our enemies will destroy us all."

Jacen Solo stood riveted to the spot, his eyes as wide as they could be. Everyone in the chamber was rooted to the spot. Twelve million people. They had one chance to make this work, and it would fail because they couldn't give the right numbers to a seven-year-old kid.

"Wait a second," he said to himself. "Who needs numbers?" He turned toward his brother, still seated at the console. "Anakin," he said. "It felt too heavy, right? Can you fix it? Can you close your eyes and *feel* it? Make it feel right, make it go right?"

"What are you saying?" Ebrihim asked. "You want him to *guess*?"

"Not guess," said Jaina. "Feel. Reach out to it, Anakin. Let go of your conscious feelings. Reach out with the Force."

Anakin looked at his brother and his sister, and swallowed hard, and then he shut his eyes. "Yeah," he said. "Yeah."

Eyes still closed, he held out his hands for controls that weren't there, controls that took form under his hands even as he reached for them. Glowing grids of orange and purple and green appeared and flared up and vanished around his head, but Anakin did not see them.

Deep beneath their feet, a deep, determined vibration began to build. They heard the crash of thunder from the repulsor, and the sound of power being gathered, of unimaginable force being channeled and focused and held in ready.

The joysticklike control materialized, slithering up perfectly into Anakin's grasp. He pushed the control stick slowly forward, and a cube of perfect blazing orange appeared before his still-closed eyes. He made tiny, imperceptible adjustments with the controls, and the orange cube flickered once and grew brighter. He held the stick forward for a long, long moment—

And then he pulled it down, as hard as he could.

The chamber shuddered with power, and a stream of lightning blazed down the corridor and out into the chamber.

*   *   *

They could not see it in the control chamber, except for Anakin, who saw everything perfectly from behind closed eyes. But those on the surface and those in space could see it. They could see the repulsor thunder and roar with repressed power, power that seethed and pulsed and flickered in its eagerness to be set free. They saw the power in that repulsor that built up and up and up.

And they saw it leap out of the repulsor chamber, tear across space, land square on the south end of Centerpoint, just as practically every countdown clock in space reached zero, just at the moment Centerpoint was to fire. The South Pole lit up with the energy that was supposed to stream out invisible, unseen, undetected, into hyperspace, was supposed to reach out across space and murder a star.

But the repulsor beam broke up the opening into hyperspace, defocused the beam, detuned it enough that some small part of its energy was converted into visible light. The South Pole of Centerpoint began to glow, began to throb and pulse with its own power. The glow spread, expanding outward, stretching itself out into a magnificent bubble of light, harmless light, that lit the skies of all the Corellian worlds, gleaming, shining, blooming, growing—and then guttering down to nothing.

Lando Calrissian watched it all from the North end of Centerpoint, and started breathing again. He hadn't even realized he had stopped.

"Now," he said to Tendra. "Now, it's over."

Epilogue

I don't even know why you were so eager to have my fleet come here," said Admiral Ackbar in his gravelly voice. He turned and regarded Luke Skywalker through his goggly eyes. They were on Drall, as Ackbar had been curious to inspect the repulsor. "There was hardly any work left for my ships to do—thanks to Admiral Ossilege and Gaeriel Captison."

"Thanks to them, yes, sir," said Luke. Luke thought of Gaeriel, thought of her daughter, Malinza. Luke had promised Malinza he would take care of her mother. How was that debt to be paid? He thought of Ossilege, of the difficult, impossible man who also had a knack for *doing* the difficult, the impossible. "I will mourn them both for a long time to come. But we have won. Thanks to them, and many others. And in large part thanks to those three children, over there."

Anakin and Jacen and Jaina were racing around, climbing around the hummocks of dirt that the repulsor had forced up when it had shoved its way out of the ground. They were being chased by a laughing Jenica Sonsen and a Belindi Kalenda who was too busy making ferocious faces to laugh. They were playing in the shadow of the repulsor. Once hidden underground, the top of the cylinder now rose a hundred meters up out of the ground.

Han and Leia laughed out loud as their children

turned the tables and started chasing Sonsen and Kalenda. Mara watched the fun, smiling quietly, and even Chewbacca was enjoying the show. Not far off, Ebrihim and the Duchess Marcha were lounging on the ground, intent in conversation. Judging by their eager, focused expressions, they were either talking over some complicated matter of state or, more likely, dissecting some particularly juicy bit of family gossip.

It was probably the latter but Luke hoped it was the former. The Duchess would need the practice. Leia had told Luke of her plan to appoint Marcha the new Governor-General of the Sector.

Dracmus sat by the two Drall, apparently so enthralled with their conversation that she had fallen sound asleep.

Luke heard a high-pitched voice raised in protest behind him, answered by a rapid, high-pitched twittering that sounded far from complimentary. He turned around to see Artoo and Q9 at it again, bickering over some fine point of droid design or other. Threepio was standing between them, trying to calm them both down. Luke had a feeling Threepio would meet with his usual degree of success.

"You know," he said, "it's the beings on this plain, the humans and the Selonian and the Drall and the Wookiee and the droids right here. *They're* the ones who won this war. Not the ships or the guns or the hardware."

"You're right, of course," said Admiral Ackbar. "But no one wins a war. There are just different degrees of losing. The damage done on these worlds is shocking. Shocking. It will take them many years to rebuild it all, to sort out all the loose ends."

Luke nodded. But at least some of the loose ends were being tidied up already. Admiral Ackbar brought news of the arrest of one Pharnis Gleasry, a self-styled agent of the Human League, part of the spy ring that had sliced its way into far too many government files back on Coruscant. It had taken very little to get Gleasry singing like a bird. The whole Human League spy ring back in Coruscant had been scooped up and thrown in jail where they belonged.

There was, of course, the question of what to do about the next star on the starbuster list. The short-term solution was to de-imprint the repulsor controls so they could be used by someone over seven, be ready with the *right* targeting numbers, and simply fire this repulsor—or the one on Selonia—as needed. Once it was too little, and too late, the Sacorrian Selonians had indeed caved in altogether. The long-term solution was to get the shutdown codes from the Triad. As the Triad was in an understandably cooperative mood—what with the New Republic occupation troops already on the way—that didn't seem likely to be too much of a problem. Someone had started the completely false rumor that the New Republic Navy was going to re-aim Centerpoint straight at Sacorria's sun, and leave it that way through all the starbuster pulses until they got the shutdown code. The rumor might well encourage co-operation.

And then there was the whole question of studying Centerpoint, and the repulsors on the other three worlds. Who had built the Corellian system, and when, and why, and what had happened to them? Well, some ends were looser than others. Those mysteries might easily take centuries to be solved—if they ever were.

There was one other loose end that Luke took a personal interest in. But he had a feeling that it would get sorted out without undue delay.

"You know," said Admiral Ackbar, "you said it was the people here who won this war. I can't help noticing two rather prominent names that seem to be missing. They were on the transport with us. Where in the world have they gone to?"

Luke smiled. He knew exactly where they were, but he had a feeling they were not much in the mood for company. "I wouldn't worry too much, Admiral. They're both the sort who are pretty good at taking care of themselves."

*   *   *

"Lando?" asked Tendra as they wandered about on the churned-up land that the rise of the repulsor had produced. It was not the loveliest of landscapes, but it did have the advantage of providing a good deal of privacy behind every hummock and furrow of ground.

"Yes?" Lando asked. "What is it?" Tendra had found herself on top of a higher than usual clump of loose rock. Lando offered his hand, and she took it, used it to steady herself as she slipped and slithered down into the next little furrow of ground. He did not let go of her hand once she was on level ground, and she did not let go of his.

"Remember how I told you that a Sacorrian woman is not allowed to marry without her father's consent, no matter how old she is?"

Lando felt a little flutter in his chest, a flutter of fear, and excitement, and interest, all mixed up together. "Yes," he said, managing to keep his voice steady. "What about it?"

"Well," she said, "there's just one thing. We don't have to do anything about it *immediately,* but there's something more I want to tell you about that law. An interesting legal technicality. It's been well established by many precedents that a Sacorrian woman is not bound by that law—*if* she is outside the Sacorrian system. If she were on, oh, Drall for example."

"Is that so?" Lando asked, quickly regaining his old equilibrium. The idea needed time, and thought—but he definitely liked it at first glance. He smiled, and looked at her lovely face. "Is that a certifiable fact?" he asked.

"It is," she said, smiling right back at him.

"Then why don't we get back to the *Lady Luck* and discuss the whole matter over dinner?" he asked. "*I've* always found legal technicalities to be downright fascinating."

ABOUT THE AUTHOR

Roger MacBride Allen was born in 1957 in Bridgeport, Connecticut. He graduated from Boston University in 1979. The author of a dozen science fiction novels, he lived in Washington, D.C., for many years. In July 1994, he married Eleanore Fox, a member of the U.S. Foreign Service. Her current assignment takes them to Brasilia, Brazil, where they will live for the next two years.

THE TRUCE AT BAKURA by Kathy Tyers
Setting: Immediately after *Return of the Jedi*

The day after his climactic battle with Emperor Palpatine and the sacrifice of his father, Darth Vader, who died saving his life, Luke Skywalker helps recover an Imperial drone ship bearing a startling message intended for the Emperor. It is a distress signal from the far-off Imperial outpost of Bakura, which is under attack by an alien invasion force, the Ssi-ruuk. Leia sees a rescue mission as an opportunity to achieve a diplomatic victory for the Rebel Alliance, even if it means fighting alongside former Imperials. But Luke receives a vision from Obi-Wan Kenobi revealing that the stakes are even higher: the invasion at Bakura threatens everything the Rebels have won at such great cost.

Here is a scene showing the extent of the alien menace:

On an outer deck of a vast battle cruiser called the *Shriwirr*, Dev Sibwarra rested his slim brown hand on a prisoner's left shoulder. "It'll be all right," he said softly. The other human's fear beat at his mind like a three-tailed lash. "There's no pain. You have a wonderful surprise ahead of you." Wonderful indeed, a life without hunger, cold, or selfish desire.

The prisoner, an Imperial of much lighter complexion than Dev, slumped in the entenchment chair. He'd given up protesting, and his breath came in gasps. Pliable bands secured his forelimbs, neck, and knees—but only for balance. With his nervous system deionized at the shoulders, he couldn't struggle. A slender intravenous tube dripped pale blue magnetizing solution into each of his carotid arteries while tiny servopumps hummed. It only took a few mils of magsol to attune the tiny, fluctuating electromagnetic fields of human brain waves to the Ssi-ruuvi entenchment apparatus.

Behind Dev, Master Firwirrung trilled a question in Ssi-ruuvi. "Is it calmed yet?"

Dev sketched a bow to his master and switched from human speech to Ssi-ruuvi. "Calm enough," he sang back. "He's almost ready."

Sleek, russet scales protected Firwirrung's two-meter length from beaked muzzle to muscular tail tip, and a prominent black **V** crest marked his forehead. Not large for a Ssi-ruu, he was still growing, with only a few age-scores where scales had begun to separate on his handsome chest. Firwirrung swung a broad, glowing white metal catchment arc down to cover the prisoner from midchest to nose. Dev could just peer over it and watch the man's pupils dilate. At any moment . . .

"Now," Dev announced.

Firwirrung touched a control. His muscular tail twitched with pleasure. The fleet's capture had been good today. Alongside his master, Dev would work far into the night. Before entechment, prisoners were noisy and dangerous. Afterward, their life energies powered droids of Ssi-ruuvi choosing.

The catchment arc hummed up to pitch. Dev backed away. Inside that round human skull, a magsol-drugged brain was losing control. Though Master Firwirrung assured him that the transfer of incorporeal energy was painless, every prisoner screamed.

As did this one, when Firwirrung threw the catchment arc switch. The arc boomed out a sympathetic vibration, as brain energy leaped to an electromagnet perfectly attuned to magsol. Through the Force rippled an ululation of indescribable anguish.

Dev staggered and clung to the knowledge his masters had given him: The prisoners only thought they felt pain. *He* only thought he sensed their pain. By the time the body screamed, all of a subject's energies had jumped to the catchment arc. The screaming body already was dead.

THE COURTSHIP OF PRINCESS LEIA
by Dave Wolverton
Setting: Four years after *Return of the Jedi*

One of the most interesting developments in Bantam's Star Wars *novels is that in their storyline, Han Solo and Princess Leia start a family. This tale reveals how the couple originally got together. Wishing to strengthen the fledgling New Republic by bringing in powerful allies, Leia opens talks with the Hapes consortium of more than sixty worlds. But the consortium is ruled by the Queen Mother, who, to Han's dismay, wants Leia to marry her son, Prince Isolder. Before this action-packed story is over, Luke will join forces with Isolder against a group of Force-trained "witches" and face a deadly foe.*

In this scene, Luke is searching for Jedi lore and finds more than he bargained for:

Luke popped the cylinder into Artoo, and almost immediately Artoo caught a signal. Images flashed in the air before the droid: an ancient throne room where, one by one, Jedi came before their high master to give reports. Yet the holo was fragmented, so thoroughly erased that Luke got only bits and pieces—a blue-skinned man describing details of a grueling space battle against pirateers; a yellow-eyed Twi'lek with lashing headtails who told of discovering a plot to kill an ambassador. A date and time flashed on the holo vid before each report. The report was nearly four hundred standard years old.

Then Yoda appeared on the video, gazing up at the throne. His color was more vibrantly green than Luke remembered, and he did not use his walking stick. At middle age, Yoda had looked almost perky, carefree—not the bent, troubled old Jedi Luke had known. Most of the audio was erased, but through the background hiss Yoda clearly said, "We tried to free the Chu'unthor from Dathomir, but were repulsed by the witches . . . skirmish, with Masters Gra'aton and Vulatan. . . . Fourteen acolytes killed . . . go back to retrieve . . ." The audio hissed away, and soon the holo image dissolved to blue static with popping lights.

They went up topside, found that night had fallen while they worked underground. Their Whiphid guide soon returned, dragging the body of a gutted snow demon. The demon's white talons curled in the air, and its long purple tongue snaked out from between its massive fangs. Luke was amazed that the Whiphid could haul such a monster, yet the Whiphid held the demon's long hairy tail in one hand and managed to pull it back to camp.

There, Luke stayed the night with the Whiphids in a huge shelter made from the rib cage of a motmot, covered over with hides to keep out the wind. The Whiphids built a bonfire and roasted the snow demon, and the young danced while the elders played their claw harps. As Luke sat, watching the writhing flames and listening to the twang of harps, he meditated. "The future you will see, and the past. Old friends long forgotten . . ." Those were the words Yoda had said long ago while training Luke to peer beyond the mists of time.

Luke looked up at the rib bones of the motmot. The Whiphids had carved stick letters into the bone, ten and twelve meters in the air, giving the lineage of their ancestors. Luke could not read the letters, but they seemed to dance in the firelight, as if they were sticks and stones falling from the sky. The rib bones curved toward him, and Luke followed the curve of bones with his eyes. The tumbling sticks and boulders seemed to gyrate, all of them falling toward him as if they would crush him. He could see boulders hurtling through the air, too, smashing toward him. Luke's nostrils flared, and even Toola's chill could not keep a thin film of perspiration from dotting his forehead. A vision came to Luke then.

Luke stood in a mountain fortress of stone, looking over a plain with a sea of dark forested hills beyond, and a storm rose —a magnificent wind that brought with it towering walls of black clouds and dust, trees hurtling toward him and twisting through the sky. The clouds thundered overhead, filled with purple flames, obliterating all sunlight, and Luke could feel a malevolence hidden in those clouds and knew that they had been raised through the power of the dark side of the Force.

Dust and stones whistled through the air like autumn leaves. Luke tried to hold on to the stone parapet overlooking the plain to keep from being swept from the fortress walls. Winds pounded in his ears like the roar of an ocean, howling.

It was as if a storm of pure dark Force raged over the countryside, and suddenly, amid the towering clouds of darkness that thundered toward him, Luke could hear laughing, the sweet sound of women laughing. He looked above into the dark clouds, and saw the women borne through the air along with the rocks and debris, like motes of dust, laughing. A voice seemed to whisper, "the witches of Dathomir."

HEIR TO THE EMPIRE
DARK FORCE RISING
THE LAST COMMAND
by Timothy Zahn
Setting: Five years after *Return of the Jedi*

This #1 bestselling trilogy introduces two legendary forces of evil into the Star Wars *literary pantheon. Grand Admiral Thrawn has taken control of the Imperial fleet in the years since the destruction of the Death Star, and the mysterious Joruus C'baoth is a fearsome Jedi Master who has been seduced by the dark side. Han and Leia have now been married for about a year, and as the story begins, she is pregnant with twins. Thrawn's plan is to crush the Rebellion and resurrect the Empire's New Order with C'baoth's help—and in return, the Dark Master will get Han and Leia's Jedi children to mold as he wishes. For as readers of this magnificent trilogy will see, Luke Skywalker is not the last of the old Jedi. He is the first of the new.*

In this scene from Heir to the Empire, *Thrawn and C'baoth meet for the first time:*

For a long moment the old man continued to stare at Thrawn, a dozen strange expressions flicking in quick succession across his face. "Come. We will talk."

"Thank you," Thrawn said, inclining his head slightly. "May I ask who we have the honor of addressing?"

"Of course." The old man's face was abruptly regal again, and when he spoke his voice rang out in the silence of the crypt. "I am the Jedi Master Joruus C'baoth."

Pellaeon inhaled sharply, a cold shiver running up his back. "Joruus C'baoth?" he breathed. "But—"

He broke off. C'baoth looked at him, much as Pellaeon himself might look at a junior officer who has spoken out of turn. "Come," he repeated, turning back to Thrawn. "We will talk."

He led the way out of the crypt and back into the sunshine. Several small knots of people had gathered in the square in their absence, huddling well back from both the crypt and the shuttle as they whispered nervously together.

With one exception. Standing directly in their path a few meters away was one of the two guards C'baoth had ordered out of the crypt. On his face was an expression of barely controlled fury; in his hands, cocked and ready, was his crossbow. "You destroyed his home," C'baoth said, almost conversationally. "Doubtless he would like to exact vengeance."

The words were barely out of his mouth when the guard suddenly snapped the crossbow up and fired. Instinctively, Pellaeon ducked, raising his blaster—

And three meters from the Imperials the bolt came to an abrupt halt in midair.

Pellaeon stared at the hovering piece of wood and metal, his brain only slowly catching up with what had just happened. "They are our guests," C'baoth told the guard in a voice clearly intended to reach everyone in the square. "They will be treated accordingly."

With a crackle of splintering wood, the crossbow bolt shattered, the pieces dropping to the ground. Slowly, reluctantly, the guard lowered his crossbow, his eyes still burning with a now impotent rage. Thrawn let him stand there another second like that, then gestured to Rukh. The Noghri raised his blaster and fired—

And in a blur of motion almost too fast to see, a flat stone detached itself from the ground and hurled itself directly into the path of the shot, shattering spectacularly as the blast hit it.

Thrawn spun to face C'baoth, his face a mirror of surprise and anger. "C'baoth—!"

"These are *my* people, Grand Admiral Thrawn," the other cut him off, his voice forged from quiet steel. "Not yours; mine. If there is punishment to be dealt out, *I* will do it."

For a long moment the two men again locked eyes. Then, with an obvious effort, Thrawn regained his composure. "Of course, Master C'baoth," he said. "Forgive me."

C'baoth nodded. "Better. Much better." He looked past Thrawn, dismissed the guard with a nod. "Come," he said, looking back at the Grand Admiral. "We will talk."

The Jedi Academy Trilogy:
JEDI SEARCH
DARK APPRENTICE
CHAMPIONS OF THE FORCE
by Kevin J. Anderson
Setting: Seven years after *Return of the Jedi*

In order to assure the continuation of the Jedi Knights, Luke Skywalker has decided to start a training facility: a Jedi Academy. He will gather Force-sensitive students who show potential as prospective Jedi and serve as their mentor, as Jedi Masters Obi-Wan Kenobi and Yoda did for him. Han and Leia's twins are now toddlers, and there is a third Jedi child: the infant Anakin, named after Luke and Leia's father. In this trilogy, we discover the existence of a powerful Imperial doomsday weapon, the horrifying Sun Crusher—which will soon become the centerpiece of a titanic struggle between Luke Skywalker and his most brilliant Jedi Academy student, who is delving dangerously into the dark side.

In this scene from the first novel, Jedi Search, *Luke vocalizes his concept of a new Jedi order to a distinguished assembly of New Republic leaders:*

As he descended the long ramp, Luke felt all eyes turn toward him. A hush fell over the assembly. Luke Skywalker, the lone remaining Jedi Master, almost never took part in governmental proceedings.

"I have an important matter to address," he said. For a moment he was reminded of when he had walked alone into the dank corridors of Jabba the Hutt's palace—but this time there were no piglike Gamorrean guards that he could manipulate with a twist of his fingers and a touch of the Force.

Mon Mothma gave him a soft, mysterious smile and gestured for him to take a central position. "The words of a Jedi Knight are always welcome to the New Republic," she said.

Luke tried not to look pleased. She had provided the perfect opening for him. "In the Old Republic," he said, "Jedi Knights were the protectors and guardians of all. For a thousand generations the Jedi used the powers of the Force to guide, defend, and provide support for the rightful government of worlds—before the dark days of the Empire came, and the Jedi Knights were killed."

He let his words hang, then took another breath. "Now we have a New Republic. The Empire appears to be defeated. We have founded a new government based upon the old, but let us hope we learn from our mistakes. Before, an entire order of Jedi watched over the Republic, offering strength. Now I am the only Jedi Master who remains.

"Without that order of protectors to provide a backbone of strength for the New Republic, can we survive? Will we be able to weather the storms and the difficulties of forging a new union? Until now we have suffered severe struggles—but in the future they will be seen as nothing more than birth pangs."

Before the other senators could disagree with that, Luke continued. "Our people had a common foe in the Empire, and we must not let our defenses lapse just because we have internal problems. More to the point, what will happen when we begin squabbling among ourselves over petty matters? The old Jedi helped to mediate many types of disputes. What if there are no Jedi Knights to protect us in the difficult times ahead?"

Luke moved under the diffracting rainbow colors from the crystal light overhead. He took his time to fix his gaze on all the senators present; he turned his attention to Leia last. Her eyes were wide but supportive. He had not discussed his idea with her beforehand.

"My sister is undergoing Jedi training. She has a great deal of skill in the Force. Her three children are also likely candidates to be trained as young Jedi. In recent years I have come to know a woman named Mara Jade, who is now unifying the smugglers—the former smugglers," he amended, "into an organization that can support the needs of the New Republic. She also has a talent for the Force. I have encountered others in my travels."

Another pause. The audience was listening so far. "But are these the only ones? We already know that the ability to use the Force is passed from generation to generation. Most of the Jedi were killed in the Emperor's purge—but could he possibly have eradicated all of the descendants of those Knights? I myself was unaware of the potential power within me until Obi-Wan Kenobi taught me how to use it. My sister Leia was similarly unaware.

"How many people are abroad in this galaxy who have a comparable strength in the Force, who are potential members of a new order of Jedi Knights, but are unaware of who they are?"

Luke looked at them again. "In my brief search I have already discovered that there are indeed some descendants of former Jedi. I have come here to ask"—he turned to gesture toward Mon Mothma, swept his hands across the people gathered there in the chamber—"for two things.

"First, that the New Republic officially sanction my search for those with a hidden talent for the Force, to seek them out and try to bring them to our service. For this I will need some help."

Admiral Ackbar interrupted, blinking his huge fish eyes and turning his head. "But if you yourself did not know your power when you were young, how will these other people know? How will you find them, Jedi Skywalker?"

Luke folded his hands in front of him. "Several ways. First, with the help of two dedicated droids who will spend their days searching through the Imperial City databases, we may find likely candidates, people who have experienced miraculous strokes of luck, whose lives seem filled with incredible coincidences. We could look for people who seem unusually charismatic or those whom legend credits with working miracles. These could all be unconscious manifestations of a skill with the Force."

Luke held up another finger. "As well, the droids could search the database for forgotten descendants of known Jedi Knights from the Old Republic days. We should turn up a few leads."

"And what will you yourself be doing?" Mon Mothma asked, shifting in her robes.

"I've already found several candidates I wish to investigate. All I ask right now is that you agree this is something we should pursue, that the search for Jedi be conducted by others and not just myself."

Mon Mothma sat up straighter in her central seat. "I think we can agree to that without further discussion." She looked around to the other senators, seeing them now in agreement. "Tell us your second request."

Luke stood taller. This was most important to him. He saw Leia stiffen.

"If sufficient candidates are found who have potential for using the Force, I wish to be allowed—with the New Republic's blessing—to establish in some appropriate place an intensive training center, a Jedi academy, if you will. Under my direction we can help these students discover their abilities, to focus and strengthen their power. Ultimately, this academy would provide a core group that could allow us to restore the Jedi Knights as protectors of the New Republic."

CHILDREN OF THE JEDI
by Barbara Hambly
Setting: Eight years after *Return of the Jedi*

The Star Wars *characters face a menace from the glory days of the Empire when a thirty-year-old automated Imperial Dreadnaught comes to life and begins its grim mission: to gather forces and annihilate a long-forgotten stronghold of Jedi children. When Luke is whisked onboard, he begins to communicate with the brave Jedi Knight who paralyzed the ship decades ago, and gave her life in the process. Now she is part of the vessel, existing in its artificial intelligence core, and guiding Luke through one of the most unusual adventures he has ever had.*

In this scene, Luke discovers that an evil presence is gathering, one that will force him to join the battle:

Like See-Threepio, Nichos Marr sat in the outer room of the suite to which Cray had been assigned, in the power-down mode that was the droid equivalent of rest. Like Threepio, at the sound of Luke's almost noiseless tread he turned his head, aware of his presence.

"Luke?" Cray had equipped him with the most sensitive vocal modulators, and the word was calibrated to a whisper no louder than the rustle of the blueleaves massed outside the windows. He rose, and crossed to where Luke stood, the dull silver of his arms and shoulders a phantom gleam in the stray flickers of light. "What is it?"

"I don't know." They retreated to the small dining area where Luke had earlier probed his mind, and Luke stretched up to pin back a corner of the lamp-sheath, letting a slim triangle of butter-colored light fall on the purple of the vulwood tabletop. "A dream. A premonition, maybe." It was on his lips to ask, *Do you dream?* but he remembered the ghastly, imageless darkness in Nichos's mind, and didn't. He wasn't sure if his pupil was aware of the difference from his human perception and knowledge, aware of just exactly what he'd lost when his consciousness, his self, had been transferred.

In the morning Luke excused himself from the expedition Tomla El had organized with Nichos and Cray to the Falls of Dessiar, one of the places on Ithor most renowned for its beauty and peace. When they left he sought out Umwaw Moolis, and the tall herd leader listened gravely to his less than logical request and promised to put matters in train to fulfill it. Then Luke descended to the House of the Healers, where Drub McKumb lay, sedated far beyond pain but with all the perceptions of agony and nightmare still howling in his mind.

"Kill you!" He heaved himself at the restraints, blue eyes glaring furiously as he groped and scrabbled at Luke with his clawed hands. "It's all poison! I see you! I see the dark light all around you! You're him! You're him!" His back bent like a bow; the sound of his shrieking was like something being ground out of him by an infernal mangle.

Luke had been through the darkest places of the universe and of his own mind, had done and experienced greater evil than perhaps any man had known on the road the Force had dragged him . . . Still, it was hard not to turn away.

"We even tried yarrock on him last night," explained the Healer in charge, a slightly built Ithorian beautifully tabby-striped green and yellow under her simple tabard of purple linen. "But apparently the earlier doses that brought him enough lucidity to reach here from his point of origin oversensitized his system. We'll try again in four or five days."

Luke gazed down into the contorted, grimacing face.

"As you can see," the Healer said, "the internal perception of pain and fear is slowly lessening. It's down to ninety-three percent of what it was when he was first brought in. Not much, I know, but something."

"Him! *Him! HIM!*" Foam spattered the old man's stained gray beard.

Who?

"I wouldn't advise attempting any kind of mindlink until it's at least down to fifty percent, Master Skywalker."

"No," said Luke softly.

Kill you all. And, *They are gathering . . .*

"Do you have recordings of everything he's said?"

"Oh, yes." The big coppery eyes blinked assent. "The transcript is available through the monitor cubicle down the hall. We could make nothing of them. Perhaps they will mean something to you."

They didn't. Luke listened to them all, the incoherent groans and screams, the chewed fragments of words that could be only guessed at, and now and again the clear disjointed cries: "Solo! Solo! Can you hear me? Children . . . Evil . . . Gathering here . . . Kill you all!"

THE CRYSTAL STAR
by Vonda N. McIntyre
Setting: Ten years after *Return of the Jedi*

Leia's three children have been kidnapped. That horrible fact is made worse by Leia's realization that she can no longer sense her children through the Force! While she, Artoo-Detoo, and Chewbacca trail the kidnappers, Luke and Han discover a planet that is suffering strange quantum effects from a nearby star. Slowly freezing into a perfect crystal and disrupting the Force, the star is blunting Luke's power and crippling the Millennium Falcon. *These strands converge in an apocalyptic threat not only to the fate of the New Republic, but to the universe itself.*

Here is Luke and Han's initial approach to the crystal star:

Han piloted the *Millennium Falcon* through the strangest star system he had ever approached. An ancient, dying, crystallizing white dwarf star orbited a black hole in a wildly eccentric elliptical path.

Eons ago, in this place, a small and ordinary yellow star peacefully orbited an immense blue-white supergiant. The blue star aged, and collapsed.

The blue star went supernova, blasting light and radiation and debris out into space.

Its light still traveled through the universe, a furious explosion visible from distant galaxies.

Over time, the remains of the supergiant's core collapsed under the force of its own gravity. The result was degenerate mass: a black hole.

The violence of the supernova disrupted the orbit of the nova's companion, the yellow star. Over time, the yellow star's orbit decayed.

The yellow star fell toward the unimaginably dense body of the black hole. The black hole sucked up anything, even light, that came within its grasp. And when it captured matter —even an entire yellow star—it ripped the atoms apart into a glowing accretion disk. Subatomic particles imploded downward into the singularity's equator, emitting great bursts of radiation. The accretion disk spun at a fantastic speed, glowing with fantastic heat, creating a funeral pyre for the destroyed yellow companion.

The plasma spiraled in a raging pinwheel, circling so fast and heating so intensely that it blasted X rays out into space. Then, finally, the glowing gas fell toward the invisible black hole, approaching it closer and closer, appearing to fall more and more slowly as relativity influenced it.

It was lost forever to this universe.

That was the fate of the small yellow star.

The system contained a third star: the dying white dwarf, which shone with ancient heat even as it froze into a quantum crystal. Now, as the *Millennium Falcon* entered the system, the white dwarf was falling toward the black hole, on the inward curve of its eccentric elliptical orbit.

"Will you look at that," Han said. "Quite a show."

"Indeed it is, Master Han," Threepio said, "but it is merely a shadow of what will occur when the black hole captures the crystal star."

Luke gazed silently into the maelstrom of the black hole.

Han waited.

"Hey, kid! Snap out of it."

Luke started. "What?"

"I don't know where you were, but you weren't here."

"Just thinking about the Jedi Academy. I hate to leave my students, even for a few days. But if I *do* find other trained Jedi, it'll make a big difference. To the Academy. To the New Republic . . ."

"I think we're getting along pretty well already," Han said, irked. He had spent years maintaining the peace with ordinary people. In his opinion, Jedi Knights could cause more trouble than they were worth. "And what if these are all using the dark side?"

Luke did not reply.

Han seldom admitted his nightmares, but he had nightmares about what could happen to his children if they were tempted to the dark side.

Right now they were safe, with Leia on a planetary tour of remote and peaceful worlds of the New Republic. By this time they must have reached Munto Codru. They would be visiting the beautiful mountains of the world's temperate zone. Han smiled, imagining his princess and his children being welcomed to one of Munto Codru's mysterious, ancient, fairy-tale castles.

Solar prominences flared from the white dwarf's surface. The *Falcon* passed it, heading toward the more perilous region of the black hole.

The Corellian Trilogy:
AMBUSH AT CORELLIA
ASSAULT AT SELONIA
SHOWDOWN AT CENTERPOINT
by Roger MacBride Allen
Setting: Fourteen years after *Return of the Jedi*

This trilogy takes us to Corellia, Han Solo's homeworld, which Han has not visited in quite some time. A trade summit brings Han, Leia, and the children—now developing their own clear personalities and instinctively learning more about their innate skills in the Force—into the middle of a situation that most closely resembles a burning fuse. The Corellian system is on the brink of civil war, there are New Republic intelligence agents on a mysterious mission which even Han does not understand, and worst of all, a fanatical rebel leader has his hands on a superweapon of unimaginable power—and just wait until you find out who that leader is!

Here is an early scene from Ambush *that gives you a wonderful look at the growing Solo children (the twins are Jacen and Jaina, and their little brother is Anakin):*

Anakin plugged the board into the innards of the droid and pressed a button. The droid's black, boxy body shuddered awake, it drew in its wheels to stand up a bit taller, its status lights lit, and it made a sort of triple beep. "That's good," he said, and pushed the button again. The droid's status lights went out, and its body slumped down again. Anakin picked up the next piece, a motivation actuator. He frowned at it as he turned it over in his hands. He shook his head. "That's *not* good," he announced.

"What's not good?" Jaina asked.

"This thing," Anakin said, handing her the actuator. "Can't you *tell*? The insides part is all melty."

Jaina and Jacen exchanged a look. "The outside looks okay," Jaina said, giving the part to her brother. "How can he tell what the *inside* of it looks like? It's sealed shut when they make it."

Jacen shrugged. "How can he do any of this stuff? But we need that actuator. That was the toughest part to dig up. I must have gone around half the city looking for one that would fit this droid." He turned toward his little brother. "Anakin, we don't have another one of these. Can you make it better? Can you make the insides less melty?"

Anakin frowned. "I can make it *some* better. Not all the way better. A *little* less melty. *Maybe* it'll be okay."

Jacen handed the actuator back to Anakin. "Okay, try it."

Anakin, still sitting on the floor, took the device from his brother and frowned at it again. He turned it over and over in his hands, and then held it over his head and looked at it as if he were holding it up to the light. "There," he said, pointing a chubby finger at one point on the unmarked surface. "In there is the bad part." He rearranged himself to sit cross-legged, put the actuator in his lap, and put his right index finger over the "bad" part. "Fix," he said. "Fix." The dark brown outer case of the actuator seemed to glow for a second with an odd blue-red light, but then the glow sputtered out and Anakin pulled his finger away quickly and stuck it in his mouth, as if he had burned it on something.

"Better now?" Jaina asked.

"*Some* better," Anakin said, pulling his finger out of his mouth. "Not *all* better." He took the actuator in his hand and stood up. He opened the access panel on the broken droid and plugged in the actuator. He closed the door and looked expectantly at his older brother and sister.

"Done?" Jaina asked.

"Done," Anakin agreed. "But *I'm* not going to push the

button." He backed well away from the droid, sat down on the floor, and folded his arms.

Jacen looked at his sister.

"Not me," she said. "This was your idea."

Jacen stepped forward to the droid, reached out to push the power button from as far away as he could, and then stepped hurriedly back.

Once again, the droid shuddered awake, rattling a bit this time as it did so. It pulled its wheels in, lit its panel lights, and made the same triple beep. But then its holocam eye viewlens wobbled back and forth, and its panel lights dimmed and flared. It rolled backward just a bit, and then recovered itself.

"Good morning, young mistress and masters," it said. "How may I surge you?"

Well, one word wrong, but so what? Jacen grinned and clapped his hands and rubbed them together eagerly. "Good day, droid," he said. They had done it! But what to ask for first? "First tidy up this room," he said. A simple task, and one that ought to serve as a good test of what this droid could do.

Suddenly the droid's overhead access door blew off and there was a flash of light from its interior. A thin plume of smoke drifted out of the droid. Its panel lights flared again, and then the work arm sagged downward. The droid's body, softened by heat, sagged in on itself and drooped to the floor. The floor and walls and ceilings of the playroom were supposed to be fireproof, but nonetheless the floor under the droid darkened a bit, and the ceiling turned black. The ventilators kicked on high automatically, and drew the smoke out of the room. After a moment they shut themselves off, and the room was silent.

The three children stood, every bit as frozen to the spot as the droid was, absolutely stunned. It was Anakin who recovered first. He walked cautiously toward the droid and looked at it carefully, being sure not to get too close or touch it. "*Really* melty now," he announced, and then wandered off to the other side of the room to play with his blocks.

The twins looked at the droid, and then at each other.

"We're dead," Jacen announced, surveying the wreckage.

THE ILLUSTRATED STAR WARS UNIVERSE
Art by Ralph McQuarrie and Text by Kevin J. Anderson

Experience the *Star Wars*® universe as never before in this stunning visual journey that carries you to the farthest reaches – and into the deepest mysteries – of George Lucas's cinematic masterpiece. Ralph McQuarrie, the legendary main concept artist for all three *Star Wars*® films and Kevin J. Anderson, the *New York Times* bestselling *Star Wars*® author, present the ultimate voyage: a vivid and close-up look at the exotic worlds and remarkable inhabitants of the Star Wars universe, including two dozen McQuarrie paintings especially commissioned for these pages.

McQuarrie's breathtaking art and Anderson's delightful text are your guide to eight different *Star Wars*® locales. You'll visit: **Tatooine**, the stark, desert home planet of Luke Skywalker, as presented by Senior Anthropologist Hoole, one of the rare Shi'ido species possessed of astonishing shape-changing abilities; **Coruscant**, the great and glorious center of the Empire, described by no less a personage than Pollux Hax, Imperial advisor to the Emperor's court; **Dagobah**, the swampy world of Yoda, as recorded by scientist Halka Far-Den in her rigorous research journals; and **Bespin**, the gas planet, site of the famed floating metropolis of Cloud City, its many virtues and tourist attractions enthusiastically promoted by councilman Po Ruddle.

You'll also explore the myth-enshrouded worlds of **Endor**, the forest moon sheltering the Ewoks, as detailed in the official – if somewhat embittered – report of Imperial scout Pfilbee Jhorn; **Hoth**, the frozen wasteland which is the site of a secret rebel base, revealed by Major Kem Monnon, chief of the Rebel Alliance Corps of Engineers; **Yavin 4**, the jungle moon, nearly destroyed by the first Death Star, its significance to the Rebel Alliance recalled by the late naturalist Dr'uun Unnh; and **Alderaan**, Princess Leia's homeworld, cruelly annihilated by the same Death Star, memorialized by one of the few survivors, the renowned galactic poet Hari Seldona.

A Bantam Press Hardcover
0 593 03925 4

STARS WARS: DARKSABER
by Kevin J. Anderson

Luke Skywalker and Han Solo, cloaked by the Force and riding with the hostile Sand People, have returned to the dunes of the desert planet Tatooine in hopes of finding what Luke so desperately seeks: contact with Obi-Wan Kenobi. Luke is hoping the old Jedi Knight's spirit will tell him how to help his love Callista regain her lost ability to use the Force. Tormented and haunted, Luke cannot rest until Callista is a Jedi in the fullest sense, for only then will the link between their minds and souls be restored. Yet brewing on Tatooine is news that will shake them and threaten everything they value.

That disturbing piece of information is that the evil Hutts, criminal warlords of the galaxy, are building a secret superweapon: a reconstruction of the original Death Star, to be named *Darksaber*. This planet-crushing power will be in the ruthless hands of Durga the Hutt – a creature without conscience or mercy.

But there is worse news yet. The Empire lives. The beautiful Admiral Daala, still very much alive and more driven than ever to destroy the Jedi, has joined forces with the defeated Pellaeon – former second in command to Grand Admiral Thrawn. Together, they are marshalling Imperial forces to wipe out the New Republic.

Now, as Luke, Han, Leia, Chewbacca, Artoo, and Threepio regroup to face these threats, they are joined by new Jedi Knights and Callista. Together they must fight on two fronts, outshooting and outsmarting the most formidable enemies in the galaxy. In *Darksaber* the Jedi are heading for the ultimate test of their power – a test in which all the temptations of the dark side beckon. And Luke Skywalker must draw upon his innermost resources to fight for a world in which he can not only live, but dare to love.

A Bantam Press Hardcover
0 593 03767 7

A SELECTION OF SCIENCE FICTION AND FANTASY TITLES AVAILABLE FROM BANTAM BOOKS

THE PRICES SHOWN BELOW WERE CORRECT AT THE TIME OF GOING TO PRESS. HOWEVER TRANSWORLD PUBLISHERS RESERVE THE RIGHT TO SHOW NEW RETAIL PRICES ON COVERS WHICH MAY DIFFER FROM THOSE PREVIOUSLY ADVERTISED IN THE TEXT OR ELSEWHERE.

☐ 40808 9	STAR WARS: Jedi Academy Vol. 1: Jedi Search	Kevin J. Anderson	£3.99
☐ 40809 7	STAR WARS: Jedi Academy Vol. 2: Dark Apprentice	Kevin J. Anderson	£3.99
☐ 40810 0	STAR WARS: Jedi Academy Vol. 3: Champions of the Force	Kevin J. Anderson	£3.99
☐ 40881 X	STAR WARS: Corellian Trilogy Vol.1: Ambush at Corellia	Roger MacBride Allen	£4.99
☐ 40882 8	STAR WARS: Corellian Trilogy Vol.2: Assault at Selonia	Roger MacBride Allen	£4.99
☐ 40883 6	STAR WARS: Showdown at Centerpoint	Roger MacBride Allen	£4.99
☐ 40068 1	AZAZEL	Isaac Asimov	£3.99
☐ 40488 1	FORWARD THE FOUNDATION	Isaac Asimov	£4.99
☐ 40069 X	NEMESIS	Isaac Asimov	£4.99
☐ 29138 6	STAR TREK 1	James Blish	£4.99
☐ 29139 4	STAR TREK 2	James Blish	£3.99
☐ 29140 8	STAR TREK 3	James Blish	£3.99
☐ 17396 0	STAINLESS STEEL RAT SAVES THE WORLD	Harry Harrison	£2.50
☐ 40738 9	STAR WARS: The Truce at Bakura	Kathy Tyers	£4.99
☐ 40274 9	STAR OF THE GUARDIANS Book 1: The Lost King	Margaret Weis	£3.99
☐ 40275 7	STAR OF THE GUARDIANS Book 2: The King's Test	Margaret Weis	£4.99
☐ 40276 5	STAR OF THE GUARDIANS Book 3: King's Sacrifice	Margaret Weis	£4.99
☐ 17586 6	FORGING THE DARKSWORD	Margaret Weis & Tracy Hickman	£3.99
☐ 17535 1	DOOM OF THE DARKSWORD	Margaret Weis & Tracy Hickman	£3.50
☐ 17536 X	TRIUMPH OF THE DARKSWORD	Margaret Weis & Tracy Hickman	£4.99
☐ 40265 X	DEATH GATE CYCLE 1: Dragon Wing	Margaret Weis & Tracy Hickman	£4.99
☐ 40266 8	DEATH GATE CYCLE 2: Elven Star	Margaret Weis & Tracy Hickman	£4.99
☐ 40375 3	DEATH GATE CYCLE 3: Fire Sea	Margaret Weis & Tracy Hickman	£4.99
☐ 40376 1	DEATH GATE CYCLE 4: Serpent Mage	Margaret Weis & Tracy Hickman	£4.99
☐ 40377 X	DEATH GATE CYCLE 5: The Hand of Chaos	Margaret Weis & Tracy Hickman	£4.99
☐ 40807 0	THE COURTSHIP OF PRINCESS LEIA	Dave Wolverton	£4.99
☐ 40471 7	STAR WARS 1: Heir to the Empire	Timothy Zahn	£3.99
☐ 40442 5	STAR WARS 2: Dark Force Rising	Timothy Zahn	£3.99
☐ 40443 1	STAR WARS 3: The Last Command	Timothy Zahn	£4.99